MAINLINE

DEBORAH CHRISTIAN

A TOM DOHERTY ASSOCIATES BOOK
NEW YORK

MAINLINE

Copyright © 1996 by Deborah Christian

This book is printed on acid-free paper.

A Tor Book
Published by Tom Doherty Associates, Inc.
175 Fifth Avenue
New York, N.Y. 10010

Tor Books on the World Wide Web:
http://www.tor.com

Tor® is a registered trademark of Tom Doherty
Associates, Inc.

Library of Congress Cataloging-in-Publication Data

Christian, Deborah.
Mainline / Deborah Christian.—1st. ed.
p.   cm.
"A Tom Doherty Associates book."
ISBN 0-312-86029-3
1. Assassins—Fiction.   2. Women murderers—Fiction.
I. Title.
PS3553.H7257M34   1996
813'.54—dc20   95-53747
                                                    CIP

First Edition: June 1996

Printed in the United States of America

0 9 8 7 6 5 4 3 2 1

A first novel can be an especially uphill battle to write and sell and get into print. That you hold this book in print in your hands, is something you and I both owe to these people:

Helen Hakeem Christian, my mother, for all her love and support.
Tina Olivas Estrada, former partner, who enabled this work with love and many personal sacrifices.
Mary Walker McCants Wilton, extraordinary teacher and school administrator in Long Beach, California, who nurtured my talents at a critical juncture.
Don Miller and Chris Christian, my brother and sister, for timely aide.
Rene Ellen Feinstein, my friend and patron of the arts, who did more to help in the completion of this book than anyone will ever know.
Leta Rank and Lynn Flewelling, fellow writers, who helped midwife the process.
Kathleen O'Shea, for helping me maintain my sanity.
Nicola Griffith, David Drake, and Walter Jon Williams, for helping out a newcomer.
Stephen de las Heras, my editor and kindred spirit, for sharing the mania with me and making it happen.
Julia Cameron, whose book, *The Artist's Way*, went far to help make this book a reality.

My love and thanks to you all.

PROLOGUE

The ghost-ray was a rumor, a myth discounted by the Unmodified of Obai Shelf. The sea-children had their tales, though, of the Sea Father of R'debh, who lived phantomlike in the depths. A creature who rode the currents, a giant ghost the color of silt-sifted water, fading from sight only to reappear nearby, or later, or never. Their tales did not say what the ghost-ray's purpose was. He did not speak to them. But now and then a child was found stunned, who awakened with strange wisdom and a head full of visions.

Niva was two months pregnant, a daughter's bio-alteration already under way in her womb, when she swam to the deepwater pump station, her work assignment. It was as far out on the shelf and down as an unaltered human dared go.

Niva did not know exactly what she met. A presence was suddenly before her, massive, invisible, yet tangible. A backwash of current swirled past her, wings that couldn't be seen brushed over her. She felt the electrical potential in the water tingle around her skin like a caress—electrical potential, and something different. Something more.

She was found adrift, unconscious, deeper than she should have ventured. Sea-children pulled her to a rest dome. Like the children, she was different for a time, full of dreams and half-remembered visions, living on the verge of a great revelation, only to have it slip away like a receding wave before its meaning could be grasped.

Her daughter was born Unmodified, like her air-breathing parents. Niva did no swimming during her next pregnancy.

ONE

"A choice of realities once foregone is gone forever."

|

It was an old capital, sure, but who would live there if they had a choice? Almost 50 outside, and the sweat streamed off the few unprotected backstreeters where they wilted in the meager shade. Geoplast and steeloy and covered slidewalk to Old Town kept the rich in cool comfort. But the sideways were in the open, for those who trod the back paths and the poor who had no alternative. Outside there was no climate control, no cool—just the clinging blanket Lyndir called air and the heat, washing over from above, radiating from below.

Reva paused in the angled shadow of a vidvert panel and studied the off-main walkways of Port Oswin. Right then she lived the Timeline where the shade was thickest behind the panel, the Line where no one looked her way, and those who did were too drone to see anything out of the ordinary. It was reflex, a tiny balance, like riding a powerband in a wide margin. Easy. Not tired yet, nowhere near tired, she waited for him, for Number 12. It was break-time in the city for the next two hours. The ways were deserted, mostly, but Number 12 would be out any minute, wasting his time, squandering his money, hot on the trail of his newest Betman, an underwriter of rigged races, another warren rat in the exterior maze of Port Oswin.

She spotted him. Coolsuit on high—no condensation on the polychrome, a radiant chill as he walked by. She could see it in his walk: he thought he owned the backways, as long as his plastic paid the way. No cares, and not aware; not aware of those who stepped out of his way, and not aware he was being watched. Reva tailed him, nearby, not a safe distance back. But any distance is safe, she thought. I live between the Lines. Nothing's safer than that.

She hunted a bit, felt for the moment, waited for it, walking up to it with each step down the sideway. Then it happened: an intersection, and he paused to get his bearings. On Mainline, it was a heartbeat of indecision, and he went his way to the Betman. One Line over, he paused a minute longer, reconsidering the wager, then continued on. Two Lines over, he forgot the address; he wasted a minute dredging it from his mind, then checked his nailplate for directions.

The other Lines were unimportant. Reva took the second one off Mainline, and the other possibilities faded into nothingness as she chose her future and shifted down to Realtime. She stepped behind the gambler as he curled his fingers to read the nailplate. With one motion she unplugged the powerpack of his coolsuit, plugged in the supercharger, stood back. He turned to her, eyes wide in surprise, then rolling up in shock.

Her client was right. He froze solid in ten seconds.

Reva left on a Line that took her unnoticed through the gathering crowd.

||

Chorb. Waterworld. Imperial starship yard and Marine training base.

Reva stayed inside the starport terminal. Kirk, her contact there, stood reluctantly by her side, squinting longingly at the beckoning holosigns and feelie shops outside. She turned to him, curled a red-lipped sneer. "Seen one Startown, you seen 'em all. Vomit in the gutters, overworked cleanbots, security mechos scanning every corner."

"Whadjya 'spect?" he drawled. The hoppers were wearing off. Reva studied him, her hazel eyes amber-tinged, their hard highlights riveting his attention.

She didn't know him, really, but his problem was unmistakable. "You hit the shops too much," she criticized. "Euphorics, sensie-feelies, holorounds—they just rip your last cred from you, or maybe your last unvouchered organ. How many of those you got left?"

"Whut?"

"Unvouchered organs."

"Zthata question?"

Reva spat, accurately, and the toe of Kirk's boot was hidden beneath mucus. "The more you pay, the more it's worth."

Kirk stared at his boot toe. "Whatzat mean?"

"Shit."

Flunkies could stew whatever synapses they wanted, but she wasn't there to chat with the brain-burned. Kirk gave her the code for the call she had to make, and he was the intro to the courier. Nothing more. She scoped the terminal for the Cardman. No one looked likely, and she glanced again at her companion. His eyes unfocused as a vert for hoppers snagged his limited attention span.

She sighed, impatient for the Cardman to show up. She had one rule: people serious about using her services paid in kind, with genetic samples, retina prints, and other irreplaceables. Goods that could pay her way no matter what Line served her for Mainline. Reva had learned that lesson the first time she took a credit chit in payment. By time the hit was done, she was living a Timeline where there were no credits in the man's bank to cover his chit. When they paid in kind, it didn't turn worthless in a week's worth of heartbeats. Not usually.

A page blared distinct over the terminal interlink, echoing down broad hallways between boarding calls and arrival announcements.

"Kamisku Benulu, please authorize credcheck on Plancomm seven-niner. Credcheck on Plancomm seven-niner, please."

Metallic speaker tones, female voice. . . . The code name registered, and Reva looked for a house comm. A global credit check happened rarely enough, and this could only be the prearranged signal. But there was always room for error.

"Konib'nichwa," Reva spoke Ganandi to the vidunit. "Benulu gesko."

"Code green, please," came the response, then the ear-scritching rasp of disconnect.

Reva stepped to the public com booth, punched in the "green" vidcode for moneymarket transactions and the special access code Kirk had given her.

The screen flared to life but carried no video. The voice was distorted. As, she knew, was hers.

"A member of the Economic Council on Selmun III," a man's voice said dispassionately. "Her name is Alia Lanzig. She holds proxies and a controlling interest, and uses them.

"Your first target is her uncle, Albek Murs. He inherits her seat if she goes first, and he could do even more harm in that position than she has. After Murs is gone, get her. Any questions?"

"No," replied Reva.

"Good. Dossiers follow. Is your downlink ready?"

The voice was disembodied, factual, but the mention of Selmun III had distanced Reva already. "Oh . . . yes, of course," she said.

"Dumping now," came the response.

The download began.

Reva was ten, living in the Obai Shelf dome with her parents and younger brother on R'debh. It was not yet Selmun III to her, nor was there much more to her world than the domes, the aquafarms, and the ocean. Her brother Calin dropped through the water-lock with a wave and a laugh. A taunting laugh, for he needed no breathing gill and was always ready for school before Reva was.

She sealed her bodysuit and settled the breather over her face, a cripple arranging her prosthetics. Her schoolmates never let her forget that she was different. Reva the misfit. Reva the freak, the throwback in whom the R'debhi genetic mutation had worked no changes. Not so much as vestigial webs on fingers or toes for Reva. No nictitating eye membrane, no pressure-venting eardrum. Most telling of all, no gill-adaptation necessary for an unhindered life beneath the sea.

"It doesn't matter," her mother Niva assured her often. "The mutation doesn't always take. We get along fine without it, your father and I. You will, too."

Reva dropped through the water-lock and swam toward school behind her brother. The fins on her feet propelled her through the water as well as or better than a sea-child's webbed toes. Like other R'debh natives, she was lean, with the muscles of a swimmer. In that respect she was no different from the others, and faster than most. She drew close to Calin despite his head start.

They met Lita beneath the kelp rafts, their friend treading water slowly, her weight belt not adjusted quite right for neutral buoyancy. Reva looked for the others, caught a motion behind the kelp fronds. She slowed, on her guard. They were hiding. She had been the brunt of many a joke that had started this way before.

Her brother body-signed to Lita, asking if she wanted to race to school. She signed no, waved him on, and waited, hands sculling through blue-green ocean.

As Reva came near, Lita clutched at a sudden cramp in her leg, gills flaring in pain. Her over-weight belt pulled her down, toward the poisonous spines of the beldy, urchins that lived among the kelp stalks on the bottom. Reva glided close, grasping to pull her friend up and away from the danger. The girl uncoiled as the others burst from their hiding places amid the fronds. Hands grabbed Reva's feet, stripping the fins from her legs. Lita grinned and plucked the breather mask from Reva's face. The children laughed, an explosion of bubbles, then turned and raced toward school.

Through angry, slitted eyes, streaming tears lost in the bio-rich ocean around her, Reva glared after her schoolmates in a rage of frustration and hurt. She drew up a leg to scissor-kick her way to the surface—but before she could, the undersea scene blurred and shifted. This was not a distortion caused by stinging seawater, but unfocus of another Reva had never seen this way before.

She became light-headed. Time slowed. There were several scenes to watch instead of one, several bodies superimposed in the same place, like different versions of the same vidcast. Each figure acting like, yet unlike, the clones of its image.

It was a confusing garble: her agemates swimming to school, her gear gripped in their hands. Frelo releasing a fin and letting it bob to the surface; Frelo holding the fin, and swimming with his hand inside it. Simultaneously, Lita carrying the breathing gill, donning it for fun, letting it drop, being distracted by it, brushing too close to a kelp-crawler. . . .

Angry impetus fixed on that vision. Yes! thought Reva. I wish she were hurt. I don't care. Then the multiple vision was gone, and she kicked her way to air.

Frelo followed, screaming to Reva over the whitecaps. "Get help! Lita's bit by a kelp-crawler!" He vanished beneath the waves.

Reva was stunned, swimming without thinking to the nearest kelp platform. The men there dove, got the sea-child to medical care. But not in time. Lita lost her arm.

And Reva discovered her gift.

Reva put Selmun III out of her mind. The courier was late, and she paced while she waited, high-heeled boots clicking an angry staccato on the ceraplast flooring.

By time the Cardman showed, she was ready to strangle the man. She held him with her gaze, a trick of intensity she had perfected to an art. He was middle-aged, pale, and slim, a bureaucrat with a receding hairline and a security case bonded to his wrist.

"Next time I don't wait," she said coldly, "and you can explain to Adahn why his contract is refused."

The Cardman blanched. Before he could decide on a response, Reva pointed him toward a conference cubicle. He slipped gratefully out from under her stare and entered the chamber. Reva followed right behind him, sealing the door shut in Kirk's face. She opaqued the outer wall and motioned to the security case.

"Let's see it."

Inside were ten vials of drugs and one palm-sized AI link module. "What's the line?" Reva asked, picking up a vial first.

The Cardman cleared his throat and spoke in dealer's shorthand. "Ten vials, 50 cc per, top-batch hallendorphs. Contraband on Class B worlds and better. Psychologically addictive. Going rate after 50 percent dilute cut, 100 creds per cc to smugglers. Hijacked MCP, the newest from Renels-Lyman."

"Mind control pharmaceuticals," Reva echoed. "Imperial?"

The Cardman nodded.

A muscle tightened in her jaw, and green-gilded nails clicked against the vial. She replaced it in the case and picked up the link module. "And this?"

"Kardon-3M language brain. Ten thousand languages, program independent. Fits standard smartmechs."

Reva looked up from the unit in her hand. "Where's it from?"

The Cardman swallowed nervously. "Imperial Army smartmech."

"Hot, like the drugs." It was a statement, not a question.

The courier dipped his head. "But rated at 50K credits, conservative," he added. "It'll probably go for 100K."

She slipped the palm-sized unit back into its holder. "Tell Adahn, 'No more.' I'm tired of the risk. In the future I take only clean goods worth the same or more. You hear me?"

The courier nodded as he removed the bonded wristlock from his arm. "But he needs to move these things, you understand, and you're so—"

Steel-hard fingers gripped his throat, pushed him back against the opaque wall. The Cardman smelled her perfume, spicy and sweet, just before his air was shut off.

Reva's face came close to his, her voice low and naturally husky. "I'm so good, I don't need backblast from you or Adahn. He wants my services, he pays going rate. Clean. I'm not a clearinghouse. Gichnu?" She emphasized the Ganandi query with a squeeze of her fingers. The Cardman gurgled and tried to nod, pawing futilely at her hand.

Reva released her grip and left him collapsed and gasping against the wall. Security case in hand, she unsealed the cubicle and left.

Kirk was so fascinated by the stricken courier he forgot to follow her. She didn't ask him along.

II

Security could be tight in starports, where planetary authorities like to monitor who and what comes through their points of entry. That was why Reva seldom carried anything with her on a job but a credmeter and a change of clothes so widely mass-marketed they couldn't be traced.

The drawback was that she had to supply her needs locally. When those needs included specialty items—concussion detonators, bypass circuitry, even simple drugs—then that required a special contact: a Holdout, the smuggler or black market connection that greased the skids of private enterprise on almost every world in the Empire. It was the trade she had started in, and the one whose people she judged best.

Her preferred Holdout on Selmun III was Karuu. When she arrived in Amasl, she headed to his midtown offices, staffed by the innocent employees of his beldy packing firm. As with most good Holdouts, it was an impeccably legitimate front.

She avoided that front by using the private entrance to Karuu's lounge-suite. A keycode and a spoken password admitted her and alerted the Holdout to his visitor.

Karuu stepped out of the bounce tube, a straight drop from his office, and waddled over to join her, his flipperlike feet bare beneath the yellow R'debhi sarong. His bright eyes were almost lost behind a bristling mustache and the doleful expression common to Dorleon natives. Reva thought of the walruslike hoslodi whenever she saw the alien Holdout.

"Reva!" he enthused. "So happy you are here! Please to sit." He gestured her to a float-couch, punched for drinks on the service table. "The usual?" he asked. "Kabo juice?"

The assassin nodded, perversely taking a chair instead of the couch. She accepted the drink when it came. Staring at the glass hid her lapse of concentration as her timesense roved nearby Lines. In none of them did she pass out after drinking. In none was she rudely surprised by arresting officers bursting from concealment.

Reva let the drink stand after a single sip, waiting for the Dorleoni to settle himself. It didn't pay to rush business with this one. His display of congeniality was misleading: although nods and encouragement were always forthcoming, nothing happened until numbers and terms were agreed upon. And those agreements came only after cutthroat bargaining.

Karuu opened with a simple query. "And how can I help you this time, tall one?"

"I hear the arms trade is doing real well, Karuu."

The alien nodded benignly.

"I also hear you have toys moving through Amasl that've never been here before."

Karuu shrugged. "Many things are heard, Reva. Who knows where rumors start?"

"Is it true you can get time patches?"

The alien sat stock-still, his evasive chatter silenced for the moment. "Time patches," he echoed.

Their trade name was IDP, Inert Delivery Patch, an industrial variation on the medicine patches used to deliver drugs through the skin over a precisely timed period. Their construction was delicate: two thin sheets of inert synthetic, the center of one shaved microns thinner than the other. With an active liquid or gel sandwiched between the two, the patch degraded where it was thinnest. Mixed, matched, and measured correctly, the contents of the patch bled through a pinhole leak at an exact time: seconds, minutes, hours, or days later.

The destructive potential was too good for criminals or saboteurs to pass it up for long. Want to set off an explosion where conventional detonators would be detected? Slap a time patch holding the right catalyst on the explosive, and leave. Want someone's vacc suit to decompress while he's in it and no one's around? If you knew when he'd be in vacuum, a time patch holding acid was your answer.

IDPs caught on quick, and were outlawed quicker. But that was what Holdouts were for.

Reva verbally prodded her connection. "Come on, Karuu. Downlink."

The alien looked perplexed. "I do not know what to tell you, Reva. I cannot help you in this way, no."

"Then why the reaction?"

His mustache bristled. "I, too, hear rumors that time patches are here, yes. I do not have them; new source does."

"I need one. Who's the connection?"

The Holdout shook his head. "I cannot vouch for the source. New Holdout, new trade. Could be Customs already have finger on her. Hard to say."

He evaded her questions until Reva brought out her credmeter. She tapped out the figure "1000 CR" and showed it to him. "A one-time referral fee," she said. "For a one-time purchase. You're not losing my business, you know."

The beldy packer didn't hesitate long. "Lairdome 7. Ask for Lish. She sells cryocases for offworld cargo runs, owns the company. Ask about the 'hex-pack special.' She will know to work with you."

After the credits were transferred to Karuu's credmeter, he added, "Lish came from nowhere. We are not sure of her yet. I offer no guarantees about service or product, tall one."

Reva stood. "No guarantees," she acknowledged.

She'd lived without guarantees since she'd learned to cross the Lines. So what else was new?

III

Aztrakhani warriors didn't leave their homeworld often. No one wanted to hire them, and they were unwelcome as travelers. Xenologists said they were the victims of seasonal hormone surges so strong that Aztrakhani tribes were driven to periodic campaigns of genocide against their own race. The role this played in population control on their homeworld was notable, but was not a great enticement to tourism. Few citizens of the Empire knew Aztrakhan existed; fewer knew its dominant species by sight.

Physically, Yavobo was a typical member of his race. At 2.6 meters in height, he towered over most humans. His black and red mottled skin was leathery in texture, a perfect camouflage pattern for the deserts of his native land. His slitted pupils gave him exceptional night vision. His reflexes were desert-trained and warrior-fast.

It was less apparent that Yavobo was a eunuch, and thus not subject to the extremes of hormone-induced temper for which his race was notorious. Not that he was without temper. No. And the moods of an Aztrakhani eunuch were enough to put bystanders in the medcenter. This warrior, however, had found a creative outlet for his natural aggressions.

Yavobo was a bounty hunter. Though an accident of youthful combat made the warrior an outcast among his people, it freed him for travel in the Empire, and with years of experience he had finally hit upon this way to legitimately hunt a sentient being, his favorite prey. His clients felt he had made the best of his circumstances.

Clients like Albek Murs, Senior Advisor to the Economic Council of Selmun III.

When Murs wanted to hire Yavobo, the Aztrakhani at first refused the commission. "I'm not a bodyguard," he said flatly.

Albek held a powerful position. He wasn't used to being refused, and persisted with the alien. "I don't want a bodyguard. I want a bounty hunter. You are that, I take it?"

The comment was calculated to goad. Unfortunately, Albek underestimated how easily an Aztrakhani was provoked. Before he could blink he was staring down the muzzle of a wide-bore dart gun, the kind that holds heavy-caliber hunting darts designed for maximum damage at short range.

"If I knew of a reward posted for you, you would be dead." Yavobo's gun never wavered. "What do you want from me?"

The cockiness left Albek as the color left his face. "I've been warned that an assassin is after me. I'm posting a reward for you to get the killer. I don't know who it is, and there may be more than one. That's what I want taken care of."

"You can't post a reward before a crime has been committed," replied the Aztrakhani. "That's not a bounty."

Albek laughed, an edge of hysteria in his voice. "I'm sure not going to post one after I'm dead. I don't want to wait for this crime to be committed. Consider it crime prevention."

"It's contract killing."

The gun had not moved from Albek's forehead. He looked past the weapon to the warrior behind it. His voice quavered. "I wouldn't know who to put a contract on. Please. I need your help."

After an eternity of heartbeats, Yavobo nodded. He lowered the gun and holstered it. "We'll talk," he said, and walked away.

It was a moment before Albek could walk steadily enough to follow.

III

Smugglers know what a client buys, when it's bought, and oftentimes, what it must be used for. If there was one weak link in Reva's line of work, it was her necessary but vulnerable tie to Holdouts.

She traded only with those she had checked out personally. That included surveillance, to see how they did business when they didn't know they were observed.

Lairdome 7 and Comax Shipping Supply—"Bulk and Custom

Cryocases"—was easily found. Reva began her routine. A walk-by past the Comax freight bay pinpointed Lish, the only human among six labormechs. That's smart for a new Holdout, Reva thought, built-in loyalty and erasable memory in the "employees." That'll save her problems in the long run.

Reva squeezed her eyes tightly shut for a moment. When she opened them, the macro cells expanded on the contact lenses she wore for this work. Focal planes altered, and she saw Lish as if she were only three meters away.

Lish was slim, petite, and looked young. A pretty face, but with a hard cast to the mouth, a frown of concentration while she directed the assembly work of her mechos. The woman was not native to Selmun III: she was too fair, without the right cast to her features. Her hair was blond, buzzed short on sides and back, green-tipped at forelock. Not a Lyndir or a R'debh style, that. Reva couldn't place it.

She squeezed her eyelids shut again, and Lish receded to a proper distance. It was time to take up a surveillance post in an out-of-the-way place. Reva had already identified the security monitors and where to stand to avoid their sweep pattern. Surveillance was the boring part of her work, but without it the rest couldn't be done. It was like prepping for a hit: Reva stuck out days of observation, tailing, and data-tracing at times when she thought Lish asleep. Slowly, the Holdout's routine emerged from the minutiae of daily living.

On the surface, there was nothing remarkable about the woman's life. Then, on closer examination, the real pattern came clear: coded vidcalls, late-night runs to deep ocean, deliveries at odd hours. Reva suspected she met with smugglers ducking the Customs net just long enough to land hot on the water, drop their cargos, then lift.

That was a big risk. No wonder she could get goods like time patches. It would be no time at all before the Imperials had her trussed and spitted for her enterprising breach of the law.

Reva decided to move closer after a late-night ocean run. Undoubtedly smuggling business was going on then. It was the perfect time to slip in, have a listen, see how she liked the attitude. Did Lish take unreasonable risks? Did she have a volatile temper? Did she have good security? Against persons without Reva's talent, that is. Those and other details would tell her if this was a Holdout she wanted to deal with or not.

And I better hurry, she thought. If they're doing hot drops, time patches won't be available much longer.

Reva walked through the cargo bay, past labormechs assembling cryocases. Normally they would alert Lish to an unauthorized entry—but Reva did a fine dance between the Lines, walking forward in the moment when a mech turned away, ducking behind a case in the precise moment before it turned back. It was precognition made practical: a knowingness of what was about to happen, and the option to avoid it if she wished, or use it to her advantage.

Security is poor, she noted. Mechos easy to bypass, and the side office connecting with the main one made Lish doubly accessible.

The manual door between the two offices was laughably simple to unlock. Reva slid it open a crack, saw and heard Lish in conversation in the room beyond.

"You're not meeting my suppliers," the blond woman was saying, temper ringing in her tone. "And I'm not using your 'help' on my drops."

A cheerful voice soothed her anger. "No, no. Do not want those things. You misunderstand offer!"

Reva knew the voice immediately. Karuu continued. "Is simple-clear. I help pick up drops because your business grows so much you move more volume. Profit increases because I distribute your goods, guaranteed at least double your current distribution. All this for a reasonable share of those profits. Yes?"

Lish considered the offer. Then a calculating look came over her face. "Profit sharing will be split as if my distribution were doubled, even if you're moving less volume than that. If you move more, my share goes up. Agreed?"

Karuu squirmed in silence. "Agreed," he capitulated.

Reva sighed. Lish was taken in by the Dorleoni's sincerity.

I was like that once, she reflected. Before I learned better.

She listened at the door a moment longer, hearing the "deal" concluded on the other side, and shook her head as she slid the panel shut. She was strongly tempted to ignore her misgivings about this new Holdout.

I might warn her about Karuu, she considered, talking herself into it. Besides, I need a time patch.

Questions about the hex-pack special led Reva directly to Lish and a private conference. Lish dealt straight and to the point. Time patch delivery was promised in two days. Credits changed meters, half now, half later; a pickup time and place were arranged.

As Reva put her credmeter away, she decided to take the gamble. She caught the smuggler's eye. "By the way," she said, "that deal Karuu made with you? He'll sell your goods to his middlemen and pay your profit out of that. Then his middlemen turn around and resell the stuff for five times what you made. Karuu pockets his share of that, too, and you don't see any of it. Be forewarned."

Lish stiffened. "How do you know about my business?" she asked coldly.

"Don't worry. No one else does."

Lish didn't let it rest. "How do you know what Karuu's going to do?"

Reva shook her head. "I know him. I know this business even better. Look—Lesson Number One. It never pays unless you own the distribution. Build your own network, and watch your back. You'll make enemies while you get rich."

Lish studied her for a moment, then reached into her vest and pulled out a triangular blue chit. She tossed it to Reva, who plucked it out of the air handily.

"A guest pass into my place," explained the Holdout. "The address is on it. I'll be there after the end of this month. Come visit. Maybe we can do more business."

Reva doubted that. She glanced at the chit. TYREE LONGHOUSE, BANEKS CAPE was engraved on it. She knew Selmun III well, but that name was unfamiliar.

"Where's Baneks Cape?" she asked.

Lish pointed one sculpted nail to the ceiling overhead. "Des'lin," came her one-word reply.

Ah. Selmun IV, called Des'lin by the natives. An ice world, settled by R'debhi emigrants and others, a place of taiga, snowy wastelands, and touchy Vudesh clansmen. It was the first place Reva had gone for training as an assassin. She knew it well, and could tell Lish was no Des'lin native.

"Lived there long?" the assassin asked.

Lish smiled openly, amused. "Come visit. We'll talk about it."

"It's out of my way," Reva said dismissively.

"You ever have anything to sell? Come see me. I'll give you a good deal."

"We'll see." Reva was unsettled by the overture and the impulsive gift of the pass. She left abruptly.

His first day with Albek Murs, Yavobo checked out a government skimboat before the Senior Advisor stepped on board. The pilot resented the frisking, and the Captain protested the search loudly until Yavobo tossed him against a bulkhead. Broken ribs made it difficult to shout.

Word of Advisor Murs' new protection traveled fast. The transport office banned Yavobo from official vehicles, and since Albek refused to move without him, this necessitated the use of private transportation for his many Shelf-hopping junkets. There was never a second protest against the warrior searching a vessel the Advisor traveled in. Yet Albek found that, for all the extensive traveling he did, it was getting harder and harder to find a boat that consented to carry him and his entourage.

Soon he was forced to lease a hydroskiff and hire a pilot of his own, an arrangement with which Yavobo found fault.

"This is not safe. When you travel always in the same boat, you are easy to identify."

"If other boats would take me," Albek said pointedly, "that wouldn't be a concern."

"They will take you," responded Yavobo. "It is I they refuse to let on board."

"We've been over that already."

"If you let me follow in a second skiff, I will be more effective. I will be free to pursue any trouble once it is encountered."

"And what if it's encountered on the skiff I'm on?"

"We have agreed you are not in much danger from your countrymen."

"What? A R'debhi probably put the contract out on me, and you tell me—"

The Aztrakhani cut Murs off before he could get started. "I am referring to those who travel with you in the same vessel. They are unlikely to be hired killers. And I am here to screen them. Attack from inside the vessel is unlikely when you are traveling between deepsea domes. If I were in another skiff . . ."

Albek tuned out the warrior's lecture on what he would do in a second vessel. The alien seemed far more intent on chasing and capturing an assassin than on preventing the attack in the first place. Albek was irritated with himself. He remembered once again Yavobo's disclaimer that he was a bounty hunter, not a bodyguard.

And I, Albek thought glumly, had to insist on a contract.

The Senior Advisor's trip to the Obai Shelf deep domes was publicized well in advance. Reva had no problem learning the time of his departure. In planning the hit, she relied on Murs' reputation for punctuality. It was an obliging habit of his, since his untimely demise depended on his following a tight schedule.

Three hours and twenty minutes before the Advisor's departure, Reva began assembling the IDP materials in a workplace provided by Karuu. It was painstaking work with delicate materials; an unsteady hand could lose her a finger or a limb. But her hands were steady, and the time patch assembly went like a manufacturer's demo. When done, she had two hours and twenty minutes to plant the device in a critical place on the Advisor's hydroskiff. When Albek Murs was twenty minutes short of his destination, over the deep ocean drop, his ship would suffer a fatal hull breach.

Two hours, twenty minutes. Reva was dressed in an aqua-colored cold-water bodysuit, a breather mask at her waist. The outfit was common in Amasl, and no one paid attention as another R'debh native took the magtube to the waterfront, the thronging interface between sea-people and landers. Concealed inside her suit was the time patch, a slender packet of death lying between her breasts. A slight unsealing of her bodysuit and the patch could be pulled out when needed; in the meantime, there were no odd lines to arouse suspicion.

Reva left the tube, checked her breather, and allowed herself to submerge in the nearby watercourse. She had forgotten this feeling and reveled in old sensations renewed: the contrast of cool water against her exposed skin and warmth inside her bodysuit; city sounds carrying through liquid to thrum, magnified, in her ear; plankton and microorganisms dancing like silt in the rich water. Then, focusing on her job, she kicked out with long legs and swam for the marina.

It was supposedly a secure area, with controlled-access gateways abovewater and a caged-off boundary below. A simple bypass wire fooled the perimeter alarm into ignoring the gap Reva made with fusion cutters. She was undetected. There were few passersby in this part of the harbor, and though she was in plain sight, the depths at twenty meters were ill-lit by sunlight. And of course, she monitored the Lines, ready, if need be, to move to a Mainline where she would pass unnoticed.

She had identified Murs' slip and learned the maintenance routine long before she picked the time to do this job. She looked up to get her bearings. Docking slips hung overhead, dark, irregular grid slashes rippling against the watery sky. She headed for the slip she needed and rose slowly through the water until she could read the underhull registration marks. Yellow alloy, black markings were clearly visible this close to daylight. This was the right skiff.

One hour, fifty minutes until the Advisor's departure. The assassin rose farther, until she was an arm's length below the skiff hull. Its hydroplane struts were extended, part of the maintenance check. She moved between them toward the drive, where the repulsor nacelle joined the skiff's hull at an angle more vulnerable than most to water pressure. It was only a hazard if the skiff exceeded its rated depth, of course. Or suffered a hull rupture there.

Her hand was reaching for the seal on her bodysuit when a splash in the water made her freeze. Less than five meters in front of her, a man had jumped into the sea feet first. The bubbles of his descent swirled around him, bobbing to the surface before his plunge stopped. His back was to her. Intent on placing the IDP, Reva had not sensed this approaching event. She moved behind a hydroplane strut before the stranger saw her. Floating there, she tried to slip into timetrance. It was a useful monitor when she was at rest or barely active, and had attention to spare. But it was terribly draining to see alternative Nows if she was concentrating on something else, or being physically active. If she was emotionally distraught or exerting herself, it was almost impossible to do.

Reva's concentration was off: her adrenaline rush of surprise following the man's entry into the water made it difficult to see Lines. She consciously slowed her breathing, trying to study the intruder while staying concealed behind the strut.

He was abnormally tall and wore a buoybelt, a flotation device for offworlders, who sink because their bodies are denser than water. As he turned to face her way, Reva realized the red and black pattern she had mistaken for a bodysuit was his natural skin coloration. An alien, then. His face was hidden behind a breather, but she realized at once who this must be. Yavobo, the Advisor's new bodyguard. He was not mentioned in Murs' dossier; she had learned of him on her own. He was said to have a nasty temper, and the speargun he carried attested that he was ready for trouble.

Yavobo slowly swam the length of the hull, checking it out, looking for something amiss. He looked closely, carefully, and Reva was glad she hadn't planted the IDP yet. The device lay warm against her body, sticking to her skin, waiting to be used. All she had to do now was keep out of sight of the bodyguard until he was done with his inspection of the vessel.

She bobbed closer to the surface than she cared to be. She was out of sight of the alien, sticking close to the hull. More relaxed now than she had been a moment before, Reva slipped into timetrance. Pushing herself along the hull, she stayed as far from Yavobo as possible as he made his circuit underneath the skiff. She used her foresight to see when she should move, and when to remain in place. Her subtle dodge was soon finished. She heard the alien splash to the surface, and she sank again below the concealment of the underhull.

Cold water flowed against her chest as she pulled the time patch from its hiding place. Bodysuit resealed, she could live with the chill for her short time left underwater. One hour, twenty minutes before departure. She activated the adhesive backing with a stroke of her fingers, and laid the time patch against the hull. She smoothed it down, pressing it firmly into place, then drifted back a few meters to look at the patch.

Yavobo couldn't have missed it, not looking as closely as he had. Coincidences like that couldn't be helped, but they nettled Reva just the same. This time, at least, she didn't have to Lineshift to get out of trouble.

With a final grin at her handiwork, the assassin swam downward into the marina bay. She had time to get ashore, have dinner, and make a codecall. There ought to be an interesting lead story on the Selmun net in the next few hours. It would be a nice touch if her client could catch the vidnews himself.

The Advisor's skiff was at 800 meters and descending toward Bolan Dome when the strut mount failed.

The first warning was the groan and screech of tortured alloy, yielding to the pressure of the deep water. A klaxon signaling hull breach went on automatic alert. Power conduits shorted and orange emergency lighting kicked on inside the vessel.

Murs leapt from his jump seat, turned to his bodyguard.

"What is it? What's going on?" he demanded, managing to block the copilot's path as that officer rushed to assess damage. The woman shoved Murs rudely aside and ran aft past Yavobo.

"Blowing ballast tanks," the pilot reported tersely, barely heard over the strident alarm.

The Aztrakhani pulled away from Albek's grasp, turning aft where cold waters spewed madly up between deck plates. There had been no shock of impact: no missile or explosion. The bodyguard immediately dismissed the possibility that it was a natural accident, a failure in hull integrity. They had been hit. In spite of his precautions, they had been hit.

Aztrakhan was a desert world. Its natives were used to the thought of death by thirst, by desiccation, by the rending of a maddened herd beast or one's own clanmates during the Frenzy. But never a death by drowning. Few Aztrakhani could swim. Fewer had ever seen more water than that contained in an isolated watering hole, or the meager streams called rivers by Imperial surveyors.

A death by drowning would not happen to Yavobo.

"Tanks blown," the white-faced pilot bit out the words. "We're over the Lip and still going down."

The alien glanced once at Murs. He had a contract, but this foolish man had refused his advice to secure a second craft. If they had had one, Yavobo could be assisting the distressed vessel right now. Instead, his own life was endangered in a way that never would have happened if he had been master of his own fate.

"Ayesh-kha." The alien spat the phrase at Murs with a sideways slash of his hand.

"Do something!" the Senior Advisor screamed. The rushing waters were up to mid-thigh and continued to rise. More metal surrendered to the sea with a hull-shuddering groan.

Yavobo exposed his canine fangs in an angry grimace. "I rescind my contract," he loosely translated the ritual phrase. "I owe blood-debt to your heirs. You I can no longer help."

"We had a deal!" Murs shrieked, terror raising his voice two octaves in pitch.

Yavobo slipped into the airlock, half-filled with water, and punched the cycle button. Nothing happened. As Murs struggled after him against the rushing water, the Aztrakhani gripped the hatch and pulled it shut with brute force, overwhelming grudging hydraulics with inhuman strength.

Murs pounded on the plasglas viewport while Yavobo yanked the breather locker open. Muffled screams and pleading curses came from the Advisor while the red-skinned bodyguard affixed his flotation belt. Breather mask secure, he turned to the outside hatch. A quick jab on the cycle button showed that system was shorted, too, but for that lock there was an emergency lever to the right of the door.

Yavobo looked back at Murs, afloat now in the sea-filled skiff, his face with wide, frightened eyes bobbing in an air pocket near the top of the airlock view port. Albek's fingers scrambled for a grip on the plasglas as the Aztrakhani turned away and heaved upon the manual lever for the external lock.

The hatch gave way. A sudden rush of water slammed Yavobo against the far wall, then the pocket of displaced air belched him out of the lock of the doomed skiff.

He ignored the sudden shattering pain in his ears and smothering pressure on his chest and organs. Aztrakhani were made of tougher stuff than mere human tissues. He adjusted one float on his belt and, with lighter weight, began a slow, controlled ascent to the surface.

Remember to exhale, he cautioned himself, continue to exhale. Like the other land-dwellers he had traveled at one atmosphere of pressure, so didn't fear sudden decompression—but breather gases expanded in his lungs at a rate greater than normal as he ascended tens of meters every minute. He concentrated on his breathing and glared at the murk below.

Only one flickering orange light from within the water-filled cabin marked the vessel's final descent into the abyss. That, and a flurry of air bubbles as the broken hull was crushed in the depths below.

Reva had a good sense for these things. She was lounging in her hotel room when an androgynous vidcaster interrupted the regular newscast only twenty minutes after the time patch did its dirty deed.

"While en route to the Obai Economic Summit, a vessel bearing Senior Advisor Albek Murs experienced mechanical failure and is believed to have sunk into the Alauna Abyss. One emergency hail was received from the hydrocraft before transmissions ceased. The skiff is feared lost with all hands. Air and sea vessels are quartering the area now, searching for survivors. Stay tuned for further updates as they happen."

Reva congratulated herself, and found she had nervous energy that needed burning up. There was Alia Lanzig yet to go, but she could think about that later. For now, it was time to hit the nightlife. Amasl had been forbidden ground to her when she grew up on R'debh, but there were no longer disapproving parents, to make her stay away from the clubs and trip-dens.

Parents. She shrugged a grim note from her mood and headed for the door.

Reva was twelve and learning to control the secret she hid from others. It terrified her at times, but she couldn't get rid of it: where others would daydream, she would fall into timetrance, and see the alternative Nows like strobe-action figures overlaid one atop the other, interbranching pathways that only she could walk upon. It seemed her consciousness traveled the Timeliness, moving from this subjective point of view to that one there. Discomforted, she wanted to talk to someone about it but had no words to explain.

For a time she wondered if everyone went through this, this "seeing" of the present in different ways. Once she asked her mother, "How do you get back to the Now you used to have?" but Niva failed to understand the question.

"You can't, dear," her mother replied. "You just make the best of every moment you have, and then go on."

Make the best and go on. It was not exactly the answer Reva needed to hear, but somehow apt. She wondered, after Lita lost her arm, if she could go back to another Now where her schoolmate was whole and uninjured. But it seemed she had passed a major juncture: all the Nows around her included the crippled Lita, and she had no way to spot the stream of reality she had departed from in the kelp beds. It was sobering, and scary.

And even that knowledge didn't help in the least when she became furious with her family.

"I wish you were dead!" Reva remembered shouting from the door of their habitat, before turning and running out to the compound waterlock. She couldn't recall what started it; her temper had always been sharp. That night it flared. Wishing them gone, wishing them away, she fell into the split vision of different Nows. Her dash down the compound passage became a time-distorted run through a nightmare tunnel of light and dark, past rippling half-seen forms, gripped by a confusing sense of *shifting* as she fled the unpleasantness behind.

The family watersled wasn't at the waterlock. She stumbled to a stop, hot tears streaking her face, and looked for it, disoriented. Had someone borrowed it? Her father had just come home on it. Now she couldn't take it and go for a ride away from the horrible people she had to live with.

She kicked aimlessly around the lock for a time, her quick escape frustrated and her anger spent. Grudgingly, she turned her slow footsteps homeward.

No angry shouts greeted her return. There was a different smell in the air: beldy cakes in moril sauce? A good dish, like restaurant food, and one her mother never bothered to make. Reva walked slowly into the kitchen, expecting the storm of family recrimination to continue.

Niva wasn't there. Someone who resembled her stood at the counter, busy cooking. The woman smiled and frowned at Reva at the same time.

"You're late. Dinner's ready. Go sit."

The girl's mouth opened; nothing came out. This was her Aunt Teana, not her mother. Talking like her mother, though.

The dinner table held only two plates.

"Where is everyone?" Reva ventured.

"It's just us. Jerrik's staying overnight at the deep domes."

Jerrik. Her father. Who had just come home.

With time, Reva learned that her mother had died in childbirth. She had never had a brother named Calin. Her father had asked Teana to raise the infant, because his work took him so often away from home.

With one mad uncontrolled dash, Reva had fled her family, and gone so far across the alternate Lines that she could never hope to pick that one thread out that had been home to her and her family.

She tried to spot the Line, and failed. And didn't dare go hunting for it, for fear of losing even Teana, a familiar face, and ending up even farther from her own reality than she had come already. There was not even the crippled Lita to be her friend in school. Lita did not exist here, either.

Reva never let her anger get the better of her again. But it was weeks before she stopped crying at night, mourning people who had never breathed in this world, and whom she would never see again.

By the time Yavobo reached the surface the sky had turned aqua, bleaching into orange and yellow clouds where the sunset line bled over the horizon. In the east and overhead a high purple-gray overcast shut out sight of the stars. Dark waters rocked the drylander in a rhythmic chop, an icing of phosphorescence from the plankton-rich sea shining atop each wave crest.

He tore the breather from his face, gasped in clean ocean air with a near-claustrophobic joy, then sculled in circles and tried to get his bearings. The closest shore was at least 100 klicks to the northeast. The only habitations nearby were either too deep to dive to or so far away that Yavobo could not see their dome lights during his ascent. There was no safe haven for him to go to.

Aztrakhani are not noted swimmers. Alone on the darkening sea, only the warrior's iron will kept panic in check. After another few minutes of treading water, he loosened his flotation belt, recinching it around his chest and under his arms. In that position he could breathe without treading water, an action that would drain his reserves of energy in very little time. Able to think beyond the moment, then, Yavobo drifted with the waves.

The water did not seem too chill, and his leathery skin that protected him from loss of moisture in the desert in some ways now served like the insulating bodysuits the thin-skinned humans wore on this waterworld. The wind was hardly blowing and no storm was brewing, so he was not in outright danger from the elements. He looked to the northeast, where Amasl and safety awaited, somewhere over the curve of the horizon.

His chances of getting there were slim. But better to be striving than to surrender to a fate handed out by nature or an ocean preda-tor. As long as the glow of sunset remained in the west, he could mark his direction. He faced where the distant port must lie, and began to swim with measured, powerful strokes in that direction.

As long as he could swim, he had a fighting chance. But when the sky fell black and overcast hid the few remaining stars from sight, Yavobo had to stop lest he waste his strength moving in circles. Frustration set in, and panic, quickly subdued, and a growing anger. Anger at him-self, that he had overlooked whatever ploy had struck down Albek Murs, whom he had vowed to protect. Anger at whatever person had thrust him into this precarious situation, where even a mighty warrior was helpless against the elemental force of the sea, and only chance and the smiling gods could help him.

Most of all, anger that he was forced to terminate a contract he could no longer honor—no, had failed to fulfill—and thus was bound to repay blood-debt to some thin-skin with no understanding of in-tegrity and principle.

If he knew who had carried out this attack, Yavobo would declare clan-feud, and hunt him down like the skigrat he was.

At first it seemed futile rage, but as the hours wore on, the notion became more and more appealing. Why not? he asked himself. I am a hunter of sentients, after all. I have had no personal enemy in a long time. Perhaps it is time to renew the power of *shkei-ko*, of blood oath and feudhunt fulfilled.

Razor-keen incisors showed in a vicious grin. He vowed his re-venge to his personal gods and family totem. He forbore to slice the feud-mark on his forearm, not while he was in strange waters where unknown predators might smell his blood, but the Aztrakhani warrior swore he would take that final step as soon as he knew he would live, and be able to fulfill his oath.

For a day and a half the Aztrakhani drifted with the currents, swim-ming when he could, resting when the unfamiliar exertion cramped even his hardened muscles. On the second night, a strong briny smell hung heavy in the air. A large body bumped against his legs and he started out of a tired haze, pulling knees up to his chest. But no fangs sank into him, no tentacles dragged him down: he extended legs again and another scaly side nudged him in passing. It was too dark to see the waters, but a splash now and then interrupted the monotonous bobbing of the waves.

It must be a school of fish, he conjectured. As long as they're not hungry, I should be alright.

Unable to do anything about it if he was wrong, he returned to his exhausted doze. And that is why he did not notice the distant running lights draw nearer, or sense the thrum of pulse engines in the water. Yavobo awoke before dawn when fishy bodies collided with his once more. He tried to move his legs aside again, but couldn't.

He was caught in the net of an apaku trawler, snaring the run of spawning fish off the coast before they could dash ashore and expire.

He laughed in exultation, a rasping bark unnoted by fishermen amid the grind of winches hoisting netting. When he was dumped to the deck under bright worklights, sprawling among the thrashing apaku nearly half his own size, Yavobo slithered to the edge like a monster from the deep and found his feet with a triumphant shout. He rose from the deck, red and black skin wrinkled and waterlogged, scales glistening along his legs and flank, with breather mask at waist and flotation belt around his chest. The trawler crew gaped at the sight, and fell back from their strange catch.

Yavobo drew his knife with a flourish, and they fell back another step. Apaku flopped around his feet as he slashed the blade across his forearm, then brandished the bloody weapon and shouted an oath in his own tongue.

"By Blood Oath and Clan, I swear vengeance for this wrong that was done! This blade shall not drink again, but it be for that cause!"

Yavobo sheathed his knife without cleaning it, and laughed at the uncertain harpooner who stood portside, spear-rifle held in a threatening pose.

The Aztrakhani strode forward from the mess of fish and nets and demanded in passable R'debhi, "Let me talk with your Captain."

Reva picked through the oddments on her sidetable, bits and pieces collected in the last couple of days. A ticket tab for the holoshow, an empty ampule from Kovar's Sensorium, a wrinkled flimsy with the Murs lost-at-sea newsblurb. A stranger's personal comp number that she didn't plan on calling. An address chit.

A blue, triangular chit with a Des'lin address on it.

She turned it over in her fingers, tapped it with a violet-hued nail. Tyree Longhouse.

Reva toyed with the chit, and reckoned local time. It had taken a while to set up the hit on Murs, and it was now just into the start of apaku season, when the game fish rushed the island shallows to spawn. Just starting the last month of summer, that was.

Lish would be on Des'lin, then, if she'd stuck to her plans. Reva needed to start thinking about Lanzig, niece of the late departed Advisor, and the main reason she was back on Selmun III. She already had some ideas about how to approach this project. Maybe the Holdout would be worth talking to, see if she had some more specialty items that were hard to find—

Dolophant dung, Reva interrupted herself. At least be honest about it. That woman is making the wrong moves, and she's going to get in trouble over it, sooner or later, Karuu or no Karuu. Maybe I can give her a tip or two on the Holdout business. . . .

The thought gave her pause. Why care? Why get involved? It's not like they were friends or anything. That was one kind of entanglement Reva found easy to avoid. Even when she had wanted one, friends were too easy to lose when you crossed Lines. Her talent had taught her isolation early on, and relationships had slipped through her grasp as quickly as she could change the moment she called Now.

Still, there was something perversely likable about the smuggler. Here, in this Mainline, she reminded Reva of a younger version of herself: with an overconfidence that spoke of underlying arrogance, the kind that put you out on a limb without even knowing it. The assassin shook her head and studied the address chit in her hand. Lish wasn't a kid, wet behind the ears, but she wasn't as well set up to be a Selmun smuggler as she might think.

It was a sure bet the Holdout wouldn't want to hear that kind of thing from a stranger. Reva paused on the verge of tossing the chit.

Then again, a new business connection couldn't hurt. It would require social niceties . . . use of someone's house pass demands some kind of politeness in return. The semblance of friendship, if not its substance, to make dealings a little smoother.

She smiled to herself. She could play that game, if she wanted to. She had a mood, a demeanor, for every occasion. And it would be amusing, maybe truly useful, to turn this casual invitation into a reliable connection.

What the hell. She hadn't seen Des'lin in forever.

She pocketed the chit and punched out on the hotel room comp.

Reva traveled mostly on commercial transport. The next hop to Des'lin was the morning commuter run, outbound to the hunting lodges on Selmun IV and the crystal mines on V. She boarded the shuttle, resigned to the company of complacent vacationers and combine executives checking on fur trapping investments.

It was a routine journey she could sleep through, and did.

Three hours later saw her past Customs' cursory check for in-system passengers. She emerged into the nearly empty concourse of Freebay's small starport, unchanged since her last trip through had taken her off Des'lin and away from the Selmun star for the first time. She found the ground travel agent in the place she expected, and leaned on the counter.

"I need to go to Baneks Cape. What's the best way there?"

The agent looked up from a terminal at the unexpected customer. "The Cape?" she repeated. "Either ground car or monorail, Domna. Rail would be faster. The storm season is on us already. Though you look prepared for it."

Reva gave a false smile out of reflex to the small talk, and brushed one hand down the fur-lined kria-leather coat she'd bought for this journey. She knew all too well just what season gripped northern Des'lin at this time, and though her garment was chosen for its suggestion of local style, it offered real protection against what could be deadly cold. There was nothing warmer than kria-fur on this iceball, she knew. She had killed and worn her share of them before.

"Rail, then." She bought a one-way ticket and studied the tourist map the woman handed back with the ticket tab. The monorail line was new to her, and now that she had the topography in hand, she saw where one spur led to Baneks Cape, a narrow, curving peninsula on the west coast of the larger of the two inland seas. Ponds, they seemed, after R'debh, but the weather upon them could be just as fierce, and from the shore, she knew, the waters looked just as vast.

There were no slidewalks in Freebay's backwards terminal, part of the contrary Des'lini pride in doing things the frontier way. She strolled down a long hall toward the monorail platform, wondering as she went if Lish would be home for this unexpected visit. Though that's no real concern, thought Reva, because this isn't just an address marker I have. It's a house pass. She's either deathly naive or has very good instincts about whom to trust.

She was shaking her head over that when an odd sensation came over her and she did her best not to halt in mid-stride. Every hair raised itself along her neck and spine, and a cold wave of anxiety forced an involuntary shudder. Reva walked as casually as she could to a vendbot and turned sideways in the hall, pretending to examine its selection of refreshments.

A quick glance showed the hall behind her was empty, and just one person walked the passage ahead. Then what had given her that uncanny feeling? It seemed like it should herald danger, so stark and primeval it was. Her skin prickled beneath her clothes where every small hair had risen with electric chill.

There, in the mecho's chromed dispenser arm, she thought she saw the reflection of a moving figure. Her eyes darted that way, not moving her head, and saw nothing. She tried to slip into timetrance, but the eeriness she felt hindered her.

"May I assist with your selection, Domna?"

The vendbot's programmed query startled her again, and she moved away with two swift steps. The mecho trundled slowly back to the main concourse, and Reva stood with her back against the wall, forcing herself by will alone to center and search the Timelines for danger.

A moment later Now shattered into its parallel parts, and she surveyed the hall again. It was a disappointingly empty space, filled with the shadows of one or two passengers who could have been late or might be early. Ghosts of chance, not real for her on this Mainline, and certainly no threat.

Reva slipped out of trance, and shook her head. The incident disturbed her more than she cared for. Anything would that I can't explain, she told herself. I don't trust what I can't explain. That gets you killed.

She glanced once more around the hall, then continued to the monorail platform, doing her best to shake off the feeling the uncanny disruption had given her.

On the vendbot's dispenser arm, a reflection moved again across polished chrome, and vanished in Reva's direction.

Adahn sighed and ran his hands through graying hair, a look he kept for the added air of authority it gave him. A com light blinked insistently on the desk console before him. Even after three years as a Tribune of the Red Hand crime cartel, the MazeRat derevin and their affiliates occupied too much of his attention. There was no one to turn it over to, no one he trusted to manage the street muscle the way he wanted it run. While waiting for someone to distinguish himself in the lower ranks, he got to take calls like this one. Karuu, on subspace from Selmun III.

"A fine good day to you, Mr. Harric," the Dorleoni's voice bubbled with native cheerfulness, filling the privacy speaker in Adahn's inner ear. The gang boss wasn't lulled by it. Dorleoni always sounded cheerful, even when they were slitting your throat.

Adahn seldom let his face be seen by associates, so the vidlink was one-way only. "Karuu. You have a problem?"

The walrus-faced Holdout tilted his head in response. "An inconvenience. There is new competition here, selling Inert Delivery Patches. I am wondering in the name of good business if you can provide me with same?"

"Too risky," Adahn refused him. "Imperial Security monitors those raw materials. If we moved enough quantity to make it worth our while, we'd alert them."

"Then Imperial Bugs come to see this competitor, I am hoping. Because if trade continues, we are maybe seeing loss of old customers."

The Dorleoni did his best to look plaintive, but Adahn was having none of it. This was business-as-usual, and nothing for an up-and-coming Tribune to be wasting his time on.

"You know the game," he snapped. "If you don't like the competition, get rid of it. Was there anything else?"

He waited impatiently for the smuggler to shake his head. "Well, then. Later." The MazeRat boss severed the connection, jacked into his deck, and put out a call for Janus.

His lieutenant was in the cybernet, as usual, and responded directly through Adahn's visual cortex. Janus appeared to float in mid-air over the crime boss' command console.

"Sir?"

"Holdout operations. Karuu's having trouble with a competitor on Selmun III. Help him a little, will you? If he really needs it."

"Sure. Is it urgent?"

"Don't know. Talk with him."

"Will do."

The exchange, facilitated through the Net, took place at the speed of light and flash relays. Janus' form vanished an instant after it appeared, and Adahn unplugged from the cyberdeck. He finished the breath he had been taking when he jacked in, and returned to the affairs the Holdout's call had interrupted.

The monorail sliced toward Baneks Cape, its mag-field racing over the track ahead, bursting the thick sheath of ice and wet snow that coated it. The train was wrapped in dark and fog and veils of wind-driven ice crystals, a blizzard so dense that only flakes packing against the monorail windows could be seen.

Reva did not try to make out the snowy, forested mountains and valleys she knew lay outside. Instead, she settled into her kria-fur coat, and regarded her fellow passengers.

The sixth sense she had experienced in the terminal had left her uncomfortably wary, so she studied her fellow travelers closely: a R'debhi businessman; a mother and children with packages from a day of shopping; two Vudesh clansmen, their crossbows nearly hidden among the long strands of deska fur they wore as cloaks. She judged and dismissed each as representing no danger to her, then closed her eyes and concentrated on the soothing rhythmic vibration of the Cape-bound transport.

Vask Kastlin watched Reva from his seat across the aisle, her closest observer and yet not one she had noticed. Then again, no one else had noticed the wiry, dark-haired man, either. No one could, at this moment, unless they glimpsed him with sensors or video monitors, or were as skillful at applied psychonetics as the man himself. For Vask was a Mutate, a graduate of the Academy of Applied Psychonetics, and, like many of his kind, an agent of the Emperor's Ministry of Internal Security. "Security" to the public; "IntSec" to the bureaucrats. "Bugs" to the criminal element, a play on their abbreviated department title.

A bug, indeed, thought Vask. Like a bug on the wall, I see you; you don't see me.

It was tiring, using his blindspot skill to assure that those around him failed to see him. They glanced nearby, or looked away, or walked past, unconsciously skirting his position, never quite registering his presence. Yet it made tailing his elusive quarry much easier.

Reva's destination was clear, though what she planned to do there remained a mystery. As was she. Tall, with brunette hair today, dressed as a winter-clad Des'lini, no longer in the revealing party clothes she had worn in Amasl, he might have overlooked her in a crowd had she not already come to his attention. Inert Delivery Patches and their buyers were always of interest to IntSec.

Vask relaxed into his seat, prepared to doze along with this buyer of contraband. Tracing the IDP delivery to her workshop had not been too hard; nevertheless, he had scrambled for the last several days, using more than his share of hoppers and marshaling psi energies carefully to stay on the trail. Then he had lost her for a time, and only picked up the trail again when she straggled back to her hotel after an extended revel out on the town.

A quick data check turned up no records on Reva—not too surprising, if she worked with Holdouts. Strangely, though, he couldn't tell if she was really Normal: he sensed no active psi from her, and neither could he detect the surface murmur of her thoughts. That could be due to a cyberimplant, a psi shield, although such were tremendously expensive and rarely encountered. His telepathic powers were weak, but he should at least be able to pick up a sensation of conscious thought. Or if she were shielded by natural psi ability, there ought to be some period when she dropped the shield. So far, there was none. Reva was an enigma.

Soon it would be time for Vask the Fixer to meet Reva, and become her friend. First, though, he would follow this trail to its end. Lish had attracted Imperial attention weeks before. While other agents investigated the smuggler and her offworld connections, it fell to Kastlin to see who used the contraband she was passing, and what for. Her dossier mentioned Tyree Longhouse on Baneks Cape, so when Reva boarded the monorail there was hardly any need to guess her destination. Kastlin tagged along, inventing ways to approach her when the time came. His R'debh cover as Vask the Fixer had a lot of connections. Surely one could give him cause to go to Baneks Cape in a solstice storm.

Tyree Longhouse was an upscale version of the traditional Vudesh structure, the preferred way to build in the chill Des'lin climate. It splayed on the land like a grounded turtle, a long rectangular box two-thirds underground, with sloping earth-bermed sides and synthetic thatching. Its ridge-top position braked gusting winds and caused snow to heap roof-high against the sides.

A snowcrawler approached and stopped as close to the covered entranceway as possible. Reva got out, waded through thigh-high drifts, and pushed the call buzzer on the gate control panel.

A scanner hemisphere emerged from the panel, angled toward Reva, retracted. Her face was not among those it was programmed to admit, and so the gate remained closed. She fumbled the blue house pass out of a pocket then and shoved it into the keyslot. Panel lights turned green, and the security bars lifted out of the snow-covered ground. Reva waved to the snowcrawler. The taxi turned back toward the monorail station as she walked inside the entrance gallery.

She had no chance to try the chit on the house door. The portal that looked made of rustic wooden planking swung open before she could touch it, and Lish stood there to greet her. "Bad night for traveling," she said with collected poise. "Come on in."

Lish led her visitor into the great hall, a ground-level room that ran the length of the longhouse. Running down its center was the traditional fire trench, with real logs burning at the far end of it. Felted mats and cushions for floor seating cluttered the edges, while food warmed on a nearby sideboard.

It was a primitive yet gracious setting, reminding Reva of her own sojourn on Des'lin in her late teens. Her coarse Vudesh companions had had floor mats of the same style and a firepit just as welcoming on a cold night. The fruity Cadanessa wine Lish handed her would only be served by one who appreciated the native food and drink.

Her habitual scan of the Lines was soon done, yielding no hint of danger. Then the assassin allowed herself to do what she seldom did. She relaxed in the company of another, and enjoyed her drink.

Vask had a problem. None of Lish's street connections knew of her hideaway on Selmun IV. That meant he couldn't walk up, knock on her door as if he had legitimate Fixer business, and finagle an introduction to Reva.

You better come up with something, he chided himself, or you're gonna blow this trail and freeze to death at the same time.

He sat shivering in a rented snowcrawler, watching the gateway of Tyree Longhouse appear and disappear between swirls of snow. He needed a break in this stakeout, a way to get closer, and nothing was suggesting itself. Well, there was one way, sideslipping. . . . He shook his head. That was crazy. Draining enough even when he was rested.

No, wait a minute. If I sideslip, then . . .

He began to tick off points on his left hand.

I get in tonight, undetected. I hear what they have to say between them now, in this very private meeting. I might get a lead I can follow up on soon. The bad news is . . .

—he switched to the other hand—

I've been on hoppers too long. If I take psiboost now, I'll crash afterward, and there's nothing I can do about it. Out for, probably, a day and a half. What if I have to move sooner than that?

Sideslipping was one of the most difficult of psionic disciplines. It required concentration and energy that would deplete all his reserves and then some. Was it worth it?

He wasn't learning anything by sitting in the snowcrawler, that was certain. And there was no telling when either of the women would leave the longhouse again.

He powered off the vehicle, then fished around in his carrybag until he found the medtab applicator. Punching up a dose of psiboost, he injected the potent compound into his thigh muscle and waited while the psionic drug took effect. In a few minutes he felt refreshed, not physically, but mentally alert and once more up to his full psychic potential. He knew it was part fact and part illusion, and he needed to get moving before the dose wore off. He opened the crawler's door and climbed out into the blustering storm.

The agent walked away from the vehicle, into the snow-laden

darkness beyond a feebly glowing lightpost. Better there than toward the longhouse gate, where security cameras might pick up his disappearing act. As soon as he was in relative obscurity he stood motionless and gathered his concentration. When the next flurry of snow whipped over him, Vask closed his eyes against the sting of icy flakes. He stood stolid and relaxed, then let himself go into the trance required for sideslipping.

Soon a peculiar, skin-crawling sensation came over him as his molecular structure unphased. Like many psi powers, phase-shifting was simply a matter of manipulating the body's natural energy field. Or, not "simply." It was a difficult skill to master, and few could learn to do it.

But Vask had. Every particle, every elemental chain that composed the man on the physical plane shifted its vibratory frequency ever so slightly up-spectrum. He was there, yet not there, existing in a state more akin to light than gross physical matter. Straddling dimensions, the entity that was Vask became a semicoherent form, one no longer hindered by the physical stuff of his natural state. A form no longer visible to earthly sight at all.

The snowstorm faded to a cloud of gray mist as Vask phased out of the realm of ordinary sensation. He no longer felt cold or stinging ice. His clothing, caught within the radius of his body's natural bioelectric field, traveled with him, although it, too, lacked substance and tangible presence.

He walked in a foggy half-world where mist-soft objects glowed with a blue-gray luminescence born of radiant molecular energy. He approached the shadowy gate of Tyree Longhouse and moved through the incorporeal structure of the bars. As he pushed through, he felt a crawling sensation in the path of the earthly material. It was not a horrific feeling; neither was it pleasant. He gathered his nerve before pushing through the door of the longhouse in the same manner.

What seemed to be rough wood planking was a veneer over thick steel, with a reinforced core like a blast door. The crawling sensation came again, throughout his body. Vask closed his eyes, hating the disorientation of walking through what his mind told him should be — no, *was* — a solid object. Only when the sensation was gone and he was on the other side did he open his eyes.

At the far end of the great hall, Lish and Reva sat beside the firepit drinking wine. Vask could hear nothing of their conversation, for sound, like other physical sensations, was not perceivable in a phase-shifted state. To eavesdrop, he would have to sideslip back to the material plane, then either hide in a mundane manner or use his blindspot ability to avoid detection. Blindspotting would exhaust even more of his powers; it would be better to simply hide.

The furnishings in the room were sparse: cushions and mats, a few benches and tables along the walls, and the sideboard that held the dinner dishes. That high-backed furnishing stood behind Lish.

Vask wafted through pillows and cushions, skirting the women as he came closer to them. Moving through the inanimate was uncomfortable enough; sideslipping through living creatures was even more disturbing, and could be detected by the highly sensitive, at least as a chill or sense of presence. He took care to avoid the women as he moved past toward the sideboard.

The furniture was angled so that he would be hidden from sight behind it. The shadows there were deep. He would not be able to watch his subjects from that vantage, though he could listen to their conversation, and he could blindspot if either walked around the room.

He moved to the space behind the sideboard, assumed what would be a comfortable sitting position, and shifted the phase of his structure back down-spectrum. First there was nothing, then there was a shimmer, then a form rested in the natural gloom at the end of the great hall.

Vask clenched his jaw, tripping a molar relay, and a microcircuit implant started recording what came to his ears. It was nearly as passive a device as an implant could be, powered by a simple bioelectrical relay, recording the sounds captured by Kastlin's own inner ear. Psionicists had a low tolerance for cybersystems, which interfered with their fine-tuned control of mental and physiological processes. Vask hated using even this simple device, but some evils were necessary in order to do his job right. He listened, and let the dumb recorder do its work.

At first the women sat in silence, sipping the Cadanessa, uncertain what to say.

Before the silence could become uncomfortable, Reva forged ahead, deciding to get out one of the things that had been on her mind.

"You take too many risks in your work," she declared bluntly.

Lish raised an eyebrow. Reva felt a twinge of misgiving; that was not the kind of small talk she'd had in mind when coming here. Since there was no angry outburst to stop her, she went on. "You're doing hot drops out on the ocean. If I could figure that out, you can be sure someone else will. Bugs. The Grinds—"

"I bribe the police," Lish interjected.

Reva narrowed her eyes. "No, you don't. You think you do. They'll milk it for what it's worth, then turn you over for extra points to someone with less invested. Maybe Selmun Customs. They must be hopping mad by now. You've been doing this for, what, eight months or so? You're running out of time, Lish."

The Holdout gave her a calculating look. "How do you know all this? About the Grinds? And Customs?"

Reva set down her wineglass. "Look. First, you make these underwater runs after dark, submerged. Harbor Patrol tracks that traffic. Are your smugglers good enough to avoid detection on each run, or are they counting on being faster than Customs?"

Lish shrugged.

"That's what I thought. So on half the runs they slip in undetected. The other half, you can bet someone's put the pieces together."

Lish's brow furrowed in thought. "I'm not the only Holdout on R'debh. Customs must have their hands full with other traffic."

"Don't count on it. You keep your transponders hooked up, don't you?"

"If there's an emergency—"

"—at sea, you want Patrol to be able to help you out. So your movements are traced. It's a two-way deal, you know. You ping the navsat for your location; the navsat knows where you are by your squawk."

The smuggler paled. "Are you certain my ID is recorded? There's so much ground traffic. . . ."

Reva looked at her shrewdly. "You're not used to working dirtside, are you?"

Absently the Holdout shook her head. "Started in shipping."

"And you continue to think that way. That'll get you killed, or locked up."

Lish studied her guest with a thoughtful eye, then refilled their glasses. "Got any other suggestions?" she asked seriously.

Reva shook her head. "Too late for that. You cut a deal with Karuu, that'll keep you safe for a little while. He's connected. But when the fall comes, your cargo will be grabbed by someone else—

probably the Dorleoni—while you and your playmates get swept up by the Grinds. Or Internal Security, with the kind of stuff you've been moving."

Lish waved that comment aside. "I'm safe from Security. I've got connections."

The assassin looked skeptical. "I haven't heard of any that'll keep the Bugs off your back. Generally speaking. What makes you think you're so safe?"

Lish chewed her lip and hesitated before speaking. "Do you know of the Shiran Traders?" she finally ventured.

Reva shook her head.

"From the Empire. Sa'adani space, I mean, from before we annexed the Confederacy."

"Ahh. . . ." The meaning of that sank in, and Reva looked at her host as if seeing her for the first time. The Confederacy of Allied Systems was thirty-three subsectors conquered by the Sa'adani Empire over a century and a half ago, now lumped into one large administrative sector for Imperial purposes. Lish meant that she was from that greater Sa'adani Empire, a place that remained largely alien in culture and attitude from what predominated on the CAS "frontier."

"I couldn't tell to look at you," Reva commented. Almost all Sa'adani wore a caste mark of some sort, either visible on their skin or formalized in their clothing. To be without that mark was a crime, for then how would high-caste tell low-caste apart? It seemed impossible for a Sa'adani to have social interaction without consciousness of caste and therefore relative rank.

Yet here sat Lish, with nary a mark upon her. She blushed slightly under Reva's scrutiny, let her thumb stray to the left side of her jaw. She stroked the skin there. "I had it removed," she said, apologetically.

Reva looked closer and saw a faint blemish there the length of a finger. She hadn't noticed it earlier, and certainly wouldn't have taken it for a caste mark if she had. She rehearsed in her mind the list of identifying marks that young children were made to memorize in school. *Stylized battleslash, laser-scribed in skin of left jaw . . .*

"Rus'karfa." She identified what caste Lish must be. The Holdout nodded almost shyly. "Warrior-in-service," it meant, one of the higher-ranking Sa'adani classes. From it were drawn officials, military officers, persons with authority who were expected to oversee operations under the direction of high-caste nobility.

Reva coiled more tightly where she sat. "Isn't it a crime to be without your caste mark?" she asked, unable to resist the jab.

Lish blushed again. "That's not well enforced in the CAS Sector. You know how people are about caste here."

Reva knew: not accepting of Sa'adani efforts to force a caste system down their throats. Yet the smuggler had gone to some considerable trouble to have her mark of aristocracy removed, and Reva was curious about that. "Laser-scribe marks are permanent," she observed. "It must've been expensive to lose that."

"They do interesting things with nanobugs on Tion," Lish replied awkwardly.

Nanotechnology was one of the few areas where the CAS Sector held its own — in fact, exported products and know-how to the greater Empire. Reva hardly thought twice about it; everyone she knew took bodysculpting and other nano spin-off for granted.

"I suppose any unhappy Sa'adani can come here, lose their caste mark like you did, and start a new life," she mused. "There must be a lot more Imperial refugees in this Sector than we realize."

Lish's back stiffened and she put down her wineglass. "I'm no refugee, and this uncouth Sector is hardly a haven. I can go back if I want to. I just . . . don't want to."

The silence between them was strained. After a minute Reva asked, "So who are the Shiran Traders?"

That subject was not much more neutral, and Lish abruptly changed it. "Never mind. It was a mistake, bringing it all up." She eyed the food on the sideboard. "Want something to eat?" She jumped to her feet without waiting for agreement, loaded two plates with pepperroast, breadleaf, and radish root, then returned to the fireside.

Reva took a plate, refilled their glasses, and returned stubbornly to their prior topic. Her curiosity was piqued, and consideration for the amenities of polite conversation had fallen by the wayside.

"I said watch out for Security, and you said you're safe from them. What do Shiran Traders have to do with that?"

Lish set her mouth, disapproval evident on her features. That was no surprise to Reva: probably her sense of caste interaction was offended. Yet whatever reaction the Holdout felt she soon quashed, and Reva gave her a point for self-discipline. A smuggler couldn't afford to put too much stock in rigid observance of caste and rank; street savvy and common sense were a lot more important, and Lish seemed to have that. She took an audible breath, found her equanimity, and answered Reva's question.

"Shirani are the trading and shipping arm of House Arleon in Sa'adani space. We were one of your first trade contacts, initially in the Corvus subsector, later in other Confederacy systems."

Reva downed a chunk of pepper-roast and chased it with a drink. "That sounds like legitimate trade." The unspoken question was, how did Lish get from that into smuggling?

The Sa'adani woman wasn't biting. She skipped ten years of personal history, and simply said, "IntSec won't arrest me because of my family ties."

"Are you saying the Empire doesn't care what kind of crime you're running if you're well-born enough?"

Lish quirked a smile. "Well . . . yes, actually. Usually."

"I haven't heard of the Bugs holding back. Even when big names are involved."

"They like to clean up in this sector, but never when high-caste is involved. At least, not publicly."

"Maybe you're overlooking something," Reva pointed out cynically. "You've lost that caste mark. Maybe they think you're just another CAS Sector bottom-feeder. If they come in blasting, you could get in the line of fire as easily as anyone."

Lish let the bottom-feeder jibe go and shook her head. "That can't happen," she said, gesturing with a yellow radish. "Once they know my family connections, they're bound by law and honor to treat me like the Rus'karfa I am."

Reva was taken aback by the woman's sincere tone. "You really believe that, don't you?"

The Sa'adani looked surprised at the question, and Reva shook her head in exasperation. By the Sea Father, this woman was naive! In this business, it would surely get her killed.

The conversation wandered then, by mutual consent, a break from the intensity of the last hour. Lish revealed no more about her background, and Reva even less. The pair enjoyed small talk, another bottle of wine, and a long game of castle-stones.

While they played, Reva studied the smuggler. Lish was unaware of the attention, bent over the board, biting her lip with the intensity of her concentration. She had a fine-boned beauty about her, accentuated by the firelight. A full lower lip, red highlights from the embers shining in her blond hair . . .

The assassin felt the strings of attraction, and thrust that thought from her mind as quickly as it surfaced.

Business and pleasure do not mix, came her rote reprimand of self. Besides, I don't have time for relationships. They make you vulnerable. Good way to get close and kill someone.

She knew; she'd used the pose of intimacy more than once to do her work, with men and women alike. Lish was neither threat nor target, but the habit of reserve that kept Reva alive was not something she was about to set aside over one firelit dinner.

Don't waste time thinking about it, she told herself sternly. That's what sex-shops and quick pick-ups are for.

She forced her mind away from that line of thought, and considered the other reasons why the smuggler intrigued her. Lish wasn't too ready to listen to common sense, that was for sure. It was an irritating trait.

She thinks she knows how things will play out. Short-sighted, short-sighted . . .

It made Reva wonder if anyone could save another from herself. No one had been able to do it for her. It would be a waste of time to try it with Lish.

But she's so damn much like me, stubborn, cocky—a younger, stupider me. . . .

Again and again, Reva saw the woman's flaw illustrated in the way she played. She was too confident, too trusting in the routine way of doing things. Toward the end, when the assassin played her own variation on the Moat Gambit, Lish followed with the traditional response. Consistently she overlooked the small variables that indicated an outcome other than what she expected.

She's smart, and she's trying hard, Reva thought wryly, but she needs someone to jar her complacency. Someone should teach her the error of her ways, before she ends up dead.

A silent headshake accompanied the thought.

Why's it have to be you, Reva?

Well, you know it's not going to be Karuu, she answered herself.

That left her with a lot to think about besides the game, and it took longer than she expected to decimate the Holdout's forces. When Lish's queen was finally made to retire, Reva looked up from the board.

"Say," she asked, "want to go hunting?"

Not right then, of course, but after the blizzard cleared in several days. The kria would be out, easily tracked atop the fresh snow. The challenge lay in their ability to anticipate the human's move; who would become hunter and who the hunted was never a foregone conclusion.

Lish agreed. She had wanted to try the sport for years.

"Great," Reva said. "We can go to the reserve and rent guns there." The hunting would not be as good as in the wilds, but it would be a little safer—the oldest and most ferocious of the female cats were culled from the hunting herds before tourists and offworlders were permitted inside.

Kria were challenging enough, culled or not. The assassin remembered the lessons in survival that she had learned in the hunt; that was what Lish needed, something to bring home the unpredictability of people and events around her, and teach her to respond in kind.

Even if the Holdout didn't learn that in one or two object lessons, at least it would be a start. And for the time being, Reva promised herself that she wouldn't switch Timelines. She would take on whatever she encountered right here in Mainline, exactly as she had in that long-ago training period with the Vudesh. It was a lesson she could use reminding of, too.

Vask was out of the longhouse and back inside his snow-shrouded crawler before the second game of castle-stones was through. He felt a tremble in arms and legs at closer and closer intervals, and that was no state to sideslip in. By the time he checked in to his resort hotel he knew he'd cut it close. Shaking, he palmed the room door, then had to reset the door lock twice before he got it right. With leaden, palsied limbs and blearing eyes, he punched up a scramble code on the comnet.

"Systems Control," came the cryptic voice-only ID. It was one of Internal Security's com centers, networking agent traffic through twelve systems and numerous sublight relays. Vask didn't know its precise location, and didn't care. It was what Control could do for him that mattered.

"This is Kastlin, code Selmun-niner-three. Got a dump for you, cross-ref Tyree Longhouse. Debrief later." He fumbled with the console probe for far too long before securing it in his wrist jack, a dumb neural interface wired only for data transfers to or from the recording devices in his head. He pressed on a tooth in a certain way with his tongue, and the uplink began.

"Need some arrangements, Control." Vask was not normally terse, but exhaustion was about to slam down on him and end this conversation. He fought the slur in his words. "When you monitor coms from Tyree Longhouse, let me know when they book into a resort for kria hunting. Book me same place and message me about it."

The datadump was done. He tugged the jack from his wrist with an effort. "New news in that uplink," he added. "We got a line on the Holdout. Shiran Traders, House Arleon."

"Acknowledged, Selmun-niner-three."

Vask didn't sign off. He barely managed to tap the disconnect before passing out in his chair.

Alia Lanzig's profile and activities were common knowledge, easily tracked on newsnet and library files. It was not hard for Yavobo to discover that she was the only surviving blood kin of Albek Murs. But when he journeyed to Bolan Dome, she refused his services, and erupted at his persistence.

"I tell you again, sir, I have no need for a bodyguard!"

"Then I will sleep upon your doorstep," Yavobo assured the Councilor, "and follow where you go, with or without your permission. If you go places where I am not permitted to follow, then I will find ways in, or wait for you outside like a faithful keshun. For I must protect you, and serve you, and that is all that is to be said in the matter!"

Yavobo was unaccustomed to having his word questioned, and angered at having his honor debt dismissed out of hand by the one he intended to aid. His determination was finally coming clear to Councilor Lanzig.

"Why me?" she demanded again.

Again, Yavobo began his explanation. "I entered a contract with your uncle to—"

"—to keep him safe, yes. You are under no obligation because of a vehicular failure."

"I say again, I do not believe it was a natural failure. And I am in debt, Councilor. It is to you I must discharge that debt."

Alia sat in a net chair, her webbed feet slightly splayed on the nubbleflooring before her. There was a sheen of blue-green luminescence to her skin on arms and thighs, and on the closed gill slits visible on her neck. Soft curves spoke of subcutaneous fat, helping to insulate body heat in the ocean depths.

"You realize I do much of my work in the water?" she finally asked. "At this depth a human would need protection, at least a special dive suit."

Yavobo bowed slightly at the concession. "I would suffer some discomfort in the ears, otherwise I believe I have no problem. I am more hardy than an unprotected human."

"Well, I can't have you going deaf, can I?" Lanzig groused. "Get a suit, keep your pressure and air right, and you can stay. Get my daily schedule from my secretary console and we'll see how you can fit into my routine."

Alia's lips pursed as if she tasted something sour. "I want none of this carrying on like with my uncle, you hear? You're not going to piss off every pilot who works for me or get my people thrown in the autodoc with your tactics. You can be a chauffeur or doorguard for all I care. I want you out of my way and in the background. Is that clear?"

"If there is a danger—"

"I'm not in any danger. Stay unobtrusive. Can you do that?"

She spoke with the authority of an Aztrakhani matriarch. Yavobo bowed again, respectfully, this time.

"We understand each other, then. Now go get that suit."

Alia felt she was in no danger, and to Yavobo's practiced eye, it seemed she might be right. Her enemies were forthright and vocal, and the Aztrakhani knew those were seldom the ones you had to watch out for. Yavobo followed her movements in a separate skiff and Lanzig had no protest, nor did she care how he executed his self-appointed duties.

It was altogether the strangest escort duty the warrior had ever performed. All the while, Albek's death continued to niggle at him, and when he could find time, he did what he could to investigate the sinister mishap with Advisor Murs' skiff.

Yavobo soon found his investigation severely limited by circumstance. There was no way to recover the wrecked hydroskiff, now a piece of compact, crumpled debris in an unmarked location deep in the Alauna Abyss. Even if the wreckage was found, what was the point? It would reveal pressure-tortured metal, almost impossible to pinpoint the one spot that must have suddenly given way. . . .

One spot. Suddenly.

Maybe he could attack this from another direction. If he had wanted to take out the skiff, how would he have done it? The answer to that was easy. A torpedo, possibly tracking on a homing button attached to the hull.

Yet the warrior knew there had been no explosion when the skiff's hull breached. There was only the sudden pressure drop. A missile would have been felt; a laser or ion pulse would at least have been noticed by the crew, and required a firing platform of some sort, although there had been no other vehicles nearby. If the failure were caused by a physical flaw, dock inspection by the pilot or Yavobo should have revealed it. Nothing he invented fit the pattern of destruction that had downed the Advisor's skiff.

Maybe something he *didn't* know about was responsible. Something the effects and operation of which he couldn't imagine. Fortunately, he had a footprint, a way to trace this mystery thing. He knew its characteristics.

Hard to detect. Capable of sudden, very destructive damage to a ship's hull, short of an explosion.

That was a brief description and to the point. Yavobo had purchased his share of contraband weaponry from smugglers in the past. That was the place to start. *"I need to do sudden, destructive structural damage,"* he would say, *"maybe at a particular time, but can't risk an explosion. Can't use a laser, no phase weaponry, and it has to work underwater. What do you suggest?"*

Yes. That was the tack to take.

When Councilor Lanzig attended a three-day retreat, his opportunity came. Praying for understanding from his gods, he abandoned his charge and traveled to Amasl. The Aztrakhani needed to do a very special kind of shopping.

Reva's interlude at Tyree Longhouse was a strange idyll, the sort of break the assassin was unaccustomed to. Days spent reading, lounging, talking with another; it was an odd feeling to get to know someone over days of friendly conversation. She learned more of Lish, not facts so much as quirks of personality: what made her laugh; how she talked easily about her feelings and took care to speak precisely, so her meaning was not misunderstood. Her dry sense of humor was like Reva's own, but the glee she took in the occasional practical joke was not. It took a controlled effort to sit through a custom-coded prank at the computer, then accept her light dismissal of the assassin's ruffled feelings, as if to say, "Don't take yourself so seriously." And that forced Reva to smile, because she did take things so seriously.

She hadn't planned on being a storm-bound houseguest for so long, and realized with chagrin that the enforced closeness was slowly causing their acquaintanceship to grow into something more.

If this is heading toward friendship, she cautioned herself, then it's just something else to lose. So get ready for it now.

That harsh reminder made it easy to shelve the fledgling attraction she had felt for Lish. And it helped her view their time together as a surreal slice of life out of some noontime vidshow. Seen in that light, the leisure soon palled and she welcomed the change when the storm finally broke.

A glorious day full of diffuse white light and ice-blue shadows dawned, revealing the frozen edge of Varlek Water at the base of Tyree Ridge. After a snowbot cleaned the east terrace, Reva went outside to admire the view. The inland sea bore thick sheets of ice out into the middle distance, remaining wet in the center where thermals kept the waters too warm to freeze.

Lish followed her outside, but spared little attention for the bright-shining ice sea before them. "You ready?" she asked.

"Ready?"

"To hunt the kria? I am. Been reading up on them. I'm ready to go."

"Reading?" Reva smiled. "They're a little different in person than what you read."

"Then let's go meet one. I've already got the reservations made."

Reva nodded agreement. A crawler picked them up an hour later.

Keshnavar Resort featured a view of Varlek Water to the north and the wooded, snow-covered folds of the hunting preserve to the south. Lish and Reva checked into a private villa there, and were soon headed for the gun shop.

A scalp-shaven youth lounged behind the counter, watching a holovid on flipped-down visors. At the sight of customers he came hastily to his feet, tossing the holovisor beneath the counter. "Domnas?" he asked helpfully.

"We're going hunting," Reva said.

"Then you'll want the Safari Set—," he began, reaching for a rack of equipment behind the counter.

"Save it for offworlders," Reva interrupted. "Two sets of airshoes; two Lingon 58-50s—you have motion-sensor attachments for those?"

"Yes, Domna." The youth nodded hastily.

"Add the sensors, then. Lift beacons, two camietarps, a fight squaller, and twenty rounds for each rifle."

"Only twenty?" The young man hesitated. "A case is just—"

"Only twenty. You only need three to drop a kria."

"I suppose you don't want a guidepack, either?" he asked, shaking his head sadly.

Reva shook hers in return, passing on the robotic guide that steered tourists toward the safer nature trails within the safari preserve. The gun shop clerk assembled the goods on the counter, going into a back room for most of them. It was quickly charged to the villa account, and the pair went outside to equip.

Reva guided Lish through the outfitting. Airshoes, to lift them above the snow and eliminate tracks the kria could follow. Air beacons, to summon gamekeepers to dress out a kill. Camietarps, a chameleon synthetic used for shelter if evading a hunting snowcat. Ammo packs attached to shouldertabs, holding twenty large-caliber explosive darts. Lish affixed hers while Reva added motion sensors to the dart rifle scopes.

"Make sure you use your range finder," Reva commented. "Once propellant burns out in these darts, they drop like rocks."

"All right."

"Use the motion sensor, too. It'll blip movement in the brush up to about seventy-five meters, in a ninety-degree arc in front of you. You can see the sensor screen if you're carrying the rifle, or watch the blip track through the scope if you're aiming."

Lish handled one of the 58-50s. Reva waved her hand in front of the barrel to demonstrate the motion tracking. Lish looked up.

"Isn't this a bit of overkill for a game hunt? So kria are clever trackers." She motioned to her feet, resting on air two fingers' width above the ground. "We won't even be leaving tracks. What about a sporting chance?"

The assassin gave a mirthless laugh. "You want sporting, try this on wooden snowshoes with a crossbow. You'll appreciate the edge."

"No, really," the Holdout persisted. "Why is this necessary?"

Reva rested the Lingon butt-first on the snowpack. "You've been reading up on the kria, right? Did you come across the statistic about how many first-time hunters are killed by the snowcats?"

Lish shook her head.

"They keep that stat out of the public record if they can. It would scare off tourists. Look." She motioned to the dished relay antennae that topped the wire-mesh game preserve fence. "They run sonics along the fence line to keep aggressive cats from jumping the barricade. The few kria in there can't roam like they want to. They get cranky about that."

She waved at the preserve beyond the fence and frequency barrier. "There are probably only three or four adult kria in there, all in a nasty mood. If you stray off the tourist trails and try some real hunting, those cats will be very ready to welcome you. An angry full-grown kria charges about five times faster than you can run."

Lish was puzzled. "What about all the cats that get bagged here? You hear about it on the sportsnet."

"They're shooting adolescents, brought in to stock the park. Not the wily adults." Reva patted the dart rifle. "Use the motion sensor,

Lish. It can make the difference between dead and alive. And I don't mean the kria."

The Holdout, though sobered, wasn't about to back down. Satisfied, Reva headed for the gate, followed closely by her newly wary companion.

From inside the gun shop, Vask watched them go, and waited a good quarter-hour before he followed.

Yavobo's new requirement was not something that his ordinary weapons supplier had an answer for. Nor the next. Nor the next.

It was near the end of his three-day stay before he worked his way up the ladder far enough to talk with Spots, a bartender and frontman for the biggest smuggler on Selmun III.

Spots took his nickname from the scaly specks on his skin, a vestige of the water-breathing mutation that had not run its full course in the R'debh native. In the subdued light of the Tidepool, his disfigurement could almost be overlooked.

"There might be something like you're looking for," he replied to Yavobo's question. "For a little referral fee . . ."

Yavobo pushed his credmeter across the bar, watched while Spots tapped in a modest figure, agreed to it, and thumbed the transfer plate.

"One of our competitors handles that kind of merchandise. There's a thing called a time patch, can do the type of damage you're looking for."

"Who do I see?"

"Lairdome 7, the cryopack place. Ask about the hex-pack special. That'll get you in to the right person."

Yavobo thanked the local and left, with plenty of time to seek out Lairdome 7 before his shuttle left dock. Unfortunately, the dome was dark and the cryocase shop staffed only by mechos. "Lish is expected back by month-end," was all they could tell him.

A hunter is patient. Two weeks, and then he would return.

Karuu had heard enough. First, Reva and her need for time patches. Then some other local inquiries—the few he had heard about, which always meant there was more interest among customers than actually reached his ears—and now another serious buyer, slipping through his fingers.

The distribution deal with the new Holdout was intended to give him an in to her operations. Well, he had that now, and had heard the rumors of something big coming down, as soon as Lish was back in town. Maybe he should cash in and get rid of this competitor, like Adahn suggested. If he couldn't compete, why keep her around?

Why, indeed?

He punched up a number that lit his com unit with a holovid of native fishermen engaged in bloody sacrificial ritual. The vid faded and revealed the bronzed face of Daribi, the chief of his derevin called the Islanders. The metallic sheen of his artificial tan lent him a surreal mien, but the bone through his nose was real, as were the facial tattoos that gave him the distinctive Islander look.

"Find the boat-boys who work for Lish," Karuu ordered the chief, jovial small talk dropping abruptly from his conversation. "On the sly, no obvious pressure. Make it casual: friendly drinks, share some euphorics—you know what I mean."

"What are we looking for?" the derevin leader asked.

"Big cargo drop is coming along soon. Find out everything you can. Her movements, the timing, everything."

Daribi nodded.

"Contact me, direct, as soon as you are knowing things. And make it fast."

"Right, Boss." The Islander acknowledged his orders and the screen went blank.

Karuu pondered what he had set in motion. First he would learn more, then take decisive action, and then he would again be secure in his position among Selmun Holdouts.

With that plan in mind, Karuu started to leave his desk, then hesitated, and called up Janus instead. Karuu was going to need a bit of help with the Imperials, and Adahn's lieutenant, who had so kindly offered, was going to provide it.

XXVI

The guidepack was a small shoulder-mount unit, worn in the same spot where Reva and Lish had placed their ammo reserves. The device was an artificially intelligent construct, a brain in a box consisting of neural net, voice and sensor chips, a data library, and a variety of narrator personalities to chose from. Vask punched up the neutral docent tone, got the guide in place on one shoulder, slung the standard tourist-issue Berka 408 dart rifle on the other, and started into the preserve.

When he set foot inside the gate, the tour guide stirred to life.

"Is this your first visit to Keshnavar, sir?" it asked.

"Hmm," Vask replied distractedly, surveying the trails ahead of him to see which way the two women had gone.

The tour guide was used to ambiguous answers from humans. "May I suggest the Yeskaya Nature Walk for your first excursion, sir? It is mildly invigorating, gives an overview of the six different terrain and vegetation systems contained within the preserve, and, of course, I will be happy to comment on the nature and habits of wildlife we might encounter—"

"Quiet," Vask commanded. "Guide, answer queries only."

"Certainly, sir," the unit responded, and lapsed into dutiful silence.

He saw two hikers on a path through the brown-needled yeskaya trees, an elderly couple pausing every now and then to record vistas with a hand-held holocam. A few other strollers, singly or in small groups, could be glimpsed on other trails and one distant hillside. Vask saw no one walking eastward across virgin snow, into the rougher terrain where lodge staff said the hunting was best. And nowhere could he detect so much as a footstep straying from the snow-cleared nature paths.

"Idiot," he blurted out loud.

"Sir?" queried the tour guide, which Kastlin automatically ignored.

Intent on approaching the women in what would seem a casual manner, Vask had paid little attention to the implications of airshoes. He had never worn them before. They made snowwalking easier and incidentally eliminated tracks to discourage stalking predators.

They also discouraged stalking Security agents.

Heads on a spike, he thought, look at that. Not a damn mark anywhere, except my own, and I'm not using the liftpads right now.

He trotted along, studying the snow edge to each side of the trail to confirm his suspicion. Nowhere was there compacted snow or a footprint, only the clean, sharp line where snowbots had dissolved precipitation and sucked it away from the trail's edge. Anyone stepping off the path in an airshoe as good as vanished.

Vask had waited too long, and now it seemed he had lost his quarry. Unless they bumped tree branches and knocked snow down, disturbing the groundcover that way. Alright. That was something worth looking for.

"Guide," he addressed the shoulder pack. "Give me a map of the preserve."

The unit extruded a projection bar forward of Vask's shoulder, then displayed a holographic topo-view of the Resort.

"Mark my location." A blinking red dot obligingly appeared near the trailhead at the game preserve entrance.

"Can you track other guests?"

"Only if they have requested that their location be monitored and are carrying the correct type of homing transponder with them. Some persons with health conditions or—"

"Never mind. Are you monitoring anyone right now?"

"No, sir."

The screen remained in mid-air, depicting nearly 5,000 square kilometers of wilderness, with only a small portion covered by groomed trails. "Show me where the best hunting is," he ordered.

An eastward section of the map lit up in blue shading. "The best places to make a catch with an acceptable degree of risk can be approached along these trails. To reach the first trail . . ."

Vask let the unit drone on while he considered the map. Reva and Lish weren't equipped like people looking for an "acceptable degree of risk." He doubted they had followed this resort-planned agenda. Neither could they have gone far in only a quarter of an hour.

"Guide," he interrupted the travelogue. "What's the best place for an experienced hunter to go after challenging game?"

The contours of colored space changed on the map. Sections previously undesignated were now lit. The safe "tourist" region was not among them.

That's better, Vask thought. "What's the best way to get there from here? Draw me a route to follow."

The guide seemed to hesitate before responding to his question. It undoubtedly had him pegged as a novice hunter, which he was. But Vask didn't plan to go hunting, just socializing. If he got too far out, he'd turn back and follow his alternative plan, to catch the women in the lodge that evening when they came back in from the preserve.

"Route?" he prompted.

The tour guide marked a path for him in green, and showed how he must move from his present position.

"That's fine. Keep that map on display, will you?"

"If you wish, sir."

The unit sounded reluctant to encourage his unconventional jaunt, but comply it did. Vask switched on his airshoes, and stepped over the path's edge onto a virgin blanket of snow. With spongy steps he headed in the direction it seemed his quarry must have gone, forging ahead into potentially dangerous wilderness. The snow behind him held no trace of his passage.

Lish held the dart rifle awkwardly, not accustomed to its weight or feel. Reva showed her the best way to brace its bulk with the sling, and to walk a little to the side and rear. With both their guns angled correctly, the two motion sensors covered a 180-degree arc ahead of them.

"You haven't hunted much, have you?" Reva observed as they moved eastward.

"Not on shipboard. And I've been too busy with my work in the last few years to get out much."

"Ever spearfish on R'debh?"

"Not that, either."

"You mind killing things?" the assassin wondered aloud.

Lish shrugged. "When I was young I was in House Arleon's military academy. I wasn't thinking about it then, though I guess that was getting ready to kill people. Got kicked out for fighting. Maybe if there'd been things to hunt I would've left my classmates alone."

"You don't seem like the kind to start things."

"What makes you say that?"

"You just don't."

"You're right. I was small for my age. And Shiran, too, in a dirtsider school. That was incentive enough for others to start things. I just finished them."

They walked in silence for a while, skirting yeskaya stands and keeping to the high ground near the ridge crests.

"How about you?" Lish followed up.

"Me?"

"Yeah. Did you fight when you were a kid?"

A spasm of guilt ripped through Reva, and she bit back the truthful answers that almost slipped out. No, she shouted in her head, I didn't fight when I was a kid, though I should have! Instead, I crippled a friend with an angry thought. I killed my mother and my brother, or left them as good as dead someplace very far away from here. I don't dare fight in anger, because I can't tell who I'll hurt or where I'll end up. Leave my heart out of it, though, do it in cold blood—oh, yes, I can fight that way—

"Reva?"

"What?" Her tone was harsher than she intended, and she realized it right away. "Sorry," she apologized, trying to brush it off. "I don't like to talk about . . . about my childhood."

"Never mind, then."

They hiked in silence past leafless red-claw brush, and paused while Reva got her bearings. "Down there, I think." She pointed to a partially wooded valley running to the northwest where two ridges drew closer together. "That looks less brushy, more like a place for deska to graze. Where you find deska, you'll find the kria who hunt them."

"Can I ask about your hunting?" Lish asked tentatively. "How do you know so much about this? That looks like any other mountain slope to me."

Contrite over her earlier response, Reva smiled to show the question was not offensive. "I lived here with the Vudesh for a while," she offered. "In the north, where the kria run free and the winter is longer."

"Whatever for?" Lish was astonished. She couldn't imagine giving up civilized comforts to huddle with unwashed tribesmen in their primitive, poorly built longhouses.

Reva looked at her friend. "Because they know how to live," she explained, "and I needed to learn that at the time."

The truth of it was rather different, but Reva wasn't sharing all her secrets. "Let's head on that way," she changed the subject, "and I'll show you what a fight squaller is for."

When Reva was eighteen, her father had retired from his work in the deep domes, and took a post teaching aqualogy on Chorb.

"I'm not going with you," she had declared. "I have too much going on here."

"The hell you're not," Jerrik flared. "You come with me, or I'll have the police shut you down."

She was astonished, and furious. Angrily he confessed to spying on his daughter, to ferreting out her clandestine smuggling activities. Though he didn't know the half of it—her contact with the techrunner Karuu, the selling of cyberware to blackwire shops—he knew enough that he could get her arrested. What the competition hadn't yet pulled off, her own father threatened to do gladly: turn her over to the Grinds.

There was a stupid speech about mending her ways. Oh, he was righteous. She tried not to respond: he was not, after all, her real father, not the understanding man of her childhood, just one of these ghost-people from a Mainline that wasn't really, truly, the one she should be living in.

But it was the one she was stuck in, more or less, and since her decision to never again skip wildly across the Lines, she knew that any nearby Timeline would hold virtually the same blackmailer with the same nasty sense of recrimination.

She was tired of being a Holdout anyway. She cleared her bank account, put it all in her credmeter, and sneaked aboard the next flight out of the starport.

When she hit Des'lin, she had no place to go, and didn't dare check into a resort—her father was too resourceful to dodge that way for long. She rode a local snowtransport as far as it would take her, then cadged a ride with an ice runner hauling supplies to Keshkaric at the edge of the Great Ice.

That is where she stayed, for three years. Three years that failed to heal what was wrong with Reva's life, although the harsh demands of frontier survival pushed that to the back of her mind. The Vudesh never welcomed her, nor did they drive her forth. They took pride in their simple existence, and with them Reva learned to value anew things she had forgotten were part of life.

Those were things inexplicable and grand, like the elemental power of nature in a scouring ice storm, and the joy of food when one is near-starving. They were things one had to experience to appreciate.

The Vudesh offered many such experiences. They tested Reva, and taught her, and finally asked her to leave when she slew a chieftain's son who insisted too forcefully that he would take her to wife.

She almost regretted leaving. She had a lot to thank them for. The Vudesh were fine hunters, and excellent killers, and their student never forgot a lesson that she learned.

Vask's hope of finding the women quickly soon vanished. There was no trail of disturbed snow knocked from tree branches to suggest where they had gone, and the convoluted terrain denied a viewpoint from which he might be able to spot them.

It didn't take long before the urban-bred Kastlin wasn't entirely sure of his own path, either. The ridge folds and stands of yeskaya, the broken ground and clumps of red claw protruding through the snow, conspired to force him off the line of march described by the tour guide's green map route. After he had trudged down another snowy ridge and found himself in another brushy valley bottom, he paused to catch his breath.

He looked at the holomap. The blinking red light that was himself was to the north of the green line of recommended travel. He looked to his right, toward that imaginary line, and saw wind-scoured limestone forming the face of an untraversible ridge. There was no way to rejoin the right line of march from here.

"Guide," he said, exasperated. "Show me the best way back to the lodge."

A yellow line appeared, marking a route from his present location back to the resort buildings. As he turned to survey the path he would have to follow, movement in the red-claw brush drew his startled attention. Vask unslung his dart rifle; before he could hold it ready, a large white and russet heap of fur lumbered out of the scrub before him. He sighed. This six-legged beast, taller than a man at the shoulder and twice as long, was fat and slow-moving and herbivorous. It was a deska, walking on in-turned toes made for gripping tree limbs. It snuffled the air as it caught the man's strange scent.

Vask was reslinging his rifle when the tour guide spoke up.

"Sir, I am required by law to inform you that you are now dangerously close to kria hunting grounds. If you recall the waiver that you signed upon check-in, Keshnavar Resort is not responsible for the safety of guests who move too closely to deska grazing areas. You have now done so, and I have so duly recorded."

Vask frowned at the shoulder pack. "Why didn't you tell me this before?"

"You have been moving through brushlands favored by deska. Until I sensed this creature here, I could not be certain this pasturage was in use. It is, and you are duly notified."

Vask growled and considered turning the guide unit off. He had turned his back on the harmless grazer when a drawn-out high-pitched scream froze him in his tracks. He spun back around. It came from the southeast, from a hilly point overlooking the valley.

"What was that?" he demanded of the guide.

"That was the combat call of the kria, a challenge issued by one beast to another to fight over hunting territory."

"Great."

Vask turned back toward the lodge and began to trot over the snowcover when a second kria answered the fighting call. He froze in his tracks, horripilation raising every hair on his body. The answering call came from the brush directly ahead.

Reva let the air-amplified blast from the fight squaller echo off the ridge sides, then dropped her hand back by her side. Lish's eyes were wide, and widened more when an answering challenge ripped through the frosty air.

"There's one down there, all right." Reva pointed. "If we can provoke it enough, it'll head straight for us instead of stalking. That's what we want." She held the squaller out to Lish. "You want to give it a try?"

"Sure." Lish reached gingerly for the palm-sized device, as if it, not the kria, could bite.

"Aim the speaker plate down the valley, like so, and press," Reva explained.

Lish did, and another fearsome squall rang out before them.

Instead of the hair-raising yowl they expected in reply, they heard something else: a distinctive human outcry, and a crashing in the brush. Lish's smile faded as the pair watched the small figure of a man burst from the brush and run toward the edge of the wooded valley.

A kria pursued, its six-legged gait eating up the ground at an impossible rate of speed.

"Squall again!" Reva snapped the order and Lish unthinkingly obeyed. The assassin threw her gun up to her shoulder and fired off three rounds at the great white-furred predator.

The fighting squall rang out again, ear-piercingly loud. The explosive darts flew almost to the limit of their range, a good 100 meters away, and missed the cat—then exploded on impact with the snowpack at its feet. The squall and the explosions were enough to distract the hunting beast, and it hesitated in its charge. It swung its head, glancing about to see if there was an immediate danger. There was not.

As Reva pulled darts from her ammo pack and hastily reloaded her rifle, the snowcat was back on the trail of the man. Even so, the diversion had bought a little time. The strayed tourist reached a yeskaya tree, and began to climb as fast as he could.

"Sea Father!" Reva exclaimed. "Kria can climb, too!" She turned to Lish. "Don't use the squaller again, we don't want that cat coming after you. Lay down here on the snow and brace your shots. Shoot at the kria. If you can hit it, fine. If not, aim for the tree trunk over its head. Keep it out of that tree until I can get close enough to deal with it better."

There was no discussion. Lish threw herself down in a prone firing position. With nervous fingers she set up the ranging adjustment on her scope, and fired as the cat squatted at the base of the tree.

Her first shot went wild, leaving an impact explosion in the snow, as before, that caused the kria to start.

Reva went over the lip of the ridge and headed down into the valley in a long, controlled, snowy slide.

"Guide," Vask gasped, scrambling for the next-higher branch, "call for help."

"I can't, sir. We are out of my limited communications range with the resort lodge."

Kastlin yanked his rifle sling free from a grasping needle-clump, and pushed an arm's length higher up into the dense conifer. "What do you mean, can't?" he snarled. "Don't you have an emergency channel?"

The kria leapt into the air, and made a swipe at Vask's foot. Kastlin leapt up the tree trunk as well, pulling his feet clear, and snapping the projector bar off the guidepack. "Damage to this unit will be added to your bill, sir," the guide commented in its neutral-docent tone.

"Vent that! Do you have an emergency channel!?" he almost screamed at the tour robot.

"No, sir. If you would like your movements monitored, you need a transponder with an emergency call button on it, and an extra fee must—"

"Shut up!" If the kria didn't get him first, the guidepack would drive him crazy. Vask pulled himself a little higher, then saw he was reaching the limits of his escape. Branches grew too closely together, and the brown, pricking yeskaya needles grew into a dense, impenetrable mass higher up the tree trunk. He had come as far as he could.

Vask looked down, right into the amber, hungry eyes of the squatting predator. The kria hunched on four of its legs, and used the forward pair to grasp the tree trunk a mere four meters below Kastlin's feet. The beast gave the yeskaya a shake, and then a harder one. The tree swayed enough to be unsettling, though not enough to dislodge the agent's death grip. The kria withdrew its front paws, claws slicing effortlessly into the bark and leaving a trail of curled green pith where it had gripped.

It coiled as if to spring up the trunk. Vask felt something twist tighter in his guts. "Guide," he panted, "can kria climb trees?"

"Yes, they can, sir."

Vask dropped his forehead against the rough bark of the trunk. Can I sideslip out of this? He assessed himself quickly, and knew the answer in an instant. No. There was too much adrenaline bracing his system; he was too uncentered. A body's survival imperative almost always shut off the higher mental faculties needed for psionics. If he had time, he could do it, and time was what he didn't have.

Vask had to get his rifle in hand. It would take some maneuvering and it would be hard to aim amid the close-grown branches, but it was his only hope.

First, he needed a distraction. Kastlin reached for the tour guide and pulled it from his shoulder. Aware that something unusual was going on, the unit asked, "May I be of assistance, sir?"

Vask looked down. The kria was hunched and staring intently, poised in that peculiar stillness of a predator right before it grabs its prey. "Guide," he said to the silvered device in his hand, "tell me about the kria."

"Certainly, sir. The kria are warm-blooded, six-legged predators native to Des'lin. . . ."

He held his hand out. The droning guide was right over the kria's face. Maybe this would work.

Before he could release the guidepack, something impacted the trunk beneath his legs, shuddering the tree and causing wood and bark slivers to burst through the air. Startled, Vask's arm jerked forward to brace his grip.

The next impact took him squarely in the ankle. The breath went from him in a shocked hiss, and the guidepack dropped from deadened fingers. Vask felt only numbness in his lower leg, where his foot was nearly blown off by the hunting dart. Close to fainting, he clung in blackness to the tree trunk.

The kria had ducked away from the spray of splinters, and paused to blink at the silvery object on the ground. Sound came from it, and that made it of curious interest. Then the snowcat looked back up the tree, where the strong scent of blood was more compelling. This quarry had become wounded, and was weakened. Now was time for the kill.

✦   ✦   ✦

Lish cursed her nerves. She didn't have this problem handling a ship's guns. She took an extra breath, aimed at the cat that was stretching full-length up into the tree. She squeezed off a round, and the dart flew true, right between the shoulder blades of the hunting beast.

The kria did not drop dead. It spun about in an explosion of blood and fur, its quarry forgotten, as it sought its attacker. It was wounded, and it was angry. It fixed its sight on Reva, loosed a hair-raising squall, then charged.

The assassin was thirty meters away when the wounded snowcat turned on her. She stopped in her tracks, rifle at the ready, and faced the furious hunter that bore down upon her. At twenty-five meters her first round flew, and caught the snowcat in the chest. The kria kept on, hardly slowed, its organs so well protected and its anger so great that a critical wound was difficult to score. These were the feared prowlers that kept fighting for minutes after they were dead. They had to be killed several times over before they realized it and lay still.

This kria was not that dead, yet.

Lish drew a bead on the snowcat as Reva aimed her second shot. The assassin fired at fifteen meters, and the explosive dart struck the kria's sloping brow right above the eyes. Silky fur and the curve of the skull deflected the round enough that its explosion caused only an irritating flesh wound. The beast came on, enraged; if anything, faster than before.

A blip from the motion sensor distracted Lish. She glanced over toward the tree and saw the man, lying senseless in the snow at its base. Blood stained the snow by one leg. She bit her lip. Through the thick needle-cover she had not realized she had wounded him.

She looked back, and shot to her feet. "Reva!" she cried out, to no avail. The cat was on the other woman, and there was no way to shoot. Her kria-fur coat blended into the tussling blur of motion that kicked up snow and obscured the action. Lish dropped back down to the ground and trained her scope on the scene, trying to make out what was happening.

Reva had a far better view. Shot twice and flesh-wounded once, the kria had plenty of fight left and leapt upon the assassin as she fired a third shot. The round went wild. With no time to think, Reva did what every Vudesh tribesman is trained to do. She leapt over her attacker and let the snowcat pass beneath her. She twisted, cat-like herself, and came down atop the charging monster.

There is only one safe place to be, near a wounded kria, and that is on its back. Kria do not like to roll over, so their reflex is to twist and snap. Hope you can strike a fatal blow before it can claw you from its back, and you will live to tell about your adventure.

Kria fur is a good protection against the beast's own claws. Reva felt the bruising blow of its rake, but was not gutted as it scratched at her wickedly. Her vibroknife was in her hand, snatched in a moment of unthinking reflex. She smelled the cat's rank breath and the scent of hot blood where she grappled with the beast, squarely atop the shoulder wound in its back. One hand gripped its ruff, her legs gripped its ribs. The knife hand sought a good place to strike.

When an energy field stiffens a monofilament wire and vibrates it thousands of times a second, the resulting weapon cuts through steeloy like a laser through gel-soup. Yet it was only a 20-cm blade, only two hand-widths long. It took two tries before her slashes at the kria's neck found a vital spot. The beast crumbled beneath her, and Reva rolled gasping off the third kria kill of her life.

The Vudesh count only the ones taken in personal combat, without a missile weapon, and so did she.

Vask awoke in the resort autodoc, aching but whole again. After he recognized the two women keeping him company, he realized who must have saved him from the snowcat.

It was not how he had planned to make their acquaintance, but it would do.

Reva looked at him strangely, and asked quietly about his health. Lish apologized for the wound. There was no trace of his injury left, only healed bone and regenerated tissues, but she remained disturbed by the accident that had almost cost him his life.

She was the one who drew him out in conversation, let him work in the ploy he had planned to use. "You look familiar," he said, off-hand. "Don't we have a mutual friend? Spots?"

It was an in to the Holdout community. Lish seemed to recall seeing Vask around and with a little psionic nudging—very subtle, that—she had the impression he was the friend of an acquaintance, with whom she may have done business once or twice. Thus their "secret" was out, and they could all relax a little more in each other's company.

Reva appeared uncomfortable, and regarded him pensively. Vask wished again that he could pick up something of her thoughts. Even close up there was no hint what she was thinking. If he could have gotten inside her head, he would have been surprised.

She had never saved a life before. The feeling was a lot different than taking one.

"We have most of it," Daribi reported back. "What Lish is shipping, how it's moving, who's buying, when it arrives. We don't have the drop point yet."

Karuu was pleased. "That is maybe not necessary, if you have the rest. Tell me more."

"This run is big, alright. So big that it's shipping on a regular cargo freighter."

"What is she moving?"

"A strange thing, Sa'adani-built. Borgbeasts."

Irritation wrinkled the soft fur over Karuu's eyes. He hated to admit there was something worth smuggling that he didn't know about. Yet one more reason to get rid of this unwanted competitor. "What have you found out about borgbeasts?" he asked unhappily.

"The Sa'adani take a neural net unit, like a mech brain," Daribi answered, "and interconnect it to an organic brain. Don't know how it works on humans, or if they're even trying it. They do it with animals, and end up with borgbeasts."

"What is the advantage?" Karuu asked, fascinated.

The Islander scratched his polished brow. "Mostly it makes an animal's behavior controllable and programmable, like putting a guide-pack in charge of an organic body. As a side effect it seems to jump up the animal's intelligence. Works best with near-human intelligence, though."

Karuu had a faraway look as he considered the potential in this new technology.

"Would you like the specfile?" Daribi offered.

"Yes, that would be most enlightening. What kind of borgified beast is Lish bringing to lovely R'debh?"

"Cetaceans, Boss. A number of whale-like creatures from some Sa'adani world, supposedly compatible with this ecology. They come with a few handlers to help them adapt and relay orders to their borg units."

"What kind of orders would that be, do you know yet?"

Daribi smirked. "Some kind of political thing is going on. These beasties are intended for people with ties to the AAP."

"The Aqua-Agric Party? Using modified sea intelligences? Well, well. This is becoming more interesting, indeed." Karuu beamed at the Islander. "How does our resourceful friend plan to bring these very large creatures here?"

"The Aqualogy Trade Fair begins next week on Avelar Island and Shelf," the chief reported. "A lot of cargoliners are shipping goods for the event. Her ship is posing as one of the exhibitors. Once it's in unregulated atmosphere, it can take off and head for the ocean drop site."

Karuu was smiling as Daribi finished. "You know the make of freighter she is using?"

"Yes."

"Arrange to buy us a vessel of the same type, my wild native friend, and hide it somewhere safe. At the fringe of the asteroids, perhaps, where its profile will not be noted on sensors. Our freighter will dock at the same time as hers. If you can do that for me, I will handle Customs. Then we will be several borgbeasts the richer for it."

"As you say, Boss."

"Good work, Daribi. There is a bonus in this for you when we are done. Consider if you would like to take over Lish's operation, will you?"

The Islander smiled avariciously. "I'll consider it," he agreed.

"Good day, then."

Daribi signed off, and Karuu leaned back in his chair, content. This was shaping up quite nicely. Borgbeasts! What a thing. Perhaps he would not sell them all to the AAP; maybe he would keep one or two aside for other buyers. It was important, after all, to maintain a balance of power. As long as he could dictate the balance.

Karuu punched up the specfile on his desk console and began to learn more about borgbeasts.

After their kria encounter at Keshnavar, Vask had invited his saviors to go ice-sailing as his guests. Having had their fill of hunting, the women accepted the offer, and a casual friendship had sprung up among the three. When Lish returned to Selmun III the others came along. Lairdome 7 became their informal meeting place.

"I need a cyberdecker." Lish addressed the air in her Comax Shipping office.

"What happened to the one you had?" Reva asked.

The smuggler frowned. "He's dead. Don't know if it was ICE in the Net, or a personal attack."

"I could look into that for you," Vask offered.

Lish looked at him appraisingly. Since their first dinner together the Fixer had been offering his services, casually angling for work. "I have someone on it, but if you'd like to check it out, I could use the help. Maybe you'll find out something different than my boy Zendo."

Vask lacked the cyberware that some agents used to track a database of criminal elements, but his mnemonic tricks and highly trained memory served a close double. "Would that be the Zendo who used to freelance as a datarunner, two, three years ago?" he asked. "Wore a gold data spike on his temple?"

Lish nodded when he described her streetboy. "He's lost the data spike—got it hardwired, now. That's Zendo, though. Why?"

Vask spread his hands. "If he's investigating for you, I know I can do better."

"Oh?"

"I know more places to look and ask better questions. What's it worth to you?" He followed up the bid with a charming smile.

Lish tilted her head. "You find out for sure who offed my runner, how and why, before Zendo does, and I'll pay you the straight service fee. Usual rates."

"I do it inside two days, and you'll pay me double," he countered. Lish gave a small laugh. "Done."

"What do you need a netrunner for?" Reva asked.

Lish shook her head. "Details are confidential, if you're not the runner. I don't mind telling you, though, it's to finalize some arrangements for my next drop."

"Big, is it?" Reva recognized the gleam of anticipation that Lish had been walking around with for several days now.

"Big enough." The Holdout smiled cryptically. She thanked Vask for his offer and asked pointedly when he would get on it. Taking the unsubtle hint, the Fixer noted down the dead netrunner's vitals, and said good-bye.

When he was gone, Reva offered to refer Lish to a good decker.

The smuggler looked sidelong at the tall woman, today a platinum blonde with flickering holographics on her nails. "You." She waved an admonishing finger. "You know the same people Karuu knows."

Reva tensed at the chiding tone. "What do you mean? Everyone knows the same people Karuu knows, if you've worked here long enough."

"I need someone with absolutely no contact and no personal interest in Karuu, that's what I mean. An offworlder, I suppose. The last one was."

So this wasn't personal. Reva fought down her angry reaction. It sounded like the younger woman was thinking about guarding her back, and that was long overdue. The assassin ventured a guess. "You're cutting the Dorleoni out of your distribution deal, aren't you?"

"I'm doing something of no concern to the Dorleoni. Yet." Lish flashed her an innocent smile, the one reserved for warehouse inspectors and people she was about to bankrupt at Shaydo cards. "I took your advice about a couple of things, though, and I made some changes in my operations."

"Is that right?"

"Yeah, like covering my tracks, and leaving myself more than one way out. Let's say I don't want to get treed by the snowcat I'm hunting."

Reva's lips quirked. Score one lesson learned. "I know offworld deckers, too. Could be here from Lyndir on the next liner, say, tomorrow."

"That's more like it. No relationship to the Dorleoni?"

"None at all."

"I need to hire the best."

"Then you want the FlashMan. Here's the call code." She jotted down a scrambled comnet access number, and the decker's ID. "He's worked with me before. His referrals are good, too."

"Terrific. Maybe Vask can pin down who killed my last netrunner by then."

"Maybe." Reva was noncommittal. "Are you comfortable trusting him with this job? You don't know that much about him."

"I deal with a lot of people I don't know much about." The Holdout looked sharply at Reva, who took her point.

"Still—it's risky."

"Everything's risky. You have to take the chance now and then. I go by my feelings about a person. I'm not usually wrong."

Reva thought of the house pass in her carrybag, and steered the subject on to a different track. "I've asked around about Vask. He's known, but he's low-profile. No one seems to know much about him."

Lish smiled. "You sure that's the only reason you checked him out?"

Her humor evaded the assassin. "What?"

"Maybe you're interested, too."

The tall woman stiffened. "Interested?"

"Come on, Reva, you know how he looks at you. Puppy-dog eyes. He'd follow you around all day, if he could."

"He better not try it. Besides, it's you he talks with all the time."

"That's because you aren't exactly conversational. You barely say 'yes' and 'no' to him. It's hard to talk with someone like that."

Reva tapped her nails on the chair arm, the pressure turning the holovids on and off again. "Don't be ridiculous."

"You act like you regret not letting the cat eat him. Is that it?"

Reva's fingers paused in mid-air. "Is that how it seems to you?"

Lish gestured. "You saved the man's life. He asks about you, tires to talk with you, and you pretty much ignore him. That's all."

"I don't dislike him," the assassin said. "I feel a little . . . awkward around him."

"Because you saved his life? And now you don't know how to act with him?"

The shrewd guess hit home. Reva was quiet.

"That's an easy one. Drop your business front and loosen up."

"I don't plan to loosen up around Vask."

"Your choice."

"And if he tries puppy-dogging me, he won't live to try it twice."

"I'm sure he won't."

"Hmph." Reva left in a huff, trying to flee the unease she carried inside.

The sunset sky was aglow with red-washed clouds and streaks of purple, fading to a greenish-yellow at the far edge of the ocean horizon. Lish waved good-bye to the last of her legitimate customers, two kelpie hunters returning to Avelar with a load of cryocases, and paused to enjoy the view out the back loading bay. The humid breeze bore the coolness of early evening, and she savored it on her sweat-damp face while smartmechs packed up shop for the night.

Reva would be by soon; the pair would freshen up and go out for dinner, and Lish had agreed to give one of the holodens a try afterward. There would be no sensie-feelie entertainment, with its hallucinogenic drugs, she was promised: just good solid external illusion to fill a few leisure hours.

She was debating what pheromones to wear when a mech interrupted her musings.

"Lish, a customer wishes—," it began, then the customer's own booming voice overrode the deferent machine.

"You are Lish?"

She turned to face the visitor, and looked up, and up, into the leathery red and black mottled visage of an alien. A minimal bodysuit revealed lanky muscles on arms and legs of the same oddly marked flesh as his face. Piercing yellow eyes stared unblinking from a countenance of harsh planes and angles. His intensity was unsettling.

"What can I do for you?" she asked, hiding behind the cool facade of a disinterested businesswoman.

"I need to discuss the hex-pack special."

Though it was a little late for that kind of trade, it was what really paid the bills. "Sure," the Holdout said. "Let's step into the office."

She motioned the alien toward the door and accompanied him. They were soon inside and Lish sat behind her desk. Her customer shut the door behind them, then came to stand before her. She pointed to a chair; the alien ignored her and remained standing, straddle-legged, his arms crossed upon his chest. "My name is Yavobo," he declared, "and I will ask you this only once. Do you sell time patches?"

A sudden fear gripped Lish's heart. This was not how clients approached a Holdout when they had to dicker over price and delivery arrangements. She could bet this fellow didn't want anything she had to sell.

"Are you interested in buying one?" she countered, stalling for time.

Yavobo gave a half-shake of his head, almost regretfully, then reached out with a long, quick arm and grabbed her by the front of her jumpsuit. The slender woman flew through the air to slam against the plassteel wall on the far side of the room. She slid down the partition and slumped on the floor, stunned, winded, with her right shoulder nearly out of joint.

Yavobo was standing over her again. "I am not repeating my question. Answer, yes or no."

It was beyond Lish to answer anything at all. Curling forward around her middle, she gasped for air, a paralyzed diaphragm failing to cooperate in her efforts to breathe. The alien waited patiently, until, a moment later, air wheezed back into her lungs.

"Yes . . . ," she managed to choke out to her interrogator.

"Good." Yavobo leaned down, pulled her to her feet with a grip on her clothes, and pushed her back up against the wall.

"Second question. Who bought a time patch from you last month?"

A feeling of terror stirred in her. Taken unawares, she'd had no chance to defend herself, and was not psychologically prepared for such an assault. This Yavobo was clearly ready to hurt her. If she didn't talk, she might end up dead.

And if she *did* talk, she might end up dead. The shadow community of backstreeters and fronts would never buy from her again, and some individual might well decide to eliminate her as an untrustworthy link.

Yavobo reached down, grabbed her left little finger. "You are taking too long to answer," he said, and snapped the bone like a twig.

Lish screamed.

The pain and the fear had already sent adrenaline coursing through her body; now this wanton injury gave her conscious intent as well. With a mental command directed through a select cybercircuit in her brain, she activated the adrenal boosters she had equipped herself with long ago, when streetfighters sought out an unwanted young smuggler and brawling had been her only defense in the byways of Raffin.

Finger and shoulder became mere throbs, to be ignored. She gained no muscle mass, and did not grow to a height to match Yavobo's, but boosted reflexes and temporary strength flooded her system in a wave never matched by natural biochemistry. Lish yanked out of Yavobo's grip and before he could react, she darted across the room and had her hand on the latch of the door.

She was halfway through the door when he pulled her back into the room. His reach and speed were remarkable as well. Iron fingers sank into her injured shoulder, magnifying the throb back into a spear of agony. Her collarbone broke under the pressure of the alien's grasp as he lifted Lish off her feet and threw her across the room again one-handed. He was growing angry, and this time he put his strength into it.

Plassteel does not dent. Skulls do. Lish's head crunched against the wall loud enough to drive the sickening sound echoing through her own ears.

Yavobo kneeled before her. Through red spots in her vision she saw him draw a utility knife from its sheath, hold the blade threateningly near. "You will give me a list of your customers now, or I will kill you." He said it matter-of-factly.

Lish tried to collect her thoughts, too much adrenaline to fall unconscious, too little reason left to remember the client file names. Trying to form words, trying to explain how hard this would be . . . nothing coming out.

"Do you wish to die, then?" The question was dispassionate as the alien's face receded down a black tunnel.

"No one's dying here, you bastard, except maybe you."

Reva's voice rang out in the confined office space. It was the last thing Lish heard as she slipped from consciousness.

Yavobo spun in a knife-wielding crouch to face his new challenger, and paused, assessing the ordinary woman who dared defy him. Tall, slim, red-haired; garbed in a sea green, body-clinging weave of semi-cellophane, one arm clad, the other bare: the fad of the month that humans considered alluring. Hazel eyes met his squarely.

"Leave us," he barked. "I have no business with you."

"You do now." Reva stepped out of her unstable high-heeled shoes and moved away from a toppled chair, balancing her weight on the balls of her feet. She recognized Yavobo immediately from her stalking of Murs and Lanzig. She knew of his great strength and reputation for a violent temper, and knew she must be ready for anything. She pulled her vibroknife from the sheath concealed on her fabric-covered arm, and thumbed the power tab. The blade became a deadly vibrating blur in her hand.

In all his years among the human-populated worlds, this was the first time that a thin-skin woman had ever challenged Yavobo as an equal, taking him on with a knife in a stance that called to combat, warrior to warrior. If his mission had not been so grim, he would have been amused.

He stood up slowly from his crouch, lowering his blade slightly to one side in a disarming gesture. "What is this to you?" he asked. "Leave, and I will do you no harm."

Reva did not alter her stance one bit. She stood silent, caught between two warring instincts. Catching this brutish creature in the act of murdering her only friend left the assassin with an angry bloodlust she had never experienced on contract hits. This was different. This was personal. She wanted to kill the Aztrakhani and do it now.

And this was problematical. Reva seldom killed with her bare hands. She used technology, carefully staged accidents or apparent flukes of circumstance. Oh, she *could* kill with the knife, was quite good at it, really. But she was more comfortable moving between Timelines, leaving her victim in a different Now when the hit was done. But this time was different. For once, when it might be convenient, perhaps vital, Reva felt reluctant to move between the Lines.

She didn't want to risk losing the Lish she knew in this Mainline, or leave her on the floor in this Now, dying, while Reva killed Yavobo a Line or two away. That wasn't good enough. She had to stay in this Mainline, with the newfound friend whose personality she knew, where she could hurt in turn the same Yavobo who had hurt Lish.

That made everything a lot harder. There was no easy way to duck out, if she didn't switch Lines. There's no room for error, she told herself, and her knuckles whitened as she gripped the knife hilt harder.

Yavobo watched her grip tighten, and smiled. He risked a glance at the Holdout, and scowled at the sight of her eyes rolled up, a pool of blood collecting beneath her blond head. "Do you work with this one?" he demanded. "Answer my questions and I will let you live."

The Aztrakhani's reach was longer, but Reva thought she was more agile. She needed to draw him out of the office, where she would have room to maneuver. She thought of his temper, and decided to talk.

"That's my partner," Reva lied. "You can't kill me, you backwater slimeworm."

He ignored the insult. "Tell me who bought time patches last month," he demanded, "and I will not kill your partner." He toed the defenseless body at his feet.

His words hit Reva like a physical blow.

He was on her trail.

She struggled to slow her breathing, grown suddenly fast and shallow. There was no point in holding back. Lish's life was on the line, as well as her own. This erstwhile bodyguard had to be taken down now. *No one* had ever gotten close to catching Reva at her work. No one would.

"Time patches?" Her mouth was dry and she forced the words out. "There's only one you're interested in. That's the one I used."

Yavobo went utterly still, with the quietude of the stalking kria.

"The next one will get you, and Lanzig, too."

With a ululating battle cry, Yavobo sprang at Reva.

Ready for an extreme reaction, she leapt sideways and backward, through the office door and out into the warehouse. Labormechs were unresponsive to the uproar and continued to stack shipping components. Reva tumbled past one, dodged around a stack of cryocases, Yavobo close on her heels. In the open loading area near the back bay door, she spun to face her attacker.

Yavobo was on her with a lunge. She sidestepped and momentum carried him by; before she could connect a slash with his ribs, he twisted and was facing her once more. The two stood poised for the blink of an eye, and then began to circle warily in the ancient dance of knife fighters.

Mechos had shut the dome lights off for the night. The warehouse held dusk and the red glow of sunset, casting the combatants' shadows far along the loading bay floor. When they turned so that his back was to the twilight sky, Yavobo stabbed toward Reva's midsection. It was a trick she would have used herself, and she was ready for it, sucking in her stomach as she leapt backward, slashing toward his extended arm as she dodged the thrust. She nicked him with the vibroknife, not feeling any resistance, but seeing the ocher gleam of Aztrakhani blood as he drew his arm back.

They continued to circle. She feinted, he dodged; he tested her reflexes with a swipe and a lunge. Each getting the measure of the other.

Then Yavobo came in for the kill. A feint; another feint; he reached out as if to grab Reva's free arm, and she leapt to the side— straight into his slashing blade, that laid open the flesh of her thigh.

His jubilant war cry echoed off the warehouse dome walls. It would not be enough, of course, until he had her head, but it was a start. Unlike the wound he bore, this one was deep, and bleeding freely. Soon she would tire, and then she would be his.

Reva sidled away to avoid the sticky-slick spot where blood ran down her leg and onto the floor. The wound was numb for the moment, not yet burning, and she couldn't judge its severity. She sensed it was enough to take away her edge of nimbleness, though, and slow her to a deadly pace. If he got his hands on her she could not hope to fend him off. Now, before she was noticeably weakened, she had to do her best.

The next flurry of exchanges showed that that was not good enough. Her leg began to buckle when she put weight on it, and without footwork she was hard put to avoid the alien's blows. He, on the other hand, was very good at avoiding her vibroknife. She tried to slice through his blade to disarm him, and failed. Another slash from the warrior's knife took her in the left forearm, not a crucial wound by itself, but one that would further slow her down by blood loss.

A triumphant smile bared the Aztrakhani's vicious canines. "I will drink your blood!" he taunted, as Reva stumbled behind a stack of cryocases. Her options were looking grim, and she wondered with a growing tinge of desperation if she could get away. It didn't matter if she wanted to move between Lines now; the fact was, she was too full of fear and anger to control a shift. Yavobo was between her and the closest exit, the broad bay door that gave out onto the ocean.

The twilight shadows that baffled the dodging assassin were no obstacle to the warrior. He anticipated her next evasion and vaulted shipping boxes to land by her side. She made a wild slash with her knife; Yavobo effortlessly grabbed her wrist, slammed it against the stack of cases behind her until the weapon flew off somewhere into the darkness. Towering over her, he ignored the wounded left arm that dangled by her side as he brought his blood-flecked blade up to Reva's throat.

The assassin saw death approaching. She tried the only thing left to her, something she knew would work on a human. She had no idea how it would affect this alien body, but it was all she had left to try. She thrust out with her wounded free arm, gritting her teeth against the pain. She stabbed in and up with one stiffened finger, then clutched at a nexus of nerves that in a human would be near the solar plexus. A human would have convulsed, and fallen, stunned or dead, at her feet.

Sobrani nerve-fighting techniques were deadly, but tailored to a certain physiognomy. Yavobo did not share that design—yet being humanoid, his structure and central nervous system had much in common with that of the scorned thin-skins. His eyes widened, his muscle tone loosened, and he stood swaying, virtually senseless, while Reva wriggled from his grasp and limped hurriedly away.

Beyond the Lairdome entrance on the land side were intruder alarms and slidewalks. Ways to call the Grinds or escape her pursuer. She was heading for that door, uncertain what to do on the other side, when Vask strolled into the Comax Shipping warehouse.

Reva had never been really glad to see the Fixer before. Shock appeared on his face as he registered her condition. Her hasty words cut off his questions.

"You carry a gun, don't you? A needler? Is that all? It'll have to do. Come on." She turned to lead the way back to Yavobo.

"Wait! What's—"

The Aztrakhani saved the need for further questions. What would have laid a human low had bought Reva only a short respite. The alien, regaining his senses, followed his quarry out of the cryocase area and now strode purposefully across the darkened warehouse floor. Between the lingering twilight and the office glowrods, there was enough illumination to make out his imposing form.

Reva staggered, then stumbled to her knees. "Shoot him, Vask. Don't let him get near. He's incredibly strong."

The Fixer hesitated, and Yavobo came inexorably onward, knife in hand, intent on the assassin half down on the floor.

"Hold it right there," Kastlin ordered, readying his needle gun. Yavobo came on.

"That's it, friend." Kastlin braced and aimed the needler with two hands, and fired a burst of three closely spaced shots. To Reva's surprise, the silent, slender projectiles arced blue as they struck their target, peppering the tall alien's chest. She looked up at Vask, revising her opinion of the Fixer. Those were electro-charged needles, illegal for general use, and capable of doing greater damage to the target than the standard puncturing rounds. Vask fired again, one well-placed needle spearing Yavobo's wrist. The knife dropped from suddenly-lax fingers, and hung dangling from its wrist cord.

Yavobo looked at Reva's friend and growled low in his throat, a primal sound eerily unnatural in a sentient being. "My fight is with you, woman, no one else. I will meet you again another time. You and I, alone."

He turned, and moved rapidly toward the docking ramp that gave into the ocean.

"Freeze!" Vask ordered. "You're not going anywhere!"

The alien kept walking, his back turned contemptuously to the man's needler. Vask took aim, and pulled the trigger. Hits peppered Yavobo's back, but as before, they had little visible effect. A moment later a splash came from the docking ramp.

Smooth green phosphorescence curled over the ripples where the bounty hunter had plunged into the sea. Vask took a halfhearted step in that direction.

"I think we better help Lish," Reva called to the Fixer. "Autodoc's fine for me, but her—I think you better call the medics."

As much as cyberscience had learned with thorough neuronic mapping, brain tissue injuries could play havoc with a patient's system. So while Reva was out of the autodoc by midnight, feeling mean enough to pick a fight and get thrown out of her favorite holo-den, Lish passed the evening unconscious in a real hospital, with real humans supplementing the medibot care she received in the Head Trauma unit.

Vask stood guard during Reva's recovery, puppy-dogging her steps before, during, and after her raucous sojourn in Gaspar's Holo Heaven. He lived to tell about it, too, in spite of her threats, and asked in the predawn hours if she would like to go visit Lish. Reva snarled about that, too, but finally took a detox pill and sobered up enough to go along to the hospital. By then the Holdout was drugged but conscious, tended by a medibot, and setting her own visiting hours. She admitted her callers.

Seeing Lish surrounded by healing devices brought back an image of blood and bone fragments and a crumpled form lying near death on her account. Reva swallowed past a sudden uncomfortable lump, and had to clear her throat before she could speak.

"You're looking a lot better," she said.

The smuggler's voice was soft, hard to hear. "They say I was in shock, and going fast. Thanks, to both of you."

Again, saved lives. Reva avoided that loaded subject; she nodded instead toward the crystalline half-globe that covered Lish's head in the blue glow of an aseptic field. "What's that?"

"That wallop I took against the wall crushed bone, and that destroyed some tissue. They grafted on some gray matter from the tissue bank, took a synaptic dump from the old stuff. This is monitoring the healing process now. Can't accelerate the brain quite as fast as they do a finger." She waved her little finger, the compound fracture autodoc-healed and as good as new. "What was that trouble all about, anyway? Do you know?"

Assassin and Fixer sat by the bedside, conscious of the nearby medibot monitoring instruments and voices in the room. "Seems like your visitor had it in for one of your special customers," Reva said circumspectly. "Remember the last big thing I bought from you?"

The Holdout nodded her understanding.

"So I had some words with him about it. I don't think he'll be back to bother you, Lish. It was me he was after."

"You? Why?"

"Let's say he didn't like how I used that last special purchase."

"He tried to kill you for it," Vask remarked.

"Had a little knife fight," Reva explained to Lish's questioning look. "The Fixer helped me out on that one. Thanks, by the way," she tossed off—her first, and only, acknowledgment of the aid he had rendered.

"Don't mention it," Kastlin dismissed the remark, "but what are you going to do when your visitor comes back?"

"Yeah," Lish agreed. "That's what I want to know."

Reva's face changed, her eyes gone hard. "He won't be back. I'm taking care of him tomorrow—or, I should say, today."

"Don't do anything hasty," the Holdout cautioned.

"I had something planned anyway," Reva said. She spoke curtly, uneasy about discussing her work. "It should be easy to make my friend part of it, instead of just a bystander. He won't be a problem afterward."

"You know who that alien is?" Vask asked with amazement.

She continued to play it close. "Knew of him. Tonight was our first meeting. I expect later today will be our last. Lish, in case I'm wrong about him coming back—will you keep out of sight until I take care of this problem? One day should be all I need."

The Holdout shook her head, a limited movement within the healing globe. "I'll be out of here by midmorning. I have something going on, too, so I won't be around for a day or so myself. Don't worry about me." She turned to Vask. "By the way—did you ever find out about my netrunner?"

"Um . . . the netrunner?" Vask switched mental gears. "Your guy met some bad neurons in the Net. He got ICEd trying to access a certain established businessperson's shipping registries."

Reva started. She looked at Lish and mouthed the name *Karuu?*

The Holdout gave the smallest nod, an affirmative. "Do you know if he was found out and backtraced? Or was it a routine defense program?"

The dead hire was not the first decker to run afoul of Interactive Counter-Espionage programs in the cybernet, and wouldn't be the last, but his end had been particularly ugly. Vask omitted the details. "That target is aware of only low-level probes from casual Net travelers. It was a defense program that fried him, not an offensive decker protecting assets."

"You're certain?"

"Positive."

Lish relaxed visibly; a moment later, her eyes fluttered closed. Accelerated healing or no, it was clear that she was exhausted, and needed to sleep. Leaving her on that reassuring note, that her dataprobes had not been traced back to her, they said goodnight and left the hospital behind.

"Say." Vask stopped Reva near the slidewalk. "You know that special thing you bought from Lish?"

Reva's eyes were uninviting. "What of it?"

"I think I can guess what that might be—"

"Don't bother."

"No, Reva—I mean, if that's what you're using, and you're going to use one again, I can help."

"Help? Trying to drum up more business, Vask?" Mercenary motivation she could understand, even if the prying irritated her.

He gave a too-casual shrug. "I know how to put one together. Can get you a lab to work in if you want to do it yourself. Whatever."

He looked up at her hopefully, a Fixer bidding for more work.
Reva's hard eyes softened. "Thanks for the offer, but I've got this
taken care of already. Maybe later, yes?"

"Oh. Later. Sure.

"I'll give you a good price!" he added reflexively.

"I'm sure of it," she agreed, and waved good-bye as the slidewalk
carried her away.

The *Savu*, a huge Peryton-class freighter, eased onto one of the
large-cargo pads at Bendinabi Field. R'debh's number-two starport
served only freight traffic many klicks north of Amasl's urban sprawl.
Karuu was on the pad with Daribi to watch the ponderous cargo car-
rier settle to the ground.

One of the largest designs capable of landing on a planet, the Peryton was a skeletal structure with a spine and traction arms that resembled ribs or gripping fingers placed at intervals down its length.
When loaded with a bulk container module, the arms would hold the
cargo firmly in place against the flight structure. Massive glowpads
fore and aft marked the powerful repulsors that enabled heavy cargo
lifts through gravity wells. The *Savu* was empty, though, and as she
set down her skeletal fingers boxed nothing but air.

The Captain was Celia Natic, a mercenary out of Chorb who
worked wet worlds and water drops. "Down and secured," she reported over the Port Authority channel. Karuu monitored that traffic
from a com booth at the edge of the docking area.

The usual contingent drove out to the ship, a Port Authority and
a Customs official on their way to check the vessel's papers and manifest. The inspection was quick. Customs had no interest in empty container vessels, and Karuu had paid well—very well—to ensure that
today's activities would not be derailed by misplaced zeal.

When the port authorities were gone, the Holdout punched up
the Custom Chief's private code. Walvert Edini came online, a beefy
career bureaucrat who maintained his well-fed appearance largely

with the help of Karuu's "gratuities" for "assistance" with complex shipping matters.

"Can't talk now!" he said in a hurried undertone. "Internal Security is walking through the door."

Karuu was oblivious to the man's nervousness. "You have everything in order?" he asked.

"Of course —"

"Security makes the arrest, and you confiscate the cargo, that is certain?"

For the fourth time that day, the aggravated Customs Chief assured Karuu that it was so. "And you can transport for us, like agreed. Later."

The com went dark.

"That was impolite," Karuu said to the screen. But perhaps understandable. Today's coup would be the biggest of the Holdout's career, and one of the richest of Edini's. The Customs Chief had to placate Security. Naturally he would be a little nervous.

"Daribi." The bronze-skinned Islander glanced around. "You have a boat-boy on hand, like I asked? One who knows the seaways from the air?"

"Like you ordered."

"Is good." Karuu washed his hands together. "We have best-ever deal, then. As soon as Lish's cargo is impounded, we are contracted by Customs to haul it to their holding yards. We have only heavy hauler capable of taking that cargo container. This is convenient, no?" The Holdout beamed at the Peryton.

"If this cargo ends up in Customs' hands after all, why the boat-boy?" Daribi asked gruffly.

Karuu cocked one furred eyebrow at his underling. "Who says Customs keeps their claws on this? Is simple, my primitive friend. Cargo is perishable, so needs seawater circulation after a while. Customs must store this in their wetdocks at far edge of Obai Shelf. They are not checking container contents too closely until after cargo is in their holding yards.

"To get there, we are navigating by eyeball and buoy trace over the Bennap Run, a little-used seaway. That is why boat-boy, to help pilot with dead reckoning."

The Dorleoni grew effusive. "On the way we see distressed seamen in skiff. Peryton sinks into ocean to help them out. Some borgbeasts are released then, to our water-breathing friends beneath the surface. Once seamen are rescued, we go on to Customs wetdocks with same cargo module, only a lighter load."

Karuu slapped a flipper-shaped foot on the plascrete, a mark of the alien's excitement. "Later, depending who gives best price for it, unknown terrorists can break remaining cargo free. Borgbeasts are powerful enough and follow directions—they can push right through the perimeter fence at the holding yards, and are out into free ocean.

"If Customs must save face, I pay indemnity for faulty cargo grips or some such that made it easy for thieves to work havoc." Karuu waved a webbed paw dismissively. "Compared to the profit made on cargo picked up for free, indemnity is nothing. Customs has not personally inspected full cargo load, can't verify its contents or value. Apologies greased by credits make Customs go away. Internal Security is no problem: they have their master criminal and by then have already taken Lish to trial for her evil smuggling ways. We are all happy."

"Won't Customs give the ship some kind of escort?" Daribi frowned. "Or tell her what heading to steer?"

"Escort, yes. Interested only in making sure the *Savu* doesn't stray too far. Heading or altitude? No. They are hand-picked crews who have worked with us before." Karuu emulated a human wink. "They will understand our humanitarian need to help distressed seamen, and won't be too intrusive while we effect a rescue."

"Sounds like you have it all covered, Boss."

The Dorleoni nodded decisively. "And you know what the very best part will be, Daribi? The look on Lish's face when her unscheduled import is uncovered, and she is taken away." A seal-bark of mirth escaped the Holdout. "I want to see that, and the docking schedule shows the *Delos Varte* is third in the landing roster. Let us go watch."

The *Delos Varte* settled onto another large-cargo pad at Bendinabi, one of many freighters arriving for the Trade Fair and the second Peryton-class hauler of the day. Experienced spacers nudged their younger counterparts and pointed. It was rare to see two such behemoths in ground port simultaneously, not likely to happen again for years.

The *Delos* appeared all the more impressive because of the gargantuan cargo pod she bore. Its modular units were configured into one long contiguous space by irising open the interior bulkheads.

Supplemental repulsor pads were affixed beneath the freight container, the better to support the tremendous mass of the water-filled module during atmosphere maneuvers. The lean lifting framework of the Peryton groaned as she set down, and weight and stress shifted throughout the structure.

Lish waited amid the growing crowd of onlookers as the *Delos* secured stations and shut down power. Healed but drained of energy, the steady chemical fuel of stimtabs kept her on her feet after a too-early release from the hospital. The Holdout stood alone, outwardly collected—for the sake of any observers—and inwardly nervous, as she once again rehearsed Plan A.

In a while, if things went as scheduled, the heavy freighter would be cleared to Avelar Island with other exhibition traffic, and would make her lumbering way through atmosphere. Her manifest claimed she was carrying a sample aqualogy, a self-contained ocean environment to be toured by Fair-goers. Any Customs inspection conducted in a breather would confirm as much. The borgbeasts, after all, knew to hide within the container's artificial terrain, and the venloy lining of the waterproof compartments had been specifically chosen because of its slewing effect on sensor readings. Short of swimming up on a borgbeast that didn't want to be found in the bottom of a lake, no ordinary Customs inspection was going to pin down the nature of the real cargo inside the *Delos Varte*'s gigantic container. If an inspection was more thorough than that, Lish had other problems, and Plan B to address them with.

Once the module was in the water, the beasts would exit; later, tourists could, indeed, come in. They might not find the aqualogy very impressive, except for its sheer size, but that was alright: by then, the container pod would have done its work, and public approval at that point would not matter in the least.

Finally the deck elevator dropped the length of a gantry leg, and the ship's captain emerged on the pad. The port authorities had not yet arrived, and Lish wanted to talk with the officer before they did. She pushed out of the crowd, and walked toward the tall, middle-aged man reviewing ship's records on his datapad.

"Devin!" she called out. The officer smiled warmly, Rus'karfa battleslash and the silver at his temples lending his face a look of distinction.

"Lish!"

The pair met and embraced, old friends renewing their acquaintance. To Lish it was something more: if Plan A didn't work, this might be their only chance to talk.

Yet she couldn't resist the temptation to stand back, grip the Captain's arm, and grin admiringly at him. He shifted, uneasy at standing inspection in the trim gray jumpsuit he wore, what passed for uniform dress among Free Traders. It was his standard garb since he, like Lish, had taken an independent path from his Shirani clanmates.

"Thanks." Lish had to say it.

He brushed the words off. "Couldn't ignore an offer from an old shipmate, could I?" Now that he had arrived, Devin was anxious to drop his contracted cargo and spend time with his kinswoman.

But it was not to be. Lish became aware of stern eyes trained upon them, and looked around. The port authorities had arrived. And a lot more, besides.

A police cordon gathered around the *Delos'* landing pad, separating spacers and ground crew from the approaches to the freighter. Nearby stood a contingent of Customs enforcers, the kind of armed guards who expected trouble from smugglers and illegal immigrants, and were prepared to squelch either with the least provocation.

Lish turned and faced three men, two of whom she recognized. They were Tammas Hevrik, Port Master; Walvert Edini, the Customs Chief; and a third, black-haired, lean, and unsmiling, in the crisp white jacket and bodysuit of Internal Security. Flanking Lish and Devin were a number of musclemen who could only be IntSec in unmarked white and gray service tunics.

Her blood ran cold. With an effort she kept a pleasant smile on her face. Plan A was out the airlock; all her hopes were riding on Plan B, now.

Devin stepped forward, behaving just as a ship's Captain should. "Gentlesirs." He half-bowed. "You have a rather large escort for a routine docking. Is there a problem? I have my documentation right here—"

The Port Master waved aside his extended datapad. "We'll get to you shortly, Captain." He addressed himself to the woman. "I take it you are the woman known as Lish?"

The Holdout stood straighter. Hevrik and Edini alike both knew her; she did enough routine and legal shipping out of this port. If they wanted to act like she was some unknown, they'd better rethink their routine.

"I am Shiran Gabrieya Lish, if that is who you mean." Though she placed subtle emphasis on her clan names, there was no flicker of expression on the Security officer's face, no response to her obvious Sa'adani rank. Sudden doubt assailed her.

"Then, madam," the Customs Chief drew himself up importantly, "your vessel is impounded."

Lish concealed the equally sudden relief that flooded through her, and put on the face that made her so deadly at Shaydo. She ignored the pompous Edini and addressed the Port Master. "I'm sorry? I don't believe I heard that right."

"You did," Hevrik said tartly. "Your vessel is impounded for inspection, and you and your Captain are in the custody of Internal Security."

Lish let bafflement play across her features. "There must be some mistake," she protested, then had to bite her tongue to avoid smiling. Here came Karuu, too excited to stay away, pushing as far as he could to the forefront of the onlookers held back by the Grinds. He stopped there, his thick mustache pulled up in an incisor-revealing grin.

"There's no mistake," growled Edini, in no mood for coy smugglers. "You are Shiran Lish, you've admitted. And this is your ship, the *Delos Varte*. You are under arrest for—"

"You're wrong," Lish said sharply, her voice carrying to the spectators who were pressing closer to the curious encounter. It was time to make her insurance pay off. "This is not my ship, gentlesirs."

The Port Master and Imperial Security man exchanged glances. The Customs Chief grew red in the face. "This *is* your ship, and you claim you are carrying—"

Devin spoke up and cut the burly man off. "A simple inspection of my documents will confirm what the domna is saying." No matter what Lish was up to, he thought, they could at least get their facts straight. Once again he extended the datapad. "This most definitely is not her ship."

The Security officer took the pad, examined its contents with keen gray eyes. Chief Edini stared at her accusingly. "How can this not be? What are you doing here, then?"

She smiled up at the captain and moved a step closer. "Why, we're old friends, aren't we, Devin?" She reached out, rested her hand on his arm in an intimately familiar way. The ship's officer played along and leaned a little into the embrace. Lish regarded her inquisitors, and said, "When I heard he was going to be in port for a while, I came to meet him. That's allowed, isn't it?"

The Port Master avoided her gaze, while Edini turned a deeper shade of red. The Security man looked up from the ship's datapad, and fixed Port Master Hevrik with a stern glare. "What data does a ship beam you in its docking request?"

"The standard, Commander." Hevrik cleared his throat. "Port of origin, port of destination, ship's master, debarking passenger list—"

Security held up a hand and the recitation stopped. "And you, Customs Chief? What do you receive?"

Edini sputtered at the unexpected question. "Last port, outbound destination, quarantine status, manifest declarations. That sort of thing."

Security frowned at the two. "You don't check ownership, mastery, or home port against Imperial ship registries?"

The Port Master was taken aback. "That's not a official requirement, Commander Obray! We'd have to check with Central Registry at Neville, and by time our queries cleared and returned, most of this shipping would be long gone anyway. We watch the hotlist for stolen ships, of course, and if those vessel ID numbers come up—"

"I don't care about stolen ships," Obray cut him off. "I care about this ship, and its owner, and its cargo." He motioned the ship's captain over, held out the datapad's edge to him. "Give me your thumbprint," he ordered. "I think we need to confirm some data around here."

The ID panel glowed green, a confirmation that Shiran Teskal Devin was indeed the contracted captain of the *Delos Varte*. "Now you." He crooked his finger at Lish. She pressed her thumb on the datapad. The ID check glowed red. She was not mentioned or authorized in any way in the ship's registry or contract papers.

The Security officer's brows drew together. Edini stood with mouth agape, and Hevrik had the grace to seem mildly embarrassed.

"Do you know the owner of this vessel, Captain, or are you a blind hire?" the Imperial investigator asked him.

"We've never met in person, but I've seen him on the holovid. He's named right there on the ship certificate—" Devin waved at the datapad, then obligingly noticed a unique face in the crowd. "If I'm not mistaken, he's standing right there, too. Good day, sir." The Captain tipped a finger to his brow, and nodded to Karuu.

Every face turned to stare at the Dorleoni. The Grinds passed him through their screen, and the IntSec men adjusted their stance to include him within their threatening circle.

"Karuu?" cried the Customs Chief in disbelief. "*You* own this ship?"

The Dorleoni stood, flat-footed, mouth open. "Of course not!" he protested. "I have never seen it before in my life!"

Captain Devin pursed his lips and looked pointedly at the ground. Commander Obray extended the datapad toward the sarong-clad Holdout. "Give us your print," he demanded.

Aghast, Karuu took half a step back. "No! I have nothing to do with this, I tell you!" A Security agent stopped his backpedaling retreat, and forcefully held out the short alien's webbed paw to the datapad.

The ID light shone green. The *Delos Varte* belonged to Karuu, the registered owner, with ship's mastery assigned on a delivery contract to Captain Shiran Devin out of Bailpoint, Corvus.

"No!" wailed the Holdout. "This cannot be!"

Obray lifted a finger, and an escort of plainclothesmen encircled the Dorleoni. Static bonds were placed on Karuu's wrists while the Commander addressed Lish.

"Domna Shiran Gabrieya, I suggest you remain on-planet until our investigation is complete."

"Sir," she inclined her head, "I'm sure the Port Master can direct you to Comax Shipping. That is where you will find me."

"I expect so. And you, sir —," he addressed the Captain. "Please see to it that your crew is off-boarded at once. A security screen will be attached to your airlock and Customs will be taking charge of your vessel. You will be coming with us for questioning."

"Am I under arrest, Commander?" Devin was worried, an earnest and honest spacer caught up in a broil not of his making.

"Not yet, Captain. Do you know what cargo you carry?"

"Only what it says on the manifest."

"That's why we're questioning you. Customs will escort you as the ship is cleared out."

An Internal Security scanner team joined them, to assure the crew sweep was thorough. Devin squeezed Lish's hand good-bye, then ascended the deck elevator with his dour companions.

Obray called the Port Master and Customs Chief over to him. "I want that lockout in place immediately. No tampering with the cargo, no boarding or other investigations until I'm here to conduct it personally. Is that understood?" He glared particularly at the Customs

Chief. The two planetary officials bowed to Imperial authority and accepted his orders.

"What about the crewmen?" the Port Master asked.

"Detain for questioning."

That mollified Hevrik, who conferred with his security forces.

Lish made to leave, and Edini reached out to stop her.

"Is there a purpose to this?" she bridled. "I have nothing to do with this ugly affair."

"We'll see about that—"

She turned to the Internal Security officer, whose stylized red armband on his uniform jacket indicated his lower-caste status. He was Kenushi, the Authorator class, about midlevel in Sa'adani hierarchy: high enough to hold responsible office, low enough to be impressed by a Rus'karfa bloodline.

"Sir," she spoke boldly. "If you know my name, you know my House. Do you plan on detaining a Shiran Trader without grounds to do so?"

Internal Security taught their people to ignore caste, so that a suspect's bloodline should not unnecessarily affect their investigations, but such indoctrination was not always enough to counter a lifetime of habit and perception. Commander Obray seemed about to oblige her, until he looked at her jawline where the missing Rus'karfa battleslash should be. His question was apparent in his eyes.

Lish colored slightly. "Would you like to see my identification?" she offered, distantly polite. Her infraction was self-evident once she claimed her rank. But as she had hoped, Internal Security had bigger concerns than enforcing caste law today.

"That won't be necessary, Domna," Obray declined. He took in her haughty, offended stance, and the casteless, blustering CAS Sector Customs man next to her.

"Let her go," he said.

Edini flushed red and tightened his grasp on her arm.

Obray fixed him with a look, and the Chief pulled back his hand as if burned. "We have a big operation staged for today," the Security officer reprimanded him. "Even if some intelligence was in error, we can still proceed with our clean-up mission. Let's make sure we direct our attentions to the right target, shall we?"

The Customs Chief stood speechless. While he fumed, the Commander bowed to Lish.

"We'll be in touch, Domna."

The Holdout dipped her head, almost regally. "I will be glad to speak with *you*, Commander. Perhaps we can leave inappropriate parties out of it, shall we?" She cast a disdainful glance at Edini, and swept past as if leaving a House Arleon audience chamber.

It wasn't until she nearly reached the terminal entrance that her nervous stomach made itself felt, and Lish had to seek out a public fresher. Afterward, she stood for a while on the viewing terrace that overlooked Bendinabi Field. High on the flight structure of the loaded Peryton freighter she finally discerned the faint shimmer of a force screen on the main crew entrance. The ship was secure, then, and holding for Obray's return investigation.

Nodding to herself, she entered a com booth, punched a number, and in her haste apparently entered the wrong code. A disconnect tone came back to her. She waved her hand at the uncooperative unit in disgust, and went on her way—that last small performance intended for tails or security spyeyes that might be observing her.

In fact, Lish was perfectly content with the disconnect tone. She took the magtube out to Lairdome 7, suppressing her joy all the way there. By time she walked into Comax Shipping her face ached, but she had succeeded in looking like the victim of an unpleasant brush with authorities. Until she did a victory dance in the privacy of her office.

Security agents marched Karuu down the concourse past whispering onlookers. The mortified alien could barely put one foot in front of the other. Never had he been arrested, not once in all his years in R'debh, or before. Now the Bugs were ready to flay the importer unlicensed bioforms and catch themselves a juicy unscrupulous rolling Holdout, and here he was, trussed up and ready to roast. crack his private files open and see more than they could imagine about his operations, and then he would be dead, dead, dead—

Dorleoni cannot sweat, like humans, when they are nervous. They pant like dogs. Karuu breathed through his mouth in short huffing gasps as he was led to a holding chamber reserved for starport security.

Obray joined him a short while later. All Karuu could do was deny; all the evidence the Commander pulled up showed that he was lying. It made the Holdout desperate enough to take an awful gamble.

He leaned earnestly across the narrow interrogation room table. "See here, Commander. You are so doubting of my truthful word, I volunteer for this: use drugs on me, or use one of your mind-readers. You will discover I say the truth."

That seemed to give Obray pause. Drugs and mind-probes weren't reliable with nonhumans. It gave him the chance to appear innocent and yet not give anything of import away.

He could see those considerations turning over behind the Security officer's eyes. Obray favored his prisoner with a tight smile. "We'll see."

He left the room, and left Karuu to squirm.

FlashMan cost 100k a day, plus expenses—enough to break Lish, if she needed him for more than a few days' work. As it was, she was in the hole, out on short-term loans to a Scripman to finance Flash's services.

It was a big game of Shaydo: certain wealth or certain bankruptcy. Or, in this line of work, probably something worse than bankruptcy. It was worth it to pay for the best.

A few nanoseconds after Lish's call, he collected his virtual self and joined a data stream flowing at light speed into the orbital comnet. There he jumped into a high-frequency burst that put his electrons in a satellite handling subspace communications over Amasl.

The netrunner reassembled his consciousness into a virtual entity, a construct that mimicked an animated bolt of white lighting. The representation pleased him. In this sim-form he tripped some circuits and locked open a secure channel on a narrow beam planetward.

FlashMan jumped into that channel by entering a virtual room in the net matrix, and sealing the door behind him. In the center of the featureless chamber was a keyboard. Playing it like an organist, Flash pounded out a code, a rhythm, a series of subspace notes. Music swirled about the room, became visible light, became data stream in his virtual analog of consciousness.

An encrypted message transmitted on tight beam to the *Delos Varte*. On board, a subspace radio with an independent power cell responded to the transmission, and locked a com channel open to receive it.

As this happened, the artificial intelligence that monitored subspace communications noted the unexpected transmission. FlashMan split his spark of consciousness in two: a diminutive lightning-man ran to the door of the chamber, engaged the data policeman who appeared there in confusing doubletalk and what amounted to minor programming. The AI concluded it had heard only white noise, a low-priority anomaly, and went away. Relieved, Flash's second spark sealed the virtual room's door shut once again.

As FlashMan merged back into one consciousness, the floor dropped out of the chamber. The netrunner and his keyboard floated atop another tunnel of white light, this one pouring down to the *Delos* where subspace radio linked satellite/sender and ship/receiver. The decker played more chords, changing the tune he sent to the ship's waiting systems. The data stream pulsed, color going from white to the crisp blue of program instructions.

In the flight deck control panel, energy shunted from the subspace power cell to a physical relay. It tripped, activating the rigger jack that interfaced with the ship's cybernetic controls. FlashMan's simulacrum leapt down the subspace channel, to reassemble inside the jack. The lightning-spark grew leads and wires from its virtual head, and the rigger connection was complete.

FlashMan maintained the data stream. Lish had provided the shipboard jack. She also sprang for the 300k worth of add-on chips the netrunner wore slotted into his brain: they lent him the temporary know-how to remotely pilot and engineer the giant freighter.

With ship's sensors for eyes and ears, and ship's systems for hands,

FlashMan reached out with a flicker of attention and dogged the air-locks shut. No unwanted visitors would force their way past the security screen and come aboard while he was preparing to lift. Item by item he went through the internal checklist, getting systems flight ready. In less than an hour, the internal preparations were complete. Only then did he risk the external ones—the obvious things that would alert everyone near the landing pad that the ship was taking off.

Things like disengaging the service umbilicals, and running up power on the repulsor pads. The *Delos Varte* lifted, snapping uncleared cables and nearly dinging a landing gantry. Guards fired uselessly at the mighty ship while FlashMan chided himself for overcorrecting against wind drift. He wasn't listening through external speakers, or he would have heard the screams and curses as the impounded ship rose into the sky.

Obray was grave as he spoke with Captain Shiran. "I'll be blunt with you," he said. "You're hauling a cargo that violates too many Imperial regulations to count. You can be fined and have your flight certificate pulled for any one of these crimes."

Devin heard that with growing concern. He'd known nothing of this.

"The environmental endangerment charges carry criminal penalties," Obray continued. "The shipper is in serious trouble, and you are, too, if you had knowledge of these violations."

Devin was troubled by this turn of events, but all he could do was tell what he knew, and that was very little. He considered the simple room he was in, sure to hold concealed spyeyes and be recording his every word and gesture. The diplomatic approach was best. "I'll cooperate, Commander. I've nothing to hide."

"I'm pleased to hear that, Captain. What's your story?"

It was not a "story," a fabrication, and Devin resented the implication. He'd signed on for the freight run through the Free Traders' job pool on Corvus, and said as much. Recorded briefing, a capsule contract handled through the Net, no acquaintance with the owner. It was a not-uncommon arrangement.

"Where did you pick up the cargo?" Commander Obray asked.

"I didn't," Devin explained. The ship was already in orbital dock, fully loaded and awaiting a crew. The contract briefing said the owner was paying a bonus for "quick and discreet"—the common spacer phrase for things a little on the shady side, where no questions asked assured no problems were encountered.

"Come now, Captain. Am I supposed to believe you took on megatons of cargo and had no curiosity about it? Especially one requiring 'quick and discreet' handling?"

"Of course I was curious." Devin frowned. "So I did what most captains do. I read the manifest. It said 'aqualogy,' heading for a trade show. I work waterworlds from inside a ship—I wasn't going to take a dip in the container module to check it out. I left the cargo secured, which is standard practice, and shipped for Selmun."

Obray glowered, but ignorance was no crime, and the Security officer seemed to know he had no real hold on the spacer. More questions and a few acerbic comments made it clear that this was one contract Devin wouldn't be completing any time soon.

The spacer was disgruntled. Loss of delivery bonus, maybe an official note of suspicion on his record—

He could not discuss these things with Obray, who was distracted in that instant by the sizzle of an energy bolt against the door and the sound of a body hitting the hall floor.

The Security man surged to his feet as the door opened, reaching for the service blaster under his jacket.

"Karuu is gone!" his aid shouted. "Edini's on the run with him!"

"Stop!" exclaimed a Security man. The entourage of Customs men and short, furred Dorleoni receded farther down the hallway.

"Stop!" he ordered again, pulling his blaster. "Or I'll shoot!"

There was a brief exchange of fire, and the Security agent went down. Edini and his men ducked around a corner and into a service tunnel while the Imperials were in turmoil.

"Hi, Boss," Daribi greeted Karuu inside the passageway, and hurried the group down a branching corridor.

Loyalty! The Islander had not deserted him after all, and it seemed he had rounded up reinforcements as well. With the chance of freedom in his grasp, the Holdout felt despair slipping away. He talked to the Customs Chief trotting along heavily beside him.

"Where are we going?" the Dorleoni asked the human.

"To the *Savu*. My boys are on it. I told your Captain Natic to have systems on standby. If we move fast, surprise will get us out of here before anyone can respond. We have to try it. We're dead if we stay here."

"Why are you running, too?"

"Beldy spines," Edini growled, "do you think I'm a free man after they inspect your records? They'll find your payoffs and if they don't shoot me just for fun, then I'm on D'rgul along with you! Better to get out of here now, while we're free to run."

Karuu could not refute that. He let himself be swept along, down service lifts and mech corridors, into the network of maintenance tunnels beneath Bendinabi Field. The hidden service routes were traversed mainly by mechos and programmed gravsleds. They hopped a sled destined for the large-cargo area, and journeyed into the warrens beneath the starport.

Obray charged into the hallway. His men were trading fire around the corner with Edini's rearguard. A blue-green bolt of coherent energy speared one of the Customs renegades; he went down with a cry and his companion retreated. The way into the terminal's service corridors was free.

The Commander thumbed his comlink to the cargo-pad security team. Before he could explain the situation, an excited voice chattered over the device.

"Sir! The *Delos* is lifting!"

Obray clenched the comlink. "Lifting?! How can that be?"

"Don't know—it's at about three hundred, four hundred meters and heading northwest. Picking up speed."

"Who's aboard?"

"Unknown—there was no one left after we cleared and scanned the ship!"

"Then you missed something. Clear this channel—no, wait. Karuu has escaped custody and Customs Chief Edini is aiding him. They may be heading your way, or to the *Savu*. I want all local Customs off guard detail until we sort this out, only IntSec and Port Authority in place. Repeat: Karuu and Edini are fugitives. Stop them if you see them."

"Acknowledged."

Obray gestured his aids to follow, and headed for the Port Master's operations center.

"Master Swimmer Sharptooth, do you hear me?"

FlashMan's synthesized voice issued from submerged speakers in the *Delos'* cargo hold. Sharptooth's answering chitter was converted by his voicelink translator into Common.

"Who speaks?" the otter-shaped Vernoi native asked. "You are not my partner."

"Who is your partner?"

"Edesz."

FlashMan searched his memory of Lish's briefing, recalled "Edesz"—a water-breathing R'debh native who had trained for weeks on Vernoi, learning from the handlers how to work with cyberbeasts in ocean waters.

"Edesz awaits you in the ocean below, as agreed," he reassured the alien. Edesz and others were supposed to open the main cargo airlock—or, when submerged, waterlock—releasing the Vernoi handlers and their borgbeasts into the Selmun ocean. *"However, there's a problem,"* FlashMan explained. *"We're arriving earlier than expected. There may be no R'debhi waiting to release you from the hold."*

"When will we be freed? We need to roam. All of us."

"You'll be free as soon as this container is submerged. If you'll help me, we can open the cargo hold from inside, and then you can go."

"Will Edesz and the others be there?"

FlashMan had no information on this, and made his best guess. *"Not right away. They're not expecting you this soon. If you follow the slope of the shelf into deep water, they can find you there."*

"Very well," said Master Swimmer Sharptooth. He gave a whistling summons to his fellow handlers. "Tell us what to do."

From the Port Master's office, a ground search was set under way for Karuu and Edini. The Holdout's flight was the best admission of guilt that Commander Obray could ask for: two coded calls directed the waiting strike teams of agents, not to Lish's premises, but to the Dorleoni Holdout's businesses, where a major search-and-seizure operation began.

Captain Verana assumed command of planetary Customs, deploying her ground units in backup positions around the starport, and putting orbital forces on high alert. Bendinabi Air Control tracked the progress of the pirated Peryton freighter, and reported its approach to Avelar Island.

Hails to the pilot went unanswered.

"Shall we shoot it down, sir?" Verana asked.

"Not yet," replied Obray. He studied the massive freighter on a satellite monitor as it navigated northward at an altitude of 2,000 meters. Sensors showed no one aboard, which left only one way the freighter could be piloted in this manner. . . .

Port Master Hevrik anticipated his thoughts. "If the *Delos* is drone-controlled, we can't cut her off over inhabited terrain. Look where she is." He stabbed a finger at the status board, tracking the ship's position. "We've got inhabited shelf and surface land all along her present path of travel."

Obray locked eyes with Hevrik, then nodded sharply. "Air Control," he reactivated the comlink. "Relay subspace data to me here, this com channel. I want frequency, point of origin—good. Keep it coming."

He punched a new number on Hevrik's console. "Systems Control," came the familiar voice.

"Commander Obray, Selmun-trio-four. I'm ordering a net scramble on this subspace channel, patching freq and origin through to you now." His fingers hit key sequences while he talked. "When rigger control is assumed, inform me this channel."

"Acknowledged. Dispatching now."

Obray turned to Hevrik. "Now we'll see how far that bastard gets."

Alia Lanzig sat on the waterfront dais with other speakers, waiting to extend greetings and welcome to the exhibitors gathered at Avelar Island. The crowd was restive. The spread of food and drink was a lot more appealing than speeches from politicos, and the Councilor planned to keep her talk brief.

The Trade Fair committee had chosen a site even wetdome-dwelling Councilors could enjoy. The lagoon beside the small-boat marina was the perfect setting for this crowd. Peaceful green waters lapped shady terraces, a pleasant spot for land- and water-dwellers alike.

Unfortunately, the idyllic setting did little to ease Councilor Lanzig, who was bothered by the energy screen unit Yavobo had insisted she wear to this gathering. She had omitted the ballistic mesh jacket, wearing only her quilted overtunic, like a guilty child hiding the body armor in a closet drawer so the alien would not notice it left in her room. The screen unit she grudgingly wore, certain that every eye noticed the small powerpack at her belt. Alia didn't want to appear paranoid, but with her bodyguard looming nearby she had little choice in the matter.

She made the best of things that she could, affixing a diplomat's smile to her face. Her eyes wandered the horizon, waiting for her turn at the podium, when she glimpsed an airborne dot moving through the offshore haze. The dot resolved itself into the surrealistically large framework of a Peryton-class freighter, and Councilor Lanzig smiled contentedly.

Soon the Free Ocean faction would be struggling to keep their shipping lanes open. They wouldn't have the leisure to grasp for new routes, new encroachments—

A round of ragged applause signaled her introduction. Alia stood and approached the rostrum, unable to take her eyes from the freighter, drawing steadily nearer. There was something strange about its arrival now, at this moment. It was early. Definitely early.

Distracted, Alia did not notice Yavobo hovering not far behind her. Nor did she notice the tall brunette with the zanned hair and the green semi-cellophane dress who stood amid terraced planters overlooking the reception area.

Yavobo did. He had been systematically scanning high places and sheltered places, then every face in the crowd, looking for her. Her wounds were not fatal, and he fully expected to see her here with a weapon in hand. Her threat about a time patch did not ring quite true, somehow, and though he hunted for one, it had been a cursory search at best. No. This keshun-cub would want a confrontation, would want eye-contact with her prey. He was sure of it.

And there she stood, almost at the limit of weapons range. The warrior straightened, cursed himself for not spotting her sooner.

It didn't matter to Reva. She saw him, unmistakable on the speakers' platform, never straying far from Lanzig's side. That's convenient, she thought. Stay close to her, and my job becomes a lot easier. Because for this one, special hit, I don't mind doing things the good old-fashioned way. Shaped charge, minimum bystander injury, and a very big bang. Right beneath your feet, asshole, a two-for-one special. No IDP at all, Yavobo. Fooled you.

She squelched her lingering nervousness, born of a promise to herself not to switch Timelines. There would be no shifting off Mainline after this, no walking away in unnoticed shadows paralleling the present moment.

No problem, she thought. I'm good enough.

When he spotted her, their eyes met, and the small hairs at the back of her neck stood up. She had worn the dress for him, so there would be no mistaking her across the intervening distance. The alien should know without a doubt who it was who killed him.

Reva waved a hand casually. Yavobo whirled and started to move. In that moment, the assassin pushed the button of the detonator in her hand. The charge beneath the speakers' podium exploded in a gout of flame and plaspanel shreds.

She walked away through gathering crowds as she had so often before. This time the uproar behind her felt more compelling, the moment not buffered by her timesense as it carried her through safe Lines. She fought the urge to go back, inspect the damage, verify the kills.

Vidnews was fine for that. It would even give her a replay if she wanted.

Most netrunners who worked for Internal Security were once criminals themselves. All had been smart enough to take the Emperor's reprieve and sign on to work for the Bugs for a while.

Obray's scramble team was no exception. The trio assembled at the junction where FlashMan had first paused to get his bearings: Captain Brace, a rated pilot with chip-enhanced flight reflexes; Zippo, a young datarunner up on decryption and interference protocols; Nomad, experienced in offensive and defensive countermeasures, netrunning in person on Selmun III. His dirtside location gave him nanoseconds of advantage in offensive combat. Their virtual selves were near-uniform, each a glowing blue wire-frame figure, health and status readable at a glance by the condition and color of its frame. It was Security's standard Datacop representation, showing allies at a glance.

Zippo, with the rebellion of the young, threw in a program enhancement. His figure became a blocky raster image, squat and low, looking like a blue bulldog. "The better to hound our target," he quipped to Captain Brace's stern gaze.

Brace let the non-uniform look pass. For now—

"After you, Nomad."

The Nomad construct, taller and skinnier than the Captain, approached a data gateway. He tasted the flow of electrons, picked the stream coursing to the right subspace transmitter, and leapt into it, his substance melting into the torrent of data as soon as it touched. Zippo and the Captain followed.

They reassembled before a virtual door, closed and sealed with caulking around the edge. The door was a piece of program code intended to divert access from the subspace frequency it guarded.

Nomad motioned Zippo forward. While he interacted with the virtual reality of the Net matrix, his cybercircuits on another level analyzed the code, wrote a counter program, ran it in the satellite to unblock access. From Zippo's bulldog point of view, he sniffed, nosed the door, grew a wire lead from his paw that probed the lock. "It's open now," he reported.

Nomad grabbed the latch and pushed.

A booby trap exploded with a bang and a cloud of virtual smoke. The bang did minor damage to Nomad, bleaching the blue on his wireframe hand to a nearly green hue. The smoke was sucked past a keyboard and through the floor, down the tunnel of flickering light where subspace tied satellite to the *Delos Varte* below.

FlashMan raised up his lightning-pointed head, with its crown of leads and wires. Deep inside the neural jack in the ship's control panel, the acrid smell of smoke came to him, borne blitz-fast through the subspace channel from far overhead.

"Shit." He spoke so intensely the words echoed through speakers in the freighter's empty corridors. *"Company."*

ЖЖЖIЖ

Bystanders pulled Yavobo out of the blood-tinged waters of the lagoon. To their surprise the lanky alien was not only mostly intact, he was still breathing. The mesh armor under his water-insulating bodysuit had saved his life.

When medics arrived he was rushed into the autodoc in the care van. The missing fingers and half a foot could be regenerated; flesh wounds and burns would be repaired by medical machinery.

"You're very lucky, sir," a medic reassured him while pulling plaspanel shrapnel from his wounds. "You'll be fine in a day or so, and you should have those limbs back in a few weeks."

Yavobo heard nothing through burst eardrums. Although he fought the painkillers that lulled tortured limbs to sleep, he was too injured to resist the autodoc ministrations for long. The Aztrakhani fell into restless slumber and dreamed of vengeance.

Alia Lanzig was not so fortunate. A screen unit is worthless against the destructive kinetic energy of an explosion. Her end came so rapidly she never realized that simple fact, and never had second thoughts about the neglected wardrobe Yavobo had set out for her.

✿   ✿   ✿

Vask saw the wave of Reva's hand, the explosion; saw the tall woman turn and walk coolly away from the scene of destruction. He turned from shattered platform to vanishing assassin. For that was what she was, he suddenly realized. She was not another Holdout, in spite of her smuggler's stories. She was a killer, plain and simple, and deadly efficient at her job.

He followed with uncertain steps. Could he find out anything vital at the crime scene right now? No, not with the uproar that reigned there at the moment. He had caught the moment on his sound and vid cybersystems, anyway.

So why was he letting her stroll away?

It was shock that held his feet in place, shock as he reconciled the puzzle pieces he had picked up about Reva with the person she really was. This woman who had saved his life, who harbored a prickliness that seemed to cover a strange sensitivity—she was all this, and a ruthless killer, too.

The pieces fit. Her skill at kria hunting. Her fight with Yavobo, who could probably have slain most other opponents out of hand. Her knowledge of time patches, and other things hinted, not said. . . .

Something tugged at the back of his mind, snippets of briefings and a criminal profile he'd read a few months before. Something that reminded him of Reva.

He let the assassin go, and took himself to a secluded corner where he could cease the distracting drain of using his blindspot ability. Sitting in the shade of a tree fern, he relaxed, head in hands, and rolled back mental pictures of briefings, reports, ready-room bull sessions. . . .

There, it came in bits and pieces. His mnemonic disciplines served him well, offering up the scattered segments he had not put together in any kind of association. Until now.

There have been a series of assassinations, Killer unknown. Perpetrator does not show up on surveillance sensors, and leaves no psi trace. High-tech devices are used to commit the murders: IDPs, coolsuit turbochargers, lethal bio-injection. Death is usually made to appear accidental. Victims are political figures or related to organized crime—assassinations that fit this pattern have been identified as far back as four years, with a high likelihood of sharing same perpetrator. . . . No leads. If you find suspect matching this profile, contact Calyx IntSec HQ, Special Investigator Kye. . . .

A chill went over Vask. Reva left no psitrace. Used high-tech devices. Had just killed a political figure.

Vent the contraband investigation. That didn't matter anymore. If she was the mystery assassin, half the Ministry of Internal Security believed she didn't exist, and the other half believed she was impossible to catch.

Suddenly Vask was very anxious to uplink his video log to Systems Control, and review the results on his comp.

He fidgeted, hoping to catch the next tube train, and then gave up the lengthy wait. He grabbed an air cab instead. If he was on the case he thought he was, he could easily justify the expense later.

Ground crew emerged from a subterranean power bay near the *Savu.* The gargantuan freighter was inert on the pad, her captain in heated exchange with a Security agent on the ground.

The techs approached the deck gantry and the Security man who stood there.

"Pardon me, sir," one said. "We're here to pull the batteries."

Agent Jorris turned angrily toward this new problem. "What's that? Batteries?"

"Yes, sir. Port Master said pull the power to the ignition circuits so they can't lift out of here. He wants this ship grounded."

"Batteries. Right." Jorris stabbed a finger at Natic. "See, Captain? No need for you to stick around. You can come back with me, now."

"Oh, no!" the ground tech spoke quickly. "We need the Captain to help us."

"Help you? Why?"

"She needs to override the phase lockout," the tech said matter-of-factly, "and maintain pulse alignment from engineering when we pull the tachyon leads."

It was only technobabble, but Jorris was no spacefarer, and hardly knew a warp coil from a vacc patch. He scowled. "Go ahead, then. As soon as this ship is grounded, you're with me, Captain."

Natic boarded the deck elevator with the ground-crew-that-was-not. Workers came aboard the broad-floored lift, pushing a gravsled, carrying lead extractors. Two muscled a heavy cable box along. One lifted power couplings off the last gravsled, then fumbled his load and spilled the equipment at Agent Jorris' feet.

The diversion nearly served to keep all eyes from the rest of the crew—but not quite. One of the Port guards watched idly, noted the fat man struggling with the cable box. Something about his movement was familiar. . . .

The guard normally worked the terminal, and knew the Customs Chief on sight. "That's Edini!" he shouted, and pulled his blaster.

Edinin dropped his end of the cable box, jarring Daribi's grip, leaving Karuu to spill out ingloriously onto the ground. The Chief dashed for the elevator, fishing for the blaster concealed inside a cargo pocket of his coveralls.

Startled by the shouts, his men abandoned him. One punched the lift button, and the heavy cargo doors swung ever so slowly shut. Blaster fire assailed their position; men snatched weapons concealed on the gravsled, and returned fire while Captain Natic dove for cover. Edini stumbled, then dove to the ground, taken down by one of Agent Jorris' well-aimed blaster bolts.

Karuu sprawled on the plascrete, ionizing charges crackling through the air over his head. Now, *this* was a diversion. The Dorleoni bounced to his feet.

"Come on, Boss!" Daribi said, running back the way they had come. He shouldered into Jorris, sending the Security man staggering to the ground. Of one accord, Islander and Holdout jumped into the waiting skimmer. Daribi punched the power, and the speeder shot off across the pad.

Wild blaster fire followed them about the same time a concussion grenade detonated inside the elevator cage. "Edini's dead," Jorris reported to Commander Obray. "Karuu and one accomplice fleeing eastward across the field in stolen skimmer."

Security forces rushed to intercept.

Karuu ducked down in the seat, the wind of their passage ruffling his body fur unpleasantly. He risked a peek forward, saw the woven mesh of the starport perimeter fence rushing toward them.

"We can not push through that," he squeaked.

"Not going to."

A blaster bolt from pursuing skimmers crackled through the air, range too long yet to be a hazard. Overhead a Customs patrol ship began a rapid downward spiral, anticipating their heading and closing on it.

"What are you doing?"

"Hang on!" The skimmer gave a leap, angled sharply upward, and rocketed for the top of the ten-meter-tall retaining fence.

A skimmer is a ground effect vehicle, but speed, momentum, and a sharp-enough angular adjustment could make it airborne. Not long, not far, but just enough to count.

They cleared the perimeter fence by so little, Karuu thought he felt gravpads scrape the top. They plunged to the ground on the other side and continued their high-speed run to the sea beyond.

The Dorleoni felt faint. "What now?" he choked out.

A crash came from the fence behind, a pursuer either trying their trick or failing to swerve aside quickly enough. The derevin chief didn't look back. The Customs flitter was closing overhead, and the edge of Bendinabi Field lay before them.

"Get ready to jump, Boss."

"What!"

"Jump. See that?"

Karuu peered forward, saw the sea cliff approaching, and slammed his eyes shut. "Edge."

"Water's deep below, we'll be alright."

Their intention to go over the cliff was apparent to the Customs ship. The vessel settled down, trying to block their route and force them to turn aside.

"Are you crazy?" squalled Karuu. "You are trying to kill us!"

Daribi shook his mane of wind-whipped hair. "I'm trying to save us. Get ready." He locked the throttle and, steering with one hand, began to pull his feet up onto the seat.

"Don't worry. You can swim." Daribi continued straight ahead, not swerving or turning aside from the Customs flitter. It loomed suddenly large before them.

"I hate this water," Karuu forced out miserably. His eyes were open again, fixed on the rapidly expanding wall of an atmosphere ship's hull. He tensed for impact and cursed his unkindly fate.

At the last possible moment the Customs vessel eased up a little to avoid the disastrous collision. The skimmer shot beneath it and over the edge of the cliff, sailing far out before it began its downward plunge.

Daribi held Karuu's webbed paw and the pair jumped clear, flailing and falling in a timeless moment into the green waters below. While he fell, between one long scream and another, the Holdout finally realized why the wild man had chosen this route for them to follow.

Offshore floated a sprawling, thick mat of woven reeds, an artificial island of the type that old R'debh natives called home.

XLI

*"**Are your handlers** on the pressure valves, Master Sharptooth?"*
There were no humans outside to work the cargo airlock so borgbeasts could swim clear. FlashMan knew the only option now was to remove the entire end of the Peryton's cargo container. Sharptooth and his companions were preparing to do so.

The end seal could be opened underwater, if pressure was equal on both sides. As soon as they were submerged, it would be. "We are standing by," the Vernoi assured him, his otterine fellows in position by the eight massive pressure seal clamps that secured the end of the container.

Flash turned his attention elsewhere. The Bugrunners were giving him trouble upstairs, hammering out dissonant music on his virtual keyboard, trying to interrupt the data flow that carried his cyber consciousness from physical body to ship's rigger jack.

Already he had had to split his attention and send a second spriteself back upstairs, to play a countermelody that bolstered the subspace channel and kept his link with the body strong.

Not every decker could do that, split his consciousness and be in two places at once. It took a specialized deck and custom programming, and a lot of practice. FlashMan cavorted in a tiny circle inside the rigger jack, and prepared to split again.

Soon the Bugs would be getting nasty. If they couldn't interrupt his subspace channel, they would use countermeasures to fight him inside the ship's cybernet. Like opening a door with a grenade, it would be messy and might hurt him.

It was time to change the rules a little.

While part of his mind considered his problem, the rest of Flash-Man handled the space freighter on reflex so intuitive it seemed unthinking. The *Delos Varte* lost altitude, touched water, settled only 100 meters until the container jarred against the bottom on the Avelar Shelf. The lifting framework of the vessel remained above the water. With a fraction of his attention FlashMan compensated for wave action, and kept the ship balanced and steady, its cargo fully submerged.

While the ship was settling, he split his consciousness again, and a lightning-shaped sprite-self secured an alternate route back to the FlashMan's cyberdeck. The second sim dissolved as the netrunner focused all his attention within the *Delos Varte*.

"*Cycling power, now,*" he announced to Master Sharptooth. The Vernoi floated by the locks as hydraulics eased clamps back. The handlers swam in excited circles, then gathered near the pressure seal valves.

Captain Brace paused, listening to a change in subspace harmonics. "He's doing something with the ship. We can't waste time." He tapped the bulldog on the head. "Backtrace. Try to locate his source."

Zippo nodded and snuffled off, moving upstream along data pathways, seeking the trickle of electrons that kept the intruder tied to the body.

Brace turned back to the floor-that-was-not, a tunnel mouth dropping down into the *Delos'* subspace receiver. "I think . . . data sharks," he mused, and reached into his virtual utility belt to pull out a handful of cherry-bomb-sized capsules. He tossed them onto the tunnel mouth, where they flowed like quicksilver, then solidified into many-toothed, crawly creatures vaguely fish-like in form. In a distant cyberdeck, a Borer program ran, creating data dropouts in the FlashMan's secure channel. In the Net, data sharks snapped and gnawed, and holes appeared in the fabric of the subspace tunnel.

The going was slow, but it was going. The sharks ate their way into the mouth of the conduit, and then down. Nomad followed and Brace came after, floating through the patchy data stream behind them.

✧   ✧   ✧

FlashMan grabbed his pointy head and yowled. It felt like someone was pouring acid on his synapses. It was hard to keep in touch with the body, and hard to focus on the ship. Time to bail out of this channel.

As quickly as possible Flash split his consciousness and sent a sprite-self racing ahead, using his back-door route to the inert body that housed the netrunner's brain. With a sprite there to serve as stepping-stone, Flash withdrew his focus from the satellite comnet, and turned instead to a route through vidphone lines.

The Bulldog's trail disappeared, and Zippo howled in frustration.

The encryption scheme on the subspace channel vanished; data sharks blinked out of existence as the need for them fled. Captain Brace plunged after Nomad through the cleared frequency, free of data or netrunner presence except for their own.

A moment later the deckers were in a round white room, with a single door leading out of it. It was the passage to the rigger jack, the only exit this particular channel could reach. Nomad marched up to it, and pulled the door open.

When FlashMan was distracted, hydraulics quit pushing and locking clamps bound in place. When his attention came back on line, machined parts grudgingly gave way. It remained for the Vernoi to vent the pressure seals, and then the massive endplate of the container should fall away.

Valves turned, gases vented. The container groaned as gravity tugged the endplate from its seating ring. It slipped partway open, and lodged there, stuck.

FlashMan twirled to face the intruder. All leads except one vanished from his head, as ship's systems fell into standby or failed entirely.

Nomad's hands came up and a sheet of blue fire lashed out at FlashMan. The lightning-man was slammed back against one of the wire-covered walls of the rigger jack. Before he could shake his head and recover, the cyber-static hit him again.

FlashMan lay on the floor, his lightning-form flickering with random discharges of energy. This isn't good, he thought. He far preferred to run and hide, dissuade and misdirect, than to outright fight an enemy in the Net.

Which is not to say he couldn't if he had to.

He threw his virtual self down the vid channel, leaving a self-destruct behind that, for the briefest moment, looked like a lightning-man tied in to the rigger system.

Captain Brace entered the room in time to share the firestorm with Nomad. The physical rigger system burst into flame and burned out in the *Delos'* control panel, and the Security netrunners fled for their lives back up the subspace link, reaching the satellite overhead as the channel went dead.

The behemoth that was the Peryton-class freighter, suddenly devoid of control, overbalanced. With the slow-motion list of megatons of mass, the gargantuan structure tilted shoreward, rolling over on the axis of its cargo module. For a moment it seemed the swell of the ocean would balance it. Then it slipped too far off-center, and began to fall.

The Vernoi tasted strange ocean waters mingling with their native seas. Strange, yet not unpleasant, and very welcome after weeks of confinement aboard. They swam back toward the lake-bottom grottos and gave long whistling calls.

The borgbeasts came. Together, in action concerted by their handlers, the whale-like creatures massed at the far end of the container, then, on signal, rushed forward as one. Blunt heads made for ramming collided with the unseated seal. The blockage jarred free, and tumbled out onto the cultivated silt of an aquafarm.

Neither borgbeast nor handler lingered. Each gripping a fin, the Vernoi were towed beside their companions into deeper water off the Avelar Shelf. They were soon so far away that they could not feel the tug of the flood wave created by the capsizing *Delos Varte.*

XLII

As soon as he drifted near consciousness, Yavobo forced himself awake. He pulled himself out of the autodoc, ignoring the red-flashing alarms that activated by interrupting its cycle, and headed directly for the door.

Medics from the clinic came running, and he pushed them easily aside. "You're not healed!" one protested, bigger and bolder than the rest.

Yavobo's wounds were raw, and he was in pain. His eardrums were restored enough so he could hear, though, and one hand was well enough to grip a knife.

"Where is my knife?"

The medics dithered until he threw one of them through a window. It took an effort, although they didn't know that, and the thin-skins hastily abandoned their protests. They gave him his knife and credmeter and what was left of his clothing and let him go.

He took an air cab piloted by a mecho, so there was no revulsion at his appearance or refusal to take the fare. Just as well. People were giving him a wide berth on the street, and it was certainly more pleasant to fly.

It was near twilight when the cab landed near the exhibitor plaza, the area roped off and abandoned pending further investigation. While the conveyance waited for his return, Yavobo limped painfully to one of the fern trees, and reached with gangling arm into the foliage above. He pulled out a spyeye, one of three he had set up around the ill-fated speakers' platform.

I may fail in my oath to protect, he thought critically, but I know how to hunt. Let's see what image I've captured.

He reset the image record and played it at fast forward, the globe that recorded becoming a playback sphere for a small holographic image.

There she was, that woman. He cropped and expanded the image, then froze the frame like that. Now he could show others her face and get an ID on her. Yavobo returned to the air cab, and gave it directions to Lairdome 7.

#

Daribi's islander heritage was not entirely pretense. He and Karuu swam mostly submerged, trusting in near-surface thermals to obscure them from Customs' overhead scans. Soon real islanders found them, men out working the yellow kelp beds. Daribi greeted them as cousins, and he and Karuu were spirited away into the root-mats of the floating, woven island.

Within the hour, a sea and island search had begun. As negative progress reports came back to Obray, the Commander knew with a sinking feeling that it was too late. Somehow Karuu had evaded him.

"Put out a planetwide alert. Karuu's description, a want and warrant. Don't let him get offworld."

Islanders are clannish, and despise the land-dwellers. They were glad to help a relative who was also in flight from unjust pursuit. Karuu and Daribi were smuggled away on a hydroskiff, traveling kelp-crowded byways unfamiliar to the surface searchers.

"Where to, Boss?" Daribi asked.

"I need to get away from here," Karuu grumbled, meaning Selmun III, "but first there is a stop I am needing to make. You have a gun, my wild friend?"

Daribi nodded, equipped by his Islander cousins.

"Good. Let us go to say good-bye to Lish."

XLIV

By time the Islander skiff neared Amasl, there were checkpoints at starports and transit stations, and the Holdout's furred image was broadcast hourly. Karuu sagged as he realized that simply walking ashore would leave him a marked man.

"Don't worry about it, Boss," Daribi reassured him. "We'll slip ashore in the twilight through Islander country on the docks. We'll pick up a car there, and you can stay in the back, out of sight. Comax Shipping isn't far from there."

True to his word, Islanders cleared the marina and secured them a car. Daribi drove them through darkening side streets. It was an air car this time, with Karuu tucked down like a small child in the rear seat. He saw the frown on the Chief's face, the first of the day to stay there for long.

"What is wrong, my friend?" he asked.

Daribi was not one to dissemble if asked. "I'm a little worried about getting offplanet, Boss. Your private ships were impounded this afternoon, and all the ports are watched. Things are snugged up tight."

Karuu had visions of another running battle through a starport, a fruitless attempt to reach a ship. He tore his thoughts from the picture before it could depress him.

"One thing at a time," he sighed. "First, Lish."

Yavobo's air cab settled around the corner from Lairdome 7. The Aztrakhani paid the fare, and turned his feet toward Comax Shipping. He saw the troops on guard duty before they saw him, and the tall desert warrior stepped into the shadows of an alley mouth to observe them. He watched for a while, light-adapting eyes taking in a myriad of detail.

They weren't exactly military, he noted. Hired muscle, then — from their appearance probably Skiffjammers, a derevin of military veterans, well equipped and cyberenhanced.

He shook his head in disgust. The thin-skins didn't have the patience to hone their own reflexes, so relied on purchased enhancements to do the job. A coward's way out.

Could I walk right in, past them? he wondered. Maybe this guard force is here to keep me out. . . .

He shifted aching shoulders and kept the weight off one badly damaged foot. If I were more fit, I could infiltrate through the seaway. But I fear even my keshun-cub could kill me tonight. This would not be a fair fight. . . .

He glanced at the holopix in his hand, then leaned against the alley wall and stayed there, for once uncertain about his next course of action.

Karuu saved him the need for a decision. He and Daribi had studied the approaches to the warehouse from several angles, and were on the verge of giving up their quest. Lish's sudden acquisition of hired help left her too well protected to attack. Now, outlined by the street glows, a tall alien of unique form and coloration lounged at the mouth of the alley.

Their air car came up gently behind him, the quiet hum of gravplates alerting him to its approach. Yavobo stared coldly at the vehicle hulking beside him.

Karuu lowered his window as the car cut power and settled to the ground. "I believe I am knowing you, sir," he said politely. "You are the bodyguard and bounty hunter, are you not?"

Yavobo regarded the warehouse again, ignoring the Dorleoni.

They had never met, but the Aztrakhani was such a distinctive person everything from his buying habits to his personal appearance left an impression on those in the Holdout's line of work.

The smuggler cleared his throat. He didn't like conferences in alleys. With Lish reluctantly scratched from the agenda, there was only one concern left in Karuu's mind: escape. Yavobo showing up like this was a stroke of good fortune.

"I need an escort off-planet," he told the alien. "I will make it worth your while."

Yavobo angled his body so the wounds he bore could be more fully seen. "I know who you are, Holdout, and I do not care. I do not guard people anymore, since I do not seem to be very good at it."

Karuu's brows drew together at the sight of the warrior's injuries. "Then do not guard me," he countered. "Get me to a ship and get me out of here."

Oh, this is coming out all wrong, the Holdout caught himself.

Put it all on the line, you silly sand-pup. This isn't the way to bargain!

"Leave me," the alien said flatly, and studied the 'Jammers once more.

Karuu fished for something that might appeal to the Aztrakhani. Daribi couldn't get him to a ship, and he had to get off R'debh. There wasn't a safe place to hide on all of Selmun III when the Bugs were really after you. He knew that; he'd watched others scraped out from under rocks kicking and screaming, and he didn't plan to be one of them.

"Maybe I can do something for you, Yavobo. Surely there's something you want?" Not the best bargaining position, either, but a sincere one. Hopefully the desperation he felt didn't come through in his tone.

The alien considered, then lifted a small spyeye globe with a holopix on display. "Can you help me find this person?" he asked, his unblinking yellow eyes fixed on Karuu's brown ones.

The smuggler leaned out of the window to see the pix more closely. Yavobo pushed the globe near, and Karuu jerked his hand back as if it were poison.

"You know her." The hunter's voice was chilling. He dropped the globe and grabbed Karuu's shoulder with his good hand, pulling him forward to the edge of the window. "Tell me who she is, where I can find her."

Karuu wanted to babble out anything that would get this creature's iron hooks out of his arm—yet if he did, he'd have no bargaining chip, no way to use Yavobo. All the other rough-and-ready types who could smuggle sentient contraband offworld on short notice were people he had screwed one way or the other in the past. Any one of them would be glad to hand him back to Imperial Security. Only someone like this, unattached and viciously efficient, could help him now.

Karuu flailed a paw and finally squeezed out some words. "I know her name. It's Reva."

"Reva." The alien tasted the word. "How else is she called?"

"That's all I've heard. I don't know where to find her—"

Yellow eyes narrowed.

"—but I know who does."

Yavobo released his grip. "Tell me more," he rasped as he scooped up the spyeye.

"My boss knows. He knows how to contact her. He can put you in touch with her."

"Who is your boss?"

No name, no name! Karuu gave a little prayer. "I am sworn not to say," he lied. Adahn would skin him alive if he blabbed the crime boss' name to derevin chiefs and streetcorner thugs like the Aztrakhani. Let Adahn deal with this fellow; Karuu's objective was to get offworld.

"You are certain he knows this Reva? How I can find her?"

"I swear it."

"If this is untruth, I will kill you."

Karuu took the alien at his word. "He will help you. I can promise that. If you get me out of here and take me to him, he will owe you."

Yavobo nodded once, sharply. "I came here tonight for another purpose," he said, "looking for the smuggler, to question her. I will trust to your information now, Holdout. I don't feel like fighting all of them—" he gestured toward the Skiffjammers, "—merely to ask a question."

Karuu opened the door and let the Aztrakhani into the air car. "Where to?" Daribi asked as he powered up.

"The frontage road north of Nahara Field," Yavobo said, referring to one of the small private ship pads on the outskirts of Amasl. Daribi considered the best way to evade checkpoints on the way, then guided the air car into traffic.

"You have a ship here?" asked Karuu.

"Yes."

Soon they were at the frontage road. "Get out and wait here," Yavobo ordered his companions as he climbed into the driver's seat.

Karuu looked distressed. "How are you going to—?"

"Be ready to board when I return. I hope you run fast, little Dorleoni."

The Aztrakhani drove away and arrived shortly at the landing field. On board his ship, his first stop was the medical locker, and a hefty dose of painkillers and stimtabs formulated for Aztrakhan bodies. He started the pilot's checklist, put in for lift clearance, got a window for half an hour later.

By lift time, Yavobo worked with icy clarity and drug-induced precision. Acknowledging lift clearance, he powered up the engines, and repulsors pushed the *Deathclaw* slowly skyward. Angling so the nose of the armed scout ship pointed north, he punched the maneuvering thrusters, and the *'Claw* shot across the small landing field. Before Traffic Control noted his deviation from flight plan, he was down on the frontage road with boarding ramp extended.

Karuu waddled rapidly up the ramp, leaving his derevin chief in the shadows. "Is he coming?" Yavobo demanded.

"No," the Holdout said. "I need him to stay here."

Yavobo cursed. Precious seconds had been wasted. "Strap in!" he barked, not looking to see where Karuu landed. He retracted the ramp, continued to gain altitude on repulsors.

Traffic Control was hailing him on several frequencies, demanding to know if he was in distress or out of his mind. Yavobo tapped a transmit button intermittently, shouting about communications malfunction, then turned off the volume on coms entirely.

Status lights showed his passenger was secure. "Hold on," he warned, pulled the nose up, and engaged main engines.

Normal lift procedure is to gain altitude on repulsors, then maneuver into an orbital traffic flow, and then out into space. Not to point for the stars like you were parked on an asteroid, and then slingshot into the void.

Yavobo laughed as acceleration pressed him into the pilot's chair. With the planetwide hunt for Karuu going on, even small craft would be inspected before they were released from orbit. His deviation from flight plan had been noted; surely a patrol ship was already maneuvering to intercept. The faster Selmun III was left behind, the more thoroughly that risk was avoided.

Sensors showed a clear path ahead. The *Deathclaw* shot toward the stars at maximum acceleration, and the Aztrakhani reveled at leaving the waterworld behind.

As Vask headed for Lairdome 7, he had lots of time to think. When he arrived, his plans had changed a little. He found a com booth, sat inside, opaqued it for privacy.

If Reva was the mystery assassin sought by Internal Security, he wanted to know that before uplinking to Systems Control. He jacked into the booth, keyed the image recorder into playback mode, and watched his point-of-view impressions move across the booth's flat-pix screen.

There was Reva, triggering the bomb. A still-frame and close-up revealed a small rectangular device held in her hand. Detonator.

Even more apparent: there was the assassin. Caught on surveillance pix.

Agent Kastlin deflated and pulled the plug on the neural jack. Case histories noted the killer's image had never been captured during a hit, even when done in full view of surveillance devices. How the assassin evaded or altered the record of sensors and pix recorders was unknown, but Reva, by the fact of her image capture, wasn't the one.

Guess it doesn't matter, though, Kastlin considered. Whoever she is, this assassin will take some watching.

Given his special qualifications, Vask was allowed unusual latitude in picking his own duty. The visual evidence of Reva at work was disappointing in one way, challenging in another. It wasn't every day you caught an assassin in the act.

Obray can have someone else trail contraband, he thought. I'm changing assignments.

Vask approached Lairdome 7 cautiously.

No police uniforms cluttered the loading bays; no Security presence hovered. There was something new in sight, though, and entirely unexpected: Lish had hired muscle.

She was prepared for some kind of trouble; that was clear. If IntSec wasn't here by this time, they must have called off the sweep operation for some reason. This derevin could be an obstacle, though. What did they call themselves? 'Jammers, something . . . Skiffjammers, that was it, for hire for water or land work. They had a paramilitary air about them, composed as they were of military veterans. Buzzed heads, army helmets with optics and ranging gear; not too many cyber modifications in evidence, though you could be sure they had jacked-up nerve reflexes and enhanced targeting systems.

The 'Jammers had set up checkpoints at all entrances to the Lairdome. The young men and women of the derevin were polite and formal; it almost made you overlook the blast rifles they carried.

Kastlin's name was on their access list; he was passed through their lines without being frisked. He walked into the Comax office shaking his head. "Looks like you're ready for some serious trouble. What's going on?"

The Holdout was playing computer games behind her desk, and losing at Shaydo by the look of it. She darkened the screen when Kastlin walked in.

"We're waiting," she said. Her face looked drawn, an effect of her lack of rest and the stimtabs winding down.

"Waiting? For what?"

"News."

Vask nodded sagely. "Any particular kind of news?"

"I'll know it when I hear it," Lish murmured cryptically, glancing at her desk console as if the vidphone should power up any second. "Meanwhile—I have some news for you."

"Oh?"

"Karuu's out of business."

Sitting down saved Vask from losing his footing. He contained himself with an effort as he heard the bare elements of the tale from Lish. He could fill in the blanks from what she didn't say. If anyone in Karuu's organization wanted to cause trouble, she'd be Number One on their hit list.

The street enforcers seemed like a very good idea.

While he was trying to digest this turn of events, her com unit finally signaled a call. Lish took it in the clear, apparently trusting the Fixer with what he might overhear.

She leaned forward over a darkened screen, no vid transmitted from the other end. "Yes?"

"*Delivery's done, baby, quick as a Flash.*" It was a synthesized voice, direct from the cybernet.

"Trouble?"

"*Enough. I'm a little fried. I expect that bonus we discussed.*"

An emotion flickered over her face, impossible to read. "Same account?"

"*Yeah.*"

"It'll be there."

The line disconnected. Lish played with a writing stylus, then threw it on the desk. "Halfway home," she said. "Now to get paid for it."

She eyed the screen meaningfully and leaned back to wait.

The reverie was interrupted almost immediately by Reva, appearing abruptly in the doorway.

"Muscle?" she inquired angrily, unhappy with the ID drill the 'Jammers had tried on her. "It's a good thing my name was on their list. If they'd tried to print or scan me, someone would be out there right now with a broken neck."

Vask started; Lish smiled nervously. "Sorry for the inconvenience. Thought I might need the protection," she explained.

"Why?"

"In case any of Karuu's people come hunting."

"You don't want trouble with Karuu's people."

"I don't think I'll have any. It's a precaution, that's all."

The strange tone of Lish's voice caught her attention and again Reva asked, "Why?"

The smile came on full-blast. "I've put Karuu out of business."

The words were nearly the same she had used on Vask, but the reaction was far, far different. Reva froze, turned pale, then flushed bright red. "You what!?" she shouted, leaning over Lish's desk, nearly screaming in the smuggler's face.

Lish shrank back, then sprang angrily to her feet.

"What in the seven hells is wrong with you? I thought you'd be glad to hear it."

"Glad to hear it? Are you crazy?" Reva took a step back, trembling with anger or some other reaction Vask couldn't identify.

"Yeah, glad to hear it." Lish spoke defiantly. "I took your advice, you know? About covering my butt, and making sure I had more than one way out. It worked, too. Better than I imagined. And you know what? If it wasn't him, it would've been me. I'm happy to be free and out of Security's hands."

Reva inhaled, a great lungful of air. "You have no idea what kind of connections Karuu has," she began.

"That's what you keep saying, 'Karuu has connections.' So what? I have connections, too, and I used them a lot better than he has."

Reva's eyes flashed. "You stupid bitch, you're going to get yourself killed."

"Is that supposed to be a threat?"

The tall woman recoiled. "I'm not threatening you," she spat. "I'm warning you."

Lish gripped the edge of her desk. "What's gotten into you, Reva? I thought you'd be happy for me. This is like castle-stones; I played a gambit that knocked my opponent off the board and made a fortune while doing it. Are you jealous that you couldn't get rid of that short pond-paddler yourself?"

"Jealous—?" The assassin waved her hand like she was waving off insects. "I'm pissed, that's what I am. You don't know the risks you're taking. And what's this about a fortune?"

Lish didn't share details in a spirit of camaraderie, as she had nearly done with Vask. Her words were terse, and she told little, yet it was enough to cause Reva to undergo another change of coloration. Her angry flush left her and she stood stock-still.

As Lish's words registered with Vask, he, too, paled, then looked away.

"What?" The Holdout stopped in midsentence. "What's wrong?"

Reva licked her lips. "You didn't sell to the AAP, but to a private person. In case there were political repercussions."

"So?"

"Only one person was contracted as your buyer. Alia Lanzig."

The Holdout gritted her teeth. "So?"

"So I killed her today. You won't be getting that pay authorization, Lish. She's not alive to make the call."

Lish remained standing. Vask could read every emotion on her face. Disbelief. Fear. Fury.

It was the fury that stayed, ringing in a voice that was tight and controlled.

"Do you have any idea at all how much I'm in debt to the Scripman? How soon payment has to be made? How many people will be collecting out of my hide if there's no money there?" Her voice was steadily escalating, until finally she was shouting. "Do you have any idea how much this shipment was worth?"

Reva was not one to take another's temper calmly. She flared right back. "Don't cry to me about your lost fortune. You're so clever. You took out Karuu." She spun on her heel, headed for the door. "I had a job to do," she said over her shoulder. "I took care of my business. Now you can take care of your own."

Lish slammed her fists down on the desk, and Vask came to his feet. He looked back and forth, between the trembling smuggler and the receding figure of the assassin. He made his choice, then, unhappily.

"Sorry, Lish," he murmured, and followed Reva out the door.

TWO

"You can't cross Lines if you want to keep a friend."

XLVI

It was a fine voyage until the sea-monsters appeared.

The misty predawn run to the north of Avelar Island started simply enough. Captain Orvan conned the *Eliset* through the foggy morning water of the straits, leaving behind a wake of green phosphorescence in the plankton-rich sea. The big cargo freighter plowed through the mild chop, then turned northward with the current. As the sun rose through orange- and green-washed clouds, the ship cut across a gentle easterly and followed the homing signal of a nav beacon toward Gambru Shelf.

The freighter ran heavy with her mixed cargo of machined parts, drums of sealant, tanks of processed oxygen. The *Eliset* was no racehorse, like the speedy but cargo-light hydroplanes that carried passengers and small goods on this run. She worked her way steadily through the buoyant waters of R'debh, in the traditional way that seagoing vessels have for countless millennia.

The attack came two hours out from Gambru Shelf, over the deep submerged canyons that channeled the warm-water current along this route. The sun was just high enough in the east to blind the Captain in the deckhouse. He turned his head from the green-yellow rays. The helmsman, eyes forward, squinted one eye half shut and never glanced to that side. Only Feron, the Mate, fetching another cup of osk from the dispenser, glimpsed something out of the ordinary through the sun-streaked glass. She lifted a hand to shield her eyes against the glare, then dropped her mug crashing to the floor.

"Helm hard a-port!" she shouted over her shoulder. "Helm hard a-port!"

The helmsman's trained reflexes obeyed the command before the Captain could question it. The yoke grip spun to the left, and the *Eliset* wallowed with reluctant inertia as rudders and repulsors nudged her downwind.

Orvan jumped from the Captain's chair. "What is it?"

Feron shook her head, mouth agape, and simply pointed.

To starboard, now toward the aft quarter as the ship slowly turned, three large shapes could be seen heading directly toward the *Eliset.* Only portions of them surmounted the waves, enough to show broad, flattened heads and bodies of a stunning length, each easily as long as the freighter. They moved so powerfully their wakes were clearly visible. They were less than 100 meters away and closing rapidly.

Captain Orvan stood paralyzed in amazement and disbelief. The oceans of R'debh harbored no large life-forms. What they were seeing was impossible.

The impossible was upon them in a moment. Before the ship could turn fully away, the alien creatures crashed mightily into the side of the freighter. Striking close together, nearly in unison, the tremendous power of their impact stove in the plating and spun metal alloy of the ship's side. Crew throughout the ship were thrown to the deck as the *Eliset* lurched noticeably sideways. Compartments began to flood below the waterline, and bulkheads jarred out of alignment failed to seal.

The creatures circled about to ram again.

The *Eliset* sank after the second attack, barely leaving time for one lifeboat to be launched. The few bedraggled crew who clung aboard choked out whispered prayers when the monstrous sea-beasts neared their boat. Then the creatures moved away and slipped beneath the waves.

"By the Sea Father," one sailor breathed. "What are they?"

No one had an answer.

Out of sight, many meters below the surface, the water-breather Edesz and his companions laughed in celebration of their success. Silver bubbles burst free from their mouths and floated toward the surface.

"Not so hard after all, was it?" body-signed Frevin.

"They're even stronger than we thought," Edesz concurred, signing back.

Overhead and to one side a single small oblong marred the light-refracting wavetops. Edesz looked toward the sole lifeboat that drifted on the surface, and gave an elaborate shrug.

"The loss of life, more than just the shipping, will drive our point home," he remarked.

Nela signed agreement, the gill slits on her neck flaring in excitement. "For independence," she said.

"For independence," the others echoed. Independence from surface traders and air-breathing industry magnates. Independence, so that water-breathers could come into their own on the planet they dominated in population.

It was an offensive that was long overdue, and the means of their liberation was approaching now. Edesz tapped the sonic receiver, a streamlined cup attached to his left ear, and pointed toward the deep canyons. He and his friends floated at fifteen meters depth and stared downwards, still astonished by the brute size of the three cetacean-like creatures that rose to meet them.

The slab-browned leviathans were guided by their handlers. Master Swimmer Sharptooth released his beast's fin and swam closer to the humans. "Our friends wish to feed, now," he whistled and clicked into the waters. "It is necessary, to reward them for their work."

"We understand," the terrorist replied. "Let them." He glanced about through mote-filled depths and asked, "Where are the others?"

There were eight borgbeasts in all, and one handler for each. They were to rendezvous after this trial run in the busy Gambru shipping lanes.

"Feeding already," Master Sharptooth whistled in reply. "Have found a school of fish."

"Go then," Edesz signed. "We'll meet you back at the dome when you're done. Good hunting."

Master Sharptooth whistled orders to his fellows. Handlers and beasts sank back into the depths, heading toward the apaku their hungry companions had already located.

XLVII

In the deep, distant waters of the equatorial belt, in a canyon charted by satellite but never visited by man, something stirred in the dark waters. Something ghost-like and large, barely visible, sensed more than seen.

The ghost-ray beseeched sometimes as the Sea Father, subject of rumor and myth, came awake. He listened without ears, sensing on a half-materialized membrane that served him as skin the distant vibrations of sound, borne faithfully for long days through the ocean waters.

Here was a sound like none he had ever heard. Like none that should be there. For long ages none had challenged his supremacy in these waters.

The ghost-ray listened to the long drawn-out wails, the booming bass notes of alien life. Large life.

For one day, then two, sound waves washed over the creature's deep grotto. Time did not mean to the ghost-ray what it meant to humans, and thus he had infinite patience. On the third day the sound changed, bearing with it not only the alien whistles, but a clamor and cry of distress wafted like pheromones upon the current.

The Sea Father could not feel a sense of threat from physical things that could not touch him. An alien presence alone was not enough to make him emerge from his lair. The scent of distress, though, close-tied to those clicks and wails, was something else. Curiosity stirred awake in the creature, and he contemplated whether or not to investigate.

Time runs differently for the phase-shifted. The ghost-ray considered.

In the human world, days passed by.

Shiran Devin entered the Comax Shipping office without knocking. He glanced at Lish, looked unhappily around the room, and slumped frowning in a chair.

"Devin." The Holdout's recognition carried with it a note of surprise. When he failed to respond, the woman abandoned her desk and came around to take a neighboring chair.

Her clanmate looked much the worse for wear, ground down nearly to the comportment of a common spacer. "Did they get rough with you?" she asked.

"Only the usual Bug tactics," he replied. "Tell the same story five times, then three more on truth juice."

Lish's lips thinned into a tight line.

"Don't worry, Domna." The captain used the honorific with bitterness. "I didn't tell them anything. I didn't really know anything to tell, now, did I? You were pretty careful about that."

"Oh, Devin," Lish began. "It's not like you think—"

"Save it for Obray. We're both Shirani. Clanmates; once shipmates. I didn't think you'd set me up."

Lish turned from the accusation in his eyes.

"Tell me this: was your offer to do business with me legitimate, or was that part of the lure, too?"

The silence stretched between them before she spoke. "If you really want to know what's going on, I'll tell you. If you only want an excuse to recriminate, you can leave."

Devin spoke tiredly. "I'm not leaving. I acted in good faith, and it got me into a pile of shit with the authorities. I never heard of this Karuu fellow before he hired me, and it nearly lost me my pilot's license. I covered for you and I don't even know what for. I think you owe me an explanation."

The Holdout considered his demand. "You're not going to like it."

Devin's lips turned down. "I already don't. At least I'll understand it if you talk."

She sighed, carelines deepening around eyes and mouth. "I admit I sort of used you, Devin," she regarded him seriously, "but that's not what I started out to do. I really am looking for a shipping partner, like I offered. I saw your name on the for-hire roster on the Net, and I remembered you'd gone independent, too."

Devin waved a hand dismissively. The fact that he still did not own his own ship rankled. Stupidly, it was the prospect of gaining a ship of his own that had lured him to Selmun III.

"I was also working a little sleight of hand with ship records," she continued. "Karuu made it to the top by setting up and taking down smaller Holdouts along the way. I think I was next. So when I had a really big run coming in, I wanted some insurance, so he couldn't finger me and grab my cargo. That's his pattern."

Understanding began to dawn on the ship's Captain. "By Juro's brass balls. And you hired me to pilot that mess for you." Anger flared in Devin's blue eyes. "Thanks a lot, shipmate."

"Devin, look. It was my chance to make a fortune. Millions. Really."

He ignored the stress in her voice. "On borgbeasts? The same happy swimmers that are starting to sink ocean shipping?"

Lish blinked, surprised.

"On the news this morning. One ship down, and credit taken by some group called the Gambru League. Security put out a flash, warning seafarers about alien life-forms in Selmun III waters. Sounds like they sat on the knowledge a little too long to do those sailors any good."

Lish's brow creased.

"What?" demanded Devin. "Nothing to say? No explanation? Innocent people killed because of what you smuggled onplanet, Lish. How can you do work like this?"

"You know there's not much logic to import laws. There's demand. I supply. That's all." She frowned. "It's not like you refused to move the cargo. I figured that 'quick and discreet' clause would warn you off if you weren't interested."

Devin sat silent. She was right about that much. Like most cargo spacers, Devin supplied demand, and didn't always think far past that criterion himself.

"I hope all this was worth your while." He motioned vaguely over his shoulder with his thumb, toward the street where hired Skiffjammers patrolled Lairdome 7. "Looks like you've bought a lot of trouble."

A shadow passed over the Holdout's face. "If you can't help me out, Devin, I'm probably not buying a whole lot of anything."

"What does that mean?"

She told him, then, of the payment arrangements for the borg-beasts, and how she could no longer collect. "I'm overextended," she concluded grimly, "and time's running out."

Devin cocked his head and studied his kinswoman. This was not the optimistic, ambitious Lish he remembered. Her trouble was big, alright, for it to weigh on her so. Old habits of concern for one's clanmate came to the fore, and his tone softened. "How overextended is that?" he asked.

"A couple million," she said softly.

His eyes widened. Scratch helping her out of his personal savings. "Millions?" he breathed.

"Loans from the Scripman, due in a month. Well—six weeks now, that's all that's left." She referred not to a Selmun month, but to the bureaucratic standard set by Imperial fiat. Intentionally blind to any planet's natural cycle, calendar increments of twenty-five hours a day, ten days a week, ten weeks a month, made for convenient accounting across several hundred diverse sectors.

She seemed to leave something hanging. "What else?" he prompted.

"Short payment to the netrunner who finished the delivery for me," Lish conceded. "He's a dangerous one to shortchange. There's not much cash left, either. I've got enough to pay the derevin another two weeks. After that, my protection's gone." She gave a sick laugh. "I may not be alive for the Scripman to kill for his money when it comes due."

"What about your smuggling runs?" he asked. "The hot drops?"

"No one's getting through to do ocean drops these days. Security's too tight right now, unless . . ." The Holdout spoke again, tentatively. "I don't suppose you'd want to do some runs for me . . . ?"

"Runs?"

"Off-planet, on-planet. You're a great pilot, Devin, better than the others who work for me. You could beat system patrols." She warmed to the topic. "If I move cargo, I might be able to pay off some of this debt, buy some time—"

He shook his head once, emphatically. "No."

"But—"

"No, Lish. I don't like the price you pay if you're caught."

The Holdout's expression darkened. He went on, to soften his refusal. "Maybe there's some other way. You say this Lanzig died. So, why don't you demand payment from someone else?"

She snorted. "Like who?"

"No, wait." What he had said casually began to make sense to him. "Why not approach the people using the borgbeasts? They took delivery on the cargo and they're benefiting from it."

Lish thought it through and a shadow seemed to lift from her face. "Say . . . you might have something, there."

"Who are these Gambru Leaguers?"

"The terrorists? Don't know. I don't follow local politics."

"Maybe you should start. As I see it, they're the ones owe you a couple million."

"A lot more than that. Two mil and change is what I owe the Scripman, that's all. This was a high-risk, very high-profit venture."

Devin ducked his chin. "Then demand that payoff from the ones who are using your cargo. That's my advice."

Lish caught his eyes with hers. "Will you help me?"

Contradictory answers flew through the spacer's mind, locking his mouth tightly shut. She watched the war behind his eyes, as recent irritation warred with old loyalties. The clan ties won out.

"Dammit, Lish." He let out a breath and scowled at her. "Yes, I will."

When things went wrong, it was Reva's habit to leave. There was no need to stick around in an ugly moment when you could move to a Now that avoided the difficulty. So it was strange that she didn't skip across several Timelines after her fight with Lish, abandoning the Holdout and her problems in a Mainline that no longer existed subjectively.

Reva pushed that thought aside, puzzled by her own behavior. She didn't fight with people like she had with Lish. She killed them, or she ignored them. There was no one she cared about enough to fight with that way.

Leaving Selmun was a reflex, her best way to escape a difficult situation besides using the Lines for a reality shift. She passed fluidly between moments, staying always close to Mainline, and left Selmun as an unseen passenger on the next ship out, a sector liner bound for Ard.

At the Lyndir stopover, she left the ship and made some calls, then returned as a regular passenger with a claim to cabin and service. And was as good a place as any to receive final payment for the work on Selmun III, and she was overdue to collect.

She met the Cardman in a bar near the Startown gate. She didn't wait long. The courier remembered her last fit of pique and was prompt in his delivery. He slipped into the booth across from her, and began without small talk. "Mr. Harric would like to know why the work took so long at your last location."

Reva raised one incredulous eyebrow. A hit took however long it took to ensure untraceability. On R'debh, of course, there had been the minor distraction of an unscheduled trip to Des'lin and time spent with Lish—and that was none of Adahn's affair.

"If he has time limitations, he needs to specify that when contracting. Fast costs twice the price, paid in advance. He already knows this, but you can remind him of my terms."

The Cardman flinched at her unblinking gaze, and ducked his chin hastily. He lifted the security case to the table.

Reva laid a hand atop it before he could open it. "Describe."

The balding fellow swallowed audibly, and began his dealer's spiel. "Fifteen cuts resonant crystal, type N3, graded through 1,000 centierg amplification. Local product, quality-tested and cleared for transshipment offworld. Certificate's inside. Cash credit chit for 50k. That's all."

"Crystal?"

"Yes."

She reconsidered the case. "Open market goods, clear and legal?"

"Yes."

Satisfying. "Open it," she ordered.

He showed her the lock codes as he unsealed the container and force screen. Reva examined the contents.

"Impressive," she conceded. Crystal prisms nested snugly in morphfoam, blue-green lights scintillating off the smooth-ground facets on their sides. A handspan long and a finger wide, they were the power conversion and output element essential to devices as various as medcenter scanners and subspace com systems. Larger versions powered blast cannon and warp engines; smaller shards focused the output of hand-held energy weapons. Reva was looking at about 150,000 CR worth of perfectly legal and valued components she could trade anywhere.

The silver-hued plastic chit in a corner of the security case was almost easy to miss. She plucked it out and studied the green-hued hologram embedded in the surface; 50,000, cash. Then she dropped the chit back into the case and closed the lid.

The courier breathed a little easier, and went on to his next item of business. "I'm supposed to ask when you'll be available for any new work that may come up."

Her long-nailed fingers gripped the carry handle, but left the case on the table. She pursed her lips and a moment of silence passed. "Tell Adahn I'll call when I'm on the market again."

The Cardman blinked, unhappy with the noncommittal reply.

"Was there anything else?"

He cleared his throat. "No. That's all."

Reva nodded in satisfaction, then collected the case and left without another word.

She started back to the starport, but a nervous clenching in her stomach slowed her footsteps. She tried to place the feeling, then paused in the inky shadow of an alley mouth and slipped into the mode between Timeliness. Surveying the multifaceted Nows, she saw nothing threatening near her or in the near future. Slowly she realized it was not anticipation that she felt; it was a nervous kind of dread, a formless anxiety that left her back in Mainline, standing aimlessly near the walk that led to the starport.

She took a few slow steps until ennui arrested her motion outside a restaurant. She stared thoughtfully toward the dome and the transport it offered offworld, unable or unwilling to continue on her way.

I don't want to go, she suddenly knew. If I go, I decide. On to Merith, where I can fence these goods. Or back to R'debh.

I don't have a choice, she considered. I've got to move these goods; Merith is the place to do that, and it's a good long distance away from that woman and her deathwish.

She stepped into the nearby restaurant then, and ordered something she didn't plan on eating, to gain time.

Time for what? she wondered. To make up my mind? I thought I already had.

She had been through this once before, on the flight out from Selmun III. It was simple enough: collect payment; trade it for cash and percentage through the Merith fence; spend time there to regroup. Forget about Lish. Reva's anger at the Holdout's actions had unsettled even herself.

I need distance, she told herself. I don't have to go back there again. I can just go on. . . .

Right, a cynical voice sneered in her head. That's why you've been careful to stay in the same Mainline as the Lish you know. You can go easily enough, but you don't really want to get away.

Why's that? she challenged the voice, but the cynic was quiet, leaving the assassin to fill in the blanks for herself. She toyed with her food while she turned over possibilities, and knew all the while she was evading a simple truth she hated to express.

Lish has become my friend. I don't want it to end like this.

Reva forced a swallow of recycled water past the tightness in her throat. Her past was checkered with all kinds of unfinished business and abandoned relationships, but this time, things went deeper than that, and it didn't take much pondering to get to the heart of the matter. The answer was there, anxious to intrude into her conscious thoughts.

I feel more toward her than I would toward a friend, Reva admitted to herself. Not that she knows it. Not that I'll ever act on it. Everyone I get close to I lose, and I don't need to lose more people than I already have in my life.

It was that attraction that had fluttered to life on Des'lin, buried these many weeks but not languishing in the back of Reva's mind, seeking a life of its own in this coloration of what had started as casual friendship. She laughed suddenly, sharply, a short ironic bark that caused other restaurant patrons to turn and look at her, then look away.

If I'd just slept with her, I'd be over it by now, ready to leave this Line and all these people behind. Wouldn't I?

She sighed ruefully. Not so sure that was true, either. She loved neither men nor women, surely never fell in love with either. She amused herself with both sexes, and that one time she'd loved a lover . . . well, he was unplanned, an accident that chance had snatched away from her soon enough. It was all pretty damn confusing, especially when you added in Line-traveling and tried to return to someone who didn't know you anymore. And at the base of it all, underlying these tangled caring webs she tried to avoid, was a foundation of friendship. She wasn't very good at doing friendship.

But not for lack of trying. Maybe that was the thing with Lish: Reva might never be more, but at least she could be that, a friend. And her friend had never even heard her reason for anger, for her concern over the smuggler's latest actions on R'debh. Lish was dangerously ignorant of Karuu's connections to Adahn, and the crime boss' power and taste for retaliation.

Reva chided herself for letting the incident linger on her mind. You can't baby-sit every new Holdout on the block, she thought, and in the next heartbeat told herself to quit whining about it. Lish wasn't every Holdout. She was the one Reva had invested time and energy in, and that made her different from everyone else.

Reva began to pick at her food, grown cold during her internal debate. She mulled over the alien idea of friendship, wondered if Lish was still mad at her.

Would she even listen to me if I went back?

It was a subject to leave to the future. Acknowledging the issue had freed her steps for now; today it was enough to go on to Merith, and once there, Reva could decide how to deal with the Holdout. Her friend.

L

"Listen good," **Daribi** boomed out to Islanders from a tabletop in the Dive, their bar and headquarters.

Faces looked at him expectantly and he continued.

"You know who shut Karuu down?" he declared. "Shiran Lish, the Holdout in Lairdome 7. Some kind of trick. She set him up, let him get snagged for a cargo she brought onworld. And you know who's our biggest threat on the docks right now? Same person.

"It's been a long time since we had a war here." Daribi spoke louder, more excitedly. "I say it's time for another. Time to get our revenge for being made to scurry from the Bugs. Time to make sure we won't be challenged on the docks. And time to take a bigger piece of the action from this offworlder who made trouble for us!"

"She signed the Skiffjammers," a voice in the crowd volunteered.

"That's right, she did." Muttered curses swept through the assembled Islanders. There was no love lost between the derevin.

"With the cargo she landed, and the maneuvering she's done, she's making a bid to run the show here on R'debh."

"So?" challenged one. "What's it to us?"

The Chief waited until the crowd silenced to hear his reply.

"She's not established yet. If we move now, we can take over before she's entrenched. If we don't, she'll move in with Skiffjammers sooner or later to cut us out of the waterfront." Angry grumbles agreed with him. "So here's our chance. Streetwar."

By the end of his speech he was exhorting them in shouts, and they were shouting right back with him. A chorus of approval came from the majority, fists raised and ritual victory steps danced in anticipation. In the end all were in agreement.

LI

Lish's habit of travel had once been to use public transportation, sleep in public dorms, become lost among crowds, and so gain the anonymity of the multitude. Since her talks with Reva, that had changed.

While setting up Karuu she took private lodgings, two apartments in the city and one villa outside of it to ensure her location on any particular night could not be easily predicted. She slept more easily at night.

Until the night she went to dinner at Pasgo's. Vask had cajoled her into it, hoping to ease the tension and the obsessive overwork the Holdout had retreated into. Escorted by a team of 'Jammers, they traveled the magtube and walked through the rain-wet streets of Old Town toward the restaurant. Lish was nearly to the door when her street-side guard dropped bleeding at her feet, shot through the temple with a silent-flying sniper's needle that exploded on impact.

She stared in astonishment at the gore-spattered walk; Vask and the Skiffjammers carried her forward in a surrounding rush and through the double doors of Pasgo's. More needles exploded against the glas doors, and one caught a 'Jammer in the back of the calf, dropping him sprawling to the floor. Diners recoiled and waiters rushed forward, only to retreat hastily as the hail of fire continued. The right-side door shattered and needles flew into the dining room. Customers fled with shocked outcries, stampeding for the kitchen and rear exists. Three 'Jammers took cross-fire stances concealed near the entrance, blast rifles sweeping the building skyline across the street with random fire, seeking the hidden assailants. The injured man stayed with Lish and Vask on the floor by a shielding wall, and called for backup.

The Fixer had his needle gun out, though he stayed out of the killing field near the door. "You alright?" he asked the Holdout.

She dipped her chin, white-faced, and the pair hunkered together while Islanders sniped and 'Jammers returned fire. Reinforcements arrived and provoked an intense firefight a block away. In the confusion, Lish was hustled away in an air car that headed straight for Evriness Highlands, the secure villa community that was her designated retreat in case of personal attack. Captain Levay arrived a short time later to offer her report on the situation.

"Word's out," Levay said. "It's full-blown streetwar with the Islanders. The same time they tried to hit you, they attacked the Comax Shipping office. No significant damage taken," she was quick to reassure, "but that's where most of my troops are located. The Islanders are going after warm bodies."

"Streetwar?" The Holdout had heard the term but never lived through the event.

"Yes. I advise you to stay inside this compound for the duration, Domna," she said. "It's not safe to travel, and the warehouse is too exposed. You're best off right here."

Putting a further crimp in her Holdout operations. "How big a danger are the Islanders, really?" she asked.

Levay looked grim. "If you want us to stay strictly defensive, it could go on for weeks. They're out to kill you, and us, and they're good enough to come close to it."

"What alternatives, Captain?"

"Give us the all-clear for offensive action. We could wrap this up in a week or two."

If it went on longer than that, Lish knew, the mercenary derevin wouldn't get paid. Then they would walk out and leave her easy pickings for Karuu's old street gang.

"Make short work of it, then," she agreed. "I don't have time for this nonsense."

Levay pushed herself back from the table. "Let me see to some combat-issue supplies for my 'Jammers. Then I'll be back."

Vask waited until she was gone to clear his throat. "Maybe I should leave," he volunteered.

Lish lifted her chin. "Why? Afraid?"

Vask squared his shoulders. "Thought I might be in the way. There's nothing I can do here for you."

"Come on. You're in and out of my office all the time. Think the Islanders won't toast you as soon as they would me?"

His brows pulled together. "I hadn't considered that."

"Consider it. You're as much a target as I am. You're a friend, Kastlin, or at least you appear to be a damn steady customer to any observers on the street. That makes you a target too. You better stick around where it's safe until this is over. You have a problem with that?"

Problem. Yeah. Like, how to report in? How to call for help if things turned bad? How to use his psionic abilities without detection when living too close to the subject of his investigation . . . ?

Then again, there were worse places he could be. Like out of touch with the Holdout completely. He sat back in his chair. "You're right. I'll stay. So what's the plan?"

Lish made a face. "As long as we have communications I'm in business, if that's what you call emptying warehouse stockpiles. I suppose I should work on staying solvent."

"Anything I can do to help?"

She gave a faint smile. "Maybe. Let's see what Levay has to say when she gets back."

He nodded, already deciding on what mix of help or hindrance he could legitimately offer. Meanwhile . . .

"Want to play Shaydo?"

"Sure."

It was as good a way as any to wait for Captain Levay's return. Lish got a deck of cards, dealt the first hand. Kastlin studied the table layout, reviewed his hand, and grimaced. It was, as always, an all-or-nothing game.

If he was going to play in this league, he needed to get much better at it.

Vask awoke suddenly. There was something disturbing about his dreams.

At first he thought it might be the streetwar, that something untoward had happened in the physical world around him. He listened, extending his sleep-heightened psionic sensitivity throughout the villa. Except for the guards, the world slumbered around him.

What was it? he wondered. Something made me tense, forced me awake.

He replayed the last dream fragment that drifted in the back of his mind. A corridor, a bounce tube, the mezzanine level of Reva's hotel. That was it, he thought, I was following her again. Nothing out of the ordinary about that dream. Except right there, at the end. . . .

The image replayed in his mind's eye, his trained recall easily restoring details lost to the ordinary waking mind. A flicker of motion clued him that Reva was on the mezzanine. He followed, stepping out of the bounce tube's gravfield, and looked down the corridor—

—where now, in dreamy slow motion, Reva walked, shimmered, and faded from sight.

The vision galvanized Kastlin and he jerked upright in bed, fully awake. With unfocused eyes he stared into the dark, not-seeing the Now, replaying the image in his head.

A shimmer, and gone from sight. He'd seen it before, though never so fluid or fast, when he had observed other Mutates shift into the unphased state called sideslipping. He did the same thing. A shimmer, a fading away, as he had seen Reva do, yet which had registered on the subconscious level.

With certainty Vask knew this was a memory, replayed by his mind so he could observe what had eluded his physical eye. He had trailed her, and lost her, and this was why. Reva was psionic, and moved unphased and undetected by sight.

She is the one, the agent thought, certain now of his assessment of the assassin's abilities. The one who moved invisibly to commit impossible murders. They had not thought to look for a Mutate, for they were known and accounted for.

Kastlin's hand strayed to his forehead, stroked the bare skin above his brows. All were accounted for, except for those in Imperial service, like himself. Law dictated that psionicists should be marked with the symbol of their special powers, each with a *rus* of various codified designs, laser-scribed in plain sight on the brow, so the unsuspecting would be forewarned of the great and often dangerous powers borne by the extraordinarily gifted.

All but a few, like Vask himself, a valued field agent who worked undercover, passing as a Normal when needed.

Sometimes criminals removed the *rus* with a nanotech fix, but that was an expensive and not widely available incognito. Others, like wild talents, were never detected and marked in the first place.

For all he had studied Reva's face, Vask had never noticed the faint blemish left by laser-scribe removal. He knew, or sensed, that she must be a wild talent, with a skill untrained and hitherto unde-

tected. Or a few skills, for that would explain why the assassin left no
psionic signature, no detectable trace of broadcast mental energy as
most all living creatures did. A natural psi shield? How very rare. . . .

He rubbed a hand over his face. Reva the mystery assassin, and
elusive wild talent; Reva, who had saved his life and might never return to the scene of recriminations and ruined hopes.

At least now I know what to be alert to, he told himself. If I ever
find her again, I'm following, wherever it is that she goes.

"You're late."

The synthesized words cut into Lish's conversation with Captain
Levay, grating through the earlink and disconnecting the Skiffjammer
in a fuzz of white noise. Lish knew the voice immediately, raw from
direct cybernet transmission.

She lowered the volume with trembling fingers and took a deep
breath.

"You don't want to owe me money," the netrunner said. There was
no threat in his tone, just confidence.

"I'm sorry. I . . . ." This was the conversation Lish had been dreading. There was no telling what havoc FlashMan could wreak on her
and her operations if he wanted malicious revenge for a short pay-
check.

"Don't tell me you underbudgeted. Tsk, tsk."

She had a strategy in mind about how to deal with him. Would
he go for it? It was time to find out.

"Look." Lish leaned forward as if she were talking to the cyber-
jock across her desk. "My buyer stiffed me. They don't want to pay
for the goods you helped deliver."

"Too bad. Not my problem."

"I'll be honest with you, Flash." She had to be; he could verify
many of her records himself. "That was the major source of income I
had on the line. The Bugs have tight security upstairs and I'm not making cargo runs. My regular customers have all gone to ground while

Security finishes its rampage. This isn't business as usual: this is no business at all, anywhere, until the heat's off. The only way I have to pay you is to collect from the buyer."

"*So collect.*"

"I've tried that." She braced herself and plunged in. "I have an offer for you."

"*With bonus pay? No thanks.*"

"No. For a share of the profits."

"*I don't work on speculation.*"

"With your help, this wouldn't be speculation." She plunged on before he could interrupt. "The buyer is hiding out, very effectively. He's using comlinks, though, and could be traced that way, by a good netrunner. A very good netrunner." That was obvious bait; she hoped it wasn't too obvious. "Muscle isn't going to turn the trick with this man. I have to convince him that it makes good business sense to pay up. With an exceptional decker on our side, we can pressure him in ways he won't be expecting."

"*You haven't tried to squeeze this buyer yet, have you?*"

"No." She had been on the verge of ordering 'Jammers after Edesz several times, but the streetwar kept heating up, and uncertainty about how to pin down the terrorist's location had held her back.

"*How do you know it's going to be this simple?*"

"I'm not saying it's simple. It'll be challenging. And worth your while."

Challenging. Lish had said the magic word. She finally had his attention.

FlashMan let her languish an uncomfortably long time. He came back online as she was beginning to think he had disconnected.

"*Difficult thing you contemplate. It would have to be worth my while.*"

"Double your usual fees."

"*Triple the fees, and I want a cut of your payment. Ten percent.*"

Automatically, Lish counteroffered. "Double your fees, plus 5 percent." Only as she spoke did she have second thoughts, hesitant to antagonize the netrunner.

She needn't have worried. "*Triple and ten,*" he came back.

"Triple and five."

"*Eight percent.*"

Lish knew when enough was enough. "Done," she agreed, and let out a relieved breath. "What we need to do, is—"

"—is put the screws to Edesz and the Gambru League. I watch the news, babe."

She gritted her teeth.

"I have some things to look into. I'll get back to you soon. And that 100?"

The hundred thousand credits, his belated bonus. "Yes?"

"I want that added to the bill."

White noise flared and faded from the earlink, and the channel went dead. Lish leaned back weakly in her chair.

If the goddess of luck really exists, she thought shakily, Lakshan is smiling on me today. I just hope FlashMan sticks to his word, and things go right.

And if they didn't . . .

She punched another comcode, marshaling her escort of Skiff-jammers for a quick trip to Akatnu Field.

The **Kestren did** not look like the speedy raptor her name implied. There was nothing swift-seeming about her boxy hull configuration, and the blasted hold unit gaped like an open wound, tortured plating and burn scoring mute testimony to a ship caught unawares or overtaken by pirates.

Lish's car pulled up near the Mershon-class trader at Akatnu Field. 'Jammers flanked the ship as she stepped out of the vehicle, picking her way through spare parts and loose plating, walking up the ramp into Cargo One, the primary hold unit.

Her clanmate barely acknowledged her presence. "These things are worthless," Devin grumbled over the charred link module in his hand. "Half of them fried when the shields overloaded and collapsed. We have to replace them."

"That's what I'm here to talk about. Status, and update."

That nudged the spacer out of his preoccupation with the damaged module. "So let's talk." He led the way into the crew unit, collecting Vask as they went. The trio sat around the galley table, lit by glowstrips.

"Power's out?" Lish asked.

"Just offline. The drive and power system is the best thing about this junker. Dual Calyx-Primes, full warp rated, 5.5 acceleration for impulse maneuvers."

Lish whistled in admiration. Vask looked lost.

"Very fast for the class," Devin explained. "And they used every bit of it running away from the firefight that holed them. How much did you pay for this heap, Lish? Besides the obvious, there's a lot of systems damage."

"Got it in trade for moneys owed," she explained.

"Well, I can fix her for you," Devin looked at her thoughtfully, "but this isn't going to be cheap."

The Holdout forced a smile. "I have the credit line, and that's just as good for now. How long will it take to get her flightworthy?"

Devin considered. "We'll need an outside crew to repair the hull damage. Otherwise we can do most of this ourselves. Pull and plug parts, calibrate shield generator, new guns . . . two or three weeks."

"Skip the guns. How long would that be?"

"Two weeks."

She gave her clanmate a tight smile. "Order the hull team today, and the replacement units you need. You have a week."

His protest was immediate. "Ten days isn't enough time to do this right. You have to consider—"

"I have to consider that we may not *have* any more time than that, Devin." Her voice was firm. "You read me?"

Lish hadn't discussed the possible need to flee Selmun III in so many words, but he took her point. "I need some 'Jammers, then, to speed up the work. A lot of them were Imperial Navy."

She agreed to that. "And you can captain this ship after she's back together," she continued.

"With contract and ownership," the spacer replied automatically.

"Contract," she said. "We'll talk about ownership."

"Ownership, Lish." His voice took on a harder edge. "You know why I'm here."

The remembrance of what had brought Devin to Selmun III hung between them. Lish gave in. "Owner shares. We'll talk details later."

"Done."

Kastlin stood and Lish slipped around the galley table, ready to leave. Devin held her by the arm for a moment. "Thanks," he said.

She met his earnest gaze, eyes dark blue under the glowstrips. "You're welcome," she replied, suddenly awkward, and hurried to leave the *Kestren*.

LIJ

A blue bulldog snuffled around virtual corridors, and finally caught what registered as a familiar scent. The scent turned to a yellow shimmering ribbon on the floor, a data-trace crafted by Zippo's deck inside the Selmun Net.

Captain Brace paced behind the hunting dog. There was nothing in the yellow ribbon to suggest the object of their quest. But soon, he knew, they would find doors and branching passages, ways that led into the part of the matrix used by Edron Behr, Governor-General of Selmun III.

It was not common to investigate a person so highly placed, but neither was it unheard of. The Governor-General had demanded that Internal Security help deal with the borgbeasts and bring the Gambru League to heel; he'd threatened Obray, unwisely invoking hostile political connections to force the Commander's compliance. That was more than enough to earn the wrath of a career-minded Sa'adani officer. Captain Brace could guess how the logic went: Behr had leverage to use against Obray; now Obray wanted leverage to use against Behr.

Up ahead, the dog-shaped decker gave a bound and closed on a red door with coded access panel in it. Here was the first hurdle, and a suspicious one it was: long before any ordinary person would institute system lockouts, Behr had something to hide.

As usual, Obray's instincts were good. The Governor-General seemed to think he had something worth concealing. Captain Brace and Zippo exchanged looks; this minor obstacle would delay them, but was not a serious hindrance. Given enough time, they could lay bare all the secrets of the Selmun ruler that had root or trace in the planet's cybernet.

Brace started to work on the door.

Karuu coughed nervously. "Don't forget you have to check in with Traffic Control," he volunteered.

Yavobo shot the walrus-faced Dorleoni a withering look, and the Holdout shrank back into the navigator's chair. He fidgeted with chair settings while his bounty hunter companion returned to the task of piloting the *Deathclaw.*

Karuu studied the pilot as he aligned the armed scout's flight path with the orbital insert pattern on the instruments. Days in the ship-board autodoc had restored Yavobo's condition admirably, though that time spent locked in his cabin had been wearing on Karuu. And the bounty hunter's mood remained indecipherable: the red- and black-skinned alien had an angular visage difficult for the smuggler to read. Karuu was used to human faces, furless and mobile, easily be-traying emotions and intent. Yavobo, with leathery skin and the mer-ciless eyes of a predator, was unreadable, and resolute in what he was about to do.

The Dorleoni heaved a sigh, and resigned himself to fate. He was well and truly dragooned into the bounty hunter's strategy, and fully believed Yavobo's threat to drug him unconscious if he continued to protest.

If worse comes to worst, he reassured himself, *I can always get a message to Adahn. I'm sure of it.*

That thought made him fidget, too. The crime boss would not be happy that Karuu knew where to find him. His address was not something he gave out to business associates, and it had been only the smuggler's insatiable curiosity—and urge to have something on everyone—that had prompted him to research Adahn's number.

Netrunners had made several tries before they pinned down the destination of that call code, and one had died in the effort.

Yet surely his arrival would not be unwelcome, the Dorleoni comforted himself. By now Adahn must have heard of the fiasco on Selmun III, and would be wondering where his most profitable Holdout had gotten to. He could be too angry, when he found out Karuu was alive and his secrets were safe.

The smuggler kept that reassurance in the forefront of his mind as Yavobo docked at the Bekavra orbital station. By the time inspectors boarded the scout, Karuu was secured in the galley/lounge area, wearing his static bonds with an expression of dread that was not feigned.

"So you're a bounty hunter?" the port inspector asked Yavobo, reviewing his datapad.

The alien grunted, and waited for the inspection to proceed.

"What'd he do?" The Customs man made a cursory check of storage lockers, glancing at Karuu as if the Dorleoni were cargo.

"Wanted for smuggling." Yavobo measured his words, yielding the minimum possible.

The official reassessed harmless-looking Karuu, continued into the small, empty cargo bay, and out again as rapidly. A bounty hunter who arrested smugglers was not likely to be smuggling himself; the inspector dismissed the *Deathclaw* as a vessel warranting serious inspection.

The Port Authority officer thumb-printed the datapad and associated landing permits. "Do you need arrangements for an escort, or a holding cell?" The man glanced back at Karuu.

"No."

"Here you are, then." The inspector handed back the datapad. "If you change your mind, the Ministry of Justice in Peshtano issues any licenses you'll need. With your record, you shouldn't have a problem getting one."

Yavobo inclined his head, saw the inspectors silently to the airlock. When they had gone, he lost no time in gaining clearance and departing the orbital dock.

"Well?" asked Karuu. "Aren't you going to release me?"

His heart sank as Yavobo refused to look at him. "Stay there. We will soon be on the ground. You remain my prisoner until we are out of the port area and well into the city."

That's what Karuu was afraid of. He sat, slumped, and struggled to belt his webbing in place with bound wrists. The Aztrakhani offered no help.

Play it your way, my friend, Karuu thought. You won't be so in charge of things once Adahn gets his hooks in you.

His bristling mustache turned up at the ends.

We'll see how you like things then.

"Salutations, Mr. Harric. It is I, your long-lost associate." Friend? Servant? Karuu had agonized over the right choice of words, though it was too late to make a difference to the agitated stream that poured from his mouth. "I am in touch once more, as you see. I have much to tell, and am desirous to be telling. What should I be doing, as you wish?"

Karuu wrung his webbed fingers below the line of sight of the vid pickup. The viewscreen remained blank, as it always did during his calls to this number. After Adahn's initial greeting and the Dorleoni's burst of words, there was silence on the channel. The Holdout shifted weight from one flipper foot to the other, awaiting acknowledgment from his master.

"Where are you calling from?" Suspicion tinged Adahn's slow words.

"Um . . ." The Holdout swallowed. "We're near Belitcia. In a park north of the river."

"We?"

Damn. How to explain the bounty hunter?

"The person who helped me get away is—"

"Save it until we see each other." Adahn's voice was cold, decisive. "You're in Vordenya Park, are you?"

"That may be the—" Karuu looked to Yavobo, outside the com booth, who nodded when he heard the name. "That is where we are, yes. By the waterfall pond."

"Stay there. I'll have someone pick you up. Look for a secure skimmer."

"Secure?" Karuu wasn't certain what he meant by that.

"Armored. Screen-shielded."

"Ah. Secure."

"Within the hour. Don't move."

"No, sir." The blank screen stayed blank, and Karuu could tell by the click of the resetting link that Adahn had disconnected. He leaned half out of the booth, looked up at the towering bounty hunter. "A ride is on the way."

Yavobo crossed his arms on his chest. "Good," he said. Blocking Karuu inside the com booth, he faced the road approaching the pond and settled down to wait.

The bulldog queried the Net, and the record of Behr's investments spread itself in the air before them. It was obvious that the Governor-General made hefty returns on his money.

Captain Brace looked more closely, ran a calculation in his cyberdeck. "Something's not right, Zip," the agent said. "He beats the market."

"Sure he does. Wish I could invest like that."

"No. I mean, he *beats* it. The chances of earning dividends like that in the last two months alone are 727,800 to 1. More or less."

The bulldog snuffled at the graphed payouts. "How?"

"Exactly. Let's look at the stock companies and megacorps involved, and their performance records."

That produced a revealing graph. The bulldog craned his neck upward to study it. "They don't match."

"Astute, my stubby friend," Brace agreed. "They don't. When Lovana Shipping loses money in a quarter, Behr gets a dividend check as if their stock had gone through the roof. The same with most of these other firms."

"They're all shipping or manufacturing concerns," Zippo noted.

The decker let the graphics fade away, and nudged the bulldog. "How about this? I'll do background checks on these companies."

"And I can . . . what?"

"This series of deposits." He refreshed the virtual display once more. "Do a pattern analysis on it. Obviously it's not tied to stock performance. Maybe it matches something else."

Zippo snuffled his agreement. The two parted ways, each armed with high-level security overrides, each taking a different path that led farther into the labyrinth of global finances.

A subsurface convoy escorted freighters east through little-used Bennap Run. Scouts swept surrounding waters and sensor scans pulsed the ocean, checking for the approach of Gambru League marauders. It was not a question of when they would strike, just where.

The convoy came upon the "where" of it momentarily. Four large-profile leviathans were clearly outlined on sensor screens, surging upwards from the cold-water chasm at the edge of Bennap Shelf. The submarine security force hired by Lovana Shipping reported their readings. Surface freighters began evasive maneuvers, a broken, randomly zigzagging pattern, while submerged craft fanned out in the direction of the approaching attackers.

The borgbeasts were distracted by the hydroskiffs, and paused to plunge after their gadfly opponents in short, powerful underwater lunges. The skiffs evaded, firing explosive missile rounds at point-blank range.

The beasts, tipped off by sensor devices inside their AI-enhanced craniums, avoided the rounds. Jamming circuits radiated counter-measure distortions at high intensity in the nearby area. Missiles skewed off-course or exploded prematurely; skiff sensors picked up ghost images and spurious readings.

The borgbeasts retreated, drawing off some of the Lovana security vessels. Other skiffs remained with the convoy they guarded, confused by false sensor images, unable to halt the three other leviathans that emerged from warm-water thermals and sped toward the evading freighters. Two ships sank outright; one listed and went under by time the alien life-forms retreated. It was another victory for the Gambru League, another nose-thumbing at the would-be protectors of surface shipping.

Master Swimmer Sharptooth gathered with his podmates in the Bennap chasm. The seven who participated in the attack regrouped there, the joy of battle gleaming in the leviathans' small, intelligent eyes. The

Vernoi swam away from their companion beasts, and gathered together for a mid-ocean conference.

"Where were you, Swimmer Brightfang?" Sharptooth addressed a laggard figure in the whistles and clicks of their water-borne language. "Four were to strike the airships. Two vessels escaped us, because of your delay."

Brightfang swam to the edges of the group, hung listlessly in cloudy green water. "I know not why we delayed, my life-friend and I," the Vernoi confessed. "I am tired, so tired . . . I don't know why." The others sculled uneasily. They were all tired, more than they should be, but it was not their way to admit weakness, to be a burden on the pod. Brightfang spoke truth for all.

The Vernoi continued. "And I fear something is wrong. Wee'ska is not well. When the time came, she could not charge."

Sharptooth looked toward Brightfang's life-friend, the female borgbeast who lingered shyly at the edges of the chasm. She was smart enough to sense her failure, and hung back, reluctant to join the others. Her hide seemed mottled, the slick black skin appearing roughened and patchy even from tens of meters away.

"Is she ill?" the Vernoi leader inquired.

Brightfang rolled a quarter of the way over and then rolled back, body language showing uncertainty. "I do not know, Master Swimmer. If so, it is nothing I have seen at home. But she is not herself, that I can say."

Again, the other handlers sculled nervously. Several other borgbeasts moved more slowly, charged less aggressively, than before. Each Vernoi hoped it was a temporary problem, an adjustment to alien waters and alien diet. No one had confessed the shortcoming, until now.

Sharptooth swam to inspect Wee'ska, and saw foreboding signs in the condition of her skin and her lackluster eyes. Such a patch had already appeared on his own borgbeast. He had dismissed it as reaction to the bio-rich seawater of R'debh.

Perhaps he had been wrong.

He studied his companions and saw that neither they nor their life-friends were ready for another assault on the humans' shipping. The condition of the borgbeasts was of paramount importance, more vital even than the nagging tiredness that was beginning to plague the handlers.

"I shall talk to Edesz about this," Sharptooth reassured his pod-mates. "Let us seek him out now. We all need time to rest, and surely he will be able to help."

The Vernoi agreed, and left the Bennap Run for the deep dome where they could find the Gambru League terrorists.

LIX

Reva slipped through Amasl's entry port in the same way that she had many weeks before: as a nondescript local traveler, nothing on her except her credmeter and a change of mass-market clothing. The brine-rich scent of R'debh's sea air filled her nostrils. In a perverse way, she was glad to be back home. Now, at least, she could resolve matters with Lish once and for all.

All the way back to R'debh she had rehearsed various overtures, practiced what she would say, then discarded each approach as juvenile and inappropriate.

Face it, Reva. You're no good at making up to people. Never wanted to do it before.

With no experience in that kind of interaction, she would have to rely on her wits and common sense. Nervous anticipation clutched her stomach and she fought off the kind of butterflies she had never been plagued with for such a simple thing as impersonal execution.

Salvaging a friendship was going to be much harder than she thought.

She slowed her rented skimmer as she neared Comax Shipping, startled by the burned-out shell of Lairdome 7. A heartbeat later, Now split into echoes of itself, a panorama of possibilities quickly scanned for dangerous upcoming moments.

Then she gave a small laugh. That was a pointless exercise. No more would she map out an exit from the moment, not until she'd cleared things up with the Holdout. It was too easy to lose track of one Mainline that way. She shifted back to Realtime, collected herself, and eased the skimmer forward.

Mainline

The Skiffjammer who emerged from an observation post was expected, a shadow she had seen in the near-future. "Tell me where I can find Lish," she demanded of the guard. "I have business with her."

Soon enough she was escorted to the Holdout's villa, ushered into a comfortably appointed room off the foyer. There they left her. Guards posted in the hall made it clear that Reva was to await the Holdout's pleasure in this chamber.

Spotting Vask in the hallway cut short her growing anger at this treatment. The Fixer stopped inside the door, clad in a soiled gray work jumper, a torque socket and static bands hanging carelessly out of one cargo pocket. His dark hair was rumpled, but his grin was as broad as ever.

"Why am I left sitting here, and what in the Deep is happening with Lish's business?" Reva blurted.

Vask, unruffled by her greeting, filled her in on the streetwar with the Islanders, how the combat had progressed from the waterfront and now revolved around the besieged headquarters of the enemy derevin.

"So how does that explain why I'm waiting on Lish? Does she even know I'm here?"

Vask spread his hands. "She's on the Net. I'm not sure—"

"You mean those 'Jammers didn't tell her I'm here because they don't want to interrupt her?" Incredulity raised her normally husky voice a half-octave. "Beldy shit. I'm announcing myself, right now."

The assassin surged to her feet and headed for the door. Vask rushed close behind, waving guards back to their posts. Half directing Reva, half following her, Kastlin took the assassin through the living area and into the office wing of the villa.

Reva glowered at Lish's door panel as if it were responsible for barring her from the dreaded, anticipated meeting with the Holdout. "You stay here," she warned Vask with a brusque aside. The Fixer, hovering solicitously, took a step away. Reva gathered herself, and walked in on the woman she had thought of as friend.

LX

*"**This afternoon surface** freighters of Lovana Shipping Corporation were sunk in the Bennap Run,"* the message began. *"Like others of their kind, they carried surface-made goods at monopoly prices to water-breathers who can, and do, manufacture most of these items for themselves."*

Freighters. Shipping. Sunk. Context recognition programs identified the message and sent an alarm-frequency pulse into the cybernet. FlashMan was jolted by that alarm. He launched himself after the neon-pulsing pink trail that blitzed along the data feed of the terrorist message, in search of its source.

"No longer will we pay extortionist prices for the goods we need to live. No longer will we support the shipping monopolies of surface interests. Until intradome trade is approved and fully legal, no surface enterprise will be permitted to keep water-breathers at their mercy . . ."

The diatribe continued, extending the transmission time for precious nanoseconds. Flash chased electrons down the yellow spiral corridor of a tightbeam relay.

When the alarm sounded, Nomad welcomed it, and awaited the personal nudge that would direct him to the burst of the terrorist's transmission.

That nudge didn't happen. He heard the alarm down a distant corridor in the data net, and took an intuitive leap to land in a newsnet junction where the pulsing pink neon trace marked the terrorist's data trail.

What's going on? he wondered, just as a lightning-formed sim blurred past. The backtrace vanished as the data-jacker raced by.

Nomad threw himself after in close pursuit.

Through the spiral corridors of tightbeam transmitters, down the fuzzy highway of a broadband frequency, Nomad raced behind the FlashMan. The wire-framed decker recognized the sim-figure from the *Delos Varte* hijacking.

I'm gonna get you, he vowed, and put on an extraordinary burst of speed that moved him a little closer to the FlashMan.

Abruptly the funhouse complex of an encrypted relay system hove into sight ahead of them. FlashMan blitzed into the mirrored complex. Nomad tried to follow, but by the time his decryption programs were online, the League transmission was no longer there to trace. There was nothing but dead air, and the lightning-shaped renegade had given him the slip again.

Cold rage threatened to overcome Nomad, a decker not used to one-upsmanship. Working as an independent on R'debh, he had beaten all the local talent. Who was this newcomer, who twice had slipped through his fingers?

Angered, it took a while to realize where he stood—but when he did, a thin-lined grin split his blue wire-frame face.

This was the relay nexus for the Embari Dome complex. Any transmission that passed through here could only have originated among those domes.

Nomad waved a triumphant fist at the faceted walls of the relay. One dome or fifty to search, it made no difference. Finally, they knew where to start looking.

The Gambru League's days are numbered, the decker thought. And so, my spiky friend, are yours.

It was too much to bear, the incessant noise, the long-range moan of alien intruders. For a time the ghost-ray phased out of the sea waters of R'debh, later to return and find the assault on his senses more abrasive than before. There were more sounds now, more distress—and something new. Pain, a silent groan, an ephemeral discord of the self. From the aliens?

The waters spoke not of a challenge, but of death. Something morbid flavored the currents.

The ray phased into his semisolid form and floated out of his deepwater grotto. The time for listening to ocean whispers was past. Now was time to see for himself what was amiss in the sea.

Staying to ravines and deep chasms, the Sea Father of R'debh moved slowly toward the source of the sounds.

The data-trace faded as FlashMan ascertained which Embari com unit had transmitted the message. He deciphered its point-of-origin code, and hopped a tightbeam to Kesic Dome.

His hunch checked out. The video pickup on the target com unit came to life for a brief moment, activated by the Flash inside the system interface. Edesz was there alright, watching the League message rebroadcast on a screen across the room.

Home, the FlashMan congratulated himself, *and just a-waiting on a vidcall. I'll see if I can't arrange that.*

Reluctantly, Lish had decided to unload wines and exotic foods she had saved up for the storm season festivals, a quarter-year away. The money brought in by luxury items was needed for essential day-to-day expenses. Medcare for wounded Skiffjammers. More ammo. Replacement armor. She hated to spend the brief infusion of cash for such transient benefits, but had no choice. It was called staying afloat. If anything, the Holdout had to seem capable of business as usual, or every debt she owed would be called due immediately, and the quietly observing Scripman would be the first to pounce.

She had just concluded terms of delivery with an Avelar wholesaler when the FlashMan's telltale white noise severed her connection.

"Dammit, Flash!" she barked into the comunit. "Don't interrupt my calls like that. I need to finish talking to that man!"

"Would you rather talk to him, or talk to Edesz?" the netrunner asked sardonically.

Lish's breath caught in her throat. "Edesz?" It was not unexpected, but it was happening sooner than she was ready for. But this was a talk she'd rehearsed and prepared for. "Put him on," she agreed.

A moment later, Edesz' face filled the vidscreen on her console.

The water-breather wore a distracted look, giving more attention to his newsnet telecast than to his vidcall. His age was indeterminate, all the cues Lish knew to expect erased by his sea-adaptation. Edesz lacked eyelashes and hair and had only the finest of fuzz where an air-breather's eyebrows would be. His ears were small and tucked; his neck gills were closed in the airdome of his coms room, but pink striations marked the flaps that would flare when he was submerged in water. The edges of his protective eye membranes showed when he blinked, as he did when he saw Lish.

"What is it?" the Gambru League leader asked automatically, at the same time that he realized the woman he spoke with was not one of his friends or contacts. His eyes narrowed suspiciously; that expression remained wholly human. "Who are you?" he demanded. "How'd you get this code?"

Lish returned his gaze coolly. With a Shaydo gambler's poise, she said, "This is Shiran Gabrieya Lish. We haven't met, though we've done business."

"You!" Astonishment was clear to read on his pale face, his nictating eyelids flicking down, then up in a reflex of surprise.

"Yes, me. You owe me money. You don't want to do that." Her declaration was flatly confident, sounding much like the FlashMan's initial threat to her.

Edesz' thin-haired brows furrowed deeply. "I don't owe you a thing."

"You took delivery of a cargo. You're using it. You owe. I expect payment—"

"Sea Father take you!" he interrupted. "You had a deal with Alia Lanzig. Leave me out of it."

"Alia's not around to deal with anymore, Edesz. Hadn't you heard?" She shook her head, as if over a misbehaving student.

"I'm not talking with you," he snapped. His hand reached out and the vidscreen went blank.

Before Lish could take a breath, the screen came to life again. Edesz' image, half turned away, whirled back in consternation. "How—?"

"You're talking with me right now." Lish followed up FlashMan's silent assist with a harsh glare at the terrorist. She stabbed a finger at the water-breather. "You pay up, or I give you to Internal Security. They're hunting for you now, you know."

The man opened his mouth, shut it. A sly look came over his face. "If the Bugs get me, they get my datachips, too. Like the ones recording your agreement with Lanzig to import borgbeasts. You won't get paid, and you'll be put away along with me."

Lish gripped the armrests of her chair. Was it true? Was it a bluff? Could FlashMan verify, to see if Edesz really had such information stored in his comp somewhere? Before she could lose the initiative or stall for time, a status window lit on her console, and a text message from the FlashMan scrolled past on the screen.

"Tell him this. Read these words exactly."

At a loss for strategy, Lish played along with the gambit, and spoke the scrolling words as her own.

"Let me put this another way. Your borgbeasts are dying. Within two months, you won't have any left to work with. Only I know what's wrong with them, and only I can give you a cure for it. You pay for the beasts, you get the cure. If there's no money . . ." Lish shrugged expressively. "There'll be no borgbeasts."

Edesz flushed, a subtle color change on his sea-adapted skin. "What are you talking about? The beasts are fine."

"Insist you're right," the FlashMan's screen prompt read.

"Check with your handlers about that," Lish replied boldly. "I'd say you have just a few weeks before it's too late to help your pets."

She leaned closer to the vid pickup. "So you think about how long you want to put off paying me, Edesz. That's 10 million, in case you don't remember. Cash. If Alia left you her datachips, I'm sure she left you some account codes, too. And next time I try to reach you?" She raised an admonishing finger. "Don't duck my calls."

She slapped the disconnect, then spoke into the comlink with her next breath. "You care to tell me what the hell that was all about?"

A small static burst announced that the FlashMan was back on the channel. *"It's about a fortune, baby."* The netrunner sounded more smug than usual.

"Is this a bluff or is it real? What's wrong with the borgbeasts?"

"All in good time. Before we do show and tell, let's talk about our terms."

"Terms? We already have a deal."

"And I honor my deals. But I came across something worth a lit-

tle extra, a tidbit about the beasties hidden in Lanzig's personal net files. What's it worth to you?"

"Dammit, FlashMan—" Lish sat up stiffly, a muscle clenching in her jaw. "Don't try to leverage me like this."

"Leverage you? Wouldn't dream of it. But I've come across something a little unexpected, and I know what it's worth to you. He owes you 10 million, you said?"

The netrunner's mildly mocking tone got on every raw nerve Lish had been nursing for the past two weeks. She came to her feet, blind to the door panel that slid open at that moment and the woman who walked boldly into her office.

"By Juro's brass balls! Where do you get off putting words in my mouth and then backing down when it's time to deliver the goods? What kind of spineless, conniving, honorless datajacker are you, anyway?" She was heating up to her topic when she saw Reva standing near her desk. "You agreed to get . . . to help . . ."

"Still yelling at people?" the assassin observed dryly.

FlashMan, monitoring Lish's office through her com system vid pickup, spoke through the external speaker. *"Heya, Reva. Talk sense to your friend, will you?"*

The conversation gone suddenly askew, Lish looked from the console that concealed a manipulative netrunner to the woman she had never thought to see again, now standing across from her. The smuggler threw up her hands in surrender and sat down.

Reva frowned at Lish's reaction. "FlashMan, you bothering the Domna here?"

"Bothering? Me? Naw—merely drumming up some business."

"Like you've drummed me a time or two? I think not. Leave us for a while, will you? You can talk later."

"I'm not working for you this time, Reva," the netrunner said petulantly.

"Yeah? Well. Humor me. You might work for me again sometime soon."

"Hmph." Mercurial as always, the FlashMan took the hint. *"Sure thing, babe. Talk to you soon, Lish."* A static burst signaled his disconnect, and the smuggler heaved a sigh of relief. Reva dropped into a chair opposite, sitting with studied ease.

"Timely interference, as usual," Lish said, knowing Reva had just spared a rift with the FlashMan.

The assassin took the remark differently.

"I didn't mean to ruin your deal with Lanzig," she said forthrightly. The words tumbled out rapidly, at odds with the aloof look she struggled to keep on her face. "I didn't know you had business with her. If I had known, I would have waited until you got paid."

Lish pressed her hands to her temples, leaned her head back in her chair. "Lords of Ice, this is a surreal conversation." She dropped her hands and locked eyes with the assassin. "What are you doing here, Reva?"

"If you want me to go, I will. We don't have to talk." The tall woman sat up, chin held high, preparing to stand. She seemed uncertain, ready to let her pride carry her back out the door she had just come through.

"Oh, sit down." Lish waved her to stay, came around the desk, and sat on the float-couch nearby. She pulled her feet up and leaned on the couch's arm. "You caught me at a bad time," she said, "but any time seems bad, these days. I'm just surprised to see you again. I want to know why you came back."

Reva looked startled, as if prepared for any question but that one. She licked her lips nervously before speaking.

"I wanted you to know I wasn't trying to hurt you, by what happened. I wouldn't do that to a, a friend, if I could help it." She stumbled over the words. "There are some things you need to realize, about Karuu, about—"

Lish shook her head. "He's gone to ground, and we're beating the Islanders back. There's nothing to worry about, Reva."

"So I shouldn't have returned, is that what you're saying?"

Lish bit her lip. "I'm not mad at you anymore," she sighed. "You were right. You didn't know about my arrangements with Lanzig. It's just that now I have to dig my way out of a hell of a hole, and I don't know if I can do it. You understand what I mean?"

Reva took in her words and seemed to relax a little, as if a blow she had been braced for had not fallen. She sat in silence, processing what the Holdout had just said, and a sympathetic expression came over her face.

"I understand." She finally nodded. "And there's a few other things *you* need to understand."

"Like what?"

"Like the fact that Karuu is not his own boss. He works for someone named Adahn."

"What's this to me?" Lish asked.

"Adahn is a crime boss," Reva said. "He won't simply roll over and let Karuu go down like this. He'll do something to reestablish his power on R'debh, and that makes you a target."

Lish quirked a lip. "Seems like I'm everybody's target these days. I can't be concerned with some offworlder who bankrolled Karuu. It's bad enough with the FlashMan trying to squeeze me."

The pair sat for a bit, each uncertain how to proceed or what she could share with the other. Lish finally broke the impasse. "Have a drink with me?" she offered. Reva gave a noncommittal bob of the head.

Lish went to a cabinet, came back with a decanter of Cadanessa. She poured two glasses of the fruity ruby red wine, and Reva sat more comfortably in her chair. It was a plain effort to recall the camaraderie of Des'lin, and the assassin took it with good grace. They touched glasses and drank for a while in silence. "What kind of trouble is the FlashMan giving you?" Reva finally ventured.

Lish twirled her glass by its stem. "He's trying to rewrite our terms," she said, and explained the deal she had struck with the netrunner. Finding Edesz was half the battle, but the unexpected threat about dying borgbeasts had left her puzzled, and things had gone rocky with the FlashMan before she could learn more.

"How are things, otherwise?" Reva prodded, and the Holdout found herself unburdening her worries on someone she had once spoken freely with every day.

At the end of her recital, she refilled their glasses and sat in glum reflection. "Every time I see this mess, it looks as bad as before," she remarked. "Can I squeeze money from Edesz in time to pay the Scripman? Probably not without FlashMan's help. The streetwar's not half done, and the Skiffjammers' contract is up in five more days. Still can't run cargoes offworld, so there's no new income there. After the protection's gone, I'm fair game for the Islanders." She snorted. "You sure picked a hell of a time to come visit."

Reva spent a long time studying the contents of her wineglass, and Lish left her to it. Suddenly the assassin drained the glass and set it down. When her hand came up again, she held a silver-hued credit chit between her fingers. "I'm not here just for a visit," she said. "Here. Take this."

"What is it?" The Holdout didn't reach for the chit, so Reva tossed it at her. It landed in her lap. She picked it up and eyed the hologram that denoted its 50,000 CR denomination. "I can't take this," she protested quickly, and extended the chit back to Reva.

"You have to," the assassin replied. "How else are you going to renew the Skiffjammer contract for a couple more weeks?"

Lish scrutinized the woman across from her. "I don't want to take your money."

Reva shrugged that off. "Then consider it a loan. There's more where that came from. I don't want to see you go under because I fixed it so you can't afford protection."

"It's not your fault that—"

"It is, dammit." She rushed on before Lish could say anything. "Let me do what I can to help you. It's not a lot, and I can't pay off all your debts, but I do have some influence. Let me use it, will you?"

It was both entreaty and angry challenge, but the smuggler heard beyond the words to the anguish underneath. It was like her own turmoil, buried in the rush to save her business and her life, no time left to pay attention to unresolved people issues, not Devin, not Reva . . .

And here was a second chance, come knocking on her door all of its own accord.

She looked at the money in her hand, and back to the assassin. It's not that easy, she wanted to say. Apology accepted; fine. If you want to help, alright. But given this way, it's more than help. It's *roi'tas,* honor-debt—and I don't hold *roi'tas* with anyone.

Then cash flow and debt-ratio and payment schedules for the Skiffjammers intruded in her thoughts, and Lish knew she had no choice. Without this money, she'd be out of business before the week was up.

She closed her fingers around the credit chit, and nodded her thanks. "If you're sure that's how you want it, fine. Let's see what we can do together."

"It was most unscrupulous setup, very foul," Karuu insisted. He slapped a broad, flat foot against the carpet in agitation. This interview was not going as well as he had expected. This man did not seem to grasp the depth of perfidy his Holdout had suffered on Selmun III.

"Lish is ambitious, grasping, surely big-time threat to us on

R'debh. Worst-ever smuggler I have ever crossed paths with . . ." His voice died away under Adahn Harric's unblinking scrutiny. He had met the crime boss twice before, and the man had changed little. Grown beefier, with grayer hair, but still with the cold, heartless eyes of a street killer.

Those eyes riveted Karuu, and brought the Dorleoni stuttering to a halt. Effortlessly Harric took charge of the conversation.

"I've heard enough of your blustering. Answer a question for me, Karuu."

The Holdout gaped, then forced his mouth shut. Blustering, was it?

"Do you know why this Shiran Lish picked you to set up as shipowner for the *Delos Varte*'s smuggling run?"

"No, I cannot guess—"

"No reason at all, hm? The biggest Holdout on Selmun was simply the most convenient target?"

The acerbic comment punctured Karuu's pretense of ignorance. "Perhaps because I was going to turn her over for the smuggling . . . ," he confessed.

"Taking out the competition, were you?"

"As you suggested, sir!" Karuu declared, briefly defiant. "She was far more tricky than we gave her credit for."

"Than *you* gave her credit for, you mean." Harric's expression matched the sour note in his voice. "You were responsible for making sure that surface shipping moves untroubled in Selmun waters. Do you remember that, Karuu?"

The Dorleoni started to nod, then shrank as Adahn's voice grew in volume. "What do you think borgbeasts are for, you dimwitted excuse for an overseer? You learned all about them. What do you think they're intended for?"

Adahn's tone became ominous, sarcastic. The smuggler spluttered and spread his hands. They had been over this territory already; what did Harric want him to confess?

"You were going to let the borgbeasts land, and then release them yourself, you ignorant turd! Have you followed the news on your way here at all? No? Listen to this."

Adahn jabbed a button on his desk console, and a newsnet announcement played into the darkened room. Karuu stood under the glaring lights and listened to the words with growing disbelief. *"This afternoon surface freighters of Lovana Shipping Corporation were sunk in the Bennap Run,"* the recorded voice began. *"Like others of their kind, they carried surface-made goods at monopoly prices to water-breathers. . . ."*

Adahn let the message play through. By its end, Karuu was panting with nervous tension. "I—I didn't know. Couldn't know! They're using them to sink shipping, *your* shipping? I, I would have stopped it if I'd known. I—"

"Shut up."

Silence fell, punctuated by the Dorleoni's gasping breath.

"Do you know what this means?" Adahn's voice was deceptively gentle. "It means your Holdout operations are of the very least importance to me anymore. We have just one interest of overriding importance on Selmun III. Do you know what that is?"

Karuu forced words out, an inarticulate mumble.

"What?"

"The shipping concerns," the Holdout repeated more clearly.

"Indeed. Or, more properly said, the shipping diversions." Harric rose to his feet, strolled slowly around his desk. "You knew borgbeasts were coming, and you didn't bother to find out why. You let the shipment land; you let yourself be set up. You've lost your smuggling operations, and endangered the real reason the Red Hand is present on Selmun III in the first place. *The shipping trade.*"

Adahn's large hand flew out, caught Karuu heavily against the side of the head. The Dorleoni staggered to the side and back and sat down suddenly on the carpet. He lifted webbed fingers to a ringing ear and blinked up at Harric with liquid, frightened eyes.

"You were too busy trying to cut down one smuggler to see the big picture," the crime boss spoke down to him. "That's not what I was paying you for. You are a very big, very sad disappointment to me."

Harric returned to his seat behind the desk, motioned Karuu to his feet with a flick of his fingers. "What should I do with you, my friend?"

The Dorleoni knew it was a trick question, that Adahn must have already decided what to do with the Holdout who had endangered his globe-spanning operations on the waterworld of R'debh. Was there any way out of this, any way at all? Karuu was suddenly conscious that time was running out. How to make himself so valuable that it would not make good business sense to kill him?

"Well?" Harric prompted.

Karuu swallowed. "Maybe I can be of help, sir."

"I doubt it."

"Please." He tried to control the urge to babble, though hasty words, beseeching in tone, slipped past his lips anyway. "Of help I can be. Lish. Let us start with her. She is your real problem, or one of them. She it is who brought the borgbeast hazard. She it is who is responsible for the gutting of our Holdout operations. A minor concern compared to the shipping, yet large enough in its own way—and the perfect way to manage the cargo diversions you rely on."

Adahn pursed his lips at that thought. He did not cut the smuggler off, and the Dorleoni continued while he had the chance.

"Then there are the political forces behind this foolish move to sink shipping. They are surely of great concern to you. You will be wanting the Gambru League destroyed, I am sure? I have the connections on R'debh to make that happen for you. And this unfortunate persecution by Internal Security. If we were to give them a sop, a fellow Dorleoni, for instance, whom they mistook for me, they will stop looking for me on R'debh and cargo movements will be able to continue as normal. You will need to rebuild the Customs connections that have helped us over the years, and I am the perfect one to help you there, too, I know so many—"

"You know so many ways to wriggle out of a net." Adahn motioned him to silence, and shook his head. Karuu was a fast talker, and he had almost been taken in by the smuggler's weave of offers. He did touch on a point or two of real value, but this was something to ponder later, when the irritating alien was out of his sight and he had Janus handy to discuss solutions with.

Harric drummed his fingers on the edge of his desk. No use letting Karuu be at ease when he might yet choose to kill him. It was better to keep him off his guard, to retain the psychological advantage.

"Tell me about this Yavobo."

The sudden change of tack took Karuu unprepared. He explained what he knew of the bounty hunter's history, his failed bodyguard missions on R'debh, and how the clever Holdout had lured the Aztrakhani into smuggling him offworld. "I did not want to speak for you, sir. I promised him nothing. I simply said you would acknowledge that he did a favor by bringing me off of Selmun. . . ."

Adahn's lips turned down. Some favor. True, if Karuu had been caught and questioned on Selmun III, the Red Hand cartel would have far bigger troubles than a handful of borgbeasts to contend with. Yet to have the Holdout here, wheedling and whining for consideration, was no special service to the crime boss, either.

On the other hand, the Aztrakhani was a killer, and Adahn always had a use for killers.

"What exactly does he want of me? Do you know?"

Karuu nodded eagerly. "Reva."

"The assassin?"

The Dorleoni ducked his chin. "He is not telling me reasons. He has sworn an oath of some sort—"

"Did you tell Yavobo she works for me?"

There was a dangerous gleam in Adahn's eye, and Karuu was glad for his closemouthedness. He shook his head rapidly from side to side. "No, sir, I said merely that you knew who she was and how to find her. There was nothing else from my lips, not even your name, I said—"

Adahn's hand gesture caused him to bite off the words.

"Go, now." Harric ordered his underling. "I'll talk to you again later."

Nervous, yet glad of the respite, Karuu bobbed his head in the awkward Dorleoni half-bow, and waddled to the door. There two MazeRats escorted him down a hallway and out of Adahn's sight. Even before Karuu was locked into his room, Yavobo was called in to face Harric himself.

Heeding Karuu's warnings of the alien's nature, Adahn discreetly powered a shield unit that created a force field between his desk and the rest of the room. Only if the stranger came too close or fired a weapon would he discover the invisible protection that guarded a Tribune of the Red Hand. Adahn hoped it would not come to that, and awaited his guest with interest.

Yavobo strode purposefully into Harric's informal audience chamber. The crime boss leaned expansively back in his plush padded seat, and ordered a float-chair to his guest's side. The Aztrakhani ignored the furniture, standing with feet spread before Harric's desk. It was a stance neither confrontational nor relaxed, ready for action should it be needed.

The alien gave the seated human a meager nod.

"You are Yavobo," Adahn said; a statement, not a query.

"Yes. I do not know how you are called. Karuu would not tell me, because of his oath."

So the Holdout had said true. He was more discreet than Adahn gave him credit for. Oath, indeed.

"You may call me Mr. Harric," he said.

"Mr. Harric." Yavobo repeated his nod "I have returned to you your Holdout, who was in danger of his life on Selmun III."

"So you have."

"In reciprocation, I ask that you tell me how I can find this woman." The alien held out a flatpix. Adahn made no move to take the picture but studied the face across his desk. High cheekbones, brunette hair, hazel eyes, firm jaw. It did not strike him as the face of a killer, but that just added to her charm.

"I am told her name is Reva," Yavobo added, "and that you know of her."

Adahn suppressed a smile. Funny thing, that. He had hired Reva through Karuu's recommendation. He knew about her, and she knew about him, but they had never met. The flatpix was the first he had ever seen of the face of his prize assassin.

"I know of her, yes," he conceded.

"Tell me how I can get in touch with her. I have business with her."

"I'm sure you do. Would you mind telling me why you are interested in her?"

The alien drew himself up, his jaw clenching for a moment. "Is it not enough that I ask?" he responded.

Adahn licked his lips. No, that was not enough. Nor would he blithely admit that he used this assassin's services, not until he knew more about what was motivating Yavobo. He recalled Karuu's successful ruse of being oath-sworn, in order to stay silent on a subject, and that gave him an idea.

"You must understand," the crime boss improvised, "that I am under oaths to others. I am not free to share information about Reva, unless your case has superior merit. . . ."

The alien took the bait. "She caused me to fail in my duty," he declaimed, "of guarding two persons who entrusted their lives to me. For this I have sworn Blood Oath. I must find her."

O ho! Adahn's eyes retained the same, serious gaze he had decided to cultivate for this meeting, but inside he smirked. The alien didn't explain Blood Oath, but he could pretty much guess what that meant. Yavobo was clearly referring to deaths on Selmun III. And Reva had gone there on Adahn's contract, to eliminate two gadflies he had wanted out of the way.

What would Yavobo do if he learned Adahn was behind the death warrants of his charges? Would it matter, or did he merely want the head of the assassin who had opposed him? Reva was Adahn's favorite killer. Harric had tried to hire her permanently just last year, but she liked to stay independent.

That means I don't owe her a lot of loyalty, he thought. It also means she's good, and I want to use her again. No, my colorful alien, I am not giving my best assassin to you to kill.

In that case, how to keep Yavobo on a leash? A flat "no" would send him away, to seek the woman out by other avenues. A "yes" was out of the question. According to Karuu, the alien thought of nothing outside of his self-appointed mission since leaving R'debh. Maybe there was a way to turn this to some benefit. . . .

Adahn nodded gravely to the red and black mottled figure before him. "I understand your needs. Perhaps I can help. Please." He gestured to the chair again, and this time the alien took it.

"Reva is an assassin of great power," Adahn said. That much was true; how she carried off some of the seemingly impossible hits assigned to her was beyond imagining. "She is not contacted lightly. No one can reach her who is not trustworthy."

Yavobo bridled. "I am Aztrakhani. My trustworthiness is not to be questioned."

Adahn held up a hand while thinking furiously. "That is not in question, my friend. I mean, only warriors of proven merit are allowed this sort of knowledge. You are a warrior, although I have not yet seen proof of your merit."

Yavobo's back stiffened. To question a warrior's prowess must push the limits; the bounty hunter looked like he wanted to launch himself over the desk and throttle Adahn right there. Yet he controlled himself with no more sign than a flaring of nostrils, and asked, "What sort of proof do you require? Let me confront your best fighters; you will see my merit soon enough."

"Let me think on this thing," Harric replied. "I'm sure there is a way whereby you can show your mettle, and I can grant you what you want. Will you give me time to consider?"

The alien stared flatly across the desk. "How much time?"

"I do not know. This will require serious thought, and an appropriate measure of your skills."

Yavobo stood once more and selected his words with care. "Apparently a debt of honor does not run as deeply with you as it does among my kind. You have one week in which to gauge my merit. After that, I will find Reva with or without your help."

Unaccustomed to such speech, Adahn watched in amazement as

the alien turned on his heel and walked from the room. Or to the door, anyway—the portal did not open until Adahn depressed a locktab on his desk console. Yavobo waited stiff-necked before the blast-insulated door swung inward, then passed into the antechamber beyond.

"Janus," Adahn murmured into the comlink, "see that our Aztrakhani friend is made comfortable for the next several days. Make sure he's shown the gym and weapons rooms."

He switched off the force screen as the door sealed shut, closing him into one of the many command centers of his diverse organization.

This was evolving into a revealing day. Very revealing. He plugged into the rigger jack on his desk and sent a mental call out to his lieutenant. Janus joined him shortly on a virtual veranda, overlooking the simulated pleasure gardens of the Emperor's Palace on Calyx.

"What do you think?" the crime boss asked his associate.

The slender red-haired man leaned against a broad marble balustrade, surveying red-orange sunset skies and the rippling firewater splashing in fountains below. "Think? About which?"

"Yavobo."

"Dangerous. Don't string him along; he could turn. He'll bite like a snake if he learns you're playing with him."

"So who's playing?" Adahn flashed a smile, a cold expression that left his eyes untouched. "Funny he should give me an ultimatum, isn't it? One week. You know, though, I bet you I can hook him in that week, get him to work for me. I could use a straightforward terror like that."

"You aren't going to give him Reva, are you?"

"She's never crossed me before." It was one of Adahn's constant concerns, and one of his highest endorsements. "No, I'm not giving him Reva. So what's your opinion about Karuu?"

"Our old friend?" Janus traced patterns in the marble with one finger. "I still think Tion, let him run nanotech."

"You don't think he can help back on Selmun?"

"Maybe. Maybe it's safer to keep him far away from there."

"If he can rebuild a Customs net, he's almost earned his life right there."

"True," Janus agreed. "Our warehouses are filling up on R'debh—there've been no cargo lifts since the Security crackdown. This can't go on; it's hurting us too badly."

"Hm. Security is forcing a housecleaning of Selmun Customs. After the dust settles we could put Karuu back in, let him grease palms again so our cargo channels stay open. He was the best we had. . . . I'll have to think about that."

He stared into the distance, where orange-hued flights of mating grieko twined and plummeted in midair. "This Lish, though. She's pissed me off. Big headaches started with that one." His deep-set eyes narrowed as one bird stabbed a rival with its lengthy beak, and the wounded grieko tumbled from the sky.

"I don't want her cluttering up the landscape anymore," he added. "Take care of it, Janus."

The investigation into Behr's dirty linen had revealed a bigger puzzle than Commander Obray had expected. Finally they were close to making sense of the big picture.

The payoffs in the Governor-General's accounts correlated to only one thing: when freighters delivered cargo to the deep domes, a stock company kicked out a payoff for nonexistent "dividends." Storage warehouses were at maximum capacity near Amasl and other port cities. Together with a few other tidbits, it added up to one distinct footprint.

Brace surveyed the data and came to the same conclusion. "Maybe it goes like this," he offered. "Freighters carry land-made goods out to the wetdomes. Somewhere along the way, they stash half the cargo. The other half a shipload is delivered to dome-dwellers, who are charged double the price for their goods. That way the freight run brings in exactly as much money as it's supposed to. From the dome-dwellers' viewpoint, they've paid twice what an item is worth, but no one is listening to their complaints anyway. Interdome trade is so restricted, they're compelled to buy from surface manufacturers. They must think inflated prices are the norm."

Obray traced the warehouse graph with a sim-finger. "Meanwhile, diverted cargos are lifted offworld. They can't do it these last two or three weeks, since we're watching for smugglers, so storage is getting used up."

"Right." Brace pointed back at routine warehouse figures. "But when those goods sell offworld, they must clear a huge profit on every cargo load they got for free."

Obray whistled. "That could be it," he mused. A routine diversion of cargo, leaching the economic lifeblood from the single biggest market on R'debh—the undersea population that numbered in the billions.

The netrunner surveyed the graphics again, looking for holes in their theory. "Don't you think this would have been discovered by now?" he wondered aloud.

The Commander shrugged. "I bet not many individuals have put this whole chain of events together. Dockworkers might suspect some local smuggling is going on, but that seems to be R'debh's favorite pastime, wouldn't you say?"

Brace nodded agreement as Obray turned from the incriminating databits. "If this is the right scenario, it's up to us to prove it."

"More digging?" Captain Brace looked pained.

"More digging. I want to know where this money trail leads."

"I'm on it."

Obray unjacked from the desk console and smiled with elation. Soon they would have proof of wrongdoing that reached from the waterfront to the Governor-General's office.

And that, he knew, could be much more rewarding than a routine hunt for terrorists.

"Alright, Flash, cut the crap. A late payment on 100k is no reason to undercut a Holdout's well-earned profit. You want to work for Lish again, or not?"

The assassin spoke as if the smuggler were not in the room, even though that was not the case. Lish stood beside the desk, letting Reva use the comlink to wrestle FlashMan into some semblance of agreeability.

"Don't care about working for her again, babe," came the flip

reply. *"If she doesn't have my help to pull this off, there won't be a next time."*

The Flash was ever-faceless on a comlink, but Reva knew he could see her through the vid pickup. She put on a cold-eyed glare for his benefit, the edges of her mouth going hard.

"Do you want to work again, ever?" she asked him.

There was a beat of silence from the com unit. *"Aw, Reva. Don't start—"*

"Don't you start, Flash. Here, take this." She pulled her credmeter, fed it into the data transfer slot, and keyed a number into the datapad.

"What's that?" Flash asked, echoing Lish's unspoken question.

"It's the belated bonus, plus a little for your patience. We're renegotiating this contract. You don't mind, do you?"

The question seemed ominous, coming from the assassin. *"Um . . . no. Guess not."* It was the first, and probably the last, time Lish would ever hear FlashMan sound unsure of himself. Before she could protest Reva's unwanted generosity, the tall woman thumbed the transfer tab, and 110,000 credits fed from her meter into the FlashMan's net account.

She tugged the card out with flick of her wrist. "Now let's get down to business."

The talk was terse and to the point. In the end, FlashMan agreed to the same deal he had with Lish, plus 1 percent more profit. His news, it turned out, was worth it.

"Here you go," he said on the room speaker. *"Found this in Lanzig's personal files. A little snippet you might like to hear."*

The log recorder switched on and a holographic projection bloomed to life over the top of the desk console. It was Alia Lanzig, captured as pale-skinned and calculating as in life, speaking into what she thought was her inviolate personal log.

"The work on the borgbeasts is done, except for the final step. I told the Camisq not to bother; I want that adaptation saved for later. That way, if they prove uncontrollable, or anything else goes wrong, they're easy to get rid of. . . . I suppose for the record I should say more."

The miniature Lanzig leaned forward, pressed some keys on her console, not visible in the recording. *"Encryption routines,"* FlashMan muttered. *"Decoded for you on this segment."*

Lanzig leaned back and continued. "The borgbeasts have a fatal flaw. For that matter, so do their handlers. Namely, natives of Vernoi cannot digest the foodstuffs in the oceans of R'debh. They lack a particular enzyme required to absorb nutrients from this food. They'll eat, they'll feel full, but they will in fact be starving to death, unless and until this enzyme is introduced into their systems. Once this adaptation is made, they can flourish and survive in our seas. I haven't mentioned this to anyone else, because Edesz and his friends will want to have sole control over the beasts. They may think they do, but they won't." A smug smile played about Lanzig's mouth. "The Camisq know what enzyme is lacking and can manufacture it with self-replicating nanotech. They're waiting back on Tion for the order, should I chose to issue it. I haven't done so yet. I'll wait and see how things go first."

The holovid faded to black, and in the silence that followed, Reva heard Lish inhale and hold her breath.

"You stay like that, you're going to explode," she remarked over her shoulder. "Thank you, FlashMan. I owe you a dinner for that one."

"You're too kind." Flash sounded both flattered and unhappy at the extortion that had brought him to share his data. *"Well—I'm off for now."*

"Wait. The order codes and Camisq contacts?"

"Already downlinked and in your console."

"Thanks, Flash," Lish spoke in a rush of breath.

The netrunner was already offline. Reva swiveled in the chair and was pleased to see the sudden difference in Lish's face. Gone was the shadow that had dogged her demeanor since she first learned of Lanzig's death. The information about the borgbeasts could turn this all around.

"This is invaluable, Reva." Her eyes glowed brightly as she reached out and grasped her friend's shoulder, concern over *roi'tas* forgotten in her exhilaration. "Thank—"

"Don't say it." The assassin held up a hand to ward off the gratitude.

Lish squeezed her shoulder instead. "Well. You know what I mean."

The smuggler spun away and crossed to the door in a few strides. "Bring Devin from Akatnu Field," she told a Skiffjammer in the hall. "When he's here, have Vask join us." The sergeant saluted, and Lish closed the door.

"Now we'll get some things done around here!" she said, and grinned triumphantly at Reva.

"A run to Tion?" Devin pondered out loud. "That's about three, four days, if you stay off the shipping lanes. More space hazard that way, though."

"Can you do it?" Lish asked.

"Yes." Devin blew air through his lips. "But we've got our work cut out for us. I'll need more help at the ship."

"You've got it."

"There's one other thing," Reva spoke up. "How you gonna pay for this? The Camisq will want a credit dump, and that was a big price they quoted Lanzig."

Lish blushed. "I was coming to that. I was hoping you, any of you, could pitch in on this. You know once we have the nanotech we as good as have our payoff. But I'm a little short. . . ."

"No need to explain," Devin brushed her embarrassment aside. "How much is this going to cost?"

"One hundred."

Eyebrows went up around the table. "I've got 1k you can have," offered Vask. "It's not much, I know, but it's a start."

"Eightk," offered Devin. "It's all I have."

"Beldy spines," said Reva, scowling around the table. "Keep your small change. I'll front you, Lish."

The announcement caught the smuggler short, caused her to cough nervously. Enough was enough. She began to shake her head in automatic refusal. "You already—"

"Forget it," the assassin cut her off. "I'm in this far, aren't I? I guess I'll get it back, one way or another."

Lish saw the stubbornness in Reva's hazel eyes, and warred with herself over a yes or no. In the gift and acceptance of such aid, Lish became indebted to her far beyond the sum of money involved. Their casual ties became more formal, a bond of honor and obligation that bred countless intricacies in Sa'adani relationships—

But we're not in Sa'adani space, Lish reminded herself. And I need the money.

Plain need again overrode personal reservations, and the Hold-out finally nodded her agreement. Reva brushed off her mumbled appreciation, and transferred credits from her meter again, this time directly to Lish's account.

The party broke up. Devin and Vask went back to the ship, four Skiffjammers in tow. Reva was shown to a room, and Lish went to bed early, finally allowing herself to relax after days burdened by ever-present worries.

In the light by the bedside, behind a locked door, Reva pulled out her credmeter once again. The portable device held her fortune, for she who moved Timelines away from banks and institutions trusted only the cash or credit she could carry on her.

She studied her balance and grimaced. Five hundred CR. Not 5,000, but 500. That wasn't enough for a decent hotel suite, or a ticket offworld.

"You're broke, idiot." She scolded herself for being so loose with her funds, then thought better of it. Lish needed the help, and she was the only one who could offer it.

Besides, it was only money. There's always more where that came from, she thought, putting the credmeter away. Guess it's time to take another job.

LXVII

In the morning, Reva made a quick run into Amasl in her rented skimmer. She went to a starport com booth, punched in a special call code and waited for the subspace connect.

"Reva?" a man said. "This is unexpected."

"Janus." She acknowledged her invisible connection. "I'm back on the market. Have anything for me?"

"Ah . . . yes, we might. Can you hold for a moment?"

"Yes."

"Disconnect, please, and I'll call you right back."

She complied, knowing that Janus would reroute his call through encrypted relays outside the public comnet. A few moments later, the booth received an incoming call.

"Yes?" she said to the blank vidscreen.

"Kamisku Benulu?" queried a woman's synthesized voice.

"Benulu gesku," Reva replied in Ganandi. A moment later, Janus was back on the line.

"Special terms with this job," he said. "One week turnaround, no longer. Double fee, cash advance, as per your terms. Still interested?"

Cash advance. "I'll take it."

"Good. This is on Selmun III as well. Ready to downlink?"

"Ready."

"Dossier follows."

She waited for the subspace dump to finish. Then she opaqued and soundproofed the booth, and hit the playback.

Janus' voice filled the cubicle.

"Target," he said, beginning the standard narrative. "Shiran Gabrieya Lish. Last known business address: Comax Shipping, Lairdome 7, Amasl. Shiran is a Holdout, operating from . . ."

The words blurred together behind the ringing in her ears. Janus' briefing droned on, and Reva heard not a word of it.

I warned her, she thought. I warned her about Adahn, and now it comes home at last.

I can't do this.

She looked at the credmeter in her hand, her fee doubled and paid in advance. Exactly what she required for fast and efficient work. She'd already said yes, and taken the money. She had one week, Janus had said.

One week in which to kill her friend.

THREE

"The less you care about a Line, the easier it is to leave.
The more you care, the harder it is to stay."

"You're certain they're worse?" Edesz faced the lead Vernoi in mote-speckled depths, unhappy with the handler's news.

Master Swimmer Sharptooth gave a body-long undulation in response. "Yes. Our life-friends are worse. As are we."

"We—?"

"Us Vernoi."

Edesz frowned. If the handlers should die before the beasts, there would be no one to control the leviathans. If the borgbeasts should die first, there would be no more war against the Free Ocean Trade monopolies.

Either situation was intolerable. Damn Lish. What had she done to his borgbeasts?

"Very well, Master Swimmer," Edesz conceded to the Vernoi. "Two strikes will be sufficient this week."

"And the help you offered?" Sharptooth prompted the human.

"It's on the way. Today I make arrangements for its delivery."

Sharptooth trilled. The ambiguous tone was ignored by the sonic translator, but Edesz recognized it from his Vernoi training. It was a signal denoting thankfulness, and he offered the proper verbal trill in response. It was a poor imitation of the Vernoi sound, but the least that Sharptooth's gratitude deserved.

Lish was glad to take Edesz' call.

"I see you know something I don't about my borgbeasts," he said coldly. "I'll buy that cure from you, but I need it within the next two weeks."

It took all of her self-control to keep her expression blank. She hadn't even placed the order with the Camisq yet.

"I'm not sure I can meet that deadline," she said noncommittally.

The terrorist curled a lip. "I don't know if they'll live any longer than that. You started this, now you finish it. I want the fix for this problem as fast as you can get it to me. How fast is that, Lish?"

How fast could the Camisq produce the nanotech fix? That was the real question. "Give me a little time, and I'll call you back on this," she said.

"When?"

"Today. Maybe tonight. Let me talk to some people."

"As you say. You have my code." He frowned by way of farewell, and broke the connection.

Lish sat for a time, closing her eyes on the elation inside, and planning what she had to do next. After a while she pulled up the Camisq contact information taken from Alia Lanzig's files. She buzzed a certain cybernet frequency, and waited until the FlashMan hummed in her headset's earpiece.

"What's up?"

"Can you scramble this call for me, and the response when it comes back?"

Flash surveyed the ready-to-transmit message in the Holdout's com unit and the Tion address packets attached to it. *"Sure thing. Sit tight. I'll send it when the relays are ready."*

Lish watched her com board. A few minutes later, the message was transmitted, seemingly by itself.

Then she could only wait, while hours crawled by.

LXIX

Reva stayed far too long in the starport com booth, wracked with indecision. On the third pass of a security bot, she left the terminal, and called the Evriness villa.

She left a message on the house comp, unwilling to talk to Lish. Her target.

"I'll be gone for a few days," she had said, "but keep my room free. I'll be back."

From the starport she headed straight for Amasl's wildest holoshops and lost herself as hurriedly as she could in programmed dreams and illusions.

Illusions were safe enough; if she forgot herself, and struck out in anger, no one died, no one was hurt. But take enough drugs and you don't necessarily know the difference between dream state and real. There were blurred images of sun-filled street corners, of being drenched in the warm rain of an afternoon thundershower. Holo-program or memory? Real experience or illusion? There were the sex clubs that she liked to visit, full of willing men and luscious women, but they all seemed blond and slender with pretty yet careworn faces, and Reva left each one just before a kiss could lead to something more. And there was a red- and black-skinned figure, far across the room, who sought her but never saw her in the crowd, the silk-draped, semi-celluloid-clad crowd that laughed and partied with her, and shared her bed, and shared her wine, and left her, finally—

—alone. Alone and hungover in a way drug-dreams rarely left you. Her nose was stuffy, and a hand pressed to her face came away wet. The moisture was clear, and salty.

She'd been crying.

Aching, she uncurled from the ball she was in, rolled over and tried to figure where she was. This was no holo-shop. It was some-one's divey back-room apartment, or a public dorm lived in by a long term renter. A bodysuit was thrown on the floor, of ambiguous cut. Who lived here? Man? Woman?

Reva didn't wait to find out. Her own clothes were the worse for wear and still on her back. She left, palming the door open, not both-ering to search out the room's inhabitant. Gray corridors led out to gray overcast streets. Twilight and an incoming storm front washed the color from everything. Whether it was morning or evening was be-yond her ability to figure. She stood, swaying, wondering where to go to now.

And how to get there. What did I do with the car? she worried, then dismissed that care. It hardly mattered. Call the rental service, say it was stolen. Leave it to them.

Then she had an idea. Seeking out a com booth, she sat inside, collapsing against the backrest, and called Evriness again. A glimpse of her reflection in the vidscreen prompted her to leave the call dark; Lish answered, and Reva talked while combing fingers through her tangled hair.

"Say. Would you mind having some 'Jammers pick me up? I, um . . . I need a ride."

It felt funny to say that. Reva never asked for anything, not a ride, not a meal, not so much as a borrowed jacket.

You do what you have to, she excused it to herself, then sat, dozing, until an escort of Skiffjammers retrieved her from the com booth and whisked her out to the Highlands villa and Lish.

The smuggler, waiting on a callback from Tion, didn't notice her disheveled condition. Vask, returned from Akatnu Field, did a double take, then backed down from the single deadly glare directed his way. The assassin found her room, reported a missing air car to the agency, then tumbled into bed and welcome oblivion in a place she knew it was safe to rest.

Rest, but not forget. Anxiety punched her awake, rousing her from groggy dream to headache-filled consciousness in just a few heartbeats. The shuttered windows, secure against attack, opened at her spoken command, and daylight streamed into the room. It was some time after midday.

Reva ordered a bodysuit from the valet bot and put herself together in the fresher. Afterward she moved to the dining room, where she forced herself to eat a sparse meal of apaku and reis. In moods like this she preferred solitude, but she couldn't get a hit done that way, either. She resigned herself to appearing to be part of the normal household until this contract was out of the way.

Vask found her picking at fish bones. "How are you?" he asked, slipping into the chair across from her.

She made an effort to smooth the scowl from her face, an expression that came too naturally now. Worse, it betrayed how she really felt. She put on a mask of neutral friendliness and prepared to play the game of putting the target at ease. As long as the Fixer was so close to Lish, he was part of that game, too.

"I'm fine," she said, shoving her plate aside. "How are you?"

As soon as the trite words were out of her mouth she kicked herself. Since when do you talk like that? By the Deep, you're jittery as a kid with a kelp-crawler. Who cares how Vask is, anyway?

The Fixer took the question at face value, though, and was busy answering her. "I'm great, now that I don't have to work on the *Kestren* anymore. I was getting in their way, I guess. A bunch of spacers and me . . . not a good mix." He shrugged, ran his hands over his jacket and undertunic. "I like these clothes better, anyway."

She put a false smile on her lips. Vask's garb was unremarkable, usually the same monotonous streetwear of gray-green and black, plain in style and functionality—the better, it seemed, to blend in with backstreeters and alley-crawlers. Reva was the one clothes mattered to; her friends could all see that. Yet here she was in a standard-cut bodysuit of charcoal gray, as obscure as she could order for the bump-and-run work she might have to do. Would have to do, she corrected herself, sometime soon.

Six days, by her count, before the week was up. Adahn's contract was in standard Imperial timecount, of course. She'd lost four days already, on a drugged-out revel that had washed no tension from her body and given her no peace of mind. Ten days to a week. Lost four. Leaves six.

"What was that?" Something Vask said interrupted her obsessive countdown of time and days.

"Lish said join her when you're up. She wants to talk with you about the payoff arrangements with Edesz."

"Is that right." Her stomach gave a nauseating roll, and she regretted eating. Lish wanted to see her. Alone, in her office.

"I'll come with you," Vask offered.

"No." She said it too sharply, and he seemed hurt. "I have to see her alone." She stood hastily, nearly upsetting her chair, and slammed it angrily back in place against the table.

"Later," Kastlin murmured. Reva gestured good-bye, and strode the long hallways to Lish's office, steeling herself to her purpose.

Vask watched her clumsy departure, and heeded the uncomfortable foreboding in the back of his mind. Reva's natural movements were graceful and deft. What's eating her? he wondered. I think this needs looking into.

Retiring to his room, Kastlin locked the door and attached an additional Security lockout limpet to the magplate. He couldn't risk a visitor discovering his unaccountable absence. For he would shortly be unaccountably gone.

He sat down, relaxed, and began the process that would carry him out of the body and out of the physical plane entirely. Soon the room slid toward shades of gray and bluish translucence; when he stood, he had sideslipped into an unphased state, and was ready to move unseen through Lish's villa.

The Holdout's door was closed. The polite thing would be to scratch on it, or tap the voiceplate and announce herself. Reva faced the panel like it was an enemy, and eschewed the polite thing. She took several deep breaths, palmed the doorplate with an abrupt motion, and slipped inside.

Lish sat at her desk, engrossed in a game of castle-stones against the computer. It offered good lessons in strategy and tactics, skills she was honing these days. Her back was slightly to the door. She didn't notice it slide open, then shut, or hear the assassin's gentle tread upon the carpet.

Reva stood against the wall, far to the left of the smuggler. One long step to the side carried her behind Lish's line of sight. She would not see the assassin with a casual glance, not unless she looked back, over her shoulder.

Reva waited, heart racing. It was nothing to walk up on a target, nothing when she was stalking someone between the Lines. This was different, so very different. Personal and immediate, like everything done in Mainline. Too personal.

She took a while to regain her center, to breathe through parted lips until detachment returned, precariously achieved as it was. She was careful not to stare at Lish, though it was hard to keep her eyes off of her friend. Too much staring, and they look at you sometimes. That's not a problem between the Lines. . . .

She wished herself there, hidden at the crossroads of many present moments, away from the dilemma of this Now. She'd sorted through the Lines as soon as she'd awakened, and again here in the hallway, trying to decipher the fragments of Now, to pick out which thread of consequence offered the best resolution to her problems. But most everywhere off Mainline, Lish lay dead or dying at Reva's hand; in a minority of Nows, the smuggler continued to live, unscathed regardless of Reva's intent. In Mainline, the reality that stretched directly ahead of her, her keyed-up emotional state interfered with her ability to sense upcoming events. The next moments and the near future were a blur of fractured images, with no coherent eventline to be discerned.

Time-blind, she abandoned her efforts to sense the future, and moved directly through Realtime to do what she had to do.

She took three long, gliding steps closer to Lish, until she was standing nearly behind the preoccupied Holdout. She paused there, planning her next move, then chided herself.

You're taking too long, she thought. What are you waiting for? Quick, be quick about it.

Still she stood. What was she going to do afterward? A burst of frustration caused her to halt, fists clenched.

Fine planning. Fine. Do the hit, and after that—what? Ask 'Jammers to give you a ride to the starport while Lish lies in here, dead?

She must have made a sound at that moment, an inhalation, perhaps, or maybe the target simply sensed her presence in the room. Lish raised her head from the comp screen, and the assassin reflexively covered her tracks as far as she was able. She retraced her movements, taking two long steps backward and closer to the door, so her threatening pose behind Lish was not so easily detected. The smuggler suddenly turned, and glimpsed her friend a stride or two inside the entranceway.

She started, then relaxed as she recognized her visitor. "Reva! Sorry, I didn't hear you come in."

The tall woman walked forward, toward the float-couch beside the desk. Her pulse was racing, but her movements appeared normal enough, someone who had only that moment walked into the room and now accepted the invitation to sit. She lounged, a little stiffly, and struggled to concentrate on what Lish had to say about Edesz.

Vask had watched Reva's slow stalking movements toward Lish, seen her hesitation, her recovery on the verge of detection. Her actions left Kastlin worried about her motives and concerned for Lish's safety. He tried to puzzle out her strange behavior, but little about it seemed logical.

Did I misread what I saw? he wondered. What is she up to?

They were questions with no answers to be gleaned from an unphased state. That required ears, but there was no place to hide while he shifted down to the physical and blindspotted. He had to content himself with continued observation in his ghostly form.

The women's actions told him very little, indeed. A talk, a glass of wine, and Reva was gone. Straightforwardly, this time, with no last-minute attack or threatening motions toward Lish.

Had it all been the whim of a moment? Stymied, the Mutate ghosted back to his room, resolved to watch the assassin closer than ever before.

LXX

More Skiffjammers were put to work on the *Kestren*. With qualified techs on hand, the refitting drew rapidly to a close. Lish came out to the ship for a final inspection.

Devin's excitement was tangible; she had come to sign the vessel over to him, the better to avoid IntSec scrutiny of the freighter and its travels. For the spacer, gaining a ship of his own to command was the culmination of a dream. Their final contract gave him outright ownership, and an equal share of profits with Lish. It was one further concession, the price of his cooperation on the upcoming Tion run, an apology for his involvement with the *Delos Varte*.

Their brief tour concluded in the command unit. Lish leaned on the navigator's chair, captivated by the array of ready lights on the flight deck instruments. All systems up and running, exactly within the week she had demanded.

"Like it?" Devin asked proudly.

"You did a nice job." She smiled over at him. "Everything looks really good."

His next question caught her off guard. "This is my ship, now," he said, "so I have the right to ask. Will you share *meriös* with me?" He eagerly watched her response from beside the captain's chair.

It was something she had never considered. The pleasant expression froze on her face while conflicting emotions reeled through her.

Meriös. A ceremony of the Shiran Traders she had long forgotten, for she had never lived on a newly initiated ship, and had only heard of the ritual from her parents and clanmates. Yet every Shirani knew what *meriös* entailed. The acquisition of a vessel was never an ordinary purchase, but the start of what was likely to be a lifelong bond. The captain and his or her extended family would be born, grow up, and die on that ship, so a Shiran spacecraft was hearth, home, enterprise, and sometimes final resting place to the Traders who lived on her. It was not simply renamed when it was acquired: it was initiated, a rite of passage for the vessel, and for the crew who would inhabit her. *Meriös* blessed the ship in the eyes of the ancient gods and created the special bond needed for her successful travels.

The *Kestren* would not truly be Devin's until he renamed her; he could not rename her until *meriös* had been completed on board. A small tradition Lish had put far in the back of her mind, and one that came crashing in on her now, with all its implications.

She made herself keep the smile on her face. She was his clanmate, and the only available Shirani here, at this time. She was bound by duty and honor to say yes. She studied Devin's earnest expression. At least it seemed like a choice for him, not an obligation simply because she was handy. He had always liked her.

And after this he's going to like me a lot more, she considered. It's not at all a marriage, not like other peoples understand it, but it is a sacred and enduring bond.

She really had no honorable alternative. She pulled herself erect, and bowed before the ship's captain. "I would be honored to share *meriös* with you, Dom Shiran Teskal Devin. I thank you for your invitation."

The words came out in a normal speaking voice, at odds with her inner turmoil.

I thought I left all that behind me, she thought. No longer Shirani. But after this, more Shirani than ever. And the ties it binds . . . oh, Devin, I hope you're never sorry you asked me to do this.

Reva prowled the villa like a caged animal. Lish's extended absence at the ship left her thoroughly on edge.

Vask watched her restlessness from the security of a blindspot. She had been back on Selmun III for a week, and still he could not make sense of her contradictory actions.

First she would watch Lish dispassionately, sometimes stalking her in the halls as she had that first time she attracted his suspicious attention. Then she would stop and retreat, or make small talk with the smuggler, or discuss ordinary business. In the privacy of her room she played with her vibroknife, practicing fast-draw flourishes that looked ready to gut any bystander, but never touching the weapon elsewhere in the residence. Not once had she stepped into the unphased state he had glimpsed when she last gave him the slip. Kastlin was beginning to wonder if that mode of travel was really a part of how this assassin worked.

No matter. She didn't seem ready to carry through with the murderous intent her stance sometimes suggested, and the constant drain on his psionic abilities forced Vask to reduce his near-constant surveillance to a more moderate level.

Now, on the eve of the *Kestren*'s departure for Tion, Reva seemed more wound up than ever. Lish was gone, spending the night aboard the ship, and had asked not to be disturbed. Vask finally left his blindspot observation mode and tried to draw Reva out in conversation. It was a short, abortive exchange.

"I hear the 'Jammers have got the Islanders on the run," he remarked. "They nearly chased Daribi down this morning, but he got away in the marina."

"Umph."

He eased past the awkward silence with another subject. "How many more days until the swap with Edesz? Eleven or twelve, is it?"

"Hm."

"You're coming along, aren't you?"

"If I'm here."

Kastlin considered that. Reva had promised to escort Lish to the undersea meeting in very public Rinoco Park, where credits would be exchanged for nanotech. He'd been invited, too, as well as an escort of 'Jammers. Safety in numbers. There would doubtless be a sizable escort with the terrorist leader, and it was better to make a show of force than to look like they could be easily overwhelmed. Vask half expected the Gambru League to try to confiscate the nanotech and keep the credits, too. The 'Jammers would be along to prevent that from happening.

And then there was the raid by Security that he had to orchestrate. This was the perfect occasion for IntSec to net both Lish and the terrorists. Vask was overdue for a debriefing with Commander Obray, a conversation he faced reluctantly, and one he had to get over with pretty soon. He'd been out of touch for too long, too wrapped up in the Holdout's affairs to emerge from his cover and report in. Maybe he was in trouble for that already. Getting too close to a case could get him pulled from it.

He mulled that over while he regarded Reva. If she came to the terrorist meeting, any Security net would sweep her up, too, and that could ruin his own plans.

"Have you changed your mind?" he asked. "About coming to the meet?"

"Might be gone."

"Oh. I thought—"

"Leave me alone, Vask."

Kastlin took the rebuff in silence, and grudgingly left the room. Things are too fluid with her, he thought. I can't count on her sticking around Lish, but I better not lose track of her either. There's no way around it. Time to talk to Obray, so the smuggler's affairs are out of my hands. At least he'll know about the meeting with the League, and he can handle that however he wants.

He left the villa, compelled to face the unpleasantries of reporting in.

Vask wanted to meet quickly with Commander Obray and get it over with. As he had many times before, he would slip quietly into his superior's office, report on the spot, and leave again the same way. That wouldn't put his local cover at risk by openly approaching Security, and his debriefing would soon be over and done with.

Of course, a quiet approach for a Mutate meant something different than for Normals. Kastlin sideslipped into the offices used by Security and faded through Obray's door as a matter of course, simply to check and see if the Commander was available or engrossed in anything else at the moment.

Obray was lost in thought, eyes closed as was his habit when meditating on a problem. Kastlin sat on a float-chair by the desk, and shifted back down into the physical. He would be noticed soon enough. Meanwhile he, too, dropped into a semitrance that permitted him to recover some of his expended psionic energy.

The Commander faced a little away from Kastlin's chair. When the external com speaker on his desk came to life, he sat suddenly upright and answered his vidscreen, and so did not notice his unannounced visitor.

It was Captain Brace, from within the Net. *"Guess what? The Governor-General can't get to any of the padded deposits in his ac-*

*count. They're screened out from his terminals. With his access code,
he sees only regular banking. Nothing unusual."*

"How can that be?" Obray asked.

*"I'd guess someone is simply using his account to hide money in.
Laundering it through established accounts with big balances and a
lot of transactions. Sorry we didn't catch this before. We were so busy
putting the rest of the info together. . . ."*

"Understood. But trace those laundered funds. Let's find out
where the money trail leads."

"Sir." The decker left the channel.

Vask coughed discreetly to alert his superior to his presence.

The Commander nearly jumped out of his seat. "Juro's balls.
Kastlin, what the hell are you doing in here?"

"Came to report, sir."

Obray collected himself. "You could use the door, you know."

Kastlin gestured to his street clothes, a clear reference to not
risking his incognito. He had, after all, reported this way before.

The officer frowned at the backstreet garb on his best psionicist.
"Maybe you've been in those clothes too long, period. I was starting
to think you were going native on me."

"Hardly. I'm on to some interesting things, though. Couldn't get
away any sooner to check in, but here I am now."

"So let's hear it." Obray pressed a record tab on his console, and
their conversation became part of a permanent briefing record entered into Security files.

"I think we've got the goods on Lish, like you wanted. Here's how
you can put her out of operation."

Vask went on to outline the Holdout's planned deal with the terrorists: nanotech in exchange for the borgbeast payment; when and
where the meet would be. Yet as he divulged the information, Kastlin
felt strangely traitorous. No, he hadn't gone native, deserting the Bugs
for the company of his subjects of investigation. But he was close to
it, in some ways. If Lish had put her skills to ethical trade she'd have
made a fortune by now and been a respected member of the civic
community. Her spirited perseverance in the face of defeat had won
his admiration, and her friendship since the kria hunt on Des'lin was
sincere and unreserved. He felt like a traitor even as his debriefing
went by the book.

The briefing on Reva was less forthright, blatantly edited, in fact,
so that Vask could retain his freedom of operation. "She's an assassin,

but I'm still investigating," he said. "She has some powerful gangland connections, and I want to track them down."

"You think it's worth the risk of leaving her free on the streets?"

"I'm pretty sure of it, yes. Her connections are offworld." Kastlin quirked a smile. "She thinks of me as almost a friend—or maybe as a friendly dog. I want to develop this contact, get more into her confidence. I think we can land something big with this one if you let me work the case for a while."

Obray agreed. It was a standard kind of request from a Psionicist who could pick his own assignments, and had the street experience to judge what was worth going after. "Good work, by the way, tying Lish in to the terrorists," he added. "She's more slippery than Karuu proved to be, and the Gambru League—well, they're a headache in their own right. I'll put a commendation in your file, Kastlin."

Debriefing at a close, the Mutate stood. "Thank you, sir." He did his best to appear grateful but barely managed to disguise his unease.

It was simpler when the bad guys were really bad. This felt like setting up a friend. And Reva would be next.

Vask was glad to shift out of the physical, and leave the Security offices behind.

LXXII

The Islanders were on the run.

Their dockside hangouts were firebombed or shot to pieces, their waterfront enterprises closed by Security crackdowns or Skiffjammer raids. A paltry tenth remained of the hundred-strong force that had once anchored Karuu's waterfront action.

Daribi led a ragged retreat to Indero Island, his ancestral home and a haven for his fellows. The reed island lay north of Amasl's lee harbor, close by rocky tidepools Indero held harvest-claim to. The Islanders limped to the refuge aboard windfloats and paddleboards, a few on float-skis in a motley twilight migration.

Daribi took his fellows below the surface of the thick-woven island, into the damp sublayers where chambers were burrowed, for sleeping, living, storage purposes. They had their wounds tended to, ate, and fell asleep. Tomorrow would be soon enough to worry about the future of the derevin.

A guard was posted, and the Islander chief joined his fellows in exhausted slumber.

The night passed uneventfully. Guards noticed nothing untoward until a hollow-sounding pop echoed off the surface of the water in the early morning light. A streamer of orange smoke began to pour from a canister wedged deep into a layer of reeds. A guard shouted the alarm, but before Daribi could be roused, the enemy derevin was upon them.

Riding float-skis and skimming just above the surface of the swell, Skiffjammers homed in on the smoke that marked their attack zone. While they were moderate-sized specks approaching from shore, high-explosive warheads arrowed into the thick weave of the Indero Island mat and discharged, blowing large segments of the reed-pack to shreds and catching the surrounding edges on fire. As they drew closer they launched canisters of flourogel. The projectiles landed on the raft-like surface that remained, tearing through reed curtains and matting; where they burst, everything the incendiary touched ignited and burned with napalm-like fury.

The smell of chemical smoke and explosives hung thick in the air. Skiffjammers maneuvered on float-skis, circling the burning, sinking debris like sharks, picking off survivors and bronze-skinned Islanders with laser fire. When the strike teams were certain there were no survivors left above or below the waters, they left the ruins of the island. Grinds would be converging on the scene by a roundabout route, hoping to avoid the derevin, which was better armed than they were.

Levay ordered the pullout from her command skiff. She regretted the civilian deaths, but Daribi should have known that in a streetwar, any place he took refuge was fair game for an attack. At least she'd have good news for Domna Shiran. She could return to the waterfront, and all would be business as usual.

At Akatnu Field, the *Kestren*'s systems were powered down. Enough air circulated to lighten the cloud of incense originating in the galley, and to draw off the smoke from the waxberry candles, but little else was in service. Lish followed the spicy scent of duskthorn into the interior of the ship, and stopped at the threshold of another world.

There was no disguising the crew unit of the freighter, but Devin's preparations had gone far to create the illusion of a modest Lahaj temple. Cloth of flowing yellow draped food station, fresher, and the console of environmental controls, hiding their technological intrusion away from sight. The pull-down comp table held censer and a bowl of shredded duskthorn. Galley table had become silk-concealed altar. An inscribed wooden tablet held pride of place amid the offerings of flowers and fruit, with statuary arrayed to each side. Water and wine stood before the tablet, with white candles illuminating all.

The flickering tapers gave the chamber a warm and primitive air. Devin saw Lish enter and stepped silently into the room from his adjoining cabin. He came and took her hand with a reassuring smile. She looked from him to the modest wonders that had transformed the compartment.

"It's magical," she breathed, and squeezed her clanmate's hand.

She felt like a small child again. The altar looked much like the one her parents had brought her to on her coming of age, and again when she had left their ship to live and work aboard the old *Jacklamb.* The inscribed tablet would hold a list of names of Teskal Devin's most honored ancestors; inside might be a datachip recording biographies and more personal anecdotes, as her parents had concealed inside the ancestral tablet for the Gabrieya sept. The colors of yellow and white were the tokens of Ashani the Protector, the only possible choice for patron of the *meriös.*

The narcotic smoke of the burning duskthorn was the crowning touch, something restricted to ceremonies performed only by adult Shirani on rare and sacred occasions. Lish had left her clan before sampling those various rites of passage; the pungent scent brought home both the thrill of doing a forbidden thing, and a consciousness of joining the ranks of the adults of her clan for the first time.

Painfully aware of her feeling of vulnerability, she left it to Devin to lead the way, as befitted his role as ship's Captain. She followed his motions, beginning with ritual purification with sprinkled water, then a sharing of wine, and a time of chanting the prayers and mantras taught by the Lahaj, priest-disciples of the lau-zim philosophy. It had been years since she had chanted, or given any thought to Sa'adani spirituality. Her initial awkwardness gradually gave way to remembered routine, and she found herself caught up in the ritual of *meriös*.

Return to ancient customs came with unnerving ease to Lish, who had thought herself freed of the traditional ways of her birthclan. Joining Devin was to step back in time, to a line of continuity that bound her ancestors to her own earlier life. She found herself stripping before her kinsman without self-consciousness, as he did before her, helping each other to dress in the white robes signifying pure intentions and new beginnings. Devin faced the altar, drawing his clanmate down to kneel with him before it. Putting hands together, they bowed formally from the waist to the deities memorialized there, icons glowing in the candlelight, tokens of forces greater than man.

The figurines followed conventional forms. Devin's were of classic design, of minute carving and intricately detailed workmanship. The first was a wingless dragon of gold, twining sinuously back upon itself, every scale catching the light of the candles. The second was a miniature shelter of thatching worked in delicately carved ivory, symbol of the means to survive in a harsh environment. The third was a glittering figurine of milky white and translucent crystal, cut in the shape of a woman in windblown robes, hair piled ornately upon her head.

Devin touched the god-statues, invoking one after the other. Lish echoed him in the blessing-refrain she had learned as a child.

"Windlord's flight," spoke Devin, raising the dragon.

"Usembo's might," she recited the affirmation.

"In brave one's sight—" He clasped the shelter.

"Korbato's night."

"Protector's right." He lifted the goddess.

"Ashani's light."

Devin dropped more duskthorn into the censer, and a fresh waft of smoke coiled upward from the bowl. In the shadows of the room,

Lish imagined she could see the invoked spirits gathering to watch over them: Usembo, dragon lord of winds and bringer of good fortune; Korbato, patron of spacefarers, a hardy godling who aided survival against the elements; and Ashani the Protector, who kept people safe from dangers natural or man-made. They were beings she had dismissed in her cynical youth, but now, in the dark, with the drugged smoke of the incense in her nostrils, it was easy to believe in them once more.

She followed Devin then on a chanting sojourn throughout the ship, bearing candles and incense to bring the light of Ashani into every corner of the vessel that would be new-created that night. Forward to the flight deck they went, through the holds, the gun turrets, then aft to engineering and back again, stopping in every cubby and byway along the way.

As they went, it became a game, like the spice hunt held to celebrate the name-day of Shirani children. Who would be the first to reach the next compartment, to open the next hatchway? There was a somber moment of invocation to the Protector, a sedate chant, and then the puckish rush to cast open every locker and accessway they encountered. *Meriös* was intended to fill a vessel with joy and light, to signify happy new beginnings. The procession to dispel darkness became an uplifting and joyful celebration, the pace accelerating until they nearly raced each other back to the altar at the end of it all. There the chants concluded with a prayerful shout and a growing sense of joy. Devin shared out more wine, and Lish could not tell if the muzziness of her head was from the drink or the duskthorne smoke. No matter; both were welcome, and her spirit was lightened. Anything seemed possible now.

Setting down the wine, Devin fetched a small plaque from beneath the ancestor tablet on the altar. It was a besk, an icon of blessing and christening and good wishes combined. One like it was carried on every Shiran-owned ship.

This one was platinum, a handspan long, two fingers wide; it bore the calligraphic symbols for the deities invoked this night, the new name of the freighter, and a short prayer for safe voyages and the happiness of the crew. Lish watched as Devin purified the besk in smoke and water and flame, and asked his ancestors' blessings upon it. Then she helped him affix it over the door of his cabin, in the place where the captain's sleep could be watched over by the gods of travelers and spacefarers.

Fortune, he had renamed the ship. She knew he meant that in the sense of good luck, not greed, and smiled at his undemanding nature.

She was still smiling when he put his arms around her and kissed her. Then he bent down to kiss the hollow of her neck, and for a moment she was conscious of his caste mark laser-scribed on his jaw, and the absence of her own. Trying to disown all this, she recalled, that's why I had it removed. Was it so bad with the Traders after all?

Then his embrace carried her away, and she spared no more thoughts to the past.

Much later she thought of her kinsmen and parents and all her clanmates who had shared a time like this with their partner. Unlike those other Shirani, she would not be traveling with Devin aboard the *Fortune.* It was for that reason alone, she thought, that tears came to her eyes as she lay afterward in his arms.

He brushed her tears away without remarking on them, and for that she was glad.

Zippo snuffled through red data packets, the product of a decryption run, and recognized the name associated with every packet he found. Barking in sudden excitement, the agent ran his simself to the nearest external com link, and bayed his news to Commander Obray.

Translated through the matrix, the words came in the clear to the Security officer.

"It's Karuu!" Zippo almost shouted his discovery. "We can trace every transaction right back to him. Every offworld transfer was authorized by him or one of his agents."

"Where's this money now?" the Commander asked.

"We can't say, yet," the bulldog reported. "We need to investigate more."

"Do it. We're talking about enough money to finance a small world with."

"We're on it, Commander."

The decker left the comlink and Obray considered all that money funneled offworld. That was the trail to follow, right there.

He was on to something big, he knew—and who better to investigate a hitherto unsuspected multiworld conspiracy?

Juro's teeth, he thought, I want to ask that Holdout some questions.

That prompted Obray to do what Internal Security rarely did. He posted a reward for information leading to Karuu's arrest, and made it a figure at the very outside of his generous budgetary limits.

Someone somewhere knew about the fugitive smuggler. And Obray was going to find that person, one way or another.

The intimate mood lingered into the morning, as Lish helped Devin put the *Fortune* to rights. When they sat down to breakfast in the galley, Devin swept her hand up and kissed her fingers. "I want to thank you," he said. "There's no one I would rather have shared *meriös* with than you."

Lish colored. Devin's words put an uncomfortable spotlight on the intimacy that now lay between them.

"Thanks," was all she replied. She withdrew her fingers and busied herself with the pretense of ordering breakfast from the prep unit. "Say," she changed the subject, "when are you lifting to go on this run?"

Devin took the conversation turn gracefully. "As soon as the 'Jammers get here and preflight is done. I want to take it easy heading out, since this will be first shakedown after all these repairs." Worry tinged his voice. "We're cutting it kind of close. Four days out, four back, that leaves three days leeway. Will they have the nanotech ready for us to ship?"

Lish paused for a heartbeat, then nodded. "The Camisq designed the borgbeasts, so they already had the replication scheme calculated for the nanotech. The goods will be ready by time you get there."

She put spicey reis cakes, broth-noodles, and tea on the table, then sat beside Devin—not quite as closely as before. She fell quiet as she ate breakfast, but the real reason for her silence was enough to kill her appetite.

When she had insisted on a two-week delivery deadline, the Camisq had called it a rush order and doubled the price. Her money counted only as half-price deposit, not full payment. The rest was due before they would release the goods to Devin.

She forced the food down, involuntarily worrying at the problem that had occupied her secretly for the last week and a half, and was now, thanks to the spacer's questions, in the forefront of her mind once again.

I'm getting that nanotech, she promised herself grimly, even if FlashMan has to raid someone's net account so I can afford it.

Sergeant Eklun and another Skiffjammer named Zay came on board within the hour. As Lish stood to leave, her clanmate beckoned her into his cabin where he moved to kiss her good-bye. She hesitated, then went along with the gesture, unwilling to rebuff the man about to undertake potential risk on her behalf.

"See you in less than a week," he promised.

"Less than a week," she agreed, and departed the ship.

Devin watched her go with mixed emotions. It would be nice if she would crew the *Fortune,* too, but too much else demanded her time and attention. Struggling to keep afloat. Dealing with the terrorists.

Sinking surface shipping.

No, that's not fair, the Captain corrected the involuntary thought. She's not responsible for how those beasts are used. We've been over that ground before. But I sure have a problem with it.

He didn't like being a part of something that would help terrorists kill innocent sailors in Selmun waters. It didn't matter how roundabout his contribution might be. Obligation to Lish came first, without question. The borgbeasts, though, enabled to live in the sea and continue their rampage . . . Maybe later, somehow, he could help authorities locate the terrorists. Lish didn't care what happened to the Gambru League, not after she was paid.

It was a quandary he could not resolve yet, and so he walked away from it as he turned his back on Lish's departing figure. One thing at a time, that was the way to take care of business. First, get the *Fortune* back upstairs, where she belonged, and after that, warp to Tion.

It's easy, he told himself. Just one thing at a time.

LXXVI

Vask couldn't watch Reva psionically all the time. That would take a superhuman effort, not called for in her days of fitful inactivity. He had to pick and choose his times for blindspotting, and relied more and more on ordinary surveillance.

When Lish returned from Akatnu Field and Reva followed her behind closed doors, he left the pair to another unmonitored conversation, as he increasingly had, and merely loitered in view of hallway and door.

Lish retreated to the solarium alcove in the study, where lush exotic ferns and a small burbling waterfall made a soothing place to relax and think. Reva followed her into the room and stood inside the door that had closed behind her.

The assassin was in her traveling clothes, dress-clad, in heels, ready to blend into any starport crowd and vanish amid throngs of like-clothed passengers. The electric blue of the Lyndir-cut fashion and platinum blond hair she affected this day made her look like a stranger, not like the dark-haired, shadow-eyed woman who had been haunting the hallways for most of the last week.

Reva's garb meant nothing special to Lish, who noted her presence with mixed feelings. Not wishing to be rude, she nevertheless wanted to be alone.

"Guess what?" she said to the assassin. "Islanders are off our backs. Would you like to come back later, when Captain Levay fills me in on the details?"

Reva regarded the smuggler impassively. "No," she replied. "I only came by to give you this."

A triangular blue chit flipped through the air, bounced atop a water-splashed paving stone at the lip of the solarium pond. It was the pass to Tyree Longhouse on Des'lin.

Recognition flashed across the smuggler's face, and she left the chit where it landed. Why?" She sounded a little hurt. "What's this about?"

"I won't be using it again, and I don't want to have it on me."

"What are you talking about?"

"I'm leaving, that's all."

Her tone of finality gave Lish to understand her meaning. "Leaving?" the Holdout echoed. "You mean gone? For good?"

Reva nodded, and walked toward the door. She didn't trust herself to prolong this conversation, or to finish it with words like *goodbye*. It was easier, just out the door and gone.

"Wait!" Lish said. "You can't go like this."

It taxed Reva's self-control to hear that. "Watch me," she mumbled through her teeth, and reached to palm the door open.

The Holdout came to her feet. "Lords of Ice, what's wrong? Talk to me."

The assassin halted with her hand on the doorplate, not yet pressing it open. She hung her head, took a shuddering breath. Sea Father, she prayed, help me walk out of this room.

"Reva."

The smuggler's tone was pleading, and Reva couldn't ignore her. There were no words sufficient, and too much to say, and she couldn't stand it any longer.

"Nothing's wrong," she denied, turning slowly about, and started moving toward Lish. Her clenched fists were silent witness to the tension she held inside. The Holdout noticed, and felt a twinge of concern.

The hesitation on her face provoked Reva. "How plain do you want to hear this?"

"Hear what?"

The assassin jutted her chin towards the blue house pass. "That's yours. I don't want it. I'm not your houseguest, I'm not your friend, and I don't want to have anything to do with you. Is that clear enough? Can I go, now?"

Lish gaped, astounded, then shook her head in disbelief. "I don't know what's bothering you, but I don't think that's it. At least be honest with me."

Honesty? Reva choked back a laugh. "Here's honesty for you. What in the Deep are you thinking about, sleeping with Devin? You go off like a nervous schoolgirl and come back like a well-laid whore when your business, your derevin, your *friends* all depend on you to—" She heard her voice escalating in pitch, felt her resentment of Devin, her unreasoning anger. She stopped herself before she could say something she'd regret. "You've got to keep your mind on your business," she spat instead, "and fucking your pilot isn't going to get you anywhere. You're in so deep you're close to drowning, and all you can think about is getting laid."

Lish bridled at the personal attack. "You don't know anything about it," she retorted. "You have no business criticizing my personal life."

"Right. Guess it doesn't really matter anymore." The assassin spun and headed for the door.

"Reva, damn you, don't you walk out on me again!"

That brought her up short, and she rounded on Lish immediately. "I'm not trying to walk out on you, you infuriating bitch, I'm trying to save your life!"

It came out as a shout, a secret confession that left her red-faced and shaking.

Lish took in her friend's body language with consternation, and softened her voice when she spoke. "What do you mean by that? What's really going on, here?"

Why? Reva screamed in her head. Why is she asking me, of all people?

The assassin felt rooted to the spot and forced herself to stir. Her hands were trembling and she clasped them before her in a white-knuckled grip. What to say?

"There's a contract out on you." She forced the words past the constriction in her throat. "Your life's in danger."

Lish paled, and sat abruptly. She couldn't take her eyes off Reva's face. "How do you know this?"

"You need to shut down your operations. Get off of R'debh and don't come back."

"Shut down—"

"Better yet, disappear. Change your identity. I can help you with that, if you want."

The Holdout saw moisture glisten in Reva's eyes. She repeated her question in a tremulous voice. "How do you know about this?"

The answer came in a rasping whisper. "Because I've been hired to kill you."

Reva never knew that time could freeze like that. The moment stretched on, and on, each woman unmoving, unable to wrench her gaze from the other, both too shocked by the admission to marshal a response.

Finally Lish needed to breathe, and drew in a ragged breath. The words came, unthinking. "So are you going to kill me?"

Reva blinked then, and a single tear flowed free down the plane of her cheek.

"No."

Lish forced herself to breathe again.

The assassin felt an unaccustomed weakness in her knees, and sat gingerly in a nearby chair. She looked to the door, and back to her erstwhile target, framed by ferns and falling water.

"Do you want me to leave?" she asked, dreading the answer she might receive.

"If you're not going to kill me, I suppose you ought to stay," Lish replied. She stifled the hysterical chuckle that wanted to follow the words.

Reva sat like a statue, in emotional shock at her own confession. What have you done? a panicked voice chittered in the back of her mind. And what are you going to do now?

She struggled to concentrate on the moment, Lish pale and worried-looking across from her, her own hands aching where they gripped the armrests too hard.

"So tell me about it," her friend prompted her. "Who hired you?"

It was a straightforward recitation. Concentrating on facts took Reva's mind off the feeling that she had just leapt a terrible precipice, taken a step she could never recall. She told Lish of Adahn Harric, of his ties to Karuu. She didn't know the full extent of his activities on Selmun III, but she knew the crime boss' tentacles reached further into the R'debh underworld than the simple surface levels reflected by Karuu's smuggling.

His decision to eliminate Lish was a purposeful action, a spiteful quashing of the Holdout who had unwittingly hurt his operations on Selmun III. He was in a hurry to have it done quickly—a demonstration to others, Reva thought, and a warning not to cross Karuu, or the man behind him.

"How quick is quickly?" Lish asked with morbid interest.

"Time's up for this job right about now, on his clock."

"Oh." Her stomach gave a nervous twist. Reva had been with her for most of the week, and she found that profoundly unnerving. The assassin was beyond or beneath such codes as *roi'tas,* and had stayed her hand only because of her friendly regard for the Holdout.

It was a fragile sentiment upon which to hang a life. Lish collected herself with an effort.

"What should I do now?" she asked.

The assassin wondered that herself. She felt hollow in the aftermath of her unexpected confession; distraught, it was hard to concentrate, hard to perceive the best course of action. Should she leave R'debh? Should Lish? Lie to Adahn, fake the smuggler's death to buy time? Hire extra security?

No, Lish's best hope was in dropping from sight completely, thoroughly. Reva's first impulse had been the right one. "Do what I said," she told her. "Leave. Shut down, move elsewhere. I'll help you change your identity."

"I can't do that."

"Don't you get it?" Reva tapped her forehead in irritation. "If you stay, you'll be dead. If I don't get you, someone else will."

Lish chewed her lip. "I'm not leaving until I collect my money. And 10 mil buys a lot of protection."

"Don't count on it being enough."

"Maybe you're right. But I can't get started again without it." The Holdout buried her head in her hands. "I'll think about what you say, Reva, but I can't go anywhere until this matter with Edesz is done."

The assassin understood her point; it was hard to run far when you were broke. She had to have one more week, then, and Reva saw what she needed to do. She made her decision abruptly: a snap judgment, like most of her decisions under stress, one based on the infallible instinct that had seen her through so many hits. Or, in this case, the sparing of a life. . . .

She forced doubts out of her mind. "If you need another week, then I have arrangements to make. I can buy you some extra time."

"Adahn will extend the contract?"

"I'll tell him I ran into problems. One more week, I should be able to bargain for that. Sometimes contracts don't get fulfilled, you know? That's life."

Lish heard the offer without surprise. It was fitting, for one who unthinkingly incurred *roi'tas,* who had brought Lish under obligation, however denied, and now raised the stakes to the level of a life-debt. *Senje'tas.* There was a symmetry to it, and the Sa'adani smuggler could only bow beneath the cloak of protection Ashani chose to lay over her.

"Thanks," she made herself say.

A meager word. Only her actions now could erase the debt between them.

"You be sure you're ready to run at the end of that time," Reva added, her tone of voice harsh. "You know what that means. After the swap with Edesz, get out of here."

Lish hesitated, then shook her head. "I have to get a new warehouse set up. If I fold now, I lose everything I have. Other Holdouts will move in on my buyers; worse, I lose face, and it'll be nearly impossible to rebuild if I return. I can't appear to be on the run, or no one will deal with me. I didn't run from Islanders; I fought back."

"So what are you saying?"

Lish spoke earnestly. "That things have to look like business as usual. I have to get back on the waterfront, and not lose any time about it. I have to go on as if I had nothing to fear from Adahn or anyone else. I'll duck out for a time, like you say, get my bearings. But when I come back—"

"If."

"—*when* I come back, I have to be able to pick up where I left off. So don't ask me to burrow like a drohl. I might as well be dead if I'm going to do that."

Reva ran scarlet-nailed fingers through her hair and paused, staring at the ceiling. This woman is nearly as stubborn as I am, she thought. Alright. Let her go through the motions. The important thing is that she drop out of sight when her time is up. No use being a walking target waiting for Adahn's pleasure.

"If that's how you want it, fine," she said. "But I'm making sure you're off someplace safe when this week is up."

Lish's mouth opened.

"Just to think things over," Reva insisted.

The Holdout finally bowed her head in agreement. The assassin knew her business, and it seemed like the wisest course of action. "But only for a while," Lish added. "Until I decide the best way to handle this."

"Fine." Reva conceded. "Now listen: when I arrange for an extra

week, that's all it's going to be. One week. I can't imagine Adahn agreeing to wait any longer than that."

"He's that eager to see me dead?"

"He's that vindictive. Our time will be up on the same day you're
trading Desz for the nanotech."

"Yes?"

"Are you certain there won't be any delays? I don't want there to
be any reason why you have to stick around on this planet after my
deadline is come and gone."

Lish gave a sickly smile at the use of the word. Deadline, in the
literal sense.

"Come on," the assassin urged her. "No delays?"

The smuggler closed her eyes. "Gods. The outstanding Camisq
payment."

At Reva's prodding she confessed the snag she had run into for
the rush-ordered nanotech. "Don't worry," she added in a rush.
"FlashMan can help. We'll get that payment made."

Reva rolled her eyes, certain she would regret what she was about
to do. "Yeah, you'll get that payment made," she said. "Right now."
She held out her credmeter to the smuggler.

Lish raised her hands. "No. You've helped me out enough already."

"Vent that. Too much is riding on this. If you go account-pilfering
with FlashMan, there's always the chance that he'll get caught."

"Doesn't seem any riskier than the other kinds of netrunning he
does."

"Yeah, but there are Bugs in the Net here as long as Security's so
interested in this planet. Do you really want to risk your life and your
fortune on an unsure thing?"

Lish considered, and stared unhappily at the meter. "No," she admitted.

"Then take this. Like I said—consider it a loan. You can pay me
back in a week."

If she owed her life already, why not more credits as well? Lish
accepted the device. Remarks about blood money and buying friendship flitted through the back of her mind, but that was the residue of
fear and stress from this conversation with a hired killer. The truth
was far more complex than that, for herself, and surely for Reva as well.
She kept her mouth shut and used the card.

The credit transfer was quickly done. The pair made their peace as best they could, and gradually a semblance of normality returned to their exchanges. When Reva left the room, Lish dispatched the final payment to the Camisq account. Then reality sank in, and she collapsed into a chair in the trembling aftermath of it all.

LXXVII

Pigtail of liquid platinum; the red-lacquered button of a single rigger implant, centered in the left temple; left eye glowing green where cyberoptics enhanced the man's vision. Long black hair, buzzed in parallel lines over the ears, pulled back in the white-metal queue that marked his derevin affiliation.

MazeRats were unknown on Selmun III. Gerick enjoyed the strange pleasure of moving in anonymity, his power and influence unrecognized by locals, who thought him simply a stylish offworlder from Lyndir or beyond.

Oh, but he was much more than that.

He unsealed the front of his Bekavra-cut tunic against the unaccustomed humidity, and took a good last look at the ruins of the Islander's Dive across the street. Then he used a com booth to make an urgent subspace call.

Adahn came on the line, his face visible; there was no need for anonymity with his trusted street lieutenant. "Yes?"

"Karuu's street operations are shattered and Islanders out of play for good."

Adahn's lips thinned. "When did this happen?"

"Skiffjammers finished the derevin off this morning, local time."

Harric frowned. "Why are they still taking on Lish's enemies? They have something personal against the Islanders?"

Gerick cleared his throat. "Word is, Shiran is alive. They were acting on her orders."

"What?" Adahn's anger was plain. "Alive, as of when?"

"Heard that word about an hour ago."

Harric flushed a swarthy red and controlled himself with an effort. "Tell me about Karuu's operations," he said shortly. "Can we save anything?"

"No."

"The Bugs?"

"Off the streets now."

Harric nodded grimly. "Start putting the pieces back together, Gerick, and make it quick. The credit line's open on this one."

"I'll take care of it, Boss."

"You better. What's the word on Karuu?"

"Everything's in order."

Adahn heard that with satisfaction.

"You want me to do anything about this Lish matter?" the Maze-Rat volunteered.

A spasm of anger clouded Harric's face, then he gave a chilling smile.

"No," he told his lieutenant. "You leave that to me."

The ship that had brought Gerick and five MazeRat companions to Selmun III was the *Lady Kestafia.* Service bots and maintenance techs prepped the liner for the next leg of her licensed interstellar transport run.

Away from the preflight bustle, medical crew and a few low-ranking personnel from the steward's staff worked in the cold-storage environmental units. There they finished the last and the slowest of the passenger unloading, the process of thawing out the sleepers: steerage-equivalent passengers who traveled in cryogenic suspension.

One had flatlined on this trip, a fact not mentioned to the sleepers who rose and left under their own power. The medical officer tendered his regrets to the local family of passenger Dono Algeri; yes, the brother said, please keep him frozen. We'll see our medclinic about this matter. The doctor smiled knowingly. Some people thought there was a hope for revival, when in fact there was none.

The grieving family collected their relative and took him in his cryocase to a dockside warehouse. There an impersonal technician thawed the body; poses of sorrow and kinship quickly shed, the former Algeri family manhandled the remains of a cold Dorleoni out of the freezer.

The corpse was laid on a gravsled and taken to the marina with boxes of supplies. Later that morning, a skiff, moving submerged in the harbor, disgorged the furred body of the deceased through its air-lock.

Washed and tugged by currents, the floater surfaced an hour later by the commercial slips. The Grinds recognized the species of their corpse, and the subsequent identification was made top prior-ity.

Retina and thumbprints were unmistakable. Obray was informed directly by the medical examiner.

"We've found Karuu," the man reported. "He's dead."

"Reva." Adahn's voice was smooth and pleasant. "This is a pleasure."

Expecting to speak with Janus, as she usually did, she was unset-tled to get Harric on the line personally.

He's waiting to hear about the contract, she thought. That's it.

Never good with small talk, she skipped the pleasantries entirely. "I've run into a problem," she told her client. "I need another week to make the hit."

Subspace static filled the line. When Harric came back on, his voice was different. Distant. No longer friendly.

"You've run into a problem, alright. You've created a problem. I'm very disappointed in you, Reva."

Her lips pressed together. She didn't care whether he was disap-pointed or not. All that mattered was finessing the man into extend-ing her contract.

"I'm sorry if you're inconvenienced," she said. "I'm put out, my-self. Give me another week, Adahn. Tell you what: next job will cost half the usual."

There. That should sweeten the deal sufficiently to—

"Forget it. Your foot-dragging's cost me too much already. I don't care why, and I don't care what difficulties you've had."

"Listen, Adahn, I—"

"No, you listen." There was no vidscreen image to view, but his voice turned ugly. "One week, rush. What did that mean to you? To me it meant take Lish out in one day, maybe two, possibly three. Five at the outside, and after that you start to worry. Now we have ten, and no performance?"

Reva, calling from her room in Lish's villa, squelched the volume on the comlink. She didn't want this to carry outside the room.

"You've cost me, with this no-performance shit."

"Then you should have specified a half-week, instead of a week."

"That's crap. How could you get this done in five days if you couldn't do it in ten?"

She had no answer for that, and Harric's voice became frosty. "By leaving that bitch alive you cost me a Holdout operation and not a few global connections you can't begin to imagine the importance of. No, you're not getting another week."

She felt her heart drop right into the pit of her stomach, and panicked urgency stressed her voice. "Wait, Adahn. I can make this up to you—"

"You can't make up shit. Dammit, I want eye to eye for this." He stabbed a transmit key, and for the first time she viewed his face. Heavy-browed, florid, cold-eyed. An almost distinguished-looking man, but for the temper that curled his lips and made him seem coarse and cruel.

"I'm canceling this contract, and I want my money back. Now."

It took all of Reva's nerve not to reveal dismay on her face. Her husky voice nearly cracked as she told him, "I can't do that."

Harric's scowl deepened. "You won't return my advance?"

"I can't. I don't have it all."

His expression went blank so fast it looked like a curtain had dropped across his features. "Failed performance. And now you keep my money?"

"I can give you back half."

"Not good enough. I don't tolerate this. You're never working for me again."

"Oh, come on, Adahn." She tried to cajole the man, realizing that Lish's safety depended upon her reaching an understanding with him. "Isn't that a bit extreme? I've never let you down before."

"So the first time you do, you cost me more in one week than you would ever have made from me in contracts, if you worked your life long to do it. I can't afford you anymore, even if it is only 100k a hit."

She took offense at that. "Then maybe I should up my rates," she sniped, forgetting the need to charm the man. It seemed too late for that, anyway.

She was right. "Up anything you want," he retorted. "You won't be doing it with me or my organization. Don't call me again."

Her mouth dropped as his image vanished from the screen.

Yavobo sat before Harric, erect and proud of bearing. "Your time is up," the warrior declared first. "Have you decided how I might demonstrate my merit?"

"Indeed." Harric nodded, then gestured to Yavobo's foot, now healed. "I understand that injury was done you by this Reva?"

"Yes. And my hand, and other wounds. Healed, now."

"But not forgotten."

"Not forgotten," the alien said coldly.

"Let me ask you this," Harric said. "Do you seek this assassin only because of your Blood Oath? Or—"

"Is that not enough?" Yavobo sounded distant and offended.

"Let me finish, please. Or do you seek her also for personal injury done to you?"

The alien sat with preternatural stillness before answering. "Both," he finally said. "What is it to you?"

Harric offered a half-bow from his chair. "Because she has injured me as well. Not in body, but in spirit. So I understand your need for revenge, and will help you in it as far as I may."

Yavobo was quick to pick up on the nuance. "As far as you may? How far is that?"

"First is the demonstration of merit you have agreed to perform," Adahn replied. "And here is the task that will show it. There is a smuggler on Selmun III, a woman called Lish. She must be destroyed."

"I know her."

Harric heard that, felt unsettled. "You do?"

"I encountered her when seeking Reva. They know each other."

"Do they?" The depth of the assassin's deceit came suddenly clear to Adahn, and he was doubly glad of the course of action he had decided on. "Then, my friend, it is this simple. Kill Lish, and I will give you Reva." Janus would know ways to contact the assassin; that was not an empty promise.

Yavobo smiled in turn. Kill Lish? Friend to the honorless thin-skin, and purveyor of disreputable weapons—thus honorless herself? His wicked canines gleamed in the light.

"It will be a pleasure," he said.

Farewells had been said. It was time for the *Fortune* to lift for Tion.

Devin made himself comfortable in the Captain's chair. He pulled a neural interface cable from the linkbox, slotting it into the rigger implant concealed spacer fashion at the base of his skull. With a physical touch, he activated key systems on the console before him. Ship's units came alive, computers and AI flashing online, a cybernetwork linking them all. Each function blended with Shiran's perceptions, his consciousness becoming brain to the electronic body surging to life about him.

Instrument readouts offered intuitive knowledge, data absorbed without the effort of thought. Mechanical impulses were recast into reflexes that twitched Devin's fingertips; sensors and monitoring systems extended the man's senses until the cycling of air pumps felt like the rushing of oxygen in and out of his own lungs. The sensor image of the landing field and nearby airspace became a spectral overlay to his vision, a picture that a squint could bring into surreal existence and instinctive comprehension.

The spacer smiled happily. Wrapped in the consciousness of his ship, he became in part the ship itself.

Mershon-class freighters could be piloted by physical controls alone. But for this, the virgin flight of his first owned command, Devin wanted to experience every nuance of the *Fortune*'s travel. The cybersystem linked Captain to vessel in an intimate embrace, allowing him to make sure all was well as newly repaired systems were engaged and flight-stressed for the first time.

In the primary drive unit aft, Zay was jacked into the power rigger position in Engineering. "Systems online and flight-ready," she responded to the Captain's spoken query. Zay shared a limited analog of Devin's perception: a realm of batteries and generators, the controlled reactions of irradiated power crystals that would break the bonds of gravity and hurl the vessel through space. She settled into her position and awaited the command to lift.

Next to Devin, Sergeant Eklun sat in the navigator's seat before sensor arrays, comconsole, environmental settings. His was an unrigged position. The former Imperial Marine needed only to handle physical settings on controls, and be ready to serve as gunner or troubleshooter should difficulties arise on their voyage.

"Nav systems online," Eklun reported. "Sensors online. Pad cleared. All secure and ready to lift."

The Captain acknowledged the routine checklist with a nod. "Prepare to lift."

On his command, Zay upped output on the repulsor pads. The *Fortune* rose from Akatnu Field and climbed into the clouds high overhead. There was a slight physical jarring, and the tug of acceleration vanished as gravplates and inertial compensators engaged.

"*Fortune,* you are clear for transition," said Selmun Traffic.

"Aye, Traffic. Transitioning now."

Zay nudged the maneuver function of the freighter's engines. The Calyx-Primes came alive and the ship abruptly changed her path of travel, from repulsor-driven lift to forward-powered thrust. The vessel shot skyward in an ascending arc that would place her in the orbital traffic pattern.

Devin rested his hands gently on the flight controls. When piloting rigged, manual guidance was not needed, but he found the grip reassuring. He concentrated on the freighter's ascent, shadowing her modest in-flight maneuvers with small, practiced movements of his hands.

The waterworld shrank into a green-blue globe beneath them, and Shiran Devin smiled contentedly as he ushered his ship into space.

Reva found Vask in the kitchen, joking with two Skiffjammers come in for a late lunch.

"Hey, Fixer," she called out. "You want to do some work for me?"

For all the angling he'd done, nothing yet had persuaded the assassin to spend time with him, professionally or otherwise. The unexpected invitation left him looking exactly like a Fixer who had finally landed a long-coveted job.

He left the street muscle and followed Reva toward the door. "What's up?"

"I need a weapon or two," she said. "Something special. I'll tell you about it on the way." She palmed the door and the pair walked to the air car reserved for her use.

She had changed clothes, once more wearing the nondescript gray bodysuit, with hair more black than brown. Her nails remained scarlet, though, and the restless, haunted mien was gone from her face. Now the assassin wore a look of serious determination. It was the concentrated focus, had Kastlin but known it, that Reva assumed before doing a hit.

This time there was no hit planned, but something every bit as consuming of self: keeping Lish alive until the ocean meet with Edesz was complete. The break with Adahn could be worried over at a later time. For now Harric's intent to have the smuggler killed presented a tactical problem, clear and simple.

It was a problem Reva didn't plan on discussing with Lish.

She put the air car in flight mode and headed toward Amasl. Kastlin looked a question toward her, wondering why the haste. She was too lost in thought to notice.

I told her I'd get an extra week, Reva argued logic with herself. *How can I say I failed? If what I tell her isn't believable she'll lose confidence in me.*

It was clear the Holdout had only agreed to leave R'debh for a time because of Reva's expertise in these matters. If she doubted, if she wanted to quibble with the best way to handle things, she'd end up dead.

Keeping her in ignorance of her continued danger was a calculated risk, but Reva knew she'd been chosen for the initial hit contract partly because she was already on Selmun III. Adahn would bring in outside talent to finish this job, she was certain of it: he wouldn't let Lish go, nor would he do the hit with locals. He never did.

That gives us some time, Reva thought, before she's a target again.

"So, are you going to tell me about it?" Kastlin interrupted her thoughts.

"Tell you—?" Reva switched mental gears to talk with the Fixer. "Oh. Weapons. I want a few more weapons, besides the blade I carry. Maybe you can make some suggestions."

"I'll try. What are your needs?"

Reva tapped long-nailed fingers on the steering yoke. She didn't like to carry too much equipment; she who could step between Lines to do a hit rarely needed more than the element of surprise and her bare hands to effect a death. Protecting someone, though—that was different. She might be called upon to fight with little advance warning, and no time to maneuver.

"I need something small, concealable—if someone looks at me. I don't want it obvious that I'm armed, even if I'm ready to attack. Maybe something that acts like a missile weapon at short range, so I can strike without having to close in." Security mechs and the right kind of perimeter alarms could warn of approaching dangers; it was the unexpected appearing suddenly in or near arm's reach that she was concerned about. Of all people, she knew best how deadly such close-range attack could be.

"Multiple-shot or single-use?" the Fixer asked.

Reva shrugged. "A mix of both, maybe? I don't expect to have a firefight. I want the element of surprise, and I want a second shot in case the first one isn't enough."

"How about a gun implant?" he suggested.

Reva wrinkled her nose in dislike. "No cyberweapons," she said. "I'm not rigged, and I don't want to be. Implants are out."

"That's harder, then." Vask thought a while longer. "Would you consider a flechette plate?"

Reva knew a lot of techno-trivia, but that one was new to her. "What's that?" she asked.

"It's a finger-wide plate, articulated in three pieces, surgically attached to the inside of your middle finger." He pointed to his middle digit on the side next to the index finger. "It can be installed outside the skin, or subdermally. Either way, it's hard to notice until you use it."

"How's it work?"

"When you straighten your first two fingers together and tense the muscles, the plate segments lock in place, making one straight unit. Then, when you bend the index finger downward, the flechette is fired."

"Through the skin? Ouch."

"Yeah, if it's internal, it will cut you, but it's nothing more than a small knife slice. Externally mounted, you wouldn't notice anything. Fires up to three flechettes, one at a time as you flex the index finger."

That had possibilities. "Range and damage?" Reva asked.

"Accurate to four or five meters. Damage—well, that depends on how you aim. The blades have a monomolecular edge, so they're deadly sharp. They carry a microcharge that detonates when forward momentum stops. Does about twice the damage of a standard projectile from a needle gun. Same principle, really: a good hit in a vital organ will kill or at least drop your target right there."

"Interesting. That's not a cyberimplant, is it?"

"Not in its basic model. Anchors to bone. It's activated by tendons and powered by a bio-electric feed."

"Don't like that," grunted the assassin. There would be no leads and wires leeching energy from her nervous system, whether they were intelligent implants or otherwise. "Can you get one powered by a battery?"

"I suppose, yeah, a milli-erg button could be used. It would probably be nested at the base of your middle finger."

"Sounds good, then. Get me one of those."

The domes of Amasl's harbor complex were coming into sight; she engaged the navlock that would integrate them into the city's air traffic pattern, and lead to public parking near the skiff marina. That task done, she took her attention off piloting, and came back to the question of weaponry.

"Between flechette plate and knife I'd have two tools that cut through a personal energy screen but are hindered by armor. How about an energy weapon that'll pierce armor? Something small, like a holdout gun?"

Vask brightened. "I know just the thing. What about a Sundragon?"

Sundragon, Sundragon . . . the assassin tried to place the name, something heard once on a Lyndir vert for private protection—the image came to mind, and she shared the Fixer's smile.

A single-shot energy weapon, the Sundragon resembled a writing stylus and was as easily concealed as one. Aim, squeeze once to remove the safety, squeeze again to fire, and an ion beam blasted from the tip. Not an ordinary beam, either, but a double-energy blast from the overcharged resonant crystal that powered the Sundragon. The crystal was shattered in the discharge, but by then the device had hopefully done its work.

The Sundragon could drop a dolophant within its effective range of ten or fifteen meters. "That's perfect," Reva agreed. "Get me one of those, too."

"How soon do you want them?"

"By tomorrow morning. I want the plate installed at a tech shop first thing—you make the arrangements and let me know when to be there, but make sure it's a good place. I don't want to pay for cheap blackwire work."

Vask looked hurt. "Never. What I broker is top-grade, always."

"We'll see." Their car circled and banked for a landing, coming under Reva's guidance in the last twenty meters to drop into a parking spot of her choosing. She set down at the end of the lot near the magtube station. "How long do you need to deal?"

Vask shrugged. "Won't know 'til I start."

Reva cut the power and the car settled to the ground. "Tell you what. I'll be back here in about four or five hours. If you're done by then, meet me here, and we can ride back together."

He agreed. Moments later, they went their separate ways and Vask stepped into the nearby magtube tunnel. He was not long out of sight, however, before he moved effortlessly into the blindspot mode. Retracing his steps, he spotted the assassin some thirty meters distant and moving away from him.

He could always get the clandestine weapons later, acquired with the help of Internal Security, if necessary. Now was the time to see what occupied Reva on this, her first jaunt outside the villa since her days of moody brooding had begun. It was for this that he had reserved his psionic powers, saving them for a time when trailing her seemed worthwhile. Hurrying to close with his quarry, he followed along behind, unseen and undetected.

Devin took final astrogation bearings above the plane of the Selmun system, and initiated calculations for their course through warp space.

The feel he gained for the process, bleeding through cyberlinks from the navcomp, was nothing like the explanation of warp travel taught in dirtside schools. A ship generates a warp bubble, so common wisdom would have it, and sits nested safely inside while space itself slips past the hull.

That was a gross oversimplification, he knew. In warp, you were in another dimension, literally, fallen into the interstices between physical reality and the multiverse that bound it all together. Warp space had a reality and substance of its own, though it was a twisting, mind-bending dimension difficult to perceive or comprehend. It could drive a person insane if exposed to it without adequate protections. To transit warp safely, you needed to travel wisely, and hope for a dash of good luck on your side.

Jump ships hopped in and out of warp, skimming that dimension too briefly for its hazards to be a real threat. But continuous warp vessels—like the *Fortune*—could encounter real problems in that extraspatial void. There were things *beyond,* things native to the warp region, that could fatally interrupt a ship's voyage.

Patrolled space lanes were the safest routes to take—and the most roundabout. It would take twelve days to reach Tion by established lanes, and that was not an option on this run. Instead, their route curved spinward, past Lyndir, past the Claw nebula, and finally looped coreward to Tion. Devin confirmed the navcomp plot. The course would get them there in little more than three days.

"Prepare to warp," he warned the crew, then gave a mental command through his rigger jack. Space twisted around the freighter. Stars smeared and stretched into thin lines; then the transition to warp was complete. Visual compensators engaged, and viewscreens displayed a twisting gray fog dotted with muted blurs of yellow and orange lights. It was a computer analogue of extradimensional space, with orange for stars below the plane of the galactic equator, yellow for those above. It was nothing like the real thing that hugged the hull of their ship, but a safe and neutral illusion for the fragile human minds buffered inside the skin of the *Fortune*.

The engines had transitioned to warp smoothly; systems felt tight to Devin's rigged senses.

They were on their way to Tion.

Reva followed a seemingly random path through waterfront dives, ships' outfitters, receiving docks, a body sculpting and tattoo parlor, and one blackwire shop. Each stop, each round of questions and greased palms, led her closer to her goal: the local Street Weasel, the Watchman who worked the Lairdomes around the marina. His gutternsnipes were the skimmer-heisting, wheedling, drug-peddling children and youths who loitered near the skiff marina fence and the warehouses. They were not yet derevin, but were too street-hardened to be destined for much else.

Long before she found the Weasel, she had that odd sensation again. Hairs rose on the back of her neck, as if she were being watched. She coped with the annoyance as she had before, slipping between Lines, walking along a shadow of the Mainline she had worked so hard to stay in.

That was where Vask lost her—and where he finally found her again.

The assassin cut between two buildings, out of sight of onlookers. When Kastlin entered the alley a moment later, she was gone from sight. It was too fast, too neat, with no place to hide.

Finally alert to how she must have vanished, the IntSec agent followed suit. As rapidly as he had ever done, he let himself go into the sideslip state, hoping to catch sight of her in the ethereal world of unphased matter. He would have to hang back, for blindspotting was not possible in the energy-shifted mode, and two unphased persons appear as solid reality to each other while all around them is insubstantial.

He glimpsed Reva down a misty alleyway, and hurried to catch up. But the assassin was not as he expected to find her, and he slowed cautiously as he neared her ghostly form. That much was wrong, eerily wrong. He glanced at his hands, solid-seeming to the phase-shifted observer; she should look that way, too. But she did not.

Reva was barely visible to the Mutate's eye. He stared unbelieving at her shimmering figure, a shifting blur that sometimes appeared as one person, sometimes two or three, each overlaid one upon the other so they often moved as one. The assassin seemed to be in some realm beyond the sideslip, existing in a different vibrational frequency altogether.

No wonder I was never able to find her, he thought in amazement. What in the seven hells is she doing?

The agent followed as she walked past loading docks, moving around objects that Vask's incorporeal form could pass right through. It seemed as if she were limited by the physical landscape before her, yet in some manner transcended it.

It made no sense to the Psionicist at all, and he trailed her mostly by good luck and guesswork. Sometimes her blurred form was easy to follow; at other times she vanished entirely from sight, to reappear as suddenly several steps ahead or a moment later. Finally she faded from the shifted state completely, but this time her slow blend back into the physical clued Vask to what was happening. Being careful to shift down directly into a place of concealment, he left the otherworldly state of the sideslip as well. He moved into a blindspot and eavesdropped on Reva one more time.

The assassin scowled in discomfort. Her short jaunt between the Lines had not dispelled that crawling feeling. . . .

The Watchman took the frown as intended for himself. It wasn't a good way to start business, not with this one.

"I remember you," he said slowly. "What would a professional like yourself be wanting with the Kipper's crew?"

The last the Kipper knew of her, Holdout was her line. One who could hire a derevin for jobs, no need of street rats. No wonder he watched her with guarded curiosity.

"You've got eyes on the street," Reva said.

The Kipper shrugged. "So have the big boys." He meant the derevin.

She shook her head, a smile touching only her lips. "Your eyes are more discreet. Less noticed, wouldn't you agree?"

"Maybe so," he conceded.

"Then let's deal."

It took a while, but bargaining with the Watchman was pretty straightforward. When Comax Shipping reopened its doors, the surrounding streets and the customer traffic would be observed by the Kipper's ubiquitous street children. Hanging out, as usual; overlooked, as usual.

All for a price that was far less than a week's worth of Skiffjammer protection. Reva paid in advance, and left the Weasel thanking the Sea Father for his good fortune.

LXXXIII

Naturally Dorleoni scientists would choose Selmun III as their meeting place. A convention with the theme of optimizing marine lifeforms could hardly go anywhere else. Some convention-goers even planned to swim in the rich ocean water, to see whether its unpleasant flavor and cloying substance was rumor or accurate report from others of their race.

One of their number already knew the truth of the ocean water's feel, and had no desire to repeat his earlier experiences in that line. Okorr ducked out on his fellow travelers, right inside the starport's busy kiosk and shop area. As Dorleoni followed their guide to a waiting transport van, their wayward companion sought the comfort stations, and stayed there for entirely too long.

One hour later, a platinum-pigtailed MazeRat knocked tentatively on the door of his fresher booth.

"Come on," said the MazeRat. "Gerick's waiting for you."

"It took you long enough to get here," a sullen complaint came in response. The door opened to reveal a walrus-faced alien who thrust his carrybag at the street thug. "Carry this, will you? I am grown tired of it."

It contained his identification as scientist and conventioneer, and none of the contents mattered to him anymore. He was already past the Customs checkpoint, where ID verification and random checks of retina prints were the only real obstacle to his return to R'debh. The prints of Okorr's eyes were unknown here, and there was no way they would show up on the Selmun III computers.

Then again, Okorr's eyes were new to their wearer as well. They had been in the Dorleoni's head for barely two weeks, after an unwelcome transplant operation had removed his old orbs and hands and supplanted them with the organs and paws of his unwilling body double. He had to give Adahn credit, though: when it really mattered, the Tribune of the Red Hand was endlessly—if repulsively—inventive.

The short-furred alien formerly called Karuu stumped after his MazeRat escort. He was soon tucked into a private air car and driven off into the side streets of Amasl.

LXXXIV

Wee'ska had strayed from the pod, wending past coral-grown islands and skirting kelp patches, making her way on dull, unthinking instinct into deeper water. Brightfang, her handler, noticed her departure, and followed his life-friend eastward into the deep. Sometimes such sulks and moods took Handler and borgbeast away from the pod for a time; the others continued on their way, knowing that the pair would rejoin them when the matter was settled, and Wee'ska soothed back into cooperation with her mates.

Brightfang knew something greater was amiss when Wee'ska ignored his croons and demanding clicks, and continued her journey propelled by languid strokes of her tail flukes. She had her mind set on going away. This time, unlike the others, Brightfang detected a morbid single-mindedness to his life-friend's efforts.

O Waterlords, give her hope, he thought. He knew her illness, her tiredness of spirit and body, and shared much of it himself. But this unerring migration into the depths could betoken only one thing, something neither he nor the other handlers had anticipated in life-friends still so young and able.

It was *ekikeku,* the death-swim, the final distancing wherein a dying creature drew predators and scavengers to itself. A swift end, which kept the podmates safe and abbreviated the failing one's misery.

Brightfang followed Wee'ska's descent through downsloping ravines, hurried to keep sight of her where the light faltered at depth. There were no sizable predators in the R'debh waters, none to ease the borgbeast's passing. Her end would be lingering and slow, a doom of starvation or the slow madness of disorientation and loneliness, far from the solace of her pod.

The handler paused, crooned, and whistled back news of his task to Sharptooth and the others. They would understand he must be by her side for this event. If he could not persuade his life-friend to continue with the others, he must ease her passage from this life. Somehow.

The ghost-ray neared one of the sounds, a rasping scream in a pitch heard more with the soul than with the sound-sensing membrane of near-incorporeal hide. The Sea Father of R'debh slowed and stopped in a broad deepwater valley, hanging there in darkling waters, phosphorescent motes aswirl in his wake.

For the first time he saw what had disturbed his sleep, that which had called to him from half a world away. A slab-headed creature, nearly the length of one of the ray's wings, sizable for the puny lifeforms on this world—*no.* Not from this world, that was it, the strangeness about her. She radiated unnatural frequencies, from the broadband static of her brain to the strangely modulated pulsation of three hearts.

And beneath it all, the groan. The cry of illness and despair that had drawn the Sea Father on, even when interest had waned and curiosity had dulled to indifference. A plaguesome sound, that, a moan from the heart, a disharmony like none that should disorder the sea song of R'debh. And with this one, unlike the others of its kind, the moan had deepened, become a plea to die.

Responding to that need, the ghost-ray obliged. Moving through the water, he phased halfway out of the physical sea. A massive ripple of displaced ocean pulsed ahead of him, but not enough to shove Wee'ska out of the way. Before the borgbeast's huge body could be pushed far aside by the sudden current, she was enveloped by the ghost-ray, the semimaterial wings wrapping about her in a embrace of water and phosphorescence.

Then the Sea Father completed his shift to elsewhere, and took the leviathan with him.

Brightfang, caught on the edge of the phase effect, was stunned. The biochemical changes set off in his brain would have caused visions in a man; in the handler, they triggered excessive neural activity far beyond the being's ability to cope. Brightfang died of a seizure that affected his nervous system, then shut down his overloaded heart.

His podmates shared the moment of his passing, and stopped in midocean to gather, trembling, and seek comfort in each other's company. They sang the far-call, urgent and demanding, but of Wee'ska and Brightfang there was no further trace.

The handlers looked at one another, and were afraid.

"No," Gerick said firmly. "You don't need street muscle."

Karuu stood in the harborside office and glared at his antagonist. It was time to switch tactics.

With difficulty he smoothed the displeasure from his face. "I cannot be spending all my time on the waterfront and in office buildings," the squat alien explained in a conciliatory tone. "Okorr's movement in those circles would bring too much notice."

"Maybe so," Gerick grudgingly admitted.

"You see? I need a derevin to approach people, to courier, to deliver presents that persuade cooperation." "Presents" like blackmail or drugs, or gifts of appreciation that started small and became large over time. "You few MazeRats alone will not be sufficient for this."

Adahn's lieutenant hated to give in, but he saw the logic of the Holdout's argument. Gerick decided swiftly. "Alright, Karuu, I see your point. You wanted the Dockboys?"

"Yes," the Holdout agreed promptly. A young, inconsequential group he could mold into the shape he wanted.

"We'll have them signed up by tomorrow," Gerick decided, and put the matter behind him. "Now, this other thing—"

"Lish?"

"Yes." The MazeRat's face hardened. "Hands off. Mr. Harric is taking care of the matter, and that's all you need to know." A cold smile played about his lips. "If you defy his wishes in this, I'll kill you."

That startled the Dorleoni and he looked up into Gerick's unsettling eyes, one steely blue, the other an inhuman glowing green orb. Karuu believed the threat.

"She is yours to deal with, as you say," he conceded. "I am washing my hands of her."

"That's smart." The MazeRat motioned Karuu to his feet, and ushered the Dorleoni to the door. "Now you can start your work smoothing things over with Customs."

He left the alien abruptly on the walkway outside. Karuu bristled again. He was not a flunky, to be beckoned and dismissed at the derevin leader's whim. This time he bared his tusks, and didn't care who saw.

LXXXVI

Lish relocated to the waterfront. Reva began to prowl as much as she had in the Evriness estate, though for a different reason. Vask accompanied her, or walked a circuit she directed him to. The assassin didn't elaborate on what danger she felt threatened the Holdout, but her caution spoke for itself. For once she did not turn his help down. They both sensed that danger waited, not knowing where or when it would strike.

The waiting got on her nerves, she who had always been the initiator. Now she understood how Yavobo must have felt. He had been a hunter, too, not a guard.

It's far easier to chase your prey, she thought, than to protect it from unknown dangers.

She suppressed a shudder and kicked a piece of shattered cryocase off the edge of a dock, barely hearing it splash into the water below. Good riddance to Yavobo. We finally saw who was the better hunter there, didn't we?

She allowed herself a satisfied smile. That moment, when the bomb exploded, and the alien was blasted along with her target . . . Reva was not one to revel in gore. Most of her kills were clean and neat. But the Aztrakhani, who had caused her pain—*worse, admit it, Reva, scared the hell out of you*—that was one death she was happy to review in her mind's eye. And to take caution from.

Never let your prey outsmart you, she thought. They can, and do, fight back.

Whoever was coming for Lish would learn that, soon enough.

LXXXVII

Yavobo headed for the *Ocello,* a midsized trader chartered for a run to Selmun III. Once aboard, he went directly to the cold-storage units. The fifth freezer box gaped open, awaiting the alien who would travel inside.

It was a necessary evil. His earlier, precipitous departure from the waterworld had flagged his records in that star system. If he returned openly, he would be detained for questioning.

In this case, there was no other way to avoid the bureaucratic queries that could delay or ensnare him; no other way to close quickly with Reva, his ultimate target.

The warrior knew what to expect, but that did not lessen the discomfort of lying inside a cryobox too short for his height, knees drawn up and tucked close. Cryomonitors and AI could compensate for his alien biology, but human engineering made no allowances in the sizing of his chilly coffin.

Monitor patches were affixed to his skin, the lid lowered and vac-sealed around the edges with ear-popping suction. A gaseous hiss was the last thing the bounty hunter remembered before he fell asleep, drugged into a depressed metabolic rate before the freezer cycle began.

The bounty hunter feared neither discomfort nor danger. It was not until the lid closed on him that he thought of being buried alive, but he passed out before he could act on the panic swelling up within his breast.

LXXXVIII

Tion was a crumbling capital world of pleasure gardens and moldering palaces—a place where disused government buildings sold cheaply, where buyers rediscovered the research facilities once employed in the Satraps' Genewar. Those facilities were refurbished and leased to commercial geneers, spurring an influx of biotech, nanotech, genetech industries to the faded subsector capital.

The Camisq were hardly the only providers of nanotech on Tion. Sa'adani and CAS Sector citizens went there for things that cybertechnology could not provide: body shaping, organically enhanced intelligence or reflexes, crafting of functional or inherited genes, baby-tailoring, and more. The services for humans were myriad, and a market catering to alien species was growing up in its shadow.

Devin turned a blind eye to the sculpting stores that littered the avenue. He liked himself just as he was, and this trip allowed no time to explore the diversions of the city, even had he been inclined to do so. He concentrated instead on the drive to the Camisq mission, where a mecho led him and Eklun to the subterranean laboratories where their nanotech product had been crafted. Their wait had stretched out for nearly an hour, but Devin hadn't been pacing long when a high-pitched buzzing interrupted his circuit of the room.

"Youuuu arrr frrrummm Lan-zzzig-g-g?"

The two men faced a door that had opened in the seamless wall of the lounge. A creature taller than a man stood there, half humanoid in form, half resembling an overgrown grasshopper. The legs were segmented, arms were cocked in the style of a mantis, and vestigial wings hugged its back. It appeared part exoskeletal, part flesh-articulated, a bastard combination that made the Camisq seem like an engineered creature. For all Devin knew, it might be. Its speech was full of whirs and clicks. It repeated its phrase before the two men could quit staring and comprehend its words.

"You are from Lanzig?" it asked again. With concentration its meaning became clear.

"We are," Devin replied.

"We apologize for the delay. We had to verify a final calculation. One moment, please." The Camisq rubbed its leg spars together, giving a peculiar vibrating flexion to the skeletal members. A musical trill resulted, like that of a giant cricket. The alien stood aside, and three smaller versions of itself came into the lounge, bearing an opened shipping case between them.

The smaller Camisq seemed more insectoid than the speaker, half the height of a man, with thicker chitin and heavier wings that lifted and flexed off the surface of the back. The drones set the case down before the Captain, and one raised the rack of flasks nestled inside.

The taller alien approached. "Eight large doses have been prepared, two per flask. These are for the borgbeasts. The last flask holds sufficient quantity for the Vernoi handlers. We have verified contents and stability for shipping. When sealed, the stasis field will engage. Your export license and tariff receipts are already coded into the case's datapad."

"What is this calculation you had to verify?" Devin asked.

The Camisq trilled again to her drones, and they began to secure the case for shipping. "Administering this to adult borgbeasts requires injection of product into a food animal and feeding it to the beast. We were verifying dosage calculations—"

An inquiring trill from a drone interrupted her. She clicked a response, and the drone activated the stasis field in the container.

Before she could get back to her topic, Devin and Eklun moved toward the delivered product. "If it's all in the datapad, I'm sure we can figure it out later," Devin forestalled further conversation. "Thank you for your help, though, and seeing to such details for us." He offered the half-bow reserved for the conclusion of a mutually satisfying trade; together he and Eklun hoisted the container and walked it back to the lift. The Camisq called Esksk-Prime clicked, and one of her drones detached from the virz, rushing to show the humans the switch that activated an imbedded repulsor strip. With a nudge, the box floated alongside its human escort.

"Farewell, then," Prime told her customers. "One-Virz will see you to the surface."

The drone escorted the emissaries through the bunkers to the lift. As they ascended, One-Virz became quiescent, soon abandoning attempts at conversation. The virz-member saw them to the exit of the palace. As the Camisq fragment withdrew to seek its nestmates, Devin and Sergeant Eklun settled the precious cargo in their car, and headed directly back to the *Fortune*.

LXXXIX

Deep, bone-seated chill.

A cold with such a grip upon the limbs that jaws clamped tight in rictus, not warm enough even to chatter.

Dull recognition of light. Meaningless sounds. Being heaved upright to sit, then guided in a staggering circle in imitation of a walk, until something like sensibility returned.

Yavobo emerged from coldsleep, his desert-born metabolism protesting against the unnatural strain of cryogenesis. A torture more effective than the bite of sandlurks, more insidious than dust-lung. A torture unconceived of by the Aztrakhani, though one that would be fondly used, should they gain any notion of its potential for nonfatal discomfort.

The warrior sat far longer than a man would have, his metabolism reacting grudgingly to stimuli designed for human biology. Warm beverages in the stomach meant little to a torsal landscape dominated by cooling-efficient lungs. Steam-heated air would have been more effective in reviving the alien, but that was a recommendation the cryotech remarked on only in afterthought.

In due time the red- and black-skinned Aztrakhani stood under his own power, causing a collective breath of relief to rise from his assembled caretakers. A quarter-day later he was fully functional once more, no longer stumbling, no longer staring at his surroundings in owlish disrecognition. The bounty hunter left the waterfront, equipped by Harric's henchmen, given money and contact information for the MazeRats who would be at his disposal should he need them. Yavobo's spirits took longer to recover, surrounded as he was with the damp, cloying air and the sea-scent of R'debh's all-pervasive blanket of moisture.

Then, in the midst of his brooding, he was forced to grin to himself, a predatorial baring of fangs that caused passersby to skirt him on the walkway. Soon enough he would taste the last of this foul planet's atmosphere. Soon enough he would be shut off from its thousand inconveniences, from food, to stenches, to water-loving thinskins. Shortly, he would have his prey. He growled to himself, nostrils flaring in a snarling purr of exultation.

Yavobo was on the hunt once more.

XC

Devin triggered the crew alert with barely a conscious thought, recognizing from personal experience what sensors had just detected.

It was a stelloid, one of the several denizens of warped space: a creature like a small sun, of fusioning plasma and unlikely energy frequencies, casting off twisted harmonics barely traceable in the otherspace of warp.

There was no question it was some kind of intelligent life-form. The miniature suns acted with motivation and cunning to satisfy one clear need: hunger. Some preferred mass, to be converted into energy, and so favored the substances of hulls or the organics concealed within. Others were drawn to the radiant discharge of a warp engine or worse, the resonant crystal reactions dimly perceived within the drives themselves.

There was no communicating with such a creature, too alien to understand, too vastly different from organic sentience to reason with. Sometimes they could be bribed with jettisoned reactive crystals, lured off from the fleeing tidbit that a warp-driven ship represented. Other times they must be beaten off, jabbed with unpleasant spikes of energy delivered at distance by ship's guns or missiles.

The alarm roused Eklun, who ran from crew unit to transport outtake, from there a leaping step into the gunner's bounce tube. A moment later he was in Gunnery One, overhead and to the rear of the flight deck. The sergeant strapped into the gunner's couch and freed the gimbal lock of the laser turret.

Warp space hugged the gun turret like glistening streaks of oil on dirty water, an unclean aurora that twisted the gut if you looked at it too long. Eklun kept eyes averted while he donned his com helmet and flipped down the warp visor to compensate his vision.

The impossible void beyond the turret smoothed into a multilayered gray abyss for the gunner. He powered up his weapons module. "Gun One online," he spoke into the headset, jacking into the fire-rigger system with one hand.

"Stand by." It was all Devin had to say for long minutes to come.

The *Fortune* turned her heading away from the energy predator, but the miniature star continued to close. The warp creature radiated in the visible yellow spectrum, looking for all the world like a smaller version of the sunny primary they had just left behind at Tion.

Devin poured power to the engines, but still it drew closer.

Captain and crew had no choice then but to wait in strained silence until the stelloid came in close range—necessary for the outmoded guns they mounted. Eklun's low-power laser fired a spear of energy, a brilliant ruby beam aimed at the core of the aggressor. One laser burst; a second; a third. The miniature sun seemed to recoil, then came on stronger than before. It dropped behind the *Fortune,* directly in its drive trail, and out of the line of fire from manned or automated guns. Before the ship could maneuver to bring weapons to bear, the stelloid attacked.

It looked a massive energy discharge, plasma flaring and lightning coruscating over the aft shields, ionizing the hull beneath. It attacked again, and the freighter shuddered, taking another hit against the energy screen that protected it. One aft shield failed completely. The creature darted in to discharge against the exposed hull, as close as it could get to the resonant crystals in Drive Two.

The Captain sensed the stelloid's closing movement. If its next attack damaged the integrity of Drive One, Zay would die in vacuum. With crippled engines, they would be at the stelloid's mercy.

Their alternative was to drop out of warp abruptly, that hazardous maneuver every spacer hated to contemplate. It could take days, even weeks, to reorient, repair damage, and return to R'debh. Far too late to help Lish.

The yellow stelloid made the decision for them, vaporizing the hull protecting Drive Two's warp reactor. The engines staggered in mid-reaction as drive crystals shattered. The ship's warp bubble shrank to half its volume, rocking the *Fortune* with a sudden half warp, half real-space shift that threatened to tear the vessel apart.

The stelloid vanished as the freighter was jerked sidelong through one of the interstices of the dimensional space around her.

Alarms screamed and safeties shut systems down. Warp failure seemed imminent, but the gray twisting swirls of other-space remained on the viewscreen, and the clamor of systems status told Devin why. They had one crippled engine keeping them in warp, though the reaction creating that bubble was dangerously erratic. There was a hot-list of systems damage; subspace communications were down, and maneuver control was reduced to a minimum.

If they cut that drive to drop into normal space, there would be phase-shift effects from the erratic warp field that the weakened hull could not withstand.

"Lords of Ice," Devin muttered. Unthinking, his voice carried over crew headsets.

They were running on one engine in a ship that could not call for help. The hull could not handle the transition to real space, and the drive could not keep them adequately on course. Every spacer's nightmare had come true for Devin and his small crew.

The *Fortune* was stranded in warp.

XCI

His appearance was distinctive, and he had been there with murderous intent once before. Yavobo would not approach Comax Shipping directly, for he had no doubt that Lish had improved her security. The Skiffjammers he had seen on his last visit had assured him of that.

What other changes had she made? Where did she live? What were her movements?

They were simple questions, straightforward ones the bounty

hunter had to answer before he could eliminate the Holdout who stood between him and Reva. The difficulty was that he could not risk detection. Tipping his hand, giving a hint that he was stalking Lish or planned to infiltrate the Lairdome—that would be the mistake of an unblooded hunter.

It was a problem he had dealt with many times before—almost every time he had hunted a quarry, in fact. His tactics this time were similar. He observed at night, from a distance, from rooftops and neighboring domes, and once from an air car skirting the harbor. But he had no time or desire to make the leisurely stalk he would normally pursue. The sooner the honorless smuggler was out of the way, the sooner Yavobo could fulfill his Blood Oath. He chose, then to take a shortcut, the simplest and quickest way he knew of discovering information.

Through a MazeRat he rented a room not far from the harbor, close to boat shelters and tenements. Again through intermediaries, he bought certain basic supplies, and prepared his retreat. Then, initial observations made, he selected his target and moved ahead with his plan. In the darkness of an overcast night, the Aztrakhani stalked a perimeter guard.

The desert-born fighter leapt upon the thin-skin from behind. The tactical jammer at his belt blocked the guard's comlink and his weight bore the Skiffjammer to the ground. The Aztrakhani's strength was great enough to keep him there, long arms giving superior leverage for the neck squeeze that sank the man into unconsciousness.

Humans had such vulnerable areas on their anatomy, Yavobo observed. It was amazing they survived in combat at all. Discarding the man's blastrifle and quickly slicing off his equipment webbing, he slung the body over his shoulder and ran off into the waterfront alleys. Into a waiting car, then into the storage shed next to the rented room, and the thing was done.

The warrior had his subject for interrogation.

The Aztrakhani secured his captive to a framework he had constructed of steeloy rods. It bore little resemblance to the Tree of Truth, though its function was the same. Not knowing what his prisoner's cybersystems might be capable of, Yavobo removed the obvious ones just to be on the safe side—a quick and crude surgery done with the blooded knife he had sworn to use solely in service to his Oath.

With the excision of a cyber-eye, a weapons finger, and two rigger jacks, the former guard was bleeding and moaning even though unconscious. The bounty hunter applied synthflesh and a trauma patch to the head injuries, then administered a hopper to revive the prisoner.

The questioning took very little time. The thin-skin was as cowardly as most of his kind, and Yavobo's skilled interrogation gained him all he needed to know. Artificial though it might be, his self-built Tree of Truth had served its purpose well. At the end he was disappointed to slay the Skiffjammer, until the man groveled and asked for death.

Scornful, are the thin-skins, the warrior reflected. You do not beg for mercy; you do not beg for death.

He replaced the bloody knife in his thigh sheath, and contemplated all that he had learned. Too well protected, his quarry was, in her new trade fortress among the warehouses.

The warrior's eyes gleamed. Well protected though Lish seemed, the flaw in the smuggler's security was a great and obvious one. She planned to come out from behind her walls, and then she would be exposed. On the streets they would be alert enough, her derevin continuing their normal guard routine, but underwater—

That is where I will have her, thought Yavobo. They expect trouble from these terrorists they will be meeting with, and that is who they will be watching for. They will not be on guard against *me*.

The Aztrakhani laughed, a rasping bark from deep within his chest. The Skiffjammers were on alert for the upcoming meeting in Rinoco Park. There would be no need for Yavobo to risk himself against security bots and perimeter alarms, after all. His dislike of R'debh's sea could be put aside, and for the last time he would wear a breather and a buoybelt. It was clear that Reva was working with the Holdout now; with luck, she would be there, too.

He would strike like a dune-vipe. His oaths would be fulfilled, and he would have his vengeance. And underwater, he would not be plagued by spineless pleas for mercy or for death.

XCII

The report of the missing guard sent Reva out into the streets that night. Levay could analyze security procedures and order all the search sweeps she liked; the assassin was after immediate answers, and had her own way of getting them.

A patrol line, an intelligent perimeter, security bots, and ready squads—none of those precautions had prevented a single attack against a single guard. The missing 'Jammer, called Borser, had even been in line-of-sight to one of the neighboring guardposts, where his fellow sentry confessed that her comlink had fuzzed out of frequency.

It's starting, thought Reva. I don't know who it is, but that's a probe if there ever was one.

Some of the Kipper's crew were out there in the streets right now, kids squatting in loading dock doorways wrapped against the fog that would roll in before dawn, sucking glow-tokes to build an inner heat against the chill of the night. Maybe they had seen something. She went to find them, blending into the shadows in her black bodysuit, wearing night-eyes, special contacts that diffused ambient light so her night vision was improved without need of optical headgear or implant.

She checked the Lines now and then, and stayed in the shadows, and saw nothing out of the ordinary. She did the rounds and heard the news.

"I thought there was someone on the roof," said one street rat. "I might be wrong, though. Could've been a shrike, nesting for the night."

"There was a car, went by twice," reported another. "No, I didn't see the driver."

"I heard running," said the next. "Sounded like hazers." He meant rock-throwing taunters, hassling derevin who looked so occupied they couldn't give chase.

That sounded promising. "Did you hear them throw anything? Or call out?" the assassin asked.

The kid shook his head and hunched into his thermal blanket. Sitting with knees drawn up in a corner of the alley, he looked like a twelve-year-old derelict settling in to an uncomfortable night's sleep.

She looked and questioned for some hours more. Whoever had snagged Borser had done so unobserved, and faded away without a trace.

The assassin returned unwillingly to Lairdome 5, unease gnawing at the back of her mind.

XCIII

Nothing was worth the extortionate price Lish was demanding to cure the borgbeasts. She was trying to bankrupt the Gambru League—and that was robbery its leader could not permit to happen. So his afternoon swim with Sharptooth and life-friend up the Rinoco Baffles was a welcome experiment, to see how closely the beasts could approach Rinoco Park without detection. When the Leaguers met the smuggler in the underwater amusement park, Edesz planned to have reinforcements within easy calling distance.

"The water is shallow," Master Swimmer Sharptooth observed, whistling his concern through the sonic translator.

The average depth in watery Rinoco Park was a little less than twenty meters, and the borgbeasts would be cramped for adequate maneuvering room.

"Can you do it?" Edesz asked the Vernoi.

Sharptooth crooned to his life-friend, and the trio drifted over the ridge toward the waterpark beyond. On the shelfland the ocean was cloudy with plankton and silt; visibility was poor, and there was little threat of waterland visitors detecting the leviathan's approach. The borgbeast nosed around, and sent some kind of sonar pulse through the water, a sounding that Edesz could detect on his skin but not hear even with the aid of the translator. The leviathan finally clicked to its handler, and Sharptooth interpreted.

"My life-friend says yes, we can do it. Two must stay off the deeper shelf; they are too large to enter the park safely. The rest can navigate these narrows if we handlers are nearby to help direct them."

With those magnificent creatures at his disposal, Edesz did not care what reinforcements Lish brought with her. The borgbeasts would be on call to chase or devour or overwhelm any who got in their way.

XCIV

Zay and Eklun stared at the destruction in D2.

The wall of engineering consoles was missing. The maneuver engines and power support that lay beyond were gone as well. In their place were heaps of melted duralloy, charred tendrils of plasteel, bits of shattered ceramic lattice. Beyond that . . .

It was hard to look beyond that. A blue-black light filled the room, something strongly UV, a radiance that clawed at the nerves until you wanted to blink it away through watering eyes. You could nearly feel it on your teeth. It illuminated nothing while glaring blindingly off every surface.

The faceplates on the spacers' helmets filtered mere UV, but even the warp visors they lowered were not enough to remove the sensation of invisible irritation stabbing through the eyes and into the brain behind. Eklun tried to make out the slagged engine, but it blurred into a heap of debris, and past that a twisting color-splashed void that defied the eye to look directly at it. Like the colors and patterns seen when the hands press hard against the eyes, but with a sickly gleam to them, and the fascination of a glow-arc or laser—*"don't look at that; you'll blind yourself"*—it carried the self-destructive urge to look, to dare the impossible, to see what it was really like in that moment before you *did* go blind—

Eklun tore his eyes away. He knew the risks, and so did Zay. He had to punch her twice on the arm before she followed suit.

They switched on their suit lights and went to the maintenance airlock, fetching laser cutter and toolkit. In the wreck of the control area, the two bent their heads downward and followed standard procedure—throwing attention into one thing at a time, the SureGrip floor matting underfoot, the next meter of deck space. Best was to concentrate on something within the compass of your own arms or legs; when you saw pieces of your body, too, you stayed conscious of self, and that made it easier to resist the perverse siren call of destruction that the beyond whispered with its light, its fascinating, oppressing colors. . . .

"Eklun. Zay. Talk to me," said the Captain. "I haven't heard a word from you. What's going on?"

They both gave a guilty start. Constant talk, another standard procedure.

"Sorry, sir," said the engineer. "We're walking where the power conduits used to be. Maneuver engine is a puddle."

They skirted near-vaporized floor plates, halting beside the duralloy-sheathed reactor. Ion exciters and flux gates were reduced to char by the energy discharge. A hatch plate recessed into the casing covered the resonant crystals precisely braced within. The hatch bowed at the aft end, where it and a good third of the reactor shell had neared meltdown temperatures.

"We'll have to cut this out," Zay said. "Two hours, maybe longer." Slow and careful going through insulating layers, to avoid nicking any displaced prisms in the core.

"Go to it, then," Devin said. "And keep talking to each other. I'm listening, but leave me offline unless you need me."

Eklun unlimbered the laser cutter and they began.

Satisfied that his crew was safe and their salvage work well under way, Devin returned to the problem that demanded most of his cyber capacity and all of his unwired attention.

On what heading lay Selmun III?

There was no telling where the warp flicker had left them in relative space. Once blinded to a known starting point, further course alterations were as likely to take a ship away from her goal as closer to it. Every hour they spent pushing ahead in warp might be one light-year of travel they'd have to make up later.

Devin fine-tuned sensor systems until he had a single long, very narrow sensor probe, extending half again as far as normal long range would permit. He pointed the probe to the rear of the *Fortune,* and swept it in a calculated arc across the void. Slowly, he smiled. As he had known it would, a warbling cycle tone native to the warp dimension filled his senses. In a moment, computers eliminated the background noise and the sensors relayed nothing at all.

That's perfect, thought Shiran. Now to see if we can find anything worth hearing.

He initiated an automated routine, sweeping the sky in a pattern of overlapping arcs that, over a period of hours, would encompass every degree of space that englobed them. If a space lane was anywhere within two days of travel, the long probe should pick up the distinctive tone of a navigation buoy, log its bearing, and alert Devin.

All we need is one beacon, he encouraged himself. That, and a couple of drive crystals, and we're on our way.

"We've got two, Captain!" called Zay. "Two intact crystals, maybe three." She cradled one in her hands, a translucent emerald-green prism a meter long and two hands wide. "The third is chipped on the focal point, but I think we can refacet that end."

"Bring them all," said Devin. "Work with the good ones first."

The spacers carried the fragile crystals out of the risky environment in D2. In Drive One they unsuited, then began work on a jury-rigged power booster that would even out their erratic warp reaction. Devin continued his cyber-attentive examination of the beyond.

Two-thirds of a search hemisphere had been completed when he heard the distinctive squall of a navigation buoy. It was the 1057 waypoint marker on the Claw-Chwstyoch shipping lane—still in the Tion subsector, but displaced high above the plane of the galactic equator. Once in the lane, they were five days out from R'debh.

There's no other option, Devin decided. The *Fortune* can't survive another warp encounter in the wilds between patrolled space.

They were compelled to take the safer course back to Selmun III.

He started to relax, until rigger feedback reminded him why he should not. Even if they could stabilize the warp bubble, performance was far from optimal. The engineering computer gave an estimate of six days' travel time, not five.

One day too late to help anyone.

Devin fished into the medkit beside the Captain's chair and injected himself with Syntozac. The drug heightened synaptic activity and boosted rigger performance, and he needed every advantage possible, from this moment on, to wring all he could from the *Fortune*. They were no longer in danger of core failure, or of wandering lost. But they had yet to win back home in time to do some good.

Devin began to tap engineering and technical computers, to find a way to make five days' travel in a ship that could only do it in six.

XCU

It was the eve of the trade with Edesz, and Lish prowled like a fenced kria.

The *Fortune* had not returned. No one remarked on it; they didn't have to. Something had gone wrong, and there was no word from Devin about what had delayed him. It looked like he was not going to make the meet.

Kastlin watched the smuggler abandon her third pointless cryocase inventory and round on the service cabinet to search for a drink. At least she won't be ruined out of hand, he told himself. Without the nanotech she isn't in violation of any laws after all. A blessing in disguise, save her from herself. . . .

He saw the thunderous look in her eyes, and wisely kept out of her way.

Lish and her companions went to sleep far too late and got up far too early. In the residence quarters of the Lairdome they gathered around breakfast, a meager repast served only to divert them from their joyless vigil.

Reva rearranged the food on her plate for the third time, then finally shoved it into the center of the table. "Sea Father, let's out with it. Lish, what are you going to do now?"

She had spoken the unspeakable. The smuggler shrank back in her chair, staring into the murky brown depths of her cup of osk.

"You can't give up now," Reva prodded. "You're going to tell Desz you need more time, aren't you?"

Lish looked up, her eyes grim. "I can't ask for more time."

The assassin's brows came together. "Are you sun-struck? Of course you can."

"The Scripman won't wait for his money," she snapped. "It's due tomorrow."

"Scripman." Reva waved a hand. "If you get a little more time from Desz, you can pay the loan shark back, with late penalty."

"His late penalty on two mil is my life, Reva." She hunkered into her chair. "It's not negotiable."

"Then I'll get you offworld, if it comes to that," the assassin volunteered.

Lish shook her head. "Then I'm broke and on the run from a Scripman, and my reputation as Holdout is shot, because I couldn't hand the goods to Edesz. What am I supposed to do then?"

Reva made an exasperated sound, and Vask gave up pretending to eat. "Well, what *are* you going to do?" the assassin demanded. "Apologize to everyone and put your head on the block tomorrow?"

Lish shot her an acid look. "I'm going to get what's mine, that's what I'm going to do. We'll trade, as planned."

The others stared at her as her meaning sunk in. "You mean, a con?" Vask asked incredulously. "Fake the delivery to get your money?"

"That's right."

Reva shook her head. "If you think the streetwar was a battle, wait until the Gambru League comes hunting for you."

"But I'm not going to be here for that, am I?" Lish asked in a saccharine tone. "I'm leaving after payoffs are made, remember?"

"Lish—"

"Leave it alone, Reva. I don't see another way. Do you?"

The assassin had no answer for her friend. Neither did Vask.

"That's what I thought," Lish said. "Then let's get on with it, shall we?"

Reva watched her come to her feet, move away from the table. "How are you getting offworld, if the *Fortune* isn't here?"

The smuggler looked back. "With that much money, finding a ship won't be hard. Now are you two going to help me set up a cryocase, or what?"

They followed her to the warehouse, and kept their misgivings to themselves.

XCVI

Three hours after sunrise, Rinoco Park opened its gates. Toward noon, the trickle had become a flood of bodysuit-and-breather-wearing tourists. Anonymous among their numbers, Internal Security and R'debh Commandos infiltrated the waterland. Park Security ushered them through an unalarmed gateway that would not betray the weapons they carried, then they were directed to the air-filled entrance dome and left to mix with the crowds of vacationers.

An interlocking chain of drydomes ringed the waterland park, from the first large entry bubble where visitors were welcome to the farthest observation domes at twenty-five meters depth. Hidden glowspots and diffuse lighting raised the color density at twenty meters depth to a level normally seen only half that far from the surface. Within the air-filled ring were freshers, restaurants, aid stations, wet- and drysuit rentals, and other services. Similar facilities were offered in exterior wetdomes, for the comfort of water-breathing species touring the Park. Airlocks at intervals let tourists pass into or out of the waterland attractions as they pleased.

Half the offworld tourists and most all R'debh natives found their way outside, and stayed there for the majority of their sojourn. Others viewed the Park from the circuitous Promenade inside the drydome ring. Agents gathered there, too, to stroll near the fire spouts, oxygenated columns of water flash-ignited, then extinguished a second later as ocean overwhelmed the pillar of flame. It was a spectacular if artful creation, a series of jet igniting and dying at intervals, placed between the natural attractions of thermal spas and lava grottos.

Other IntSec agents and all of the Commandos extended the short webbed struts on their fin shoes and joined the tourists swimming fish-like through the features of the waterland. Each operative carried a laser pistol concealed in belt-bag. Each wore a pressure-adapted ear set for communications, and the full-face breather that permitted radio comms. Many tourists favored the masks as well, so the Commandos and IntSec officers blended easily into the crowds.

Obray joined Captain Survek of the Commandos at a comtemplation grotto halfway up a steep lava ridge. The impromptu command post flanked the viewing plaza before the fire geysers. Units reported their readiness, and mingled with tourists in the plaza.

Now all they had to do was wait.

XCVII

Borgbeasts milled in the Baffles, close-packed so they could move in a coordinated wave when called. The Vernoi who handled them drifted at the ridgeline, listening for the signal to advance into the Park.

The Vernoi did not detect anything amiss with their pack, nothing they had not already learned to suffer with through the long days of a gradual decline. Handlers and life-friends alike rested lethargically, worn to a point that would have taxed the endurance of any creature, large or small. Another one of the beasts was nonresponsive, showing the same signs of despair that Wee'ska had, shortly before she had gone on the death-swim. That particular life-friend would join the large pair on the Shelfland, lingering in reserve to hinder pursuers, and would not enter the Park, where swift and accurate maneuvering in uncomfortably shallow waters would be required.

Confined, the borgbeasts' discomfort became a palpable knot of agony, resounding through the Baffles into the echoing valleys and chasms of the seabed. The hurt-filled groan detected by the ghost-ray swelled into an amplified chorus of pain, a soul-felt lament radiated by creatures in subsonics and psychic cries only subconsciously sensed by their handlers.

The Sea Father heard their complaint clearly, and came to see who it was that called louder and longer than the one he had already taken.

Wafting through ravines, drifting over silted wastes, the ghost-ray flexed broad wings and sailed through turbid water. He heeded a woeful beacon clamoring through submerged valleys, rebounding off ridges of sea-carved limestone and lava.

Someone wanted to die, someone who cried long and loud. Or many someones, together. The Sea Father of R'debh heard, and was drawn irresistibly to the call.

XCVIII

Devin's long-range vision flickered and died as burned out sensors dropped offline. The spacer cursed, and reset his rigged vision to midrange, instead.

It had started with the refaceting of the chipped third crystal. The idea had seemed like a good one at the time, the only thing that could boost their speed the critical percentage points they needed to reach Selmun III on time. Zay had added the third crystal to their power booster configuration, then she and Devin had spent their waking hours in shifts, juggling performance parameters ever since in the jury-rigged overdrive system.

Zay bitched about half-assed homemade ion exciters and undefinable flow rates. Devin could feel the ragged edge to their power, and accepted the calculated risk. Yet constant extreme power fluctuations throughout the system were taking their toll. First the faulty frequency head in the sonic shower had blown. Then onboard sensors, the controllers for the cargo bay doors, scattered link modules. Now long-range sensors.

I should be glad it's nothing more serious, Devin thought. No telling what might go next. Whatever's a weak link, whatever's stressed by power surges . . .

He didn't want to think about critical systems like environmental control or engine functions. Not now, less than an hour from their goal.

Lish traveled to Rinoco Park in an air car, lost in the general exodus of Skiffjammers heading that way for the meet, on magtube, shuttle, and air vehicles. Numbers helped conceal her movement. Reva sat beside her, a watchful guard on hopper-fed energy, while armed 'Jammer escorts flanked their vehicle on either side.

The cryocases and the ruse they contained were in the boot of the car.

Convincing? Maybe so. Convincing enough to pass by Edesz? . . . Lish was uncertain, though she dared share those doubts with no one.

The comlink buzzed at her belt. She reached for it distractedly, not realizing until it was in her hand that this call signal was on her personal and private frequency. The people who knew that code were all with her in the car, except for—

"Devin!" she shouted into the link. The vehicle gave a slight jump as Vask reacted to her outcry. The others looked on with sudden anticipation.

"Where are you?" her words came out in a rush. "Do you have it?"

His end of the conversation was heard by Lish on her privacy implant. Her excitement was tangible and the spoken exchange brief. After a few words, she replaced the comlink at her belt and leaned forward to talk over Kastlin's shoulder.

"Head for Avelar Field," she announced. She grinned ecstatically at the others and said what they could already guess. "He's got the goods."

"Deadheading, were you?" the Customs inspector drawled, looking around the empty expanse of Cargo One.

"That's right," Devin said, keeping his tone neutral. This inspector had been poking here and there, making random scans with a hand-held sounder, a sensor tuned to recognize wall and sub-floor cavities that might be used as smuggling hidey-holes. His partner was in D2, suited up and walking the drive unit's slagged ruins, in case the freighter's Captain had planned on hiding something in vacuum that they might overlook.

"I'll take a look at your flight log now, if you don't mind."

Devin lead him back to the flight deck. The officer made himself at home in the Captain's chair while looking over the flight records. He paused while his partner spoke over comlink. "Seems like you've got a slag heap where a maneuver engine's supposed to be."

"That's about right." Shiran shrugged.

"We're confirming damage to Traffic Control. You won't be cited for your reckless approach. You better head straight to the yards with this ship, though. She's barely atmosphere-worthy, with that hull damage to catch the wind."

Devin nodded agreeably as if taking the inspector's sage advice to heart.

The man applied his thumbprint to the landing permit on the Captain's datapad. "I guess you're clear," he said. "Be careful heading dirtside."

"I will," Devin agreed. Eklun saw the inspector to the airlock and cleared the boarding umbilical before returning to the flight deck.

"Grinds," snorted the Skiffjammer.

"Yeah." Devin sat once more, began keying sequences on the control panel. He looked up when Eklun stifled what sounded like a giggle.

"Does it always work that slick?" the 'Jammer asked. "He was sitting right on top of the nanotech the whole time, and didn't catch on even with that sounder."

Devin allowed himself a half-smile. Another trick of the Shiran Traders, well learned and well used. "It doesn't work at all unless you modified the chair mount ahead of time," he said. "I did that myself during our refit, replacing staylocks with screw-bolts so the floor pillar comes out."

"And beneath it is just enough room for a box of select cargo."

"In a space lined with venloy, which slews sensor readings. When the cubbyhole is full, the sounder reads it like regular flooring. When it's empty, sensors read the mass of the chair's support pillar as extending that far into the floor. Not unusual in some ship designs."

Eklun smiled. "Congratulations, Captain. You pulled it off."

"Almost," Devin said, resuming course calculations. "Wait until we're dirtside, and then we'll celebrate."

XCIX

The smuggler and her escort met the *Fortune* as she touched down on the pad. Lish was first up the crew elevator, first to run into a sweaty, rumpled Devin as he walked wearily out of the flight deck.

She didn't mean to hug him, but somehow it happened. Her embrace was hard and quick. His lingered, stopping only when she pulled away. While Skiffjammers retrieved the cargo, Devin brought Lish up-to-date on the extent of their damage, and the condition of himself and the crew.

"I had planned to come with you," he said, "but now . . ."

"After five days on Syntozac and hoppers? I don't need someone falling asleep in the middle of this meet. You stay here, Devin, see to your ship."

He looked around ruefully. "See to it. Yeah. I can't take you off-world in this like we planned, Lish. The *Fortune*'s not warp-capable again until she's been in the yards."

The Holdout put a hand on his arm. "I'm paying for it. The damage was in the line of duty, wouldn't you say? And this time no cutting corners. You're getting new guns along with everything else."

Devin wasn't about to argue. He patted the bulkhead with a loving hand. "She's a tough one, worked hard to get us through. I'd like that."

"It's settled, then." Lish started to pull away.

"Not exactly. How are you getting offworld? I want to come with you."

"I'll rent a ship. Come if you want."

"The repairs here—"

"Or stay if you want. Don't worry, I'll be back." She smiled warmly. "Walking out on my business is one thing, but I'm not leaving you without a word. You're part of my team, aren't you?"

"I thought so."

"Good. Then I'll be back. Now let me go collect my money."

Her tone was gentle, and he let her go, letting her hand slip through his fingers with a trailing touch. He held off on the kiss he wanted to give her—*not yet; don't push her*—waiting for a sign from her that invited closeness.

There was none, just her last wistful look as the crew elevator dropped her out of sight through the hull of the ship.

C

"Commander, Station Four. We've got her in sight at the silt river, now. She and her escort have joined up with a sea-spider. They're heading your way."

"Acknowledged," Obray told the checkpoint, registering then dismissing report of the vehicle. Tourists could rent spiders or bring their own vehicles into the park. It shouldn't affect their plan of action significantly.

Right now Obray was more concerned about clearing innocent civilians out of the meeting place, the viewing plaza by the fire geysers.

Carefully, discreetly, Park Security IDs were flashed and clusters of tourists who had wanted to take a lengthy break here suddenly decided the floatweed ponds were more interesting. Commandos trickled out of reserve positions and swam into the attraction area in pairs and clusters, a good simulation of natural crowd movement.

Obray watched the tour trail leading from the thermal spas, and his patience was soon rewarded. Skiffjammers came through first, their attempts at incognito failing in the uniformity and precision of their appearance. All had buzzed hair or wore a snug-fitting cowl; all wore full-face masks that permitted them, like the Commander's forces, the use of comlinks to talk in privacy. Their bearing was alert and trouble-ready, and they moved in coordinated pairs, taking up posts around the viewing plaza, intimidating the supposed-civilians they encountered until they had cleared the plaza area.

Lish entered behind the lead group of 'Jammers, recognizable in the garb described in Station One's first sighting of the smuggler. She wore a green bodysuit with white flash-lines down arms and legs; her short blond hair flowed loose above a full-face mask. She swam a little awkwardly, not at ease in the ocean; then as Obray watched she dropped back to snag a handhold on the airlock of the spider that stalked beside her. A 'Jammer drove the vehicle, picking its way over the ground trail on the angular jointed legs that gave the vehicle its name.

To one side swam Vask, recognizable by his bodysuit, gray with orange spatter-streaks—the same fluorescent color as the armbands Security agents would don, when violence broke out. It was an undercover agent's way of identifying himself as friendly.

On the other side of Lish swam another woman, tall, dark-haired, her bodysuit a neutral aqua that functioned like camouflage against the blue-green depths of the water. Obray looked at her again. She was obviously no Skiffjammer, though she kicked strongly through the water with a grace and assuredness that they shared. Could that be Kastlin's pet assassin?

"Leaguers moving, sir." A sentry's report tore Obray's attention from the Holdout's group, and directed it to the lava grottos north of the fire spouts. The water-breathers emerged from the caves at the same moment that several sea-adapted "tourists" moved forward to claim one side of the viewing plaza. Skiffjammers ceded that much room until derevin and terrorists faced off across the width of the plaza, confining themselves to the edges and various heights above the seabed. Their jockeying for position was brief, then movement ceased while Lish and Edesz entered neutral ground before the fire spouts.

Edesz bothered Reva from the moment she first saw him. At first she racked it up to the hoppers she had taken, that the way he kicked and glided could itself seem arrogant. That he radiated disdain of the land-dwellers he saw before him. Yet when he came to a stop some five meters away from Lish, his look of scornful assessment was not lost on any of them.

He meant it to be intimidating, perhaps, but to Reva he suddenly seemed like nothing more than a primary-school bully. Like some of the sea-adapted she had gone to school with as a child, treating her with the dislike they reserved for land-dwellers, simply because she, too, was an air-breather.

Edesz and two of his companions wore full-face masks, the voders bulkier than usual and wired to an ear-cupped headset whose arcane communications purpose she couldn't guess. The Gambru League leader could have spoken in clear language through the voder, but did not. He signed, a language cryptic to Lish, with whom he expected to deal.

The insult was not lost on the Holdout, whose Sa'adani heritage had taught her all she ever needed to know about condescension.

Reva spoke inside her facemask, transmitting to Lish and all 'Jammers monitoring Com 1. "Do you have what you promised me?" she translated Edesz' meaning.

Lish's answer came back through Reva's earlink. "That's why I'm here. Do you have my money?"

The assassin body-signed the reply. Behind the mask Edesz' features were hard to read, but the sneer faded a little to something like an amused smile.

"Sea-dweller?" he inquired with a quick gesture, a curving motion of the hand followed by the fist-clench signifying seadomes, the quirked little finger that meant interrogative.

The unexpected exchange brought back old memories, and the sudden urge to chat in sign as she had once done with family and friends. Reva stopped herself before she revealed too much. "Interpreter," she responded shortly, and left Edesz to draw his own conclusions.

"Interpret this, then. I want to see what you've brought, and test it by using it on my sea-friends. If it works, I'll pay you the money."

Reva drew a breath before putting that into words, and watched Lish for her reaction. Her face went blank with the aloof, reserved look Reva had seen over Shaydo and castle-stones. The Shiran Trader was ready to bargain.

"We had a deal," she told him. "You pay; I deliver. If that doesn't suit, I'll go right now, and take the goods with me."

There. Bluff to call bluff.

Edesz raised a hand, the "please wait" gesture clear without translation. "No need to leave. But I need reassurances. How do I know this delivery will work as promised?"

"You don't," the smuggler replied through Reva, "except that I tell you it will. You know my reputation?"

The Leaguer signed yes. "I need more than promises, though," he added.

Reva expected Lish to grow angry. But the smuggler took it all in stride, as if renegotiation at the point of closing a bargain was a common part of doing business.

Lish made a gesture of goodwill and keyed the voder on her mask to speak for herself. "I'll let you examine the cargo documentation. You can see what you're buying. If you have someone with the right expertise, you'll know whether it'll work or not."

Edesz flicked on his own voder. "What's in the cargo?" he asked.

"Nanotech."

The water-breather glanced at a woman who flanked him; she nodded in turn. "Alright," he said.

"Good. You can take a look in atmosphere."

Edesz agreed. The sea-spider headed for the nearest vehicle lock. Smuggler and terrorist started that way, flanked by a few escorts each.

Reva was swimming that short distance when her alertness gelled into the sudden conviction that something was not right.

A quick look around gave no hint what might be wrong. The Leaguers were staying put, and 'Jammers had given no sign of alarm. Tourists drifted about the area, and shopped at kiosks.

Time to look through the Lines, she told herself.

She sought that centered place where Now would split into its close-related moments. She reached it almost at once—and inhaled sharply within her breather.

This was not the way things should look at all, and the oddness of the vision halted her in mid-kick, leaving her to slow and float for a moment in the water.

Where events should be overlaid like kaleidoscopic fractals, one possibility atop or near the other, now all was a confusing blur. A figure that she knew was Lish fuzzed into what could be a Gambru Leaguer, and then into some unknown tourist, a confusing metamorphosis: it showed too much displacement to reflect a parallel Line, and the figure was too indistinct to be certain of identity. It was not just perplexing, it was *wrong,* a vision her Lineshifting had never bestowed on her before. She couldn't tell what lay in the next moment, let alone down the Line.

Vask's hand on her arm centered her again in Realtime. "Are you alright?" he asked on a privacy channel.

"Something's wrong," she blurted, but could not bring herself to say more. How to explain the Lines to the Fixer, the chaos of the near-futures she had seen? What did it mean?

"What's wrong?" Kastlin echoed her thoughts. "What do you mean?"

The vision was profoundly unsettling. And in this moment Reva had neither time to explore it, nor understanding of what she had seen, so Vask's questions bothered her like fingers probing a fresh wound. She jerked her arm from his grasp, kicked away from his solicitations. "Don't know," she growled. "Keep your eyes open, will you? Something's not right, that's all."

Edesz hovered as his companion examined stasis box and datapad. A murmured conference took place, and the Gambru Leaguer finally turned back to Lish.

"Acceptable," he said. "Here." He held out a credit chit.

Lish took it. She examined the black and gold hologram on the small rectangle as Edesz ordered his fellows to reload the container on board the spider. The Holdout interrupted him.

"What do you mean by this?" She flourished the plastic between two fingers. "A bank transfer marker? That's not part of our deal."

Edesz faced the smuggler. "Sure it is. Ten million, on account. Any bank will verify and honor that marker and transfer the funds to you. You know that."

"Those weren't the terms," Lish said, anger creeping into her voice. Levay moved closer to the smuggler's side; Reva and Vask stood ready on the other. The Fixer licked his lips nervously, but the women stared at Edesz with deadly focus.

The water-breather didn't like their attention, either, and his nictitating eyelids flicked down in a reflex of guarded caution. "Our terms were cash. That's cash."

"Not until it's been run through a bank, it isn't. I don't like banks, Edesz. I wanted transferable credits, something to put in my meter on the spot."

The terrorist dissembled, allowed himself an apologetic smile. "Then I'm sorry, Domna. That wasn't explicitly clear according to our earlier conversation. You wanted 10 mil; you have 10 mil. I can take it back, if you like, and we can do this some other time."

Damn the man, Lish thought. He doesn't want to wait on this any more than I do. My time with the Scripman's up, and I can't risk something ruining this exchange.

She held the transfer marker for another breath, then flicked it with one nail and put it into a breast pocket. "Alright. But you leave here first. I'm watching you all the way."

The water-breather inclined his head agreeably, then reaffixed his breather mask. A Gambru Leaguer stepped inside the sea-spider. Edesz and the vehicle led the way through the airlock and out to the fire spout attraction.

Reva's feeling of something not right clamored stronger than before. On edge, she looked about the plaza for the source of the subconscious alarm.

All seemed normal enough. The sea-spider and ten Leaguers started back toward the thermals, the most direct route out of the Park. Edesz seemed in conference with his fellows near the center of the plaza. Tourists wandered by, closer than they had before.

Tourists . . . She looked again, and didn't like what she saw. There were too many full-coverage masks. They paid too much attention to the group around Lish, direct looks, now some direct movement.

Reva grabbed the Holdout's arm, not knowing what she was going to do. What was this? Another derevin? Law enforcement? This was not the kind of attack she'd been prepared for, expecting instead some shot in the dark targeting only Lish.

"Trouble," she said on Com 2. Lish looked her way; Vask and Levay heard the news as well. As she spoke some Skiffjammers had started to spread out, to haze off approaching tourists. From mid-plaza, Edesz and his friends kicked toward Lish, swimming back in a leisurely manner that quickly picked up speed.

Every combat reaction she had was screaming. "You're out of here, now," she barked, pulling Lish back toward the airlock. "Levay, get us cover."

Trusting Reva's instinct for danger, the Holdout turned her back on the plaza and activated her adrenal boosters. Her kicks became more powerful and she easily kept pace with the assassin. The pair arrowed toward the lock they had left minutes before, and the relative safety beyond it.

Cl

Get the nanotech safely away, and get the money back from Lish.

The plan was that simple, and Edesz cursed as the Holdout flitted like a sand midge away from his approaching forces. The time for subtlety was past. The terrorist gave a cry on the sonic translator, the amplified voder tone easily reaching the Leaguers near souvenir shops and the reserves in the lava grottos. His main escort came on with him, enclosing their leader in a fast-swimming wedge intended to punch through the screen of Skiffjammers.

The Holdout's swimming was amazingly strong for an air-breather who had seemed clumsy in the water only minutes before. He couldn't risk letting her escape. Edesz gave another long and whistling call, this one to the borgbeasts so close by the edge of the Park.

As he did so, he became aware that the tourists were armed and interfering in the League's attack. Amazement gave way to anger at Lish's additional treachery, and he called again to the borgbeasts, an exhortation to speed and violence. No matter if the ring dome must be destroyed to get her. Get her he would.

Chaos erupted in the plaza. As Obray ordered promenade teams to head Lish off at the vehicle lock, Commandos closed with the escaping spider. Sea-adapted R'debhi poured from the lava grottos, taking some of the laser-armed Commandos unprepared, stripping their breathers and fleeing with them before the operatives could react.

The greater fight surged before the fire spouts, where Skiffjammers fought terrorists. Concealed cyberweapons came into play, and the ocean pinked with blood-tinge from dead or dying sea-dwellers. In other places the bodies of air-breathers hung motionless, drowned by the R'debhi tactic of stripping breathers. A handful of belligerents floated helplessly near the souvenir booths, arms and legs confined with static bonds, the victims of successful arrests by officers who had returned to the fray.

With an effort Obray restrained himself from issuing orders and second-guessing his field commanders. His lieutenants could handle the situation in the plaza.

Then the Security officer made the mistake of gazing out, toward and past the fire spouts. A movement there caught his eye. He stared, then made an unprofessional gurgling sound into the comlink, followed by an inarticulate stutter that went ignored by his troops. For the longest moment of his life, it seemed Obray Paros was the only one aware of impending doom. The knowledge choked the words in his throat and turned his bowels to water.

The borgbeasts were upon them.

Reva heard Edesz' eerie voder call, heard the cacophony of grunts and voder voices and thrashing limbs behind them that carried so clearly through the water. Her sea-tuned ears could pick out the sounds, and she knew better than to slow herself by glancing back. They were halfway to the lock, now, and Lish was close beside her. Reva kept on with single-minded intent and barely registered the sudden movement in the upper left corner of her field of vision, a place obscured by the frame of her breather mask. Then that sixth sense that had cried foul for the last half hour shrieked an alarm and she glanced up. Someone in a black bodysuit had moved out of concealment behind barnacle ferns, drifting down from the ridge-face, closing on their position.

She saw the lanky build of the swimmer, then noticed the speargun, highlighted for a bizarre moment in the chance beam of a glowspot. She noticed the red and black mottled hands that held it, and recognition hit her like a physical blow. Lish kicked past her as the assassin's limbs froze and a gasp tore loose from her throat.

Yavobo.

You're dead! she wanted to scream at him, her brain refusing to accept the apparition she saw before her. She had seen him blown to bits along with Alia Lanzig, right before she left Selmun III—

Left and never followed up on news of the hit.

Sick realization washed over her. She had come close to death at the alien's hands and wanted to put the frightful memory from her. She had never discussed Yavobo with those who might have known of his survival, and in her concern over killing and then saving Lish, his fate had no longer seemed relevant. The alien was dead, or so she had thought. . . .

The smuggler slowed, wondering what was wrong, and turned belatedly to follow Reva's stare. The assassin saw Yavobo take swift aim, knew she was defenseless; unmoving, the Aztrakhani had her as good as dead in the water. Helpless again before the killer, she felt the gut-sinking feeling she had hoped never to live through again.

And then the muzzle of the speargun tracked the least bit ahead of her, and a new realization struck like the kick of a vecna.

It was Lish he was after.

The assassin kicked back into action as Yavobo squeezed the trigger. The gas-propelled spear quarrel flew through the water, stream-lined and wickedly barbed, heading well aimed and true for Lish's torso. With a scream of rage that carried through her comlink and nearly deafened those sharing the privacy channel, Reva surged ahead and shoved Lish to the side and down. It might be enough, to get her out of the path, might be—

It was. The quarrel passed just over the smuggler's ribs and sliced a ragged tear in Reva's right forearm. Yavobo cocked the magazine-loaded gun, and took aim again.

"Keep going!" Reva shouted at Lish, waving toward the airlock, ignoring the oozing blood that fogged the water around her injured arm. The wound stung fiercely, aggravated by the salt and organics in the thick R'debh water. Reva centered herself with steely determination and headed straight for Adahn's unexpected killer. To approach straight on would block his aim from Lish and leave Reva the perfect target for his quarrels. She had no doubt the alien would be overjoyed to take her out on the way to hitting the smuggler. But that was the one way she could get near, near enough to kill him with the flechette plate.

She struggled against the harsh distraction of adrenaline, trying to center and *go*, before it was too late. She sped toward Yavobo, disregarding all her own rules, and then she cast herself between the Lines, shimmering and vanishing from sight uncaring of what witnesses might be looking on.

Yavobo warred with himself for a critical moment. Here came his Blood Oath–sworn enemy, right into the death his stolen speargun carried. Beyond her was the fleeing target, whom he had vowed to slay before he had his vengeance with Reva.

But Reva should be slain with the knife, the one he had sworn his vow on. The woman came on toward him, once more the bravest of thin-skins, and the most foolhardy. Yavobo could not shoot his sworn antagonist in this way, not like a butcher killing a skigrat. That was reserved for the unscrupulous smuggler. His eyes sought the Holdout, noted she was closer to the airlock; looking back, he glimpsed another swimmer approaching from beyond Reva, a man in a gray bodysuit trying to flank him to one side.

His growl was heard only in his own ears. Yavobo prepared to fire again at Lish, his line-of-sight no longer passing through the assassin's body, when suddenly Reva faded to transparency and disappeared from view.

The effect was chilling, like the haunting of a soul-stealer on a moonlit dune. Yavobo blinked and his finger jerked in startlement; the readied quarrel hissed from the barrel and sped unhindered through the water where the woman had been a heartbeat before.

He spun about, badly disconcerted, searching for the assassin. Instead he saw the man who had been flanking him. The swimmer had stopped, floated unmoving in the water, like an injured freeling playing dead. Did he think that would keep him safe from the hunter? It was a poor ruse, with the stream of air bubbles from his breather exhaust betraying that he lived. Was this a distraction so Reva could trick him?

That was likely. Yavobo kicked off strongly, moving to close the distance toward Lish. There was no reason to linger near dead-lures and ghosts. His mission here had one goal. He would deal with his personal enemy later.

Lish was at the airlock now, and the bounty hunter took aim with a newly loaded quarrel. Then a swelling wave of displaced water slammed into him and he tumbled out of control toward the lava ridge that had so recently offered him concealment.

It took Vask a moment to recognize Yavobo; as he did, his options collapsed into a very narrow spectrum of choice. He couldn't help Lish; she was nearly to safety and destined for arrest. Reva was the one to watch out for now. She was wounded and directly in the killer's line of fire.

In the moment that she charged ahead, Vask watched her suicidal action with disbelief. A second later the dissolution of her form told him all he needed to know. She was invisible for the moment, shifted into a different energy state. Should he sideslip as well and try to help?

If he didn't, Yavobo could kill him out of hand, a defenseless target in the water. If he did, he would be betraying something of his nature to Reva.

He hung there, taking the time to control his breathing preparatory to an energy shift, searching for the concentration that would let him go, yet reluctant to make the change and reveal his abilities to the assassin. Then, as Yavobo started abruptly after Lish, Vask felt a weird and uncomfortable tingling, of electrical potential, all over his body. It stiffened his muscles and held him suspended in mid-water for a moment.

When the unseen surge of water tossed the bounty hunter toward the ridge, Vask barely noticed. He was losing consciousness of his surroundings, his senses thrust *elsewhere,* into that inner dimension that permits the trance state and energy shifts, and beyond his body at the same time. The Psionicist had a fleeting impression of an all-encompassing awareness, something large and vast that saw through dimensions as easily as through space. It was a perspective he felt he should be able to grasp, but could not.

Frustrated, he shrank back within the limits of his own mind—and was impelled to enter the shifted state in a spontaneous upscale pulse of energies over which he had no control. His consciousness followed after, an unwilling tagalong, entering what ought to be a sideslip but seemed like something more.

He quailed at the new sensations and his lack of control over them, and felt a fearful confusion he had never known during all his mastery of the psionic arts. In the foggy surroundings, every molecule of water aglow with an unaccustomed greenish light, he sought a landmark, any sign of familiarity—and there, close by was Reva. Not a blurred figure, as he had seen her before, but clear and distinct and near at hand.

He willed himself to move toward her as she twisted about, searching for her bearings. When she saw him her eyes went wide and she kicked backward, holding out hands to fend him off. Then her hands went to her head and in the soundless space of sideslipped energy, he saw her face distort in an anguished scream, the more horrible for all its silence.

CII

The borgbeasts came rapidly, giant flukes driving them through and over the kelp gardens that lay beyond the fire spouts. The smallest of the beasts came the fastest, skirting the flickering fire jets, charging into the plaza. The orderly chaos of a skirmish and mass arrest turned into havoc.

The slab-browed leviathan slammed heartily into a bunch of struggling bodies, squashing undercover officers and Skiffjammers alike into a mash of paste against the side of the ring dome. Souvenir kiosks shattered and compacted in the creature's driving charge. Obray heard the groan of stressed dome supports giving beneath the hammer-headed attack. A handful of Security agents struggled to escape the wreckage of the beast's first attack, but the creature came after them, picking first one man, then a woman out of the fleeing figures and chomping them down in two bites.

The small beings riding fins resolved themselves into otter-like sea-creatures. The handlers called back and forth to the terrorists, whistling and clicking through sonic amplifiers. The area had grown suddenly too small with two borgbeasts nosed into it, and two more circling about overhead.

A broad black-skinned hide swept past, right in front of Obray's nose, and the Commander dove back into the safety of the grotto command post. Captain Survek was wiped off the ridge by the giant's scaling flank, and ground into the lava face nearby.

When the borgbeast's side had cleared the ridge, an even stranger sight met the Commander's eyes. Something indescribably huge had joined them, hovering in the water, a hard-to-distinguish form that dwarfed fire spouts and plaza and borgbeasts alike. It was . . . made of water? Seen through the water? The thing enveloped the smallest of the borgbeasts in its substance, killer beast visible, the ghost-creature barely seen at all, and all about the plaza small bodies were whipped away like leaves through the wind as its insubstantial wings swept downward.

A great swell shoved Obray tumbling back into the grotto.

* * *

Edesz raced below and behind the smuggler and her small escort. Attack, he had urged the beasts, and counted on the handlers to help direct the action. He glanced over at crushed shops and shattered humans, taken out with one blow. When he turned back, he saw Lish swimming alone, and one companion barely moving in the water. The third, the woman who had body-signed, was nowhere to be seen.

A borgbeast skimmed the face of the nearby ridge; Edesz assumed it had snatched the woman up and stunned the unmoving swimmer. He had wanted the leviathans to hunt the smuggler, and could still call this one back, to chase Lish—but now there seemed little point, with her so near the airlock, and himself so close behind. Well, then, let them simply crush the League's enemies and ensure the terrorists' escape. Edesz would recover his fortune himself.

Intent on his goal, he was taken unawares by the Sea Father's wave, which tossed him uncontrollably toward the ring dome. He didn't see the panic in the borgbeasts, although he heard their sudden outcries of fear; two of the creatures drove toward open water, one propelling itself from the plaza with a sudden hard flex of its fluke. Massive flesh slammed against the ground in a careless fillip, flattening the sea-spider and the Leaguers and Commandos who fought around it.

The nanotech that would have let beasts and handlers survive in the oceans of R'debh leaked out of its pulverized containers, blending harmlessly and unremarked with the bio-rich waters of the sea. Ignorant of disaster, Edesz righted himself and pushed on to the airlock where Lish, thrown against the dome wall by the wave, floated stunned and motionless before him.

Reva was proud of that shift, so hard to do under pressure, letting herself slip between the Lines where she could not be traced. The electrical tingle was new, though, and disturbing, and it grew to a discomforting level as she settled into the state where she could navigate the fragments of Now. Her self-congratulations faded then, spent too soon on something that had gone wrong.

The jumbled, distorted Lines she had seen earlier were all around her. Before her was a ridge, and no ridge, and an upwelling of lava from the crust; to one side, mining domes instead of the Park's airdome, overlaid by virgin seabed. The Lines were chaotic, and she was lost.

She did not see Yavobo anywhere. The feeling of disorientation grew worse as she glimpsed realities that did not exist as she understood time—the work of the alien phase-shifter, bending and warping the fabric of dimensions to its own ends. Images flickered: people swimming, suggestions of sea-creatures that had never lived in the ocean she knew. The tingling was unbearable now, a slow electrocution, and involuntary nerve twitches plucked at her muscles. Then she turned, and saw a ghost but not a ghost, a solid form she recognized immediately from Realtime. Vask.

Vask in the flesh. Kastlin, substantial, and caught with her here between the Lines.

It was an impossibility, and she shied away from his touch, scared and hopeful at the same time. If he was real, there must be a way out of this maze of fractured realities that she had never been trapped in before. She wished she could talk in this space that didn't carry sound, but of a sudden it no longer mattered. There was a final surge of energy as the ghost-ray responded to the siren call of death, and vanished from the oceans of R'debh. Black light and stabbing pain burst out behind her eyes, between her ears. She screamed, not hearing herself, wishing for an unconsciousness that would not come.

And then it was gone.

As if some master switch had been turned off, the pain ceased, the tangled Lines were gone, and Reva was left adrift in the ocean like a spratling washed up in the surf. She was breathing hard, a race run against destruction, and she wasn't so sure she had won. Vask was beside her. Had she imagined seeing him *there,* between the Lines?

For all the agony, she didn't hurt now, nowhere a feeling of pain; even the wound in her arm was numb, the bleeding lessened. A confident euphoria filled her.

Feels like endorphins, she thought, like a good MCP trip. With a nightmarish program overlay. . . .

"Reva."

It was Kastlin's voice in the comlink, sounding alien and distant to her ears. She ignored him and cast about, remembering Yavobo, remembering a pursuit. . . . Where was he?

"Reva," the Fixer spoke more harshly now. "There."

He tapped her arm and pointed; she followed the finger to the airlock, Lish's destination, and saw the smuggler moving groggily, to one side by the dome wall. A lone figure closing with her. Edesz.

And Yavobo? She saw the alien emerging from barnacle ferns that clung to the ridge face.

"Take Edesz," she told the Fixer. "I'll get Yavobo."

Lish shook her head to clear it, and blew her breather mask dry of the water that had leaked inside. She looked about her, disoriented, remembering her intent to flee; saw the assassin swimming away and Vask coming toward her.

And Edesz.

She kicked toward the airlock, adrenal boosters still flooding her system but the impact that had stunned her hard to recover from. Her movements were a far cry from the darting agility she could display on land. She shoved her palm against the cycle pad and the outer airlock door pulled itself slowly open, a lock suited for the broad dimensions of vehicles, not intended for use by single humans. She looked over her shoulder to see Edesz nearly upon her, and Vask not far behind him.

The lock slid open far enough to admit her to the water-filled compartment. She had one hand on the moving frame and was pulling herself inside when the terrorist caught up with her. Edesz sank his fingers into her loose blond hair and jerked her back by the head, stripping her breather with the other hand so it slid up, off her face and over his arm. It stayed there where she could not reclaim it to use. She felt the man pull her back, farther into the sea and away from the promise of oxygen that the lock offered. The water burned her eyes and she struggled to strike out at her attacker. Edesz was bigger and had better muscles for swimming, webbed feet and fingers for maneuvering in the ocean. He kept her at arm's length and continued to pull her into the deep by her hair.

Then Lish felt herself yanked to the side, and the water-breather suddenly released his hold. Vask, it must be him, she thought and swam in barely controlled panic to the airlock. The door was fully open now; she palmed the cycle pad a second time, and watched the large hatchway track slowly, inexorably closed. Her lungs were burning, the effort of holding her breath in an oxygen-starved body excruciating. She could barely see beyond the door of the lock to where the two men fought; shadowy figures rolling, curling about each other in the water. How do you drown a water-breather? she thought giddily. Objects fell drifting to the sea floor—breathers?—and as the lock came near to closing, only wide enough for a man, two hands with webbed fingers grasped the frame in front of her.

She would have shrieked if she had had breath to spare. Edesz pulled himself through and launched himself upon her, trying to strangle the smuggler, to make her gasp out the last of her air. Blood pounded in her ears as her efforts to escape spun her about. Then she felt an arm around her waist pulling her back and out the airlock, a nearly sideways squeeze for her through the narrowing gap in the door.

Edesz wouldn't let go, and she tried to loosen his grip around her neck with weakening fingers. He was partway out the lock, tugged through as Vask pulled her. The terrorist seemed to realize his imminent danger in the same moment that Lish saw what to do. The water-breather relinquished his grip, tried to slip back inside the airlock where all of his body from the shoulders down remained.

The Holdout didn't let go.

With the manic grip of a drowning woman—and that was closer to fact than she knew—she clenched the terrorist's wrists in an iron hold, running on the last of the chemical soup from her adrenal boosters. Edesz pulled back, but Vask's firm embrace and a fin shoe planted on the lock frame kept Lish outside the danger zone of the sealing airlock door.

Not so for the leader of the Gambru League. The lock caught him in the upper chest, crushed ribs with an audible snap, and pinned Edesz in a deadly embrace as he jammed open the locking mechanism with his unresisting body. Lish released his arms as his muscles went slack. Vask had recovered her breather from the ocean floor and slipped it back over her head. The emergency air boost from the filter pump purged the mask of water for her. She could breathe again.

She floated, gasping, giving her racing heart a chance to come under control. Kastlin waited for her to regain her air. When she finally did, she gave the Fixer a squeeze of the shoulder in silent thank-you, then looked around for Reva.

Like a guided missile, Yavobo reoriented himself, then moved unerringly toward Lish at the airlock. Reva was in a position to intercept him, and she did so, ignoring the screaming voice of fear in the back of her head. *Almost dead, he had you almost dead.*

She didn't dare try moving through the Lines right then, though maybe there was a way to distract him, like she'd done in the warehouse that time they had tangled before. Taunts would get to him, she knew, and outright challenges. She flicked on her voder and called to the bounty hunter.

"Afraid to fight with your hands, Yavobo? Need a speargun to take out a helpless woman?"

The warrior hesitated, faced toward Reva, slowed to a near-stop in the water. Her tactics seemed to be working.

"What about me?" she continued. "You said it would be you and me again. No one else. So here we are."

Sea Father, it was bravado enough, and it made her sick to her stomach to voice the words. She didn't want an "again" with the warrior. All she wanted was time, time to get Lish away from here.

Yavobo studied her, speargun angled away. He glanced to the airlock and Reva followed suit, seeing tangled bodies and Lish without a breather inside the nearly closed lock. He looked beyond Reva's shoulder, where law enforcement was rallying now that borgbeasts had fled the plaza in fright. Some were looking their way, soon would be moving their way.

The alien's lip curled. "It seems this is not the time, soul-stealer, not for your friend, and not for you. I will see you again, when we can have more time together."

Soul-stealer? Reva blinked. *What is that supposed to mean?*

Yavobo swam back behind the barnacle ferns to the lava ridge, and was gone from sight. Baffled, the assassin stared after him.

Why was he so ready to break off? If I didn't know better, I'd say something spooked him.

With that she turned to look around, see what was worth spooking an Aztrakhani warrior. Saw the aftermath of chaos from the borgbeast attack and stopped, staggered, wondering when and how that had happened that she had not noticed it. Her friends joined her shortly, and Vask shared her shock at the broken bodies and blood-haze that filled the plaza.

"Borgbeasts," Lish explained. "I saw them right before Edesz grabbed me."

Reva tore her eyes away and looked to the airlock, where one glance revealed the terrorist's fate. She flicked her voder off and spoke again on Com 2.

"Let's go." She jabbed her chin toward the plaza, where law enforcers were separating themselves from the terrorists, Skiffjammers, and general destruction. In minutes, if that long, they would sort themselves out enough to notice and pursue the Holdout. "We need to get out of sight while we can."

She led the way beneath ferns on the ridge. Peering through screening black frond, Reva saw they were not yet followed. "You got any 'Jammers left to help us, Lish?"

The smuggler shot her an indecipherable look before querying Com 2. There were no answers. Then a call on Com 1 turned up scattered responses. Some 'Jammers had fled when the borgbeasts attacked, and retreated to the floatweed pond attraction, on the other side of the ridge.

Lish shook her head. "Call it survival cowardice," she remarked in a tone of disgust, then got back on the line with the remaining 'Jammers. "We'll meet you at the ponds momentarily," she told them. "Then we're out of here."

"Hold on," Reva said on the privacy channel. "How're we going to meet at the ponds? If you want to get out of here, I know a route through the—"

"Vent that," the Holdout cut her off rudely. "You know the plan. Let's stick with it. Over the ridge here, into new clothes and out. Leave the second thoughts for later."

Vask stared at Lish oddly, and Reva's stomach did a slow roll as she heard the woman's words.

Oh, no. I think I've been here before.

She probed carefully. "The ridgetop has a flex filter," she said slowly, "so attraction jumpers aren't tempted to take a shortcut over the hill."

Lish snorted. "Had. That's cut."

"When?" asked Vask, seeming puzzled.

Lish scowled. "What's wrong with you two? This isn't the time to rehash infiltration plans. Let's get moving."

She led the way up the ridge face. Vask looked at Reva, shrugged, and followed the smuggler kicking upward past lace fern and grasping frond. The assassin brought up the rear, her limbs leaden with dread anticipation.

Lish was correct. The flex filter had been cut at the top of the ridge. They slipped through the gap and down the other side far from Park Security's checkpoint, where visitors were being turned away from the tunnel to the fire geyser attraction. The trio met up with Skiffjammers by a water-breather snack bar where aliens like large sea-slugs dined on fresh rock limpets.

From there they detoured quickly inside a kiosk of package lockers to retrieve new bodysuits, and used wet-freshers to change in. Reva was conscious of the wound in her arm that still leaked blood, though it had not yet been noticed by tourists or Park Security as she moved amid a pack of Skiffjammers. She snagged a length of damp-patch, intended for bodysuit repair, but usable in a pinch as a crude bandage for her slashed forearm. She stripped out of one garment, smoothed the binding tape over the wound, and regarded the repair job. She could ignore the ache; the wrap should hold her until they got out of the Park and she could safely get proper treatment. Then Reva donned the new clothing, struggling with the seals in the bodysuit and the water-weightlessness that made it hard to dress. It was awkward, and it was an escape contingency Reva had no recollection of planning. "If we're taking time for this, why not go inside the airdomes?" she asked querulously on the comlink. "It's easier."

"We're more mobile out here if we're sighted," came the reply, "and 'Jammers can screen us better. Lords of Ice, Reva, stick with the plan, will you?"

When they reassembled in the water their clothes were different, Reva in a white and gray bodysuit, Vask in bronze, Lish in red with headcowl snugged close to conceal her hair. The assassin bit back her questions. There would be time enough for that when they were clear of Rinoco Park.

The Holdout wanted them to split up and travel with separate groups of 'Jammers. When Reva protested, the smuggler rounded on her on Com 1, where every Skiffjammer could hear.

"I've had enough of your contrariness," Lish said harshly. "If you're on my team, you're on my team, and you take my orders. If you're not on my team, you can clear out. Now which is it?"

Reva's lips compressed to a thin line. Vask's gaze flickered from one to the other. This was not a normal confrontation, though what motivated the undercurrent of hostility evaded him.

"How about we have this out after we're clear of the Park?" the assassin said with forced neutrality.

"How about we get things clear right here?" Lish came back. "You do it my way, or you're gone. Is that understood?"

The assassin's eyes narrowed. "I'll talk to you about this later," she said coldly, and swam off on her own. Vask followed, and left the Holdout fuming.

The escape from Rinoco Park was easy. With the waterland's main flex filter damaged by the borgbeasts' forced entry, silty bottom water was infiltrating the Park and spoiling the view. Tourists were leaving, and though visitors were kept clear of areas where Internal Security was handling mop-up, rumor of disaster and marauding beasts spread rapidly. Half the Park guests seemed to head toward the fire spouts, hoping to glimpse death and destruction, while the other half left as quickly as they could, unwilling to risk endangerment from unsafe attractions or sea-monsters running amok.

Assassin and Fixer rejoined Lish in the entrance dome. The Holdout ripped off her breather with a sigh of relief, and led the trek through the dryer stations and the exit gates. They slipped through with hundreds of other refugees fleeing Rinoco for more desirable surroundings. 'Jammers scattered to catch public conveyances, leaving the area as soon as possible on their employer's order. The smuggler seemed to have a mission of her own, striding ahead of the pair who followed her, using her comlink for communications on frequencies her friends could not monitor.

Reva and Vask exchanged puzzled looks before they caught up with Lish. She stood right-side on to them, affecting a distant pose while she watched the passenger loading lanes impatiently.

"It's not safe to wait here," Reva said, glancing uneasily around the traffic loop that fronted the Park's entrance. "Let's move on, before the Grinds show up."

Lish glanced at her sidelong, then returned her gaze to the traffic lanes. "We'll catch our ride here. Devin is on his way."

"Devin?" Vask spoke in surprise. "I thought he'd be sound asleep by now." The Fixer remembered the drugged-out pilot who had greeted them at Avelar Field.

Lish raised a brow. "Why would he be asleep? He's waiting for us."

Oh gods, oh gods, oh gods, thought Reva, looking from Vask to

Lish. The one remembers too much, the other remembers too little. Are things happening like I think they're happening?

Her questions were put on hold as an air car pulled up at the curb. Devin gave a half-wave, and Reva studied him warily. Same man, same face—and it bore absolutely no sign of days on drugs to push the *Fortune* through her tortuous travels. If anything, he seemed cool and rested and aloof. He motioned to Reva; she and Vask got into the back. Lish went around the front, slipped in beside the spacer, then leaned over to kiss him hello. It was a warm and welcoming kiss, like they'd been doing it for a while.

A kiss that showed Lish's left jaw, and the red Rus'karfa battleslash laser-scribed there.

Reva felt the ground drop away beneath her.

It's happened again. I've switched Lines.

In spite of her best intentions, she'd been swept away from the Mainline she had tried so hard to stay in. Once again she was living a different Mainline, and who knew how far she had come from the original, from the Lish who was her friend?

Her throat tightened. It hit her like the disappearance of her mother, or the abandonment of her parents, or the loss of the lover she'd had once, all long discarded on distant Lines that she could never go back to. Tears welled in frustration over her powerlessness. It wasn't fair to be yanked across the Lines like this, not when she'd made a commitment, by all the hells, for the first time in her life tried to stay, to work things out—

Lish broke off with Devin and spoke to Reva. Her voice was cold. "Your behavior today was inexcusable. We'll talk about it tomorrow, and see if we have any reason to continue our association." She faced forward as if that was the end of the conversation. Devin moved the vehicle into traffic, and Reva stared fixedly at the woman who was not her friend.

I swore I'd stay, she thought, not move Lines, help Lish out—but I didn't promise myself to help *this* woman. This isn't the person I care about. She's a ghost, like all the others when you stray off Mainline. A ghost.

She blinked the tears away, feeling a layer of protective ice settle back around her heart, a return to the safe feeling of distance she had cultivated for so long, that she had grown away from in that other Mainline. Her "real" Mainline, she was starting to think of it, she had spent so much time there out of choice. The thought was bitter and ironic. Now she would never know what happened to the people she had almost grown attached to, like Devin with his battered freighter, and the real Lish, her friend, and Vask, who puppy-dogged her—

Vask, whose hand touched her thigh, not an intimate gesture, but a hard, panicked grip. She realized the Fixer was staring at Lish's caste mark, pointing surreptitiously to see if Reva noticed.

Of course she did. But why would he?

Then it struck her. She reached out, wrapped steely fingers around Vask's hand, pried it from her leg. He looked at her beseechingly and she locked eyes with him as if she could see into the depths of his soul.

"You notice, too?" she choked out in hoarse disbelief.

He nodded, and she clutched his hand harder. "You came, too? You're the same?"

His brows furrowed as he glanced toward Lish. "The same? As I was? Of course."

"Not of course." She gave a hurried shake of the head. "There are ways to know, memories to compare . . . we'll have to talk later." Her mind reeled with the possibilities.

"What's going on?" Vask whispered worriedly. "I saw you, there, in that . . . place. . . ."

She stared at him earnestly, every bit of deadly reserve forgotten completely. Her eyes were those of a child, hopeful, astonished. "I saw you, too. I thought you weren't real, you couldn't possibly be real. I've never met anyone who could—"

She was near babbling, and Lish's sharp remark cut her off. "We'll drop you back at your place. Come to the Lairdome tomorrow at 0900 and we'll see where we go from here."

The Holdout's words were like a dash of cold water. Reva tore her eyes from Vask with difficulty, and saw now the supercilious caste to Lish's features as she awaited a response from the assassin.

Shiran Gabrieya Lish. Was she in mortal danger here, too? Do I even care? Reva asked herself, and knew she didn't have the answer. "O-nine hundred," she acknowledged. Lish nodded and raised the privacy shield that cut off the front seat from the back. Reva shot a nettled glare at the woman's back; it went unnoticed.

She let the Fixer's hand go and turned in her seat to face the shorter man. "I don't believe you're sitting here," she said, hoping to sound matter-of-fact about it all.

"We have to talk." He sounded distressed. "You seem to know what's going on better than I do. I want to understand it, too."

"I . . . I don't have all the answers." *More like a lot of questions, after what happened today.* "But I'll tell you what I can." Her vows of secrecy meant nothing if there was someone she could really share this with, this gift, this curse, of traveling the Lines. She realized as she said it that she was eager to talk.

"Good enough," Vask said soberly, and twined his fingers through hers. She let his grasp stay, for it was not a suggestive or a sensual touch. It was reassuring, like the handclasp shared by two children lost very far from home, and afraid of what they might find there.

FOUR

"Victims of circumstance owe it to fate.
Victims of choice owe it to themselves."

CIII

Reva had forgotten how it hurt, to lose the sense of the familiar. How jarring it was, to become a secret outcast amid places and people grown alien in subtle, disturbing ways.

Amasl's skyline had changed in a way she could not define. The beacon pylons that guided air car traffic were a different color, dark steeloy with green lights strobing instead of blue. The occasional security mecho on street patrol was of matte-browned steel, not the buffed white metal of Mainline. A holovert on a sign showed an androgynous couple embracing in an ad for "Breathless"—an aphrodisiac Reva had never heard of before.

Subtle changes but significant ones. The more visible the differences between Lines, the farther she had traveled. If this was anything like other times, she was nearly as far off Main as she could get and have the same bank account.

Off Main. That distant Timeline remained her reference point. This was a ghost-world, a shadow place full of people who were incorrect imitations of the ones she knew and had reluctantly grown to care for.

Yet even ghosts live out their lives, and in this Realtime, however incorrect it seemed to Reva, the analogs of people from Mainline went about their business like it was just another day.

Behaving like—but not exactly like—their counterparts across the Lines.

"Aawwwrrrrrrrrrrr!"

The Dorleoni called Okorr stumbled out the door of Storage Unit B, Lairdome 38, in the backwater suburbs of Amasl's neighboring Saleks Bay. He staggered like a blind man, bumping against the door frame, doddering to a halt at street's edge.

"Aawwwrrrrrrrrrr!" He repeated his heartfelt cry, back-arched and braying toward the afternoon sky.

Passersby walked a little faster, and Karuu closed his eyes to their indifference. He stood swaying, a furred and disconsolate figure, deciding whether the anguish in his heart warranted another outcry or not.

He decided not. He could not risk the attention he might draw to himself and so forced his eyes back open, liquid brown orbs turning to the warehouse door, drawn by the tragedy that lay beyond. His feet followed the magnet of disaster and led him back into the security-locked haven, where a wealth of stolen cargo containers had once awaited him.

There was nothing there now. The yawning expanse of empty plascrete offended his eyes as he scanned the vacant unit once again. Nothing was left, not a crate, not a packing strap. Nothing. Of hundreds of items, carefully chosen, each worth their weight in andorium in the offworld markets, especially tariff-free as only he could move them—

All gone.

Where could the goods be? Stolen? No. The security codes showed authorized entry only. Someone had come in his absence and cleaned out his stash. And this was not the first, but the last place he had checked. The best of his caches, all six of them, gone. Someone had methodically and thoroughly emptied his emergency reserves, the security Karuu had counted on to gain financial independence from Gerick's stranglehold. There was only one person it could be. Or could have been. Daribi, the only one who knew of all the Holdout's personal caches. Daribi the backstabber, now dead and irrevocably beyond Karuu's reach.

I'm ruined, Karuu fretted. I have no resources. What am I going to do?

The Dorleoni followed up the thought with another ear-piercing shriek, though it didn't help him feel any better. He needed to come up with answers, not wail about his fate. To get out from under Gerick's thumb was going to take money and cleverness. He had thought he had both, until this tour of his secret reserves proved him wrong.

Now I'm as reliant on Adahn as that MazeRat offal thought I was, he fretted. What am I going to do?

Karuu gnashed his teeth at the thought and left the warehouse, slamming the door shut behind him.

CU

Reva punched up the vidnews and left the volume loud.

"*. . . Also this late-breaking word from Rinoco Park, where disaster has struck the waterland and forced the park to close . . .*"

She listened with half an ear as she walked about the apartment, checking out the space she shared with Vask in this Line. The Fixer stood inside the doorway of the apartment suite looking lost while she investigated their rooms. Neutral upscale furnishings, nothing very personal, but cluttered with the detritus that collects after weeks of residence. A jacket slung on the couch arm; holonovels stacked by a float-chair, and one on the kitchen counter by a crumb-speckled plate.

"*. . . portion of the ring dome is damaged and leaking . . .*"

She went on down the hallway, opening cabinet doors, inspecting contents, stepping into the bedroom to see what clothes she had accumulated in this Line. Men's clothing hung in the closet, too, of a size to fit Vask, and she frowned at the only bed—ample enough for two—as if it willfully refused to tell its tale.

They had skipped across many Lines indeed, if her self in this Realtime had something going on with the Fixer. How drastically had other relationships changed? Well, Lish was probably a good indicator of that. . . .

She shoved that line of thought to the back of her mind, into the category of issues to deal with later. The first order of business was to get the lay of the land, see if the extreme timeshift had left her with any big surprises or problems to deal with. She needed to know how far from Main they'd come.

That thought brought her situation home once more, and she clamped her jaw shut on a grimace that threatened to dissolve into tears. She concentrated on the news instead, where live coverage from Rinoco showed the continuing exodus of park visitors and a heavy security presence at the gates.

"*. . . claim to have seen the mythical Sea Father of R'debh, a monstrous creature 'of solid water' which grabbed a borgbeast and then disappeared. These incredible reports are unconfirmed—*"

The words sank in, and Reva took long-legged strides back into the room where the news was on.

"What are we—" Vask began.

"Not now." She grabbed his arm, pulled him down beside her on the couch. "Listen."

The news cut to a handcam image, a stolen interview with injured water-breathers in the back of a care-van. The camera closed with the least-bloodied man, blinking with nictitating eyelids against shock.

"What happened down there?" The reporter's insistent voice came from off-camera. "How did you get injured?"

The water-breather answered unthinkingly, dazed. "Borgbeast slammed into us, trying to get away . . . was an accident. Frightened by . . . the Sea Father."

"Sea Father? What do you mean?"

"He came. He was there. Gigantic . . . took one away. Just vanished in the water, like that. . . ."

"Here, now. Get out of here. Go on!" A security escort pushed between camera eye and prisoner-patient. The lens caught an anger-furrowed brow, then jumbled impressions as the guard pulled the door shut in the face of the intruding camera.

The scene cut back to studio coverage. The exodus from the Park had slowed to a trickle, and guards were locking off gateways. "*There you have it,*" came the voice-over. "*An eyewitness report. The Sea Father of R'debh is said to have materialized in Rinoco Park, along with borgbeasts. Simply amazing! A creature of legend, and the tools of ter-*"

rorism, working together for what ends? More on this within the hour."

"Reva, what is it?" Vask put a hand on her arm, a touch he would not have dared a week before. But everything was different now, everything. . . .

"You alright?"

She heard the worry in his voice, realized she was staring blindly at the news screen. "News off," she snapped, and the room fell silent. She turned to Vask and threaded her fingers together to keep them from trembling.

"That must be it," she said. "What happened to us."

"What is?"

"The Sea Father."

The Fixer gave her a confused look. "You're not making any sense."

"No. I suppose not." She drew in a deep, shaky breath. "Look. Let's start at the start. First, I want to know this. How did you come along with me? Can you . . . shift, like I do? Move Lines?" The question came hard. It was the first time she'd ever mentioned her own ability to another.

Vask heaved a sigh. "I don't know what you mean by Lines, but shift—yes, I can do that."

"How?" Her question was urgent, the look in her eyes like a dagger.

"I'm a . . ." He hesitated. "I have a wild psi talent," he spoke confidentially. "I can do a thing called sideslipping—an upward shift in the energy frequency of my molecular state. It makes me invisible, lets me move through solid matter."

Reva stiffened. "Wait a minute. You're a Mutate?"

It was slang from Sa'adani space, and hit Vask uncomfortably close to home. He swallowed. Mutate implied a mutant identified and, by law, trained to control the psi powers that might otherwise endanger those around them.

"Not exactly," he said. "Not officially."

Reva studied his forehead. No *rus* was visible, the label imposed on formally trained adepts. "A wild talent, you say."

Vask rubbed his forehead self-consciously. "They never caught and marked me." It sounded almost like a boast.

Reva's brow creased, her thoughts in a whirl. Her natural caution was alerted, and in other circumstances she would have abandoned him that very moment. A Fixer who could walk through walls made the perfect spy.

But given the circumstances, did it matter after all?

Not right now, she had to admit to herself. Back in Mainline, maybe, but not Now.

"I saw you disappear in the water," Vask said, easing back into their original conversation, "and guessed you could do the same as me. Then with Yavobo turning to me like I was his next target, it seemed like a good idea to disappear, too. That's when I saw you, in that other space, between the physical and the not. You saw me there, too."

She nodded slowly. "And when we came out of it we ended up here. In this Line."

"Line?"

She knew she had to tell him, and shifted on the couch uneasily. "Look, Vask. This is a long story, alright? And I've never told it to anyone, not anyone who would believe me."

He gestured her to continue, and she did. She told him about her own wild talent, her ability that had cost her family and friends, that had driven her finally into work that kept her separate from any one Timeline. She knew what she said must sound wildly improbable, yet Vask had already seen the proof: a Lish who was not the Lish he knew, a Devin who was as coolly distant as any Rus'karfa high-caste, an apartment he had never seen before, keyed to his and Reva's voice-codes.

The Fixer listened in silence as her tale unfolded. She held some things back: how she could stay present in Realtime, for instance, yet split her attention to survey nearby Nows with her timesense. Vask didn't need to know everything, after all.

She caught the Fixer's uncertain expression. "Do you know about the Sea Father?"

Kastlin had heard rumors. She told him more. For R'debh natives, those who lived under the ocean waves, there was little doubt that something large and immaterial and alien was out there, something that brushed the edges of their lives from time to time.

"So, you see . . . ," Reva struggled to articulate an idea just dawning upon her, "if the ghost-ray is real—"

Vask had the same idea. "And he was there in Rinoco, near us—"

"He must have been. That energy surge—you felt it, too?" He nodded. "We must have been caught up in that energy, and it carried us across Lines."

"Or drove us," Vask agreed. "That makes sense. My talent doesn't involve a timeshift, though. I don't understand how it could affect me that way."

Reva shrugged. "Maybe any shifted state can be affected by the Sea Father. Or maybe it's because you were close to me when it happened. The fact is, you're here. Now."

Vask looked around, mild distress on his face. "Yeah, so—when *is* Now?"

The assassin laughed, short and bitter. "Be damned if I know. I told you. I can never find my way back to a Line that's too far off."

Vask struggled to assimilate all that Reva had told him. "How is that," he finally asked, "when you can see these Lines around you?"

"Think about it," she chided. "You see several variations of Now. In this one the streetboy has a jacket on; in that one he carries it; in the third there's no jacket at all. These are times that are *parallel* to you. You get there by moving sideways and just a little ahead, like, like crossing from one tree branch to another along a twig that touches both. Now, in which of those Lines, on which of those branches, are your parents alive and contracted to each other? You see?" Her tone became acid. "There's just no way to tell, not in that moment when you have to make a choice about which way to go, which Reality to live in. And if you make too many wrong choices, there's no telling where you end up."

Her voice quavered. "You get it, now? We're lost. We're stuck with this bitch version of Lish, and there's no way to get back to Mainline. What was *our* Mainline."

Tears were in her eyes again and she brushed them away angrily. I hate feeling this way, she thought.

Better the calm coolness of disassociation—though that evaded her completely now that Kastlin was with her, knowing about the Lines, a constant reminder that she was not alone in this anymore. How strange, how very, very strange, to have someone with her in this situation who *knew.* . . .

His hand reached out, fingers twining through hers, and she returned the squeeze of his touch. They sat on the couch in silence in the apartment they kept together in this Line, each wondering what to do next.

CUI

"**Boss?**"

The voice spoke twice more before Karuu heard it, an urgent low-pitched call from close by. He glanced around, saw movement in the alley he was passing, a figure hunched between warehouse wall and a broken-down skimmer idling a few centimeters above the ground.

Karuu looked, the face not registering, the voice too familiar to mistake. It was Daribi, skin bleached of Islander bronze. His shaved head bore pink scars from some kind of surgery. One shoulder was stiff and carried lower than the other, and he wore a patch over his right eye.

He was most definitely alive, not killed by Skiffjammers after all.

Karuu snarled. Daribi had left his smuggling empire in ruins. He had looted Karuu's last reserves on this forsaken globe, leaving him poor and at the mercy of MazeRats—

"Awwrrrrrr!"

He launched himself at the broken figure in the alley.

The rush overbore the injured man and Daribi slammed to the ground with sixty kilos of clawing, snapping Dorleoni on top of him. Karuu's ripping tusks were not just for show; one good fix on Daribi's neck and he would be a dead man. The former lieutenant did the only thing he could think of, slamming the palm of his hand into the Holdout's nose.

It was a muzzle structure more sensitive than a human's nose. The sudden pain caused Karuu to roll off, clutching at the blinding agony that was his face.

Daribi scrambled away and to his feet. The skimmer thumped against the ground as he jumped in, then rose and shot down the alley. Air washed over Karuu where he gripped his face with two hands, blood trickling from his nostrils, tears blinding his eyes.

The pain sobered him. As rage fell away, he realized he had made a mistake.

I'll have that traitor dead, he thought. But first, I'll have my money.

CVII

*"**Most wild talents** have been documented, but it's always possible to encounter something new."*

Vask had heard that point driven home countless times at the Academy of Applied Psychonetics. When you found a wilder, your duty was clear. *"They are a danger to themselves and others,"* the Academy position went. *"You are obligated by law and your professional oath to turn over such persons to the Academy so we can properly investigate their talent, and teach them to use it wisely."*

That wilder would also be branded as a known psi power, imprinted with a laser-scribed *rus* for all to see. The subject would be forcefully recruited into the Academy. If uncooperative, she would be thrown in prison or compelled to take psi-suppressant drugs to limit her potential to harm others.

Kastlin had never questioned the logic behind the psi laws before. It had all made perfect sense to him, until Reva.

He studied her, now changed into a casual jumper, sprawled on the couch with one long leg dangling onto the floor. It was late and they had long since talked themselves out. The assassin was lost in a sensie flick on the vid unit, the neurogrip that she wore hidden from sight among the cushions cradling her head.

Vask sat in a too-comfortable armchair and sipped a Lyndir ale. The room lights were on low; he watched reflections from the vid play over Reva's face, greens and blues outlining high cheekbones, straight nose, the curve of her lip.

His Academy masters had surely never envisioned what it would take to "turn over" a wilder like this for study. Vask was pretty sure that was a move he didn't even want to attempt.

And duty requires I arrest her, he thought. She's the mystery assassin wanted by IntSec. I can't prove it, but there's no doubt about it, now.

The killer who did impossible hits, who moved past surveillance cameras without being recorded. Now he was certain she did so in a shifted state.

He looked at her lounging figure and a cold chill ran down his spine. If I could catch her in action, he thought, I'd bet anything she wouldn't show up on the vidpix. That was why I could record her doing the Lanzig hit: she didn't move across Lines right then.

He drained the last of the ale from its chill-pack container, and got up to get another from the kitchen. When he returned to his chair, the flick had ended, and Reva was sitting up.

"Entertainment's no better in this Line than in Main," she said dryly. "See you in the morning."

"Night."

She left the room, appropriating the bedroom to herself. This Reva obviously didn't intend on sharing her space, regardless what her other self might have been doing in this Line.

Kastlin welcomed the buzz he was getting from the ale. It saved him from trying to sort out the paradoxes that suggested themselves. The assassin was no source of enlightenment; she had given up attempting to answer the unanswerable a long time ago.

"What happens when you shift Lines?" he had asked earlier. "Does your body physically move dimensions, or just your consciousness?"

Reva guessed it was consciousness, since an analog self seemed to exist in each Line she visited.

Why, then, did she physically shift into an altered state?

The assassin had only shrugged. "I don't know, Vask. I could never figure this all out. You'd have to be some kind of Mutate Master to do that, and I'm sure as hell not."

He'd swallowed uncomfortably and changed the subject. He *was* a master-level Mutate, and had as few answers as Reva did. He had plenty of theories, though. Reva didn't know enough about psi and talents to know what to look for, or how to experiment creatively, to make sense out of her ability.

Vask did.

Was her talent one that could be learned and duplicated? If he could learn it, maybe he could find a way to a specific Timeline, even though Reva had failed to do so. He was better trained, could surely think of more things to try—or, perhaps, the *right* things to try.

It was a tempting proposition, and a frustrating one. An arrest would make his career, but she wouldn't be teaching him anything, then. Then there were the ethical—and oath—claims the Academy had laid on him, about wilders. . . .

Vask gulped down half the ale. It was easier not to decide anything, yet. He needed to get his bearings before making any major decisions. Just discovering that they kept house together here was one more unsettling thing in a day full of shocking revelations.

It wouldn't be such a bad deal if she enjoyed my company, he thought wryly. So why do I feel kept at arm's length?

He regarded the blankets stacked near the couch and sighed. Finishing his drink, he quickly made up a bed to sleep in.

Reva's door, of course, stayed closed throughout the night.

Yavobo tended to his business while others slept.

The lanky warrior studied the dock and loading bay of Lairdome 5 from a sea-sled 200 meters out in the warm harbor waters. He wore a black bodysuit and rode a dark aqua-colored sled, buoyancy set so craft and rider floated just below the surface, like a submerged log. To foil any underwater sensors that might detect him, the sled mounted a thermal curtain generator, a device that diffused his shape and heat signature into the surrounding surface water. Only Yavobo's head and hands were visible, glistening with seawater sheen.

The warehouse area was quiet, no small craft in motion, no dockworkers about. Yavobo lifted the night-glasses at the end of a wrist strap and put the light-magnifying lenses to his eyes.

Lish's stronghold leapt into sharp relief. The seaward side of the complex was dominated by the bay doors of the warehouse. During the daytime, they would be opened onto the ramp that sloped directly into the water. At night they were secured and guarded by security bots inside the Lairdome. It wasn't possible for Lish to block off her dock access with an underwater fence, like the one surrounding the marina—that was against harbor regulations. But the guard he had interrogated had described an elaborate system of perimeter sensors, including some kind of underwater alert that announced incoming traffic, in operation both day and night.

She would have guards stationed underwater to back up the alarms, of course, but a few Skiffjammers wouldn't be much of an obstacle to an Aztrakhani warrior. And with the right timing, the Holdout would be in sight when he got inside. Then surprise would negate all her elaborate precautions, and Yavobo only needed a moment in which to make the kill.

This was going to be enjoyable.

CDIII

Vask awoke entirely too early. It was dark outside, a thick sea-fog hugging ground and windows, beading the glas with moisture. He pushed a hand through rumpled hair, and trudged over to the com console against the wall.

He was sitting in the chair before he realized why he was there. Gotta check in, he thought. I've been out of touch too long. Obray must be wondering what happened to me.

He glanced down the hall to the bedroom. He would make it discreet and fast; and if Reva by chance got up right now and overheard the call, he could pretend he was checking with his answering service. The terse language he used with Systems Control would be ambiguous enough if there was reason to fear an eavesdropper.

He punched in the special call code that connected with the field center. As usual, it was a voice-only link, so only the *wheep* tone let him know connection was being attempted.

"MTS," came a woman's voice. "What is your account code?"

Vask stared dumbly at the com unit.

"Money Transfer Systems," the woman spoke again. "I said, what is your account code?"

"Money transfer systems?" was all Vask could choke out.

"Yes. Are you one of our clients, sir?"

"I—no. I'm trying to reach Systems Control." It was more than he should have said, but the code he'd punched was visible on the com display. This should be Internal Security. Who was using this number?

"They're not at this code. I'm sorry, sir, I have to ask you to clear this line."

"What—who are you?"

"We're a money market broker, listed in the Services Directory, and this is a secure line for our priority clients. I'm sorry, sir, I really must clear this line."

The click of disconnect left white noise on the com speaker. Vask sat in shock. If he'd had any doubt, needed other proof of his timeshift, this was it.

And if the code to Systems Control had changed, what else had changed along with it?

CIX

Vask had long been up by time Reva came into the kitchen for food. She was clad in what he thought of as her "serious business" garb — bodysuit of charcoal gray, darkened hair — and the air of spring-tight tension about her cautioned him to keep to himself.

She sat down to eat and offered him food as an afterthought, pointing to the extra staying warm in the cooker.

He took it, and they sat at the counter together. Kastlin felt funny, and it took him a while to realize he had a nervous stomach.

Feel like I'm going on stage, he thought, without knowing any of my lines.

"So, how do we do this with Lish?" he finally burst out. "We don't know anything about her, in this Line. What kind of relationship we have, what's gone before. . . . How do you fake your way through this?"

Reva gave a tight smile. "I play it by ear."

"Isn't that kind of dangerous? Not knowing where you stand?"

She sipped from a cup of osk, wrinkled her nose at a broth saltier than expected. "That's the problem. You learn to be a good actor, and ask the right leading questions. Look — you follow my lead, alright? I don't want you saying something that'll sound too outrageous, like you dropped off a moon or something."

Kastlin frowned. "I don't usually put my foot in my mouth."

"No, but it's easier to trip up than you know. People either think you're on drugs, or get pissed at your 'forgetfulness.' Until we're clear where we stand with Lish, keep quiet."

He tilted his head in concession, and they finished their meal in silence. Reva called a taxi and headed for the door.

Vask was following her when it happened, a sudden buzzing behind the mastoid bone of his left ear. It caused him to jerk his head up, falter in midstep. Loud enough to drown out conversation, it seemed. It was a sound he hadn't heard since the implant was tested after his graduation from training.

"Something wrong?" Reva asked, looking at him oddly.

He forced himself to behave normally. "No, uh, just remembered something."

"What?"

That Mother is calling me home right now, he thought. "Nothing important," he told the assassin, and walked out the door.

This was the damnedest time for Obray to recall him. Something big was up; the recall sounder was a last-ditch emergency beacon to reach an incommunicado agent. His ass was fried now: he'd been out of touch too long, or he was being pulled from field duty, or a major emergency had happened. When recall was transmitted the standing order was disengage yourself from field activities immediately, and report back in person.

After a minute the implant fell silent. Vask knew it would sound again, repeating every hour until he returned to IntSec offices. His stomach erupted into the acid fire of stress, and he frowned as he trailed Reva down the hall.

This was going to be a very long morning.

CX

The warehouse complex looked as they remembered it, until they entered Lish's office. It was more finely appointed than the workaday shipper's office they'd known, this one with plush cream floor matting and sonic sculptures on desk and shelves. The Holdout carried herself differently, too: her body language stiffer, more formal than they were accustomed to. She turned a sharp gaze on them, one glance at nearby chairs enough to order them seated.

Vask complied. Reva managed to take a seat slowly and make it look like her own idea.

The Shirani smuggler leaned against the edge of her desk, arms crossed on chest, clothed in a red work coverall of finer make than any Reva recognized. The battleslash caught her eye again, the unexpected splash of color distracting from that fine-boned face, a countenance that now belonged to a stranger.

Lish's voice hadn't changed, at least, and the edge to it demanded attention.

"I've been thinking about our arrangement," she began. "After that business in Rinoco, I've decided we don't need a discussion after all. I'm terminating our contract." She considered something, then added, "You did well enough, on security advice. I'll give you a reference, if you need one. You, too, Fixer." That last an afterthought.

Reva's lips thinned, one brow arching in unconscious surprise. A reference? As if she did security work for hire? She didn't dare inquire about those details, but wanted to know more. Now, what would draw Lish out? Maybe playing off that imperious high-caste attitude. . . .

"Why no discussion?" Reva demanded. "If you're unhappy with my work, clarify what you expect."

Lish regarded the assassin coolly. "How often do I have to make my expectations clear? You offered to handle security. Fine. You did that. And questioned me in front of my derevin, and tried to take charge of operations. And now—"

"And now we know Yavobo is after you. This isn't a smart time to send me—to send us packing, Lish."

Of that much she could be certain, anyway. Yavobo had targeted the Holdout both before and after the timeshift in Rinoco Park.

Lish moved around the desk, answering serenely enough, in defiance of her body language. "I'm leaving when Devin's ready," she said. "I know you think I'm in danger from Adahn's hit man. But I'll be safe as long as I'm on my own turf, surrounded by 'Jammers. The ship will be ready in two days, and then I'm gone."

"But if—"

"This discussion is closed."

Reva regarded the arrogant and overconfident woman across from her. "Played castle-stones lately?" she asked on a sudden impulse. The smuggler looked at her blankly, and Reva shook her head. Her gut was telling her right. This woman wasn't making the right calls. Not like the other Lish, who'd started to smarten up and plan for the unpredictable. This one didn't play the great game of strategy in stones, or in real life.

She glanced at Vask and caught his eye. There was no reason to stick around here. If Yavobo wanted the Holdout, Reva didn't intend to stay close to this target any longer than necessary.

Lish busied herself with the desk console, then stood, pulling one plastic chit and then a second out of a slot on the console. Credit chits, withdrawn in that moment from her online account. She handed the money markers to the couple before her. Vask took his from her hand; Reva ignored the proffered card, so the Holdout dropped it in her lap. "Sorry we won't be doing any more business together," she said, her inflection imparting the opposite. "You'll want to clear out your room."

She nodded toward the wall, and the residence quarters beyond. "I expect you'll be out of here by the end of the day," the Holdout concluded. "After that your names are off the access list. Call my business number if you need a reference." Then she turned her back on them, done with an unpleasant task, and adjusted the position of the sculpture on her desk. Chiming notes rang out as her hand disturbed its sonic wave field.

It was dismissal, rude and brief.

Vask looked at Reva and she nodded toward the door. They left without farewells, and the Holdout didn't bother to watch them go.

"What do we do now?" Kastlin hissed as they walked the hallway past Skiffjammers and rooms of shipping supplies.

"Wait." The single word was all Reva would yield until they came to their room.

Lish had provided separate but adjoining quarters in that other Line. Now Vask walked into the room that had been his own—then tiptoed right back out again. In it were off-duty Skiffjammers asleep in their bunks. Reva's room, it turned out, lodged them both. Like the apartment, they shared here as well.

Vask followed her inside and shut the door.

"What are we going to do?" he asked. "She didn't tell us all that much."

"No, she didn't." Reva roamed, opening lockers and drawers, seeing what was there to salvage. "Though it would be pretty stupid to ask much more. Of her, or the 'Jammers."

"Why not? We might sound forgetful—"

"We could sound worse than that. We could sound brain-wiped."

"So?" Vask joined her in the rummage through drawers.

"If it seems like we don't remember simple things we're supposed to know on a daily basis, like someone's name, or Lish's call code, and we fuck up often enough, they'll think we've been wiped. And that means we might be spying, or turned to the side of whoever wiped us." She shook her head. "It's too dangerous. Better to be ignorant and pass as best you can than to give yourself away by asking too much."

"Uh-huh." Kastlin took in the logic of that policy, and found he couldn't argue with it. "I still don't like being in the dark, like this. There's too much I don't know."

Reva gave a small snort. "That's right. And you won't, until you have your nose rubbed in it."

"Meaning—?"

"Oh, like traffic laws change—you get pulled over for a violation you didn't know was a violation. Only it is, here. Or call codes change." Kastlin ticked that one off in his head. Systems Control, unreachable. "It's the small things trip you up. Believe me. Like asking for a kind of food no one's ever heard of. No one can help you with that."

"I'd feel better if I could hear some street talk, though," he said. "How the 'Jammers stand, what Lish's reach is on the waterfront. Stuff like that. Things we used to know."

Reva shrugged. "That couldn't hurt."

"You know what?" he said. "I don't think there's anything here I care to pack up and drag off with me. Nothing I can't replace, anyway. I'm leaving it."

"Oh?" Reva turned around, the Sundragon blast tube in her hand. "Look what I found." In this Realtime, the weapon had been left behind in the Lairdome, instead of in Lish's car. She slipped it now up the right inside forearm of her bodysuit. "Sure you don't want to look a little closer? Might be surprised at what you find."

"Maybe later. I'm going out for a while. See what I can hear."

Reva continued her search. "It's your party, Fixer. I'll meet you back at the apartment."

"Right." He raised a hand in a lazy farewell. "See you later," he said, and left the room.

A once-through of their quarters assured Reva there wasn't much she'd take with her. The holo-novels could stay there to enliven some 'Jammer's off-duty hours. A color-brush—that went into her carrybag, along with some earrings, a splash bottle of perfume, a few items of clothing. She'd pulled the electric blue Lyndir-cut dress off the rack before she realized what it was.

The dress she'd worn when she confessed to Lish that she'd been hired to kill her.

In Mainline, it was in a closet at Evriness. She sat on the bed, dress in hand, looking through it and into that other Timeline where it was charged with significance.

Why was it here, now, at the Lairdome? It was the kind of mystery that hinted at so much more. Had her actions in this Line been different?

There was simply no way to know. And no safe way to find out.

Her clenching fingers balled the dress up into her fist, and tears came unbidden to her eyes. It was always like this after such a drastic change.

I hate this, she thought. The not knowing. The lost connections. I promised myself I'd never come so far—!

She cut the self-reproach short. There was no help for it. She had had no control over it, not with the Sea Father involved.

I'll stay out of the damn water from now on, now that I know better.

She glanced toward the closed door, and imagined the hallway beyond it. Was this it? Just simply walk out of here? It felt wrong to abandon Lish, knowing Yavobo hunted this woman, after she'd spent so much time and energy on keeping the smuggler alive. The Holdout still looked pretty damn good to her, too, even though she was so high-handed you wanted to smash her face in—

But the Lish she was drawn to was a different person, in a different place, another time. It wasn't this woman.

Let it go, Reva. . . .

She sighed and tossed the dress back on the rack. That particular shade of blue she could live without.

Slinging bag over shoulder, she headed down the hall. Past lounge, past 'Jammer ready room, and out into the warehouse bay. She spent a heartbeat considering a last talk, a good-bye, anything that might bridge the distance between her and Lish—and gave it up for a bad idea. She turned then, to walk out of the Lairdome, back into the muggy bright R'debh day where she could resume her life in this now-alien place.

Then she noticed Skiffjammers forming up, blast rifles unslung and at the ready. An officer escorted someone back through the gates and into the warehouse. The officer was Eklun, wearing Captain's flashes. Reva did a double take before the stranger by his side compelled her attention.

It was a cyborg. The armored body looked like a mecho's, blued-duralloy plating and servos hinted at by streamlined joint housings. The face was human except for cyber-eyes and the skull casing, gleaming blue-silver like a helmet as he passed from sun to shadow.

She glanced back, and saw that Lish had emerged from her office. If there was danger in meeting the cyborg, she wasn't going to risk dealing with it in the confines of a closed-in room. In the warehouse bay, 'Jammers could maneuver and give her cover. Security bots swiveled slightly, tracking the newcomer through targeting sights, although they remained passive, reassured by the 'Jammer escort and lack of threatening movement.

Who could this be? Reva wondered. Then she saw the Holdout pull a credit chit from her breast pocket, a gray card with the hint of a holographic validation stamp on its surface. The cyborg reached out one gauntlet-like hand, took the large-denomination bank marker with a movement as smooth as if flesh and blood animated the armored shell.

"Tell Hajba thanks for his help." Lish's voice carried faintly to where Reva stood, and suddenly the assassin realized what she was witnessing. In that other Mainline, Reva and Vask had agreed to deliver payment to the Scripman's pickup point. In this Line, he'd sent someone to collect: a one-man task force capable of claiming his pound of flesh if necessary.

Lish had made it, just under the wire, and was in the clear by over 7 million credits. Rich, by anyone's standards.

The cyborg departed with a half-bow, a strange gesture from a creation neither man nor mech. The derevin escorted him back to the gate and the air car waiting there. Reva felt eyes on the back of her neck then, and turned to see Lish staring at her. Hands on hips, as if to say, there, it's done, it's all taken care of. Rid of the Scripman, and rid of you.

Reva returned the stare until the Holdout broke off, her slender red-clad figure retreating into her office. Then the assassin left Lairdome 5, out of the gate now devoid of car and cyborg, and went back to the meager haven offered by her north city apartment.

CXI

In Mainline, the Ministry of Internal Security had offices in a towerplex near the government center of Amasl. In this Realtime, the whole architecture was subtly off. The place where Security's highrise should be was now occupied by a small park with a leaping fish pond as its centerpiece.

Vask swore under his breath.

Internal Security didn't advertise its presence and wouldn't be listed in a lobby directory. There were eight offices ringing this plaza. Where to start?

Two hours later—and two more head-pounding recall alarms later—he was inside the third building to the north of the plaza. He found what he wanted at his third stop down from the top floor.

Instinct cautioned him to come in like an ordinary agent, in the physical, to see and be seen among his peers. So he surrendered thumb- and retina print at the door, offered his field ID code, and was admitted into the Ministry's offices on Selmun III. Obray met him personally in the door to his office and ushered him in. The Commander took a seat behind his desk, and Vask dropped casually into a nearby chair.

"What in the seven hells is wrong with you?" his superior officer roared immediately.

"Sir?"

"You wounded or hurt?"

Vask blinked in surprise. "No."

"Then get the hell up on your feet and report, man!"

Kastlin sat for a heartbeat longer and then shot to his feet. His heart was racing with sudden anxiety.

Shit. Reva was right about that. It's the little things that trip you up.

Obray studied him with flint-hard eyes, his dress whites crisp and smooth, his hands resting on the desktop spaced apart just so. He toyed with a writing stylus, the only sign of tension Vask could detect in the man.

"Well?"

Kastlin drew himself up. This was a drill from training school, reporting as ordered to the officer of the day. He remembered the drill, but went through the motions like an ill-rehearsed stand-in.

"Agent Kastlin reporting as ordered, sir. I heard the recall."

"Took you a damn long time to get here, too. What? Three, four hours? What was the delay?"

"It wasn't possible to disengage immediately, sir. I was in a meeting with our subject of investigation, Shiran Lish."

Vask heard himself say the half-lie, and winced inside. As if he'd been with Lish that whole time. That was the first time he'd ever colored the truth in a report. It was one thing to omit irrelevant info and unconfirmed theories—everyone did that, now and then, and he'd held back his share about Reva—but an exaggeration like this was as good as a lie, and lies belonged on the street, not in an official report. Thank the gods Obray was no sensitive or truth-reader.

"I want a briefing in full, Kastlin. Update me on events since the sweep at Rinoco."

"Yes, sir."

"Go on, then. What happened after the borgbeast attack? We lost track of you."

Vask wondered if the slow marshaling of his thoughts seemed as ponderous to Obray as it did to himself. Probably; the Commander was looking more grim by the moment. He said what he could, then, erring on the side of brevity—no telling what this Obray knew, or how much he himself had held back or volunteered in the past events of this Realtime. Kastlin lied by omission, and wracked himself as he heard a bare-bones narration of events pass his lips. Too bare.

I can hardly tell him about the ghost-ray and the timeshift, he agonized. Can I? I don't need to muddy the waters with that issue, not until I have it figured out for myself. Stick to the facts for now—where I was, what I did.

He related how he'd followed Reva and Lish, struggled with Desz, and later slipped out of Rinoco Park. How it had seemed important to stay with the assassin, who seemed upset over events in the waterpark—an understatement that almost made him laugh with nervous tension. Then the meeting with Lish, ending in Reva's termination, and dismissal of them both from the Holdout's association.

He made no mention of Yavobo, and hoped that was one tidbit

missing from Obray's knowledge base. Kastlin finally wound down and remained at attention, awaiting his commander's response.

Obray Parnos drew his brows together, looking for some flicker of unease in the Mutate before him, and finding none. He dropped the stylus on the desktop and pushed himself back in his chair. He didn't offer Kastlin a seat as he addressed the agent in clipped, formal tones.

"I think you've gotten too involved on this assignment, Agent. At the very least, you're out of touch for too long. At worst, you're getting involved with these criminals as if they were real people. I don't like to see you risking your life to save the butt of someone destined for brain-wipe and prison."

Kastlin said nothing, and kept his eyes on the cloud-smeared sky beyond Obray's window.

When no response was forthcoming, Obray continued. "The reason I sounded recall is this. I want you well away from Lairdome 5 this afternoon. I'm bringing the Holdout in for questioning, and I don't want you accidentally caught up in the action, if there is any."

Kastlin started. "Questioning, sir?"

Obray smiled slyly. "A grab-and-dump. Terrorists have given us cause and hearsay evidence. Now we have sufficient reason to pull her in. When we're done, we'll have all her secrets. Then we'll arrest her, and she'll be out of action for good." The Commander seemed proud of himself, as if it were a coup. From his standpoint, it was. Kastlin didn't feel the same.

"You know her layout there. Sit down with Lieutenant Adari to map it out. I want to know where Skiffjammers can hide, where her security bots are positioned—the usual."

Kastlin could only nod in silence.

"Good. Then there's one other loose end I want tied up. This assassin of yours. Bring her in. As soon as Shiran is locked down, we're off this ball of mud and on to bigger and better things. I don't want you wasting your time on some minor bomb fanatic. We'll bring this killer in and let the Grinds take it from there."

Kastlin offered a salute by way of acknowledgment. It wasn't his habit, and the old Obray would never have expected it, but this—this wasn't the old Obray.

His superior returned the salute from behind his desk. With long-unpracticed military precision, Kastlin spun about-face and marched stiff-backed from the Commander's office. It was the only way to avoid betraying himself by eye contact or speech.

Lish's taking down was inevitable; whether this Holdout or the one he knew, he'd seen it coming for a long time. Why, then, did he feel like a traitor, compelled to reveal her security arrangements?

As for Reva—she was his ticket out of this Timeline.

There was no way he was turning her in now.

He let himself back into the apartment, and found Reva engrossed in another holovid. He tapped her shoulder. "Can you stop that?" he asked. "We gotta talk."

She nodded and pulled the neurogrip from her head. "What's up?"

He ran a hand through his hair and let a studied look of worry crease his brow. "The bottom line is this. I want to go back. You want to go back, too."

"What have you got in mind?" she asked. "Made friends with the Sea Father lately?"

He quirked a smile. "No, but I think if we work together, we don't need the Sea Father to help. I want you to teach me your timetravel trick."

Reva shook her head. "It's nothing I can teach, Vask."

"Have you ever tried?"

"Well . . . no, but—"

"Listen. I've read all kinds of stuff on psi talents. I wanted to know all I could. I think I can at least ask the right questions. Maybe this is a learnable talent. Maybe not. We won't know until we try."

"Say you learn it—what then? How does that help us?"

"I'm thinking there might be a way back, that I can figure out—"

"Beldy guts, Fixer." She leaned back in the couch. "I've been trying to figure that my whole life, and if I haven't had any luck, what makes you think you will?"

Because I'm trained for this and you're not, he thought, and then invented another answer he could speak out loud.

"We each have different perspectives on our talents. I think working together we might find a way to navigate across Lines. But I can't even experiment until I know how you do this kind of shifting."

"Mm." Her expression darkened. "What do I get for this? I don't know that I want to share my skill with you, even if it is possible."

"I'll teach you how to sideslip, if you can learn it. Even trade. And we might get back to Mainline. The one we know."

She considered for a while, and finally nodded. "I'll try it. When do you want to start?"

"Right now."

"This minute?"

"Yes."

Reva looked him up and down and gave him a knowing smile. "Some old girlfriend didn't recognize you? Or someone came after you for a debt you didn't know you owed. Right?"

He grasped the excuse. "Something like that."

She nodded understanding. "If you can do anything to get us back where we want to be, that's fine by me. So let's get started."

CXII

"Ye an't freeloading any longer," Riggo said flatly. "Can't allow it."

Daribi looked up at the Dockboy from his pallet on the floor. He trembled with fatigue and the slack muscles left when too many hoppers wear off suddenly. The derevin chief was just a kid, too young to tell an old Islander what to do. He was doing it, though.

Daribi gestured around the storeroom, cluttered with packing tape, squirt cans of solvent, miscellaneous tools—the detritus of a Dockboy's odd jobs on the waterfront.

"Am I taking up too much storage space?" he rasped.

Riggo blinked. "Ye better vanish yesterday, Islander. There's a want out for ye."

Daribi sat up swiftly. "A want? The Grinds—?"

Riggo shook his head. "A Holdout, with a price on yer head." He smiled coldly. "I got exclusive rights to collect, seeing as I knew ye from Islander days."

"Oh." Daribi slumped. He could guess which Holdout that was.

"Just let me sleep for now, will you?" he said. "I'll be gone soon enough."

"See that ye are. I'm warning ye off, fer old times' sake. Later I'm coming looking, 'cause then ye're fair game."

Riggo's booted foot scraped on the floor and the door closed behind him. Daribi curled up and shut his eyes.

This was not the safe haven he had hoped for, not after what he had discovered: that the Dorleoni using Karuu's old shipping network really was Karuu. In the past, the Holdout had scrupulously avoided being seen on the waterfront, but a name-change was hardly enough to keep his identity secret from his former lieutenant.

The smuggler was working out of Verchiko's Imports, a cover office near the docks. Daribi had hoped that, under his old boss' wing again, he would have a chance at a fresh start. He needed a break to make that happen: this battered body wasn't going to let him lord it over derevin muscle again any time soon.

He shuddered on his cold pallet, remembering again the Skiff-jammer raid, the explosion that had blown him out into the water with other flotsam, thrown him clear of the enemy lurking in the ocean below. Sinking through cold, dark waters. He'd clawed his way to the surface on pure panic-driven instinct alone, struggled toward concealing headland rocks.

After that was a blur. Staggering ashore, promising too much to a streeter to take him to a blackwire shop—days in a haze, his Islander identity erased, tended by medics in a clandestine clinic that stitched up backstreeters on the run.

Since then, avoiding the 'Jammers who would finish the job if they found him alive. The loss of an eye was hardly a disguise and there was no way to buy a replacement, unless he got connected again. . . .

That's what he was trying to accomplish when Karuu jumped him in the alley.

There's no use talking to him now, Daribi thought grimly. He must have discovered the skimming. He'll want me dead for stealing from him.

He huddled into a thin blanket trying to get warm, the tremor of depleted hoppers shaking him with cold chills. A sudden inspiration tensed him up again, almost stopped the involuntary reaction that kept him aflutter on the bed.

Wait a minute. Maybe Karuu *is* a way out, after all.

He'd heard street talk, of a big reward for the Holdout, posted only a few weeks ago. Maybe the offer was still open. He mulled that over as exhaustion claimed his battered body and pulled him down into slumber.

CXIII

Waterspeak wasn't a sign language. Vask was fluent in, but basic signals were easy to pick up. His current vocabulary consisted of the terms *yes, no, stop, wait, look,* and *back to base.* Though used in the waterless void of a shift state, *back to base* meant "get out of here and back into the physical."

Reva made the signal; the Mutate complied.

Forms resolved themselves until the soft glowing outlines of molecular structures faded and solid substance gelled in its place. Vask and Reva were sitting on the couch in the apartment, in a world suddenly full of gravity and hard-edged shapes.

"Damn it, Kastlin," the assassin breathed. "This isn't working."

Reva shot to her feet and began to pace. Vask exhaled loudly and threw himself back against the cushions. It was nearly more frustrating to work with the woman's impatience than with the obscurities of her psi talent.

"We were doing fine. What do you think isn't working?" he asked.

"Shit. I don't get your trick of going immaterial, and you don't get the timeshifting. Even though we can touch, over there. In there." She referred to the ghostly handclasp they had shared, like passing one's hand through an electrical field, the tingle of energy in flux noticeable even though immaterial skin should not carry such a sensation.

"That's good," Vask sighed. "Shows we aren't as out of synch as we look." To him Reva had appeared blurred, her form overlaid on itself in varying positions. To her, the Fixer seemed similarly fragmented, as all living creatures did when she rode the Lines. He was wraith-like, also, the product of his phase-shifting: an insubstantial figure hard to perceive. Yet if they could touch, or something like it, that meant they shared some kind of frequency in common—

"So what?" She interrupted his line of thought. "You can't sense what I'm doing. I don't see you in the Lines as a single figure, like I did in Rinoco Park—that would mean you're controlling your drift, that you have time-independent motion, like me. Your consciousness isn't coming separate from it all. Except for when I touch you."

"When I seem to become more solid, you mean."

"Less time-fragmented. Yes."

"Then in that moment, I *am* in synch with you!"

"You're not crossing Lines on your own. We touch, and I can take you, like dragging you in my wake. The Sea Father Effect." She laughed humorlessly. "But I still can't tell where the old Mainline is from here."

"Wait. Wait!" Vask clapped hands to his head, squinted eyes shut as a sudden inspiration struck. If she can tow me along, he thought, I don't need to switch Lines on my own. What I need to do is see where we're going, like a guide dog—

—and I think I know how to do that.

His eyes flicked open and he sat upright. "Sit down."

"What?"

"Sit down."

Reva bit back a remark and did as he asked.

"Now. Do it again. And this time, hold my hand from the start." She shook her head but followed his instructions.

"Now, when we go—don't stay here. Move as many Lines away as you're comfortable with, and then back again, slowly."

A moment later she shifted, moving her subjective Now to a neighboring Line, and then one that branched off from that, then one more.

As before, Vask came along with her, not through his own doing. But this time, he spotted the change that had niggled at him—the oh-so-subtle variation in radiant energy that he hadn't put a finger on before. When Reva moved Lines, the molecular radiance around them changed color.

This time it was his turn to signal *"back to base."*

When they had returned to Realtime, the assassin looked at him curiously. "What is it? What did you see?"

He made calming motions with his hands as he marshaled his thoughts. Have to get this straight in my head before I say . . .

"Spill it, man. What did you see?"

He leaned forward excitedly. "When I sideslip," he said, "every-thing has a glow. Ambient light, radiating from molecular structures themselves. In the air, in objects around me. That color has always been gray, edging toward blue. Here it's green. And it changes when we move Lines!"

He squeezed her arm and sat back triumphantly, his explanation speaking volumes in his own ears. Reva struggled to follow what Vask was telling her. "So—Mainline has a particular radiance to it, a color, that you can see when shifted?"

Kastlin nodded, rubbing his hands in nervous excitement. "And this Line doesn't look the same as our original one."

"Why not?"

"Don't know. Maybe basal energy frequencies here are slightly different, a little upscale from where we were. It doesn't matter, Reva. All that matters is that this is as good as a road map!"

Her eyes lit up as understanding flooded over her. "You're say-ing I can shift us across Timelines, and you can tell by the look of things how close we are to the Line we came from?"

Vask bobbed his head eagerly. "I think so, yes. You could move out of this energy spectrum, back to the radiant frequencies I recog-nize. Then we should be there!"

"Or so close we can't tell the difference. Oh, Vask!" A broad, beaming grin illuminated Reva's face. Her hands captured his and held them tight. "You think this'll really work? It seems so easy—"

"And impossible for either of us working alone. Yes, I think it'll work. We could go right now, if you want."

"Gods, Kastlin! I love you for this!" Her hands shifted to the Fixer's face, and she planted a kiss on his lips before he could react. Then she was on her feet again, pacing once more. "We can't leave from here," she said. "It's not our apartment in Mainline—someone else will be here. We don't have to take things; everything's waiting for us in that Line already—"

"Reva."

"Best if we go right away, before Lish has more trouble on her doorstep. Bugs must be after her by now, after Rinoco. . . ."

"Reva." Vask stood, grasped the tall woman's arms, and halted her progress across the floor. "We'll go, whenever you like. I'd like to do this right the first time, though, and you've got to be rested and centered—"

She pulled her arms free and scowled down at Kastlin. "Don't worry about me. I may be wound up right now, but I've never succeeded at what we're about to try. *Never.*" Her throat grew tight. "There are a lot of things I would've undone if I'd had your sight, a way to choose between the Lines. . . ."

She turned away. "I'll be ready when the time comes. For now— why don't you help me make some plans? We've got some concerns here besides crossing the Lines."

Kastlin watched her back, then sat on the couch where she had gestured. He'd seen her go from mercurial moodiness to ice-cold nerve before. Doubtless she would do it again when she needed to. And she was right about one thing.

If Security was on the move in Mainline, too, they would both be dealing with more than a shift of Timelines.

CXIU

Agent Jorris hunched into his stained work coverall, snugging his jacket closer against the brisk harbor breeze. To the casual eye he looked like another out-of-work dockhand, burly of frame, worn of clothing. He loitered aimlessly, sheltered in the lee of a net hoist.

"Surveillance team in position," he mumbled into his collar-tab com pickup. He squinted, and the macrocontacts he wore pulled his target of observation into close-up focus. It was a waterfront office 100 meters down the street, a small operation with the sign: "Verchiko's Imports," posted beside the door.

Jorris had let Karuu get away at Bendinabi starport, when the Holdout had first run. If this tip was a good one, he could erase that blunder from his record, and bring in the fugitive who had eluded Internal Security for so long.

The big man smiled to himself and pulled an empty packing crate over to sit on. This was going to be worth the wait.

✧ ✧ ✧

"Do we need to take anything?" Vask looked around the apartment as he spoke.

"No point," Reva answered. "Everything should be pretty much how we left it, if we're on the mark with this shift."

Vask caught her eye. "This Lish isn't going to be happy to see us again."

The assassin smiled coldly. "She gave us until the end of today to clear out, didn't she? Today's not over with yet."

Vask inclined his head. He'd just as soon not return to the Lair-dome to try this experiment, but Reva's argument made sense. If events in this Line echoed those in the other, however faintly, then the Holdout might be lingering on Selmun III—a dangerous inter-lude, for whatever reason, with Yavobo and the Bugs after her. It was best if they could return to not only the time, but the place where Lish was to be found. Reva wanted to make certain she was out of the reach of assassins and Security. It wasn't a plan Vask could argue her out of.

"I guess we're ready, then," he said, and followed her through the door.

I shouldn't be here, Daribi chided himself again. I should be out of sight. Wake up later and call the drop box. If the Bugs made a deposit, I'll know they've got him. . . .

He snickered, a bitter sound devoid of humor. There was a hor-rible fascination in this, watching the Holdout he'd worked with for years get swept up like so much street garbage by Internal Security. On his tip-off. On his turncoat word.

Give it a break, he told himself. I'm no traitor. There's nothing worth my loyalty anymore, and a man's gotta eat.

He'd tried to force himself away from the impending drama, but curiosity had sunk its claws into him and wouldn't let go. So he waited with ghoulish fascination, huddled like a derelict among packing de-bris. There was Verchiko's, down one block; from the alley mouth where he lurked he could just see the entrance.

He rehearsed an imaginary conversation as he waited, things that needed saying.

It's nothing personal, Boss, he said. I need the money, real bad.

Besides, you shouldn't have tried to kill me. Then putting Dockboys onto me. That was too low.

You understand how that goes, Boss. Don't you? You'd do the same if you were in my place. I know you would. . . .

The Bennap warehouses were cleared, offworld shipments set up. There was nothing for it but to visit that bastard Gerick and ask what new thing to begin work on.

Karuu took a ground cab—the cheapest quick transportation he could afford—and ordered the human driver to take the most direct route to the office: one that cut through alleys and along back streets. It was chance that carried him past the alley mouth where Daribi lay in wait, serendipity that caused Karuu to glance that way, and belatedly recognize the figure he glimpsed huddled there.

"No! No!" he told the driver as the vehicle began to slow by Verchiko's. "Keep going. Circle around behind the warehouses and back up the alley we just came out of!"

The man made a face and shook his head but obeyed his fare's directions.

The cab emerged one alley over from Daribi's lookout, and stopped there on Karuu's order. The Dorleoni slipped out to walk gently down the sidewalk toward the next alley intersection. He fished in the belt of his sarong as he approached, pulling out something he'd invested in since starting his search for the Islander. Then, gathering himself, Karuu jumped around the corner of the building and into the alleyway.

"Ha!" he cried. "Do not move!"

The melodrama was lost on Daribi, startled near out of his skin by the sudden intrusion. The man threw himself back against the wall and tried to scramble away, packing scraps slipping under his hands and hip, denying him purchase. He recognized Karuu, saw the doubled hands clasped before the Dorleoni's rotund midsection. He didn't recognize what gleamed there until Karuu's hands jerked, struggling to hold back the thing that wanted to tug from his grasp.

Daribi's eyes widened and he quit trying to scuttle out of the way.

"Ah-ha!" the Dorleoni chortled, his eyes bright with triumph. "You are knowing what I am holding, yes? A seeker. A little sting, that wants to greet you. Talk with me, Daribi, and you may not get stung."

The seeker strained toward its target, the closest source of body heat other than the one who had activated it. Its needle-tipped injector could hold any of a number of drugs, including lethal injections. Daribi licked his lips. Karuu had tried to bite his throat out once; he didn't want to know what might be inside the robotic dart.

"Heya, Boss," he said weakly. "What . . . what's to talk about?"

"You are the good one for alley encounters, though I think we do this better elsewhere. You are please to stand up." A tug on the straining seeker emphasized his words; Daribi came slowly to his feet.

"I kindly give you a ride, now," Karuu said, inclining his head toward the corner where the taxi waited. "After you, my friend."

Daribi walked as directed, his former employer following after. A moment later taxi doors closed, and the vehicle wheeled about, heading away from the office where Karuu had been bound moments before.

"It's a Dorleoni?"

"Confirmed. Not heading our way, though." Mikos watched the departing taxi. "I'll tail him."

Jorris calculated his options. If this wasn't the right mark and he moved the stakeout team, they might miss Karuu. Yet if it was the fugitive Holdout, something was up. There was no point in letting him slip through their fingers again.

They could always come back to the importers later. "Get moving," he ordered Mikos. "We're right behind you."

CXV

Callis nudged the yoke leftward, turning his skiff into the incoming traffic pattern in Amasl's inner harbor. The hand on the controls was steady enough, though his free hand, raised to wipe his furrowed brow, trembled in passage to its destination.

Yavobo noted the fisherman's sidelong glance, a fruitless effort to spy out the Aztrakhani where he lurked in the rear of the skiff's long cabin. "A simple run, Captain," Yavobo told the man, watching him start at the unexpected voice of his passenger. "Stick to your routine, and all will be well."

Callis turned his weather-lined face forward, toward Lairdome 5. He had no choice in the matter. Toughs with green-glowing cybereyes sat with his wife, surety for his cooperation. Yavobo had invited himself aboard, then busied himself with the reserve fuel pods before the fisherman was allowed on the deck of his own boat.

Fear for his wife didn't interfere with the man's ability to pilot. It was just as well, for deviation from the course to Comax Shipping would have earned his death. Yavobo was prepared for that contingency, as for many others, and his unwilling pilot sensed it. The skiff continued true, inbound for Lish's warehouse stronghold.

Reva led the way back into the Lairdome, walking boldly past Skiff-jammer checkpoints. There was no sign of the smuggler, though mechos outside her office were readying cryocases for out-shipment. Reva glanced at her companion meaningfully, glad to avoid confrontation with this unsympathetic version of the Holdout. They moved quickly down the long hall and back to the room they had left earlier.

"So far, so good," Kastlin breathed, locking the door behind them. He was used to sneaking around in an altered state, blindspotting or sideslipping, not brazening it out in broad daylight.

Reva gave him a half-smile. "Now for the fun part. Let's see how good you are with your dimensional sense of direction, Fixer."

She sat in a chair; he sat opposite her on the bed. They clasped hands. "Do this right, Kastlin," she breathed, "or I'm going to be very disappointed in you."

Vask exhaled sharply, almost a snort. "Encouraging words."

"Fuck encouragement." Her hazel eyes held his; she was biting her red-painted lip. "I'm praying you can do this. And I don't pray."

He nodded understanding and gave her hands a squeeze. The return pressure of her fingers nearly made him wince. Then they relaxed their grip, and sat, breathing in a well-known rhythm, muscles relaxing as they altered the pulse and energy frequencies of their bodies.

Their forms shifted, blurred, then faded swiftly from sight.

✦ ✦ ✦

"Incoming, grid C-3, bearing 293 degrees," Zay read her heads-up display in a bored monotone to her second. "What's it squawking?"

"Callis, from Avelar," Novic answered. "His weekly run. A little late, today."

The battered green hydroskiff cleared the channel buoy and headed for the water-side ramp of Lairdome 5. Zay swam leisurely out to the edge of the submerged sensor cones, to meet and pace the skiff back to the ramp.

Since yesterday's attempt on the smuggler's life in the waterpark, the 'Jammers had been on alert. They'd doubled up on guards at all security checkpoints. The underwater team now numbered four; two on the loading ramp, two on the sensor boundary. They traded off every hour.

It was nearing time for that trade-off again. "We'll follow Callis in to the ramp," Zay told her team, "and relieve you at the dock."

Acknowledgment came, bored ayes to a routine procedure. Zay glanced at the vessel's path in the HUD band of her faceplate, and swam to intercept the approaching fisherman.

CXVI

"You have things that are not yours," Karuu confronted his prisoner inside Riggo's bait shack. "If you are telling me about these, now, you can come out of this alive."

Riggo stood to one side, eyes flicking from the Holdout he knew as Okorr to the Islander he'd reluctantly sheltered. Daribi looked pale beneath the shed's skylight, pink scars gleaming against the hairless skin of head and chest. The Islander glared at his former employer, belligerence and capitulation warring in his expression.

"I was keeping your stuff safe," he finally said. "Lish was scooping up whatever the Bugs overlooked. I tried to salvage what I could."

Riggo knew about the streetwar; he knew who Daribi had worked for. He suddenly realized who his boss must be, and regarded him with widened eyes.

"You are keeping silent about what you hear," Karuu spared him an aside, "or you are taking it to your resting place with you. Understood?"

"I'm deaf, Boss," Riggo hurriedly assured him.

"Good. Daribi here is deaf, too, I am thinking." He gestured with the sting, still grasped and tugging in his doubled hands. "I am not asking *why* you stole, you piece of beldy shit. I want my goods back. Where are they?"

The Islander blanched, but he had no stomach to be broken by Dockboys before he was forced to confess.

"Oh, gods, Boss," he whispered. "It's gone."

"Gone?"

"I liquidated some, moved the rest to our base, then the 'Jammers rolled over us. . . ." He rushed to explain himself. "I didn't mean to lose it all, I thought we'd be safe there. It was Lish's fault. I need money too, Boss, I need medical work real bad. Hey, maybe we can work something out—"

"Gone?" Karuu's voice broke into a higher octave. Riggo and Daribi both stared. Whites were visible around the Dorleoni's eyes, and his fur bristled. "Gone?" he repeated, eyes glazed and unseeing. Staring through the Islander, watching his hopes for redemption wink into nothingness.

"Awwwrrrrr!" The ear-piercing howl caused both men to start, distracting them from Karuu's sudden movement. The Holdout released the seeker. The device arrowed from his grasp to plunge unerringly into the Islander's thigh. Injection delivered, the cylinder went inert and remained in his leg, a tube secured by barbed prongs and piercing needle.

Daribi's scream of fear and pain joined Karuu's screech. The Dorleoni launched himself after the seeker and fell upon the helpless man before him.

The shed door cracked open. Cricker stuck his head inside.

"Bugs. Here now, Boss!"

Riggo looked past Crick's shoulder, saw approaching strangers, saw their guns. Flashing lights in the distance warned of Grinds on the way. "Evasion One, Cricker. Center here, on the shed. Evasion One. Fast!"

The youth shut the door; Riggo turned back to the tangle of bodies on the floor. "Boss!" He said it again, louder, then dared to touch Karuu's shoulder. "Dom Okorr! We've got to go, now. Bugs are here."

The words sank in slowly. Karuu eased his aching jaw muscles and looked up blankly at Riggo, blood and matter dripping from his tusks.

"Bugs?"

"Come on." Riggo turned his eyes away from Daribi's gore-spattered body. "We've got about a minute to get the hell out of here."

Karuu came to his feet stiffly, like a drunken man. Riggo pushed aside a storage shelf, and swung a plaspanel out from the wall. "This way!" He pulled the Dorleoni's arm.

They emerged behind the shed. Dockboys were mounting their airbikes; repulsors hummed as they lifted, circling to buzz with open thrusters back down the dock. Two airbikes, five, then seven wove a confusing pattern, circling the shed, threatening the IntSec agents who ducked and dodged out of the way.

Karuu was hoisted aboard Riggo's own vehicle; his bloody fingers clutched the Dockboy's jacket as they shot out over the water. As soon as they were airborne, the other bikers followed them out over the water of the harbor, evading the pair of Security skiffs rushing to intercept. They scattered in eight different directions, weaving at water-level past skiffs and boat traffic, some out into the harbor, some toward the marina, some skirting the waterfront road.

Jorris and his team were left with an empty dock, a body without a throat, and no Karuu.

"Lords of Ice!" the Security agent spat. "This isn't going to be a wash." He turned to Mikos, and the police captain beyond. "Back to Verchiko's," he ordered impulsively. "I don't know who's there, but I want them locked down before they fade on us, too. Move out!"

#

It took three Line-switches before Vask signaled *no*, this was not the direction they wanted. Reva moved again, taking her companion back through one branch of reality, then another, returning to the Line that was their starting point, then going beyond that, cutting across different parallel Nows. A direction that brought a smile and a thumbs-up from Kastlin.

She took his guidance on faith, for as always the assassin could see nothing distinctive about the different Lines she crossed. These varying Nows were not remarkable: in most all of them the pair sat, undisturbed, in the privacy of their room. It was a monotonous panorama, Vask in one pose on the bed, overlaid by a second Vask with elbow on knee, overlaid by a third with his head cocked at a different angle, and so on—each one connected to her, through the ethereal clasp of their hands. Fragmented and blurred, yet looking about with hopeful concentration for all that. She had to take on faith that the Fixer came with her, that his consciousness moved, as did hers, across the perspective of differing Nows.

Their transition was fast, and it was timeless, and from Reva's point of view, it was barely happening at all.

Vask drifted in the greenish glow native to this Realtime. Molecular energy suffused the air with radiance; bed, floor, chair dissolved into sculptures of light and mist gleaming with yellow highlights.

He glanced at Reva, seated before him, the strobe-like figures that overlaid her form—her selves in various Lines—flickering in and out of sight. He tore his eyes from the confusing imagery, and concentrated instead on the reason for their experiment, energy only he could perceive in this sideslipped state. The greenish frequency of light was not the familiar hue of the dimension the Mutate called home but, as he looked about, pulled across Lines in the wake of the assassin, the yellow highlights diminished, faded, then dropped entirely from the visible spectrum. Greens deepened, became blue-green, until blues dominated, each minute variation corresponding to a separate Timeline. Each Line with molecules vibrating at a basal frequency ever-so-slightly different from neighboring Lines. How to tell which one was the place they had started from?

Vask searched for the right mix of color and radiance, the right sheen of ghostly substance to physical objects. They both knew from the start that they might not end up in precisely the same Line where they had encountered the Sea Father of R'debh. There was no way to pick that single frequency out of the hundreds of parallel realities they skimmed through. They could only hope to come close, so close that Mainline would be nearly as they remembered it.

They relied on the Mutate's ingrained recognition, his perception of what was "right"—and so Vask readied himself for that moment, the one he sensed approaching. He squeezed Reva's hand, a gentle flexion of potential, and raised his other hand to alert her. The muted blues and luminescent grays seemed like those he had known before, or so close he could not tell the difference. Before they could drift beyond, he dropped his hand.

Reva heeded his signal, and stopped their movement across the Lines. A heartbeat later they left that state of shifted energy, returning to their bodies, now stationary in this one Realtime. Reva was breathing as if after light exertion.

They collected themselves, eyed their surroundings uneasily. The room seemed unchanged.

"So you think this is it, Fixer?"

There was a quaver to the assassin's voice he had never heard before. "Maybe," Vask answered. "Or pretty close."

"Then let's go see where we've gotten ourselves to."

Kastlin nodded, and the pair headed for the door.

"He's here, Domna."

"Who?"

"Callis. You wanted to know—"

"Ah. Good." Lish nodded to the Skiffjammer. "I'll be right there."

She had readied a big shipment of cases today for the apaku fisherman from Avelar. And this time he wanted an extended warranty on her goods. He was shipping offworld, he said, and wanted the

Mainline

safety margin. Warranty and insurance, something she didn't sell much of. It was a nice piece of extra change, worth a few minutes spent discussing terms with Callis face-to-face.

Lish plucked the datapad from her desk, eyed the warranty contract, and smiled in satisfaction. She walked out her door into the loading bay where the fisherman's skiff was approaching the water ramp.

Reva and Vask walked down the hallway, past the ready room, the lounge. The few faces in the halls looked familiar, but there was nothing yet to prove this Line was closer to home than where they'd been. They neared the warehouse bay, and a 'Jammer walked toward them, unlimbering his blast rifle as he moved to the ready room for his break.

Reva recognized his features and a quick glance at his insignia confirmed what she had hoped for. She stopped abruptly in her tracks. "Sergeant Eklun!" she exclaimed, relief evident in her voice.

The 'Jammer slowed, then stopped, puzzled by the assassin's greeting. "Yes?"

Vask waved him on. "Nothing. It's nothing." He tugged Reva's arm, got her reluctant feet moving again. Eklun passed them by with a quizzical look.

"He's not a Captain," she hissed to her companion excitedly.

"That's a good sign," Vask said, the same effervescent joy starting to bubble up in his own chest. "We need to see who else is the way we left them."

The pair exchanged a meaningful look, and without further conference turned towards Lish's office.

Timing in the stalk is everything. Move too soon, and you spook your prey. Move too late, and it has slipped beyond your grasp.

With unerring instincts, Yavobo let his actions be directed by the pulse of the hunt. His fingers held a release lanyard, and he grasped it gently, caressingly, until the skiff began to ease up the loading ramp, gliding on low-power repulsor skids. The back of the craft was still afloat, and her spare fuel pods, affixed port and starboard of the pulse engine, were out of sight beneath the murky waters of the docking bay.

Ahead was the smuggler's office. Behind were Skiffjammers underwater, and two in plain sight by the bay door. Yavobo pulled the lanyard. With a pop muffled by waves and the thrum of the engine, the fuel pods detached from the sides of the skiff and tumbled through the water, sliding and rolling to the bottom of the loading ramp in nearly ten meters of water. A time-delay trigger ticked away in each, waiting for the swift-approaching moment when the valves would blow and the contents of the pods be spewed forcefully into the water.

Yavobo moved to the rear hatch. "Steady on," he spoke a low caution to the fisherman at the helm. "Just as we have discussed it. You are almost done."

These were the critical moments, the final test of his planning and his skills. Yavobo settled the speargun slung across his back for later use, and checked the breather at his neck. Then he readied the long-barreled sniper's pistol in his hand. It gave accuracy greater than he would need at this short range, and a powerful coherent beam that could hole a light armored vehicle. It would suffice to kill a Holdout, as well.

He readied himself as the rear skids engaged. The skiff pulled clear of the water, and Yavobo set his hand to the hatch.

The warehouse was the same, as were the security bots in strategic corners of the bay. The 'Jammers on dock duty seemed familiar enough. Then the real proof of their success walked out of her office, and Reva felt a smile tug at her lips.

This Holdout was dressed in a plain work overall, not the fashionable red bodysuit favored by that *other* woman. Reva refused to apply her friend's name to the Sa'adani bitch, even in her thoughts, but this person, she knew in an instant, was the friend she had left and thought lost forever.

"Lish!" Reva called out.

The Holdout was heading toward the new-arrived skiff, but looked back over her shoulder at the hail and smiled. With a wave to the boat pilot, she detoured and walked toward her companions.

"Scripman all happy?" Lish asked as they came closer. Reva kept puzzlement from her face. In this Line, had she and Vask already made their promised delivery of payment to the loan shark? If so, was this Mainline, or only somewhen close to it?

Reva couldn't help herself. "Look at me," she said, crooking a finger. "Turn your head this way."

Lish smiled in friendly confusion. "Why?" she asked, but complied with the request.

Reva stretched her hand out, touched the other's jaw. Her left jaw, where the skin was smooth, devoid of caste mark except for the faint blemish only an expectant eye could see.

The assassin felt her voice hoarsen with emotion. "It's you," she said softly, blinking against sudden tears.

"Of course," Lish said, her brow furrowed in puzzlement. She lifted her hand to Reva's, pulled the woman's fingers gently away from her face. "And now that the Scripman is paid, we can wrap up here and get offworld. Like I promised."

Reva barely heard her words. This was too much. Vask's plan had worked. She looked to the Fixer. "You did it," she breathed.

"Alright," Lish said good-naturedly, releasing Reva's hand. "Be cryptic if you want. Let me take care of Callis first, will you? Then we can talk."

She headed for the vessel at the lip of the ramp, water dripping from its hull as engines ticked into silence.

Reva watched her go. Beyond the skiff, the two 'Jammers at the bay door dropped to the ground like puppets with cut strings. The flash of beam energy that felled them was nearly lost against the daylight outside.

Her body registered the danger before her thoughts embraced the concept. She darted in Lish's direction, pulling the Sundragon from her sleeve. "Get down!" she shouted.

The Holdout paused, turned in confusion back toward Reva. A security bot swiveled its torso, aiming at something behind the hydroskiff. Others scuttled into spider-legged motion, attempting to lock on the intruder.

Reva glimpsed a familiar red and black form. Yavobo's head and arm popped into view just long enough to fire, and to flash a feral grin her way. Then the alien leapt from sight, splashing into the water behind the skiff.

Her mind screamed at the impossibility of it, even as Lish stumbled toward her. The smuggler's chest was charred, her clothing blackened around the fist-sized hole where beam had cauterized lungs and heart. There was no trace of blood, only the stench of burned meat as token of death.

There was no friend left in the damaged shell that toppled into her arms. Reva caught at the falling corpse, was brought to her knees by the sudden weight. Lish's face was frozen in shocked surprise, eyes unseeing, mouth open. Not a sound, not a cry had she uttered. Reva stared at her burden in horror. She had come all this way, an impossible journey across countless Nows, for this.

For it all to come to this.

She heard the wail, a tortured cry from what must be a human throat. It was not until she struggled for a lungful of air that she realized that awful, gut-wrenching sound came from her. The tears came then, and she curled over the body in her arms, blind to her surroundings, mad with grief and rage. She pulled away from Vask's touch, until he managed to pry her gently from the body of her friend.

Then Reva cried like she had never cried before, huddled into arms that could only hold her as she keened her loss.

The rigged pods filled the water with marker fluid, a liquid smoke screen of inky black holding billions of particulates in suspense. Each minute flake echoed and distorted sensor pulses until no readings in this water were valid.

It was a short-lived sensor-proof veil, until dispersion should render it harmless. It would last long enough for Yavobo's purpose.

The bounty hunter tugged his breather on underwater, purging dark liquid from the face mask, and forged ahead through night-black ocean. Skiffjammers could not see him or anything else in the occluded waters. One blundered into him by chance; Yavobo had his speargun at the ready, and the bolt, fired point-blank, transfixed the 'Jammer and left him doubled over in mortal agony. The alien swam on.

Soon a manhunt would be under way around the warehouse docks, but by then, he would be long gone. His sea-sled waited submerged near the marina fence, his escape route out the harbor locks was clear, and MazeRats waited beyond to pick him up in the waters of the open bay.

He swam through the edge of the artificial gloom and into deeper waters, heading for where his sled was secured, savoring the image of his enemy, the look on her face as he dispatched the Holdout. It had been enough to smile defiance at the assassin, to let her know she was no threat to a desert-born warrior.

Enough of Skiffjammers, he thought, and of foolish smugglers. Now it is time to hunt the worthy prey, the Oath-sworn enemy.

The soul-stealer called Reva.

CXVIII

A bloodied grieko tumbled from a sunset-reddened sky. The colors matched the angry hue of Adahn Harric's virtual eyes.

"What do you mean, you can't reach anyone?" His voice grated as he spoke the unbelievable. Janus' simself retreated a half-step on the veranda of the crime boss' cyberretreat.

"Simply that," Harric's lieutenant said. "We can't raise Gerick, or any MazeRat on Selmun III."

"You've tried our shippers?"

"They're unavailable."

The Emperor's pleasure gardens shimmered, then dissolved. The men faced each other in a cold and formless void, the wind of cyberspace whistling unheeded about them. Janus cringed; it was a place he associated with Harric's killing rages. A place he did not want to visit, even in sim-form.

"Fuck that," Adahn growled. "Make someone available, any way you must. But find out what's going on. Now."

Janus bowed himself out of cyberspace and into his office chair, where a sheen of nervous sweat had broken out on his physical body. He had seen the Tribune of the Red Hand in a stormy mood before. It was risky to be too near, or too unhelpful.

He closed his eyes to collect himself before doing his master's bidding.

Kastlin imagined he knew what it was like to be a wanted criminal—to know the authorities were closing in, readying themselves to pounce, and himself helpless before their grasp. For now he sat square in the sights of an imminent Security raid, anxious to leave the area, unable to do so, and painfully aware of each passing minute.

Minutes spent ordering Skiffjammers. Moving Lish's body to a private room. Getting Reva out of the warehouse bay, away from staring eyes.

Long minutes waiting for Devin to arrive. Longer yet turning a polite eye aside from the spacer's grief, and now, fending off his need for action.

The big man sat behind the desk so lately Lish's. "Who did this?" he asked emptily. His voice was hollow, as soulless as his eyes.

Vask repeated the name Devin had not yet registered. "Yavobo."

The spacer studied his hands, resting atop the desk. His mouth pursed and the silence grew deeper.

Kastlin fought the urge to order his companions out of here. They wouldn't leave on his say-so alone. Reva kept her own council, stone-still on the float-couch beside him.

Devin pulled himself up decisively. "I'm calling the Grinds," he declared.

"They won't do anything," Vask told him flatly. "You know Lish must be wanted after Rinoco. It's only a matter of time 'til Security sweeps this place clean."

A matter of two hours, he thought fretfully, if this Obray has the same plans as his counterpart. . . .

Devin was oblivious to his concern. "We were partners of a sort, Lish and I," he said softly. "More closely bonded than you know."

"Then IntSec will rake you over, too, when they take this business apart."

A muscle clenched in the big man's jaw. His fingers began to key controls on the desk console. "Then let's start by doing what has to be done."

"What's that?"

"Securing assets," he answered tersely. "I was the closest thing she had to a partner, and her only kin in this place. I'm not letting them take everything she worked for."

Vask glanced toward Reva for her reaction. She sat, eyes reddened, staring through the wall, seemingly oblivious to their byplay.

The com unit disgorged a plastic chit, then many more: markers for cash withdrawn from the Holdout's online accounts. Apparently she had shared more with the spacer than her friends had realized.

Devin swept the markers up and pocketed them. He looked to Reva, blind to his gaze, and then to Vask. "We Shirani take care of our own," he said grimly. "I want who's responsible for this."

" 'Jammers are searching the area."

"That's not what I mean. I want Yavobo."

This was no time to plan a vengeance hunt. Vask frowned, prepared to dissuade the spacer, when a familiar voice preempted him.

"You don't want Yavobo," said Reva. "He's not responsible."

The men stared at her. It was the first she had spoken since Lish had died. Her words were measured and bare of emotion. Devin took them at face value.

"That bastard killed my—" He stumbled to a halt, realizing the Shirani term for a partner in *meriös* would have no meaning for his listeners. "She was like family," he began again. "The Aztrakhani killed her. He'll pay."

Reva turned her eyes from their distant focus, and leveled her searing gaze on the spacer. "Adahn Harric killed Lish. He put the contract out on her. He wanted her dead. That's your enemy, not the bounty hunter." Her lips thinned. "He was just the muscle. It could have been me."

Devin's eyes flicked over the assassin's body, a quick head to toe. "I know."

Vask looked from one to the other in stark surprise. The weight of the confession and acknowledgment hung between them, a shared secret that excluded the Fixer. "When did this happen?" he wanted to demand. They spoke on, ignorant of his restraint.

"Lish held *roi'tas* and *senje'tas* with you. She told me after Rinoco. Honor-debt, and life-debt."

Reva raised and dropped one shoulder, uncaring, and Devin's face grew hard. "I forgive your ignorance," he said harshly. "Those are great obligations, not taken on lightly by any Sa'adani. Lish's kin owe you duty and honor." He spoke curtly. "I stand good for my kinswoman's debt to you."

Reva frowned, the first ripple of emotion Vask had seen on her face since she had retreated into stony composure. "You don't owe me a thing." Her tone was bitter. "I didn't succeed in protecting her life when it counted, did I."

Devin's voice softened. "There were other times, other aid, not to be forgotten. Lish would want those debts honored."

The woman exhaled, a barely concealed snort, and turned her head sharply away. Devin eyed her hesitantly.

Vask was riveted by their exchange, yet the sense of time flowing swiftly past was relentless. He came to his feet. "Let's talk about this somewhere else," he prompted. "It's dangerous to stay here."

The spacer's jaw set. "I want to use the Skiffjammers, against Harric. Yavobo, too." He looked at Reva. "We should plan how to deal with them."

Reva flinched at the alien's name. "Don't be stupid about the bounty hunter. And Vask is right; let's get out of here. When IntSec guts this place they'll lock you up and everyone else they find here. Just for good measure."

Devin frowned down at the com console.

"A local derevin won't help you against Harric," she continued. "To get him, you have to strike where he lives. Offworld."

Her words drew the spacer like a magnet. "You know where he is?" he asked grimly.

Vask watched silent understanding pass from one to the other. The assassin finally spoke, eyes narrowed in calculation.

"I don't know where he is," she said coldly. "But I know how to find him."

Nomad and Zippo ransacked the house systems at Verchiko's as soon as MazeRats were cleared from the premises. Gerick's records were not as deviously obscured as Karuu's had been, and after interrogation the MazeRat had no will to hide much of anything.

Finally the source of the cargo conspiracy was laid bare. Selmun authorities were set to work shutting down the local Harric network, and Obray marshaled his agents for immediate transfer to Bekavra.

Jorris led that afternoon's sweep through Lairdome 5, a raid made urgent by a fisherman's garbled report of an attack there. The place looked like someone would return at any moment, but the Holdout's computer systems were wiped and her Net records deleted.

After pressure and bribes, street rats confessed that Skiffjammers had left the premises a few hours before, taking some goods with them. Of Shiran Lish and her usual companions, they had no word, nor could they be persuaded to share one.

Reva addressed a blank com screen. "You feel like interrupting your vacation?"

"You have work for me?"

"If you want it. It's involved. Risky, too."

"You said the magic words. Let me call you back on a secure channel." The comlink went dead. A moment later Reva took Flash-Man's incoming call.

"So, babe—what would make you happy today?" the netrunner asked.

"Two things, one small, one big."

"The small one is — ?"

"Trace a call code. It connects with a man named Adahn Harric, a crime boss, so I'd bet there's ICE on the line. It relays to another subsector, I don't know where. I need a thorough trace, down to the address where the code originates, if you can get it."

"Riding relays is tedious. I charge extra for tedium."

"Charge extra for the ICE, too."

"I will. When do you need this?"

"An hour ago."

"Time is money. Rush jobs cost more, haven't you heard?"

"You charge for everything, Flash."

"Why, so I do. What's the big thing I can bill you for?"

Reva took a breath and then plunged on. "When we know where Harric is, we're going after him. I want to take him down."

"Can't help with your line of work."

"You don't have to. Adahn runs a little empire, and what he doesn't manage with street muscle he handles through the Net. That's where I need you."

"Let me guess. Start with the basics, like security breakdown on his residence, travel plans, general eavesdropping, then move on to infiltrate his operations net. . . ."

"Information is all we need. No file wiping, no reprogramming."

"Aww." The pout was drawled. *"I'm disappointed. This sounds too easy."*

"It's not. His systems are tight, and he has deckers as well as ICE guarding against infiltration. You can count on it."

"Hm. Then I'm not so sad. I'll have to be on-site for that, wherever he is."

"So will I."

"Oh, joy. Travel expenses." Flash's grin could be heard in his voice. *"What do you want all this info for?"*

"In the right hands, it will make life very difficult for him."

A mirthful cackle poured through the com speaker. *"That's it? You're going to make life* difficult *for him?"*

"He had Lish killed."

The words hung in the air, stilling the decker's wisecracks. *"I didn't know."*

Reva let that pass. "I'll put your security briefing to good use, don't worry about that."

"Ah, Reva," the netrunner sighed, *"you are as constant as the sun and moons."* His tone changed abruptly, all business once again. *"Time, as they say, is wasting. What's that code?"*

She told him the number. *"I'm on it,"* he said. *"Later."*

Reva let white noise fill her ears for a time before thumbing the comlink off. As constant as the sun and moons. Right.

Not anymore.

If she acted as she always had, she would be after Yavobo this very minute. But now she was stopping herself. Vask and Devin thought her plan to go after Adahn wise and well reasoned. In reality, she harbored a guilty secret, the true reason for that decision.

She feared Yavobo.

Never before had an opponent scared her, she who was supremely confident of her own skills. Who had been uncaring of death, for the feeling that people were ghosts of real counterparts elsewhere had, in some way, extended to herself. Who was to say that she would really die, when she could shift Lines? Who cared if she lived? No one.

Until Lish, and Vask, and even, yes, Devin. Now a few people mattered to her, and she mattered to them. Somewhere along the way she had lost her indifference, the shield that kept her invulnerable, and cold-blooded as one must be to kill, uncaringly, for a living. The last of that Reva had died in Lairdome 5 right along with Lish. The woman who remained was uncertain about life, about direction. About her ability to kill.

Yavobo scared the hell out of this Reva. He was better than her. He'd demonstrated that already, several times over. Her grief and anger demanded a confrontation with the Aztrakhani. Her sense of self-preservation screamed at her to stay away.

Adahn was the only target that was left, the one ultimately responsible for Lish's murder. And so Reva put this self-appointed task on her agenda, to focus her attention and her rage, and to keep her mind off Yavobo. To take her far away from a murderous alien who didn't know when to quit.

The thought of flight bothered her pride, but the thought of battle with the alien knotted her stomach. Better to concentrate on other things, like getting off R'debh and dealing with Harric.

Before the bounty hunter could find her again.

Yavobo slinked from shadow to shadow with a desert hunter's cautious tread. Avelar's Kriezor Shipyard offered sufficient concealment for his nighttime prowl, if he used it wisely. He skirted pools of activity and flitted between silent workshops, seeking just the right vantage point for his reconnaissance of the *Fortune*. It would not do to betray his presence to the scattered security guards or the stray yard worker.

Yavobo was surprised to find a welter of activity around the holed freighter. Reva had come here with friends that afternoon, but surely she could not still be aboard. Needing to locate his enemy, and hoping to understand what the bustle portended, he risked spying out the offices around the work area.

He peered in window after window, until he spotted the assassin and the others, drinking osk in a refit supervisor's office.

For a moment Yavobo froze, weighing this opportunity to challenge his enemy here and now. But the traffic in and out of the office was too heavy; the trio reviewed ship plans, talked with workmen, argued with the refit super. . . .

This was hardly the privacy he needed for a Blood Oath duel. A later time, then. He retreated to the arm of an unused crane, where he could watch both office and drydock.

Massive worklights flooded the docking cradle with artificial daylight, showing the *Fortune* a-crawl with human technicians and labor mechos. The drive units were released from their interface and lifted clear of the drydock gantries. He grunted as he recognized what was happening.

Instead of repairing damage to the ship, Shiran was replacing the crippled units entirely. The warrior's eye was drawn by a hoisting derrick swiveling about. Its lifting arms held two new drive units, of the same modular design as those just removed.

He frowned as the import of that sank in. The *Fortune* would be lift-ready by morning. With the resources of an entire shipyard at hand, round-the-clock labor, and a frighteningly exorbitant bill, a ship of this modest size could be rehabbed and spaceworthy in no time at all. It was, after all, the great selling point of Sa'adani modular design. Ease of repair.

Yavobo's lip curled. If the soul-stealer sought to evade him in this way, she would be disappointed. He looked toward the office many meters below, glimpsed her well-lit figure pausing in front of a window. He studied her form with unblinking eyes until she moved back out of sight.

No matter. Whether she left the shipyard on foot or left in the freighter, he would be prepared to follow.

Kastlin studied the woman he was supposed to bring in, sooner or later. She poured another cup of osk from the dispenser by the window, stretched catlike to ease her tension, and returned to the table, blowing on the steaming drink to cool it. Small lines around her eyes seemed deeper, a crease between her brow sign that fatigue and tension were taking their tolls. She sat, the charcoal gray bodysuit that she'd worn all day blending into the drab tones of the refit super's office furniture.

It was best if he bowed out. This association had become too compelling, and now he was being carried along on a vengeance mission that he didn't want to know about. A hunt that would amount to one more murder planned and executed by the assassin.

It was something he couldn't aid, and perversely couldn't bring himself to walk away from.

As Kastlin grappled with indecision, the refit supervisor stomped back into the office. He tugged a com set from his head and spread flimsies on the table before Devin. Modifications were discussed, Shiran pointing out two hardpoints he wanted changed, the super shaking his graying head in return.

"Don't have an EMP gun for that unit," he said. "That's special order."

Devin shrugged. "Then make them both ion cannons, and boost the battery power reserve."

The man made suitable notations on his datapad, then left to oversee the workcrews.

Shiran cocked his head at the Fixer. "I don't suppose you have gunnery experience, Kastlin?"

Vask shook his head, distracted.

"You can get it if you want it."

"You've hired on 'Jammers for that."

The humor went out of Devin's smile. "So what are you going to do to help out on this run?"

That barb was unlooked for, and Kastlin regarded the Captain sharply. "There's not a lot I can do on board ship. I think you know I'm not a spacer."

Devin grimaced. "That's evident."

"That's not why I'm coming along."

The trader fixed Kastlin with a hard stare. "Then why *are* you coming along?"

The habit of acting in character as Fixer was strong, and that persona flared immediately. "What in the seven hells is that supposed to mean? Lish was my friend, too."

"Vent that. We've been sitting here all evening, talking about the ship, about supplies, about our plans, and you haven't had two words to say about any of it. Are you in? Are you helping? Or maybe you're just along for the ride?"

It had been a long day for all of them, and stress told in Devin's attitude. He had become more curt since Lish's murder, since their plan of action had taken hold of him with purpose. It was no reason to bristle at Vask, though for a calculating moment Kastlin saw he could play this either way. Shrug off the big man's remarks and go along with the plans, or take offense and make this his opportunity to bow out of Reva's newest assassination plot.

If he lost contact with her now, it might be for the best. He had no hard evidence of her past history as assassin, except for the Lanzig hit. If he did his duty anyway, she would be rehabbed for the Lanzig murder. The woman who would emerge from that process would not be the Reva he knew.

And yes, he admitted to himself, that was a concern. She wasn't his friend, exactly—could never be as long as she knew him only under the pretense of his street guise—but she had come to mean far more than a common criminal ought, to an Imperial agent.

You sympathize with her, a traitor's voice spoke in his head.

His silence had drawn out too long for the spacer's comfort. "Dammit, Kastlin," the man barked. "If you don't want to come with us, just say so and be done with it."

A hand touched his arm, and he looked into Reva's eyes as she leaned toward him, her serious intensity burning right through him. "Don't you leave me, too, Fixer," she said softly, so only he could hear.

He knew what it must cost her to say that much. He looked away first.

"I'm with you," he said, and swallowed his misgivings.

He'd leave a message with Systems Control, and deal with Obray later. After he'd seen this through.

CXXIII

The *Fortune* lifted from drydock in the early morning light, and settled easily into a parking berth in the shipyard's landing field.

Supply pods and a handful of Skiffjammers waited at the pad. Captain Levay had been eager to hire her space-skilled muscle to Devin. Suddenly bereft of employer, they needed the work, and the fact that it had something to with punishing the Holdout's killers made it doubly appealing. For Devin's part, he couldn't find crew he was satisfied with on such short notice. 'Jammers had at least shipped on the *Fortune* once before; they'd proven themselves reliable enough, and had other skills that might come in handy dirtside. He was happy to have a contingent aboard, led by Sergeant Eklun.

FlashMan had discovered their destination was Bekavra, a week and a half away by established shipping routes. Devin would stick to those patrolled routes, not risk ship and lives in the trackless void between space lanes. They would play this one by the book, like the Shirani preferred: with flight plan on file, so their departure would raise no eyebrows among Customs.

Because he knew it paid to plan ahead, he also took on board miscellaneous spares, some specialized Skiffjammer equipment, and an item from Lish's stockpiled wares: a ship's transponder, squawking a different ID code than the *Fortune*'s own, and identification files to match. That last was insurance, in case Security wanted to detain and question him about Lish. In that case, he didn't plan for his ship to be easily traceable.

The insurance was quickly stowed in the smuggler's cubby. Then, with crew and extra 'Jammers in place, and Reva and Vask secured in the lounge, Devin settled into the Captain's chair. He requested clearance to orbit.

Traffic Control spoke the go-ahead, and the spacer released the breath he had been holding. Internal Security had not put a want out on him. He and his vessel were free to leave.

When their lift window arrived a quarter-hour later, the freighter rose on bright-glowing repulsors, and arrowed skyward.

Yavobo manned the navigator's position aboard the *Faroukhan*, keeping a watchful eye on the pasty-faced man by his side. Destin Troi was the owner and erstwhile pilot of the pleasure yacht, a man now reduced to trembling obedience to the warrior's every order.

Troi's family lay bound on the floor of their plush suite in a security high-rise in Avelar, unmoving lest they detonate the vibration-sensitive bomb in their midst. When the warrior thought of the spy-eye that posed as a bomb, he almost barked with laughter. Ignorant thin-skins, and cowardly, to allow themselves to be so coerced. Had they been Aztrakhani, they would have kicked the so-called bomb to set it off and taken their captor with them. But fearing for his life and for his family, the yacht owner did Yavobo's bidding with clammy hands and wire-taut nerves. A thin-skin trait the bounty hunter had counted on.

The *Fortune*'s flight plan said her destination was Bekavra. "File a flight plan to Lyndir," Yavobo ordered the sweating man by his side.

It was quickly done. Then the warrior keyed in their real destination, the same as the freighter's, and set the navcomp calculating warp routes to their goal.

While the computer worked, the Aztrakhani wondered if Shiran's flight plan, like his own, was obfuscation for possible pursuit. Surely, with all possible destinations, the choice of this one was not chance. They must realize that Adahn Harric was there.

Yavobo bared his teeth. Reva must be after the man who had ordered the Holdout's death. Harric would not recognize the *Fortune*'s name, would not be suspicious even if she landed in broad daylight, as Shiran Devin apparently meant to do.

It made a devious sort of sense. This kind of head-on approach would be most unlooked for. He nodded approval at the tactic.

When the freighter appeared on the list of ships assigned a lift window, he ordered his unwilling pilot to request departure clearance as well. A moment later, their yacht was added to the outbound traffic list, two ships after the *Fortune*.

Minutes after the freighter lifted, it was their turn to depart—but repulsors stayed on idle. Destin's hands were locked white-knuckled on the controls. Yavobo liberated them with a prod in the ribs from his hunting knife. His Blood Oath knife, usable because this action helped him come closer to his enemy.

The *Fortune* was a blip on the yacht's monitors, already leaving orbit.

Another prod from Yavobo, and the *Faroukhan* hurtled after.

CXXIV

The *Fortune* left the transit lanes monitored by Traffic Control—then, instead of heading for a run-to-warp coordinate, she dropped beneath the plane of the elliptic and angled sunward. The primary of the Selmun system filled the forward screens, its coronal glare damped down to a viewable level by compensation circuits.

"What are you doing, Devin?"

Reva's voice on the intercom. Cool. Brittle.

"Taking care of personal business," the Captain answered.

A pause, then a sharper tone. "We need to get on to Bekavra."

A muscle clenched in the spacer's jaw, and he let irritation creep into his voice. "We can spare the time to say good-bye to Lish."

Silence on the com. To that, Reva could have no objection.

The *Fortune* held station halfway between Selmun I, a barren ball of magma flows and toxic vapors, and the brilliant yellow-green star that gave this system life. Reva looked nearly contrite as the crew gathered in the Number One cargo hold, the one that held their foodstuffs and supplies.

'Jammers pulled one cargo crate out from the others, swiftly broke it down to reveal the casket within. The funeral pod was the type used on spacecraft, streamlined, sealed, a fitting resting place for the Shiran Trader who had met her death far from the spaceborn culture that had shaped her existence.

Only Devin could ensure that her passing was memorialized as befitted a Shirani, with a bright-burning star as her grave beacon. His real prayers were kept in the privacy of his heart, not to be shared with these strangers to his clan, but as Captain it fell to him to say the words of farewell to one no longer with them. The others gathered around and he placed a hand on the cool plas casing of the smuggler's casket.

"You had left space in these last years, Lish. Now you come home at last, welcomed into the warm heart of a star, to be your memorial for all time. I'll tell your kinfolk that all who pass this way know one of us rests here, and think of Shiran Gabrieya Lish whenever they see this star. May Ashani watch over you."

He nodded to Eklun, and 'Jammers fitted the casket to a simple drone probe, set to home on the Selmun star. Ported through the cargo airlock, the probe fired its limited propellant, a brilliant spark pulling swiftly ahead of the stationary freighter. By time the rocket fires were exhausted, its burden had moved far within the star's gravity well. Those aboard the *Fortune* watched the monitor tracking Lish's remains. Long before the casket entered the envelope of gases about the star, it superheated and ignited, vaporizing in a flash of combustible gases.

The solemn gathering broke up, people returning to their stations. Reva walked beside Devin back to the crew lounge.

"When you said there'd be a funeral later, I thought you meant . . ." Her voice trailed off, and the Captain looked at her. Her eyes were bright. "That's not what I expected."

"It's our way."

"Lish would have liked it."

Devin quirked a smile. "Lish insisted on it."

Reva looked at him sharply. "Insisted—?"

"If she died. It seemed the wisest way."

The assassin was puzzled. "How so?"

"Her smuggling contacts didn't die with her." The spacer raised a hand, tapped one finger to his temple. "Neural computer. It could be recovered if she was buried, and ordinary cremation might not destroy the whole implant."

Reva halted, her mouth opened in surprise. "Her contacts were all—"

"In her head, yes." Devin shrugged. "It's just as well. Her secrets are all gone with her, now. A fitting farewell, don't you think?"

He left her in the hatchway of the lounge. Minutes later, the *Fortune* was under way.

Yavobo cursed his luck and had his captive pilot nudge the *Faroukhan* into the sensor shadow of barren Selmun I. A ship following or mirroring the freighter's movements too closely would surely be noticed, especially in this little-traveled part of the system. The bounty hunter waited and watched, the yacht's short-range sensors his eyes, hoping that Shiran had no reason to closely examine the space behind him.

A quick scan of the probe and cargo pod was reassuring. Inert organics, in a human-sized container. He could guess what this waystop was about, and he relaxed a little more.

When the freighter resumed her heading for a run to warp, the *Faroukhan* waited and then trailed behind, blurring into otherspace at the same coordinate as the *Fortune*. She was ahead of them in warp space; Yavobo let his quarry draw farther away, out to the edge of long-range sensor contact. Unless the freighter swept space diligently behind her, and carefully tracked ships there, the pursuing yacht was not likely to be detected in these busy lanes.

Yavobo placed the yacht on autopilot and turned to his unwilling companion. His pudgy captive blanched under his scrutiny. "What are you going to do with me?" the man asked.

A long-toothed smile was his only answer.

A short time later Yavobo dumped the man's body into the airlock, and cycled the outer door open. Atmosphere puffed out into the curling energies of warp space, carrying the ship's owner with it.

The warrior had the security codes for the yacht now, and didn't need the thin-skin anymore. He had to sleep sometime, and did not wish to be burdened with a useless captive.

The more one takes thin-skins hostage, he reflected, the easier it becomes.

That matter disposed of, he settled into the Captain's chair. He kept one eye on sensors, and turned his thoughts to a final issue that concerned him.

Adahn Harric was ignorant of the danger that approached.

I'm not honor-bound to help him, Yavobo considered, or even to warn him. But if I do, he will be indebted to me for both the warning and the assassin's death. . . .

A short time later he called Harric.

CXXV

Reva watched Qual slide closer on the monitors, an oily, twisting sheen of distorted energy fields marking the star system's position in normal space. It was capital of the subsector, last waypoint before their destination. She had read about it in the ship's library, something niggling in the back of her mind as she scanned the planet's profile data.

The freighter stayed true to its course. As they began to move past the distortion, the sense of unease that had been just beneath the surface for days surged strong enough to propel Reva to her feet.

She didn't wait to analyze her feeling but went forward, intruding into the dimly lit haven of the flight deck.

"You've got to stop at Qual," she announced.

Devin didn't spare her a glance. "We don't need to go there."

"I think we do."

The spacer swiveled about, dragging his attention from rigged controls and focusing on her with an effort. "Do you know something I don't?"

The tall woman paused, suddenly awkward. How to explain this feeling? It was the same prompting that urged her to move between Lines sometimes, before she actually saw a hazard—an intuitive response that helped her to avoid danger. She had learned to obey it without second-guessing her instincts.

"I have a feeling it's time to hide our trail," she finally said. "We could use the asteroid belt at Qual as a place to stop and change transponders. It's beyond system traffic lanes and not patrolled."

"Swap-out's a lot of trouble, if we don't really need it."

The assassin didn't like to explain herself. "It's not smart to go straight in," was all she offered. "Don't do it. We can't risk being identified before we move on Harric."

Shiran began to shake his head.

Reva's voice hardened. "I know what I'm asking you. Play it safe, Devin."

The pilot took in her stiff-necked stance, the serious expression on her face. He slowly nodded concession. "Asteroids, you say?"

"Mined out, mostly abandoned. We should be able to shelter on one while the work is done."

"You better take a seat then." He swiveled back around in his chair. "Prepare for transition to real space," he told the crew through his headset.

The *Fortune* slowed and dropped out of warp.

CXXVI

The problem with a stolen ship is that you can't fly it through Customs. Yavobo made his landing accordingly—in one long, erratically swooping path, from warp through local space to brown, mountain-wrinkled globe, shearing wildly through Bekavran traffic patterns, his angle of attack in the atmosphere dangerously steep and swift. A few random settings on the screen controls let the hull heat dangerously; with com systems offline the violent approach of the *Faroukhan* made the yacht seem a distressed ship with all the flight characteristics of an incoming meteor.

That guided meteor swept high over the central Bekavran plains, then low over the Harcavenian peaks, to vanish into a sheltering system of ravines. Minutes later, the ship's resting place was marked by a brilliant blossom of orange-white light. To observing eyes the string of events looked like the wreck and ruin of an already-damaged ship.

To Yavobo, sheltering in another ravine a half-klick away, the self-destruct he had initiated seemed suitable camouflage for his return to Bekavra.

Before investigators could close on the smoking wreckage, the bounty hunter was far away, heading toward the city of Harcavenia in the sheltering dusk of twilight.

CXXUII

A triple chime sounded. The tone startled Janus, and he looked around from where he orchestrated data flows in the net. He shifted to a private place where he could respond to the summons, a personal call code that only one associate had ever used.

"Janus here," he said.

"This is—," the Dorleoni began.

"I can see. I'm amazed to see you making a local call."

Karuu eyed the com screen. "I am all-damn lucky to be anywhere alive and free right now. Local is best place for that, I am thinking. Safest, anyway."

"Hm. Are you being followed?"

The Dorleoni barked. "I was escorted nicely away from our R'debh hellhole by one of our Customs collaborators, for a large and unreasonable fee, I am noting. No following, no. I am first mentally tortured by Gerick, then hunted by Bugs, impoverished by turncoats, finally packed here like smuggled cargo—but no, I am not followed. I am calling in to see how you can help me, to make right all these wrongs."

Janus absorbed Karuu's fractured tale. "I'll have to think about this," he responded slowly.

"What is to thinking?" Anger stressed Karuu's voice.

"You're in deep shit for abandoning us on Selmun III."

Karuu spluttered. "Abandon—? I am not—"

"If Adahn learns you're here, you're dead."

The Dorleoni took a half-step back, mouthed words that wouldn't come. "How so, dead?" he finally squeaked. "I am a good, loyal, hardworking Holdout—"

"—who let MazeRats get taken by Security, who saved his own hide, who's hotter than a Kashtani whore and brought his muchwanted butt right back home to sit on Mr. Harric's doorstep. The same doorstep Bugs are sniffing at right now."

The smuggler looked quashed. "Security is here, too?" His squeak was higher than before.

"As I said. Dead."

Karuu stared listlessly at the com unit; then a thought jogged him into action and he looked around, over his shoulders. "Are you—? You would perhaps be sending muscle to collect me. I am going, I think." He reached out toward the console

"Wait! I'm not sending anyone. I said Adahn's unhappy with you. Not me."

The Holdout's eyes glistened. "You are offering me assistance, then?"

Janus paused. He saw a resource where his boss saw only a problem. It might be a resource worth keeping, against a rainy day. "I'll help you out, Karuu. I think we can work together."

The reprieve made a slow impression. It took a while for Janus to recognize a Dorleoni smile.

"Glad I am to hear you are a reasonable man," Karuu said. "Happy to be working with you, my friend."

"Don't get too happy," Janus cautioned. "Let's see what I can do for you, first."

"Am happily awaiting to see that, too. What are you wishing me to do, then?"

The decker pursed his lips. "Stay out of sight for an hour, then call me back. I'll have something lined up by then." A game plan; a way to take advantage of the Holdout's reappearance. Or if not, he could set Karuu up, hand him over to Adahn, and curry favor at a time when Harric's goodwill was exceptionally thin.

That would bear consideration.

Janus ended the call, but before he could mull over possibilities, Adahn was on another channel in voice-only mode. His disembodied speech filled the cyber-air like the voice of a god. "Do you have our financial records offline yet?" he demanded.

"Almost. Another hour."

"Make it faster. Bugs have cracked level-three security and taken two defensive deckers down."

Janus looked up. "I didn't know they were so close," he said.

"They weren't. It's a random probe, I think. They got lucky. They probably don't realize how near they are to the heart of Red Hand data yet. You damn well better make sure there's none for them to find."

"Almost done," he repeated.

"Good. Then get over to my office when that's finished. Yavobo is back."

"Will do." Janus acknowledged the order before he digested the knowledge. Yavobo, here. He who had warned of Reva's imminent arrival. She was not yet sighted, though teams of MazeRats stood by to move on the *Fortune* when it appeared.

Harric barked a last curt demand. "Anything new I should know about?"

Janus nearly laughed. Like the fact that Karuu is back, he thought, and hiding from you? Like the fact that your operation is collapsing around you, and you can't seem to stop it?

He coughed in the physical body, a reflex before finding his cybervoice. "No, Boss. Everything's the same."

Adahn let the comlink fall silent.

CXXVIII

The assassin who occupied Janus' thoughts strode long-legged under a canopy of green trailing hiana leaves. She followed a walkway through a city park, patches of smog-hazed sunlight playing now and then on her white tunic-dress and offworld jewelry. Her hair was black, her style Bekavran eclectic. Now that she was away from crowds, she abandoned the leisurely saunter locals preferred, and walked with purpose toward a secluded pocket of greenery.

Vask awaited her there, looking as comfortable in his new high-collared gray tunic as he had in his R'debhi street garb. That was promising, she thought. Like herself, the Fixer could mix easily into a local setting. He would need that ability, to cut the deals she expected of him.

She sat beside him on a shaded bench. "Well?"

Kastlin gave a small shake of his head. "No buyers. I can't get a nod from anyone."

Reva felt a surge of anger. "Of course there are buyers," she said sharply. "Information is always worth something to someone. Where haven't you looked?"

Kastlin bristled. "It's not my looking that's at fault. It's the street situation here. A few days isn't long enough to crack it. There aren't any takers."

"What the hell are you telling me?" she fumed. "That you can't find anyone on this dirtball who wants a piece of Adahn Harric?"

"His organization is better connected than we knew. The small players stay clear of the Red Hand, and the big ones won't deal with outsiders like us."

Her words were sarcastic with disbelief. "We can hand someone the keys to his operations and they're still saying no?"

"That's how it looks. No one trusts us or the goods we say we can deliver. They think it's a setup."

She stood, eyes flashing, and walked a few paces away. "How are we supposed to feed a big fish to the scavenge-rays if the rays aren't interested? This is fucking ridiculous." She glared back at Kastlin, whose Fixer talents had failed her, then turned her scowl on the smog-yellowed greenery around her.

Their ship's new identity as the freighter *Westen* had gotten them safely onplanet; FlashMan was making great inroads into Harric's private cybernet. In the right hands, the netrunner's snooped information could lay the crime boss low, leaving his operations vulnerable to infiltration, to raids, to outright takeover or destruction. That would be a satisfying prelude to her final confrontation with the man. She wanted to visit him first with powerlessness and ruination, even fear. She wanted this derevin-grown lordling to know that he was the target, for a change; to know what it was like to live under siege, to constantly watch his back, as Lish had, and to fail anyway, in the end, as Lish had. . . .

Without a buyer for FlashMan's gleanings, she could offer the crime boss only death. Her fantasy of a slow and crushing revenge on Harric was unraveling before it had even begun.

"Actually . . . ," Vask broke the silence tentatively. "There might be one taker."

Reva put hands on hips. "Why didn't you mention this before?"

He sighed. "This other party, they'd want the goods quickly. Everything possible, within a few days. If we do a rush job like that, Harric will know where he's been raided, where he's vulnerable."

Reva considered the offer. "Who are these buyers?"

"An offworld interest. They'll use it to shut him down."

She looked across treetops to the hazy residential hills where

Harric's secure estate was nestled. Perhaps it was the best she could hope for. After all, they didn't have weeks or months to do this in. Yavobo was on her backtrail somewhere. Better to finish Adahn and get far away from here, as swiftly as she could.

Her anger drained from her as her grand scheme collapsed. It left her with the kind of choice she always came back to: when and how to remove an unwanted person from the world. She had formed different resolutions about that kind of thing when Lish had died, but new codes of behavior were hard to adopt while Adahn Harric drew air and her friend did not.

I can live up to those promises later, she told herself. When all this is behind me.

She inclined her head to the Fixer. "Tell your contacts yes. When Flash is back, we'll plan this systems raid. And after that, I'll see to Harric."

Vask watched the assassin's lithe figure pass from sight. Then he closed his eyes and leaned back on the park bench, at war with himself.

Back on R'debh, Systems Control had passed on a message from Obray. *"We'll be on Bekavra. Rejoin us there when you can."* Kastlin had accepted that order blithely enough; at the time, he didn't know Bekavra would be his own next stop. Apparently there was no standing order for him to arrest Reva in this Timeline, for Control had relayed no reprimand or update request from his team commander.

Yet when he came in contact with Security again, Obray would want a debriefing, and if Kastlin was to be honest in what he reported, his duty was painfully clear.

He would have to prevent Reva's next hit, or arrest her after it was done.

I'm not sure I can do that, he confessed to himself. Or that I'll even try.

Never before had he been caught in such a bind between personal involvement and duty. The friction between the two put his gut in acid turmoil. *"She gave me the slip,"* he could say, *"but look, here's the way into the Red Hand cartel, the toehold you need to break that case wide open. . . ."*

It would take Harric down, and he could redeem himself with the data he provided. In the furor, Reva could do her work, and then fade away, as she had in the past. . . .

He knew as he imagined it that she would not. He'd become some kind of touchstone for her, a nugget of solid reality that transferred between Lines as she did. She looked at him differently these days. He knew with a sinking feeling that the assassin would stick around.

And sooner or later, that he would have to take action on that.

"You said you would help me to find her."

Adahn nestled deeper into his thick-padded chair, marshaling a semblance of patience. "We will," he repeated. "We'll put out a call for her services on the Net. When she answers, Janus will arrange a meeting. Then it's your show."

The alien sitting across from him made a small negation, the overhead light shifting across angular planes of cheek and brow. 'That is not *finding* her," Yavobo declared. "That is hoping she will respond. If she does not, you have rendered me no aid."

Harric rolled his eyes, unconcerned whether the Aztrakhani understood and took offense at the expression. The loss of Selmun operations was a ruinous blow, and now the blue wire-frames of Internal Security agents had been spied in the local Net. His systems had been infiltrated two days running—already the senior Tribunes of the Red Hand were asking uncomfortable questions.

Meanwhile all Yavobo could do was yammer for this assassin, as if she came and went at Harric's orders.

"I don't know where she is," Adahn said, "and right now I don't care—"

"You should care," the alien said. "You are her next target."

Adahn's heavy brows drew together. "Yeah, you said that before, and she hasn't shown."

Yavobo's lips twitched, a briefly mocking smile, and it spurred Harric to anger. "I don't think you have anything to go on at all," he snarled. "That's why you're so damn anxious for me to find her, isn't it? Because you can't do it yourself."

The bounty hunter stood swiftly. His stance was taut and threatening.

"One last time: will you find this assassin for me, as you promised?"

Harric's jaw jutted. "I told you what we'll do for you."

"I cannot wait longer for your assistance." Yavobo's face was expressionless, his words flat.

Adahn curled a lip. "Then you're on your own."

The warrior remained poised for a long moment, balanced on the edge of violence. Then a silent decision was made and his tension broke, replaced by a chilling resolve that could be read in his eyes.

"Place your call," he said to Janus, standing silently behind his boss. "You can leave a message for me at my ship."

Without another word or a glance at Adahn, the red and black figure left the office.

Harric shifted in his chair, easing stress he had collected in his shoulders. He swiveled about to face his lieutenant. "Imperious son of a bitch. No rush with that call to Reva. She won't answer it anyway, once she knows it's from us."

"Maybe she will," Janus offered quietly.

"Yeah, and maybe she won't. Maybe she's not anywhere near here."

"What if he's right?"

That thought dredged up concerns Adahn didn't have time for right now. Concerns that wouldn't retreat obediently into the background, either.

"Vecna turds," he said in disgust. "Shake some MazeRats up. Have them search again, and make sure everyone has a copy of that flatpix Yavobo left us."

"If she's onplanet, she's lying low," Janus noted.

"If our boys look hard enough, they'll find her. Get them started."

Smoke curled from the muzzle of the impossibly large handgun gripped in a lightning-jagged hand. FlashMan grinned at his weapon of choice, then looked to the charred sim-form sprawled in the data gate before him. Flash shook his head. That man needed better equipment.

He air-holstered the virtual gun by his side. It lingered for a moment, then faded into nothingness. It would be in his hand with a thought when needed again. He stepped around the form of his enemy, a decker who would gladly have killed him outright, instead of merely stunning his victim.

Now there was nothing between Flash and the exit from Harric's third-level systems. His route lay just ahead, a glitch in a status reporting program that he had expanded into a trapdoor between levels. He grinned more widely and did a brief jig outside his personal egress. Then he slipped into the jimmied routine and cavorted out the other side—and nearly into the arms of a gangly blue wire-framed figure he knew from Selmun III.

The two netrunners froze, both startled beyond response by each other's unexpected appearance. Flash was the first to unfreeze and, true to his name, darted off, directly away from the Security hack, as fast as neurons could carry him.

Nomad collected himself a nanosecond later, and sped after.

For pure brute force, Security netrunners had Flash outgunned any day. His only hope lay in evasion. He did his best, taking unexpected corners, until one dodge sent him racing down a curving passageway. Too late he recalled the glowing static screen ahead of him: coarse but effective broadband protection against intrusive viruses and unauthorized netrunners. It filled the hall with lurid electric yellow, its field potential strong enough to tug at the lightning spikes on his sim-form.

He skidded to a halt. In the body he began to thumb the emergency disconnect on his deck, though he risked death or brainburn that way, too—when choice was taken from him. Nomad slammed into him, sliding them both along the floor, then trapping him in place with a restraint field that locked out most of his cyberdeck circuits and immobilized his virtual limbs.

"You ICE-sucking, loose-wired data weasel!" Flash erupted. "Can't you see we're too close to this static? If you're gonna fry me, at least do it in a nice quiet place where I don't have data blackouts from the signal noise!"

Nomad looked up, his crude wire-form features concealing whatever reaction he felt to the looming, crackling hazard. Instead of towing his captive to a safe distance, the Security agent sat right down beside the discomforted FlashMan.

"Fancy meeting you here," he said dryly. "I remember you. Do you remember me?"

"Can't say that I do."

Nomad grabbed Flash's spiky leg, slid the lightning-shaped figure closer to the screen field.

"Hey! Stop that!"

"Remember me now?"

Flash pulled a face. "You must be that kind gentleman who tried to toast me on the *Delos Varte*. Would that be you?"

Nomad smiled. "You *do* remember. My associates aren't with me this moment, but you have me, at least. I must say, I'm surprised to find you here. You're a very busy little terrorist."

"Ha. Bugs deserve their reputation for intelligence, I see."

"Do you work for Harric?"

"Double ha. Check your neuro links."

Nomad wagged a blue finger in reprimand. "No need to be insulting. We're just going to have a little chat. We can have it here, or I can lock you down and wait until we trace and retrieve your body."

FlashMan's head jerked. "You can't do that. If you leave me here, some roving ICE could get me. That's as good as murder."

Nomad stood. "Your work on R'debh amounted to murder, too, though I don't suppose you'd count that. Take your chances, terrorist."

The netrunner nudged his prisoner with one foot, and a blue glow bled from that spot, elongating to a single thin line flowing back to Flash's cyberdeck.

There was a time to be glib, and a time for flight. Both had passed the decker by. He heaved a sigh, resigned to unpleasant reality, and called out to the Bug's retreating form.

"Hey, wait a minute!"

The Security netrunner regarded his captive.

"Look, I've never murdered anyone. You've got me wrong with this terrorist confusion of yours. Let's talk, maybe I can clear you up on some things."

"Maybe you can."

"Could you just get us out of this subsystem first? There's too much ICE around here. And stop that deck trace. That's an invasion of privacy."

Nomad returned to hunker by his side. "In case you haven't figured it out, you have no more privacy. You're under arrest." He looked around. "But maybe a criminal's personal network isn't the best place to have our talk in. Let's go."

Nomad hoisted FlashMan's hindered figure into his arms. Before the interrupted deck trace faded, they had left Harric's system.

CXXXI

"So, how late is he?" Devin asked Reva.

"Two hours, now."

"Maybe he thought you were supposed to meet in Harcavenia."

"Come on, Devin," she said curtly. "He knows to conference through ship's systems only. It's the only place we're certain of secure comms on this end."

The spacer nodded, casting absently about the crew lounge. They'd had that discussion right here, strategizing about their movements and contacts. Agreeing to use the freighter as one base of operations, secure and anonymous among the other Mershon-class freighters at Peshtano starport. It was discomforting to think something serious may have delayed their netrunner.

"Even so," Devin reflected, "that doesn't seem like a reason to rush ahead with things."

"Two hours can be an eternity in the Net."

"I know. I'm rigged."

She waved aside the obvious. "FlashMan's never this late. Something has gone wrong, and that makes it contingency time." She paused. She wished she could talk to Vask, but without Flash's intervention she refused to entrust sensitive conversation to their ordinary comlink. There was no telling where Harric had his ears in this Net. Talk had to be face to face, or not at all.

Even face to face, Devin didn't seem to be getting the gravity of their situation. "Look," she said seriously, "when things go wrong, you either get out completely or move ahead swiftly, before the opposition expects you to move. Flash out of touch means just that: something has gone seriously wrong. Now: either we leave this for a deal gone bad, and lift out of here right away, or we move, quickly, while we have the initiative."

"Isn't that premature?"

Her expression soured. "I wish it were. Trust me on this. When you lose your netrunner you have bigger problems than you know. If he's not dead, he's being made to talk, and that means even bigger troubles for us."

"That may be, but that's no reason to jump in Harric's direction, much as I'd like to. We don't have the estate layout, security breakdown, nothing. How do you expect to get into his compound?"

"I can do it." Her confidence on that point was unassailable. She could use the Lines as she always had, moving between moments, dodging surveillance and opposition.

"Then I'm coming with you," Devin said.

She shook her head. "You're not trained for this."

"No, but I'm not a bystander, either. I want to help." The big man locked eyes with her. "She was my partner," he added softly. "I didn't bring you here because I like ferrying people around subsectors. I'm here because I want to stop this man."

"You can't help in this kind of work. Stay here. Handle our comms; keep our data safe. Be ready to get us out of here on short notice."

"I can watch your back. I want to go," he repeated stubbornly.

"Not with me, you're not."

"Juro's teeth," he flared, "you can't leave me here. I'll come if I want to."

Not knowing what to say, she said nothing. She merely shook her head, and walked away to her cabin.

"Damn you, Reva!"

His angry shout echoed down the corridors. 'Jammers looked up from their duties.

The assassin didn't respond at all.

CXXXII

FlashMan lay near-paralyzed, dropped like so much baggage upon the virtual floor of IntSec's secure program sector. The white wireframe sitting cross-legged beside him was complex enough to show disdain in its expression. Flash didn't think that was a good sign.

"So you're the independent I've heard about," the officer said.

"Hi there."

"No terrorist connections, you claim."

"That's what I claim."

The sim-form of Commander Obray frowned down upon the captive. "Don't suppose you can offer us any concrete proof of that, hm?"

"I don't have too many character references you'd believe, no."

The Security commander poked a finger at the blue deck trace flowing from the lightning-shaped sim. "We have a pair of baby-sitters with your body now. When you unjack, we can get any kind of truth we like from you. One of them's a Mutate."

"A mind-reader?" FlashMan lifted his spiky head from the floor.

"Suit yourself, Mr. Bug. That won't get you into Red Hand systems any quicker."

The officer cocked his head. "What does that matter to you?"

The Flash giggled. "I've been running circles around your deckers for two days now. Your boy only caught me because he found the doorways I made into second-level security. And you weren't there because you were looking for me. You want into Harric's systems. I can get you there."

"Why should I let you run point for a Security operation? I want you out of the way, my illicit friend."

Flash rolled his head from side to side. "Bad idea. You need me. Tell me what you're after; I've probably already found it."

"We can take care of our own business. Now—who are you working for?"

Flash exaggeratedly clamped his lips together.

"Don't make this more difficult on yourself," the Security man cautioned him. "If we need to, we'll unjack you ourselves, and start the quiz in person."

He knew they could do that, in spite of the hazard an abrupt disconnect presented to the netrunner's mind and body. Flash was appalled at the situation he had landed in. He was not free to go, yet not free to betray his clients.

"Man," he whined, "you know I can't talk. It's worth my neck if I do."

Amusement quirked the framing of Obray's sim-face. "No one can get to you where we'll be putting you away."

Put away? Out of touch with cyberdecks and Net systems, away from the virtual challenges and joys upon which he'd built his fame and career? The thought had barely occurred to him before, but he knew Security could toss him in a small cell in chains if they wanted, and no one would lift a finger to prevent it. He couldn't let himself be cut off from cybersystems if there was any way around it.

"Wait a minute," he wheedled. "Let me finish delivery to my client, then I'll help you out. Get you into Harric's systems. Take you back to Selmun, even, show your deckers my system traces. They can verify I wasn't trafficking with terrorists. After that, whatever you want—"

Obray dismissed him without hearing more. "How about this instead? You tell us who your client is, and we don't unjack you. Then you don't risk losing neurons."

"That's not much of a deal."

"That's all I'm offering."

FlashMan mulled it over. Reluctantly, he began.

"I'm working for a woman named Reva," he said. "She wanted secure files from Harric's private net." He lay braced for the next round of questions about who she was, why she wanted to plunder a crime net—but the questions didn't come.

The Security officer's sim sat with a strange expression on its face, so motionless that for a moment Flash thought the man had left his virtual self. The wire-frame leaned forward suddenly, close enough that Flash gave a little jerk of startlement.

"Is there a Fixer working with her, too?"

FlashMan hesitated only a moment. Obviously Reva was a known quantity to these people. "Yes," he admitted.

"His name is—?"

"Vask."

The officer's sim froze again, returning to virtual life several heartbeats later. No telling what frenzied offline conference had occurred during his absence, but two blue wire-frames were suddenly by FlashMan's side, pulling him to his feet.

Obray faced his prisoner. "I've had a change of heart. Here's what we'll do." He motioned to the taller of the wire-frames. "Nomad here is now your bosom buddy. He goes where you go. You can wrap up that delivery to your client. You won't be mentioning us, of course. When you're done, you can give us a dump on Reva and her friends. Then take us on a guided tour of Harric's. Nomad'll stick by your side and trace pathways as you go. You can work with another netrunner, I take it?"

Flash looked Nomad over. "I find most are too slow to keep up with me."

"Make sure that this one does, or we'll—"

"Unjack me, yeah, right. Enough with the threats already."

The officer's voice hardened. "I don't make threats, decker. One suspicious move, and you're unplugged. Is that clear?"

"Yes," Flash replied in a surly manner.

Obray nodded to the Security netrunners, and the binding field and deck trace dissolved. FlashMan flexed the arms of his newly revived sim-self and twirled once in place. "Alright, bosom buddy," he sneered up at Nomad. "Try to keep up, will ya? We've got plans to deliver."

A white wire-frame hand rested on his jagged shoulder. "Leave us a copy before you go."

Flash grumbled but obeyed. Milliseconds later he was out of IntSec systems and back into the Net, with Nomad by his side.

CXXXIII

"Any ideas about how to get in there?"

Reva looked at Vask oddly. "I'll use the Lines, Fixer. Like I always do."

"You risk losing track of Mainline that way."

"I'll take pains to stick close. This is the Adahn I want, not some copy a few realities away."

"Mm."

The pair sat in Kastlin's rented rooms. "I want to come with you," he finally said.

"Oh, gods, don't you start, too. I had enough of that from Devin."

"I'm different."

"You're not trained—"

"I can sideslip."

Her eyes flicked to his, and a slow smile cracked her determined expression. "I nearly forgot about that."

"So let me come. Walk the Lines all you want; as long as you end up in Mainline with Harric, I'll be there. Your invisible guardian, until you need me."

"That sounds tempting."

Vask looked hopeful, the eager puppy-dog gaze she had not seen in weeks. From somewhere came a desire for support in this thing that lay ahead of her, and that part wanted to say yes; the rest, which worked alone, always alone, hung back.

She approached the subject from a different angle. "There might be an easier way in," she volunteered. "I'm not sure I want to take it."

"Tell me about it."

"I have a net account under a contact name. Someone left me a message today. Harric."

Vask's mouth opened.

"It came from his lieutenant, actually. We talked. He says Adahn regrets his angry words with me and wants us to create a new working partnership. I can write my own ticket; come in and talk about it.

As gesture of goodwill, I'll have clearance all the way in—no guards, no checkpoints, no locked doors."

Kastlin made a rude noise.

"Yeah. Too eager. We could talk over a comlink, if he's that interested. Though Janus says they're letting defenses down around me to extend a courtesy, to show they're sincere. They trust me. I wouldn't be scanned or searched."

"Do you believe that?"

"It stinks like a beached beldy. How'd they know I was near Bekavra, Fixer?"

Kastlin sighed.

"But it all comes down to this: do I want to say yes, anyway? I'm walking through the same building, whether I'm expected or not. This way, at least, the doors are open and guards out of the way, at least going in. And no matter what this trap is they think they've cooked up, they don't know I can move between the Lines."

"But," Vask reasoned, "if things get ugly in all the nearby Lines, you're caught up in it, no matter which Line you're in."

Reva dipped her chin.

"It sounds too risky, then. Say no and go in like you were planning to, unannounced."

"That means going in blind. Not knowing where Harric is." She shook her head. "If they think they're luring me, then I go right to him—or close enough, anyway. Less uncertainty about his location. I won't have it that good if I make a blind run, and with limited Nows to choose from, I'm more likely to wind up in a real dead end. Unlike you, I can't float away through a wall when that happens."

His face sobered and she punched him in the arm. "Come on. He refuses to leave his estate for a meeting. This is the next best thing to Adahn putting his neck on the block for us. You want to come along, ghost-man?"

Reva seemed confident of her abilities. He couldn't say no. "I'm in."

"Good. Then come on."

"Right now?"

"Let's go before they can make themselves too ready for us. I'll call Janus on the way."

CXXXIV

"Here's your data," FlashMan chattered unannounced. *"Hot off the Net."*

The voice roused a brooding Devin from his reverie in the privacy of the flight deck. The spacer looked to the com module, blinked in astonishment at the monitor trace that showed data streaming into the *Fortune's* comp core.

"Flash?" He fumbled for words. "What are you—where've you been? Are you alright?"

"Had some delays. Got the goods for you thought, as promised."

"Look—Reva thought you were dead, not delayed. She's gone to—"

"Spare me the tale. I'm late for a date."

"Flash—"

"Later."

The grating hiss of static filled the channel. "Lords of Ice!" Shiran slammed hands down on the arms of the Captain's chair. "Can't anybody stick around here long enough to talk?"

He stabbed the disconnect angrily, then glanced at the illicit files. It was all there, what Reva should have waited for. Floor plans. Service entrances. Security scanners. Even the codes and passwords for the day's security patrols at Harric's estate.

Devin reviewed the files with growing dismay. Now what good will this do us? he thought. Reva's sudden strike is bound to fail, and worse, she'll tip Harric off to his danger.

He rubbed his eyes. Reva's plan was born of an urgency that the FlashMan's reappearance made pointless. Her ill-considered initiative would ruin the chances for a more organized assault to work, besides getting her killed in the process.

That was not the memorial to Lish's death the Shiran Trader had planned on. He put his anger aside and thought about it logically, calmly.

He'd been unable to stop Reva from leaving the freighter, set on this self-appointed mission of confrontation and death. *Her death, most likely.* Yet Devin owed her *roi'tas e senje'tas,* on Lish's behalf. He was honor-bound to help preserve her life. And now he held the key to a successful operation in his hands—though it would be useless if he waited too long to use it.

Maybe she would listen to reason yet.

He punched up her comlink code, but the call tone continued for long minutes, unanswered, and Devin cursed as he terminated the connection.

He sat upright, tense with renewed determination. He was no commando, but he had those on board who were. Here were the plans they needed, and soon, Reva would be providing a distraction for them. If they were quick, if they were good, if the gods smiled upon them—they could strike Harric in the most effective way, and save the assassin from her own rashness as well.

"Skiffjammers," he said over ship's intercom. "Assemble in the crew compartment. We have work to do."

CXXXU

Yavobo contemplated the security monitors with an unseeing eye. Harric was in his thoughts, and the man's heavy-browed face hung before him, an obstinate visage that stirred anger in the warrior's heart.

The man has no honor, the Aztrakhani realized belatedly. His word is not to be trusted.

It was even possible that he had been used, in the matter of Lish's execution, but Yavobo did not dwell on those thoughts, lest they put him into a killing rage. There was no time for such a diversion, not now, when his long-sought prey was about to give herself into his hands. Thanks to the efforts of Janus, and the gods who had prompted the assassin to call.

After he had dispatched Reva, he would turn his attentions to the man who had failed his sworn word. Meanwhile, it would be best to center himself, preparing for the combat that was soon to come.

The lanky warrior interlinked his fingers and began a small wailing chant, invoking ancestors, sending his unreasoning fury out to the desert expanses of his homeworld. He resolved to be left with a core of determination—the commitment to slay his enemy and thus redeem his tarnished honor.

He waited patiently in a small room, chanting to himself before monitors that displayed the antechamber and hall beyond one door. A featureless chamber, stripped of furnishings at Yavobo's request, for he wished no obstacles to come between him and this thin-skin. The chamber had become a dueling arena, like one of the barren red-rock amphitheaters of his homeworld.

His chanting stilled as he felt a tautness grow within him, the keying to tension that heralded changes in his metabolism, Aztrakhani adaptations to combat hormones that raised pain thresholds, increased lung capacity and stamina. It was always better to fight thus, with the body and mind properly prepared. Not as he had met her before, in strange environments, with too little combat readiness in his blood. This time she would know what it was to contend with a truly battle-ready warrior.

He smiled thinly, pulled knife and whetstone from their sheaths, and sharpened his blood-rusted blade with slow, caressing strokes.

"Too near?" Adahn sneered at his lieutenant. "If you're afraid, go hide in the Net. I've got a four-way locking blast door. Guards. A force screen. I've got business to do while we wait, and I can do that best right here." He laid a beefy hand on his desk, computerized command center and com unit in one.

"Besides," he added coldly, "this bitch screwed me around and helped lose us a fortune on Selmun III. Or several fortunes. I want her to know she has me to thank for her quick trip to hell. It'll be a pleasure saying hello, then watching Yavobo gut her."

Janus stepped away from the desk. His boss' pleasures were something he'd rather not have to see. "I'll be next door, then, if you need me."

He let himself into a smaller adjoining office and made certain the door was closed before shaking his head over Harric's folly. Adahn's interest in bloodletting would put him in harm's way yet—

"Sir?" A voice spun him about. "We found something for you."

A MazeRat darkened the far doorway; inside stood two more derevin muscle, holding Karuu between them.

"We thought Mr. Harric would like to know right away," continued the Rat. "We were shaking down tourists at Interglobal, searching for that woman you want—and we found him instead."

Janus nodded slowly, put a welcoming smile on his face. "This is unexpected." He motioned to a chair, and made a show of pulling a needle gun out of one pocket. "Sit him down there. Thanks for the good work. I'll tell Mr. Harric as soon as he's available."

Karuu shrank smaller in his seat; the MazeRats grinned congratulations at one another.

"I expect you'll keep this quiet for now, understood?" Janus said.

"Yes, sir!" they reassured him, and left, exchanging pleased looks. When the door closed behind them, Janus could hear the Dorleoni's nervous panting in the quiet room.

"You're in it good, this time," he told his reluctant guest.

The Holdout's eyes teared. "I know," he whispered.

"Turds, Karuu. What am I supposed to do with you now?"

His prisoner had no answer.

CXXXVI

Reva drove a skimmer through the wrought-iron gates of Adahn's high-walled retreat. The gates were fancy scrollwork, archaic in appearance, in keeping with the tradition of Bekavra's feudal principalities and grand fortified homes. The real security came from force fields and screen technology, roving security bots on the grounds— things that would be unseen and undetected until engaged.

She felt her heart beat more rapidly and her hands became damp where they gripped the steering yoke. Never before had she approached a job so openly. It felt unnatural to drive through an unguarded entrance, felt dangerously exposed to know that her face was known, and that sight recognition had opened the portal to her.

She swept along the tree-shaded drive, a nervous edge keeping her too wound up—a state that could hurt her reaction time, she knew. Reva compelled herself to center before she neared the residence. Made herself breathe, just so; rehearsed plan of action, just so.

"Hope you're ready, Fixer," she murmured, the merest whisper, to the ghostly presence by her side. Knowing he couldn't hear, but comforted by the sense that he was there.

The assassin pulled up before the broad steps and castle-like facade of Adahn's home. The edifice loomed, quarried granite faced with cream-colored marble; high, narrow windows of real beveled glass, solid, imposing—an ancient structure that could withstand direct physical assault and, at some times in its history, had.

Reva wished again she had seen plans for this estate, but knew that once she stepped between the Lines, this physical layout was not as limiting to her as its owner would expect. She got out of the skimmer as thick-paneled doors swung open at the top of the steps. No human was in sight, no alien servant or mecho drone. She ascended, a slender figure in somber black bodysuit, ready for any threat or surprise.

True to Janus' word, there were no guards in sight, no obvious security. Reva let her perceptions split, watched the neighboring Nows splinter into visible reality around her. In none of those Lines did unwelcome company lurk—at least not in this stretch of hallway. She glimpsed ahead some moments in time and saw no surprises awaiting her.

A service mecho rolled out of a side room a moment later. "Follow me, please," it said, and rolled along ahead of her.

Reva alternated back and forth between Line-spanning vision and her ordinary sight as she walked that broad marbled floor. She glanced at then ignored closed doorways and side passages; moved past sideboards, paintings, sonic sculptures, tapestries—the exhibition of wealth and history was noted and dismissed as inconsequential. Her real goal lay ahead, somewhere: the spider in the middle of his web, orchestrating far events and murders from within this nerve center.

At the end of the great hall was a wide bronze-embossed door. The mecho pulled it open, stood aside for Reva to enter.

A white-carpeted expanse of room lay beyond, sudden floor-muffling change from the cold marble beneath her feet. She approached slowly, looking ahead along the Lines as she lingered in the doorway. She was distracted from her examination of Nows by something in this room, something jarring to the senses, and she halted just inside the door to try to identify it.

Then she had it. Lighter spots on the walls, slight disturbances in the nap of the carpet—this room had been furnished and decorated not too long ago. That realization came as her Line sight demanded her attention: moments from now, Harric would blossom large on a wall com screen. Then shortly ahead of that—

—what she saw made her gasp.

A red and black mottled figure, knife in hand, striding toward her from the far end of the room.

The chill that prickled every hair on her body slammed her solidly back into the limited vista of Realtime. Reva spun about, adrenaline-charged, ready to dart from this vicious trap, and her shoulder slammed into the door that had closed silently mere centimeters behind her. The blue nimbus of a security screen lit the edges of the portal, locking it into its frame.

A com screen set into the far wall glowed to life. Adahn Harric leered crudely down at her, his face looming grotesquely huge.

"So kind of you to join us, Reva." He smiled, a sneer edged by a too-sensuous lip. "I'm afraid there's been a change of plans. I won't be able to meet you in person today. I will be glad to watch you die, though."

Fear clutched Reva by the throat.

"Oh, look!" Harric said, casting an artful glance to one side. "Here comes an acquaintance of yours now." The crime boss smiled a poison-sweet smile at her. "I'll let him say good-bye for me."

She tore her eyes away from Adahn's snake-like stare, turned her head toward the sound of an opening door.

Red and black skin. Long fangs bared. Rust-stained knife in hand. The alien was here, in Mainline, and she'd seen him in all the Lines around her.

Yavobo strode toward her, ready for the kill.

CXXXVII

A panther of faceted black obsidian stalked the virtual hallway, wicked head lowered, snarling at the scent of intruders. FlashMan laid a steadying hand on Nomad, who was gathering himself to leave. "Wait."

A gun appeared in his hand, pulled magically from a sim-fold. The weapon belched, and something roared from its barrel. Nomad did a double take. It was FlashMan rushing forward, or the image of him, one jagged lightning figure racing to confront the ravening beast. The sim that was not-Flash met the ICE, battled it, succumbed to it. The glassine creature ripped a clump of energy from the chest area of the inert sim-form. The Flash clone shorted out, vanishing in virtual smoke.

The panther pawed the ground, looked casually about. The intruder scent had been accounted for and dispatched. The ICE was satisfied, and padded elsewhere on its system patrol.

The real FlashMan stood by his official companion, a finger to his lips until the sim-panther was past and out of sight. "Clone and conceal," he offered under his breath. "A sim as decoy; a little virtual confusion to hide our data trace."

The ICE would have felled the real decker with a heart attack. Nomad looked at the independent with new respect. "Interesting program."

"Wrote it myself." Flash glanced about, made sure the corridor was empty. "Welcome to level-five security. Adahn's home cybersystems. If you want to look around, now's the time, before the cat comes back this way."

Nomad deferred to FlashMan's instincts, and followed close in the footsteps of the independent decker. The pair ran a swift reconnoiter of in-house command systems, down corridors and piggyback on data streams, until a red-barred tunnel mouth caught FlashMan's eye and slowed him up. "What do you think's in there?" he mused out loud.

"It's alarmed." Nomad pointed out the telltales at the edges of the security lockout.

"Not for long," Flash said. "Let's see. . . ."

The netrunners ducked around the edges of the fading lockout grid. Flash, in the lead, was the first to let out a low whistle.

"Home base," he said. "We're in his command center." The cybercenter linked security, communications, Net interface. On a dais, a fiber bundle ascended to virtual heaven, the direct link to something physical—a deck, perhaps, or command console of some sort. Flash-Man cavorted beside the construct, then stopped, grinning at his companion. "We're top of the heap here. So what did you want to snoop?"

He began tapping randomly into data streams, flicking from secure channel to channel.

"Stop that," Nomad warned. "You'll alert someone to intruders."

"Pffft." The decker shook his spiky head. "Not by random sampling, that looks like the integrity routines that do the same thing. Only if we sit on one—whoa. What's this?"

He nudged electrons, redirecting video and sound feed to a quickly crafted virtual monitor.

"What in the hells are you up to?" Nomad demanded angrily. "Come on. This'll bring ICE or deckers for certain."

"Save it," FlashMan snapped. "What's wrong with this picture?"

Together they saw the image that Adahn Harric watched on his wall monitor: a woman clad in form-fitting black, an Aztrakhani alien closing on her.

The figures moved in the syrup-slow pace of organics not in synch with the accelerated perceptions of the Net. Gradually, Reva blinked. She seemed to coil herself, to lean a fraction away from the door. Yavobo hefted the knife in his hand, too slow to be a threat, too boringly slow to keep FlashMan's attention.

Or Nomad's. "Let's get out of here," he ordered.

"I don't think so," Flash retorted. "That's my client."

Nomad studied the vid for a moment, then looked back the way they had come. "That ICE'll be down our throats in no time."

"Then lock us in," Flash said distractedly as data leads grew from his jagged head, tapping into the fiberbundles that led to the outside world. "We can let ourselves out later."

Nomad considered ordering Flash unplugged, then decided he wasn't ready to face the killer ICE on his own. He turned grudgingly and trotted off to secure the tunnel entry.

His retreat was unwitnessed by FlashMan, who floundered in the sea of new information he had tapped into. Finally he caught the rhythm and rose from subterranean processes to the instruction layers that gave it all purpose. Then understanding came, and he cursed himself for the milliseconds he had already wasted.

It was time to issue some orders of his own.

CXXXVIII

Cornered by the bounty hunter.

The shock of it echoed through Reva. Even in health, unwounded, she was not his match for strength, for reflexes. Not his equal in plain fighting skill. If she once became injured, he would soon have her dead.

She'd already seen that much in the Lines around her.

Her only hope was to put Yavobo out of the fight immediately, with one powerful, unexpected blow. She reached for the Sundragon, the supercharged blast tube concealed along her right forearm. As the deadly cylinder came into her fingers, the warrior leapt—from an unexpected distance, farther than a human would have tried. His abrupt motion forced her to react or be pinned and knifed against the door.

The reality of combat drove hesitation from her, and fine-tuned reflexes carried her away from the wall in a sideways spring. She had faced bloody death before. She would not let the look of bloodlust in Yavobo's eyes distract from what she must do.

Her dodge was anticipated and the warrior twisted in midair, to land where Reva had stood, facing into the center of the empty room. He ran after her, three, four darting steps. The assassin fell before him. His oncoming rush left no time to aim and fire the Sundragon. She feinted to one side, dodged to the other, and slipped past her attacker.

His blade nicked her right arm as she darted by, a split second too late to do serious damage. But the blooding elated the warrior and he yelled, a ululating victory cry, and paused to brandish his weapon.

Reva fired the blast cylinder at her enemy.

The Sundragon erupted with a crackling blaze of coherent light, energy bolt sizzling through space where Yavobo to all rights should be—but he was not. Impossibly fast, he dropped to the floor and rolled to one side, out of the path of the weapon's beam.

The bolt seared through Harric's monitor, vaporizing screen and plascrete, leaving a hole the size of two fists in the wall. The energy discharge ended somewhere beyond, and Reva heard muffled outcries from that direction.

Yavobo sprang to his feet, glared at the offending Sundragon in her hand, and gave another bloodcurdling cry. Reva knew that its only charge was expended. She threw it at him, hoping for a moment's worth of distraction. He batted it aside as she pulled vibroblade from her other sleeve.

Before she could set herself, or plan where to maneuver, he was upon her.

Yavobo startled Vask nearly as badly as he had the assassin. The agent's concentration wavered, his phase-shifted body slipping precariously downscale toward solidity. Willpower alone returned him to his complex energy state. He watched in anxious suspense as the antagonists engaged in a flurry of attack and pursuit, silent shadow play between ghost-soft figures of blue-gray light.

The Sundragon's discharge was a color-shifted explosion of near-white energies and trailing blue sparkles. As the bolt missed the deadly alien, Vask knew that Adahn no longer mattered. It would be the end of Reva if he could not help in some way. He hated to reveal his presence so soon, but Yavobo's answering charge stripped his options from him.

He positioned himself near the alien and let his concentration relax, the energies of his structure cascading back down to a natural harmonic, condensing his form from spectral energy into molecular solid. Ozone from the Sundragon discharge assaulted his nostrils. He wore the loose street clothes he had favored on R'debh, and from within the jacket near his chest—close enough to shift with him—he pulled a blast pistol.

The alien hulked large before him, not yet aware of his danger. He dodged Reva's vibroblade, trying to press her back against the wall of the room. Vask raised the pistol at point-blank range, and set finger to firing stud.

Feet shuffled. Reva darted past Yavobo's guard, out of his narrowing reach, and grunted as he struck home, the price paid for the evasion. They circled and she slipped out into the center of the room.

The swift turnaround put her in the line of fire. She was wounded and bleeding, backpedaling as her stalker closed. The warrior had stabbed, and caught her near collarbone and shoulder. Her left arm no longer balanced her crouching stance, but hung uselessly by her side.

Vask angled his gun at Yavobo, and fired.

Reva spared him a word in that instant. "Get out," he thought she said as the killing beam blazed from his gun—to seer a char mark on the wall, missing the bounty hunter, who sprang forward, low and extended, in the moment that Kastlin squeezed the trigger. The warrior barreled into his attacker, slamming the Security agent against the floor, winding him with a well-placed shoulder and far too many kilos of weight.

Yavobo rolled to his feet beyond Vask. Carelessly, as if disposing of a minor distraction, the lanky alien spared one hand for his unexpected assailant. Fingers grabbed jacket and shirt. The Mutate felt himself swung up from the ground, snatched in one long, fluid movement that carried him off the carpet and set him flying through the air.

Time slowed. With the disjointed thought of one caught in an accident, he realized his motion was unnaturally fast and hard, that Yavobo, in battle, could throw Security agents around for hours and not be tired at the end of the day.

That was all he had time to think, for then head and shoulders crashed into the door of Harric's office, and he collapsed to the floor in a heap.

Reva saw Vask fall and thought of Lish, skull bashed in after their first encounter with Yavobo. She squelched the twinge of caring, of sorrow, that intruded.

The Fixer's sacrifice had bought her time, valuable time, and she was busy using it.

The Aztrakhani turned back to her, reorienting on her position, the slit pupils in his yellow eyes dilating like a hunting cat's. She had not moved to take advantage of his distraction; surely he took that hesitation for cowardice or fear. Yet it was something much more difficult than those ready emotions that froze her before him, vibroblade humming in one hand, blood dripping down the fingers of the other.

She ignored the crimson spots staining the carpet near her feet. She'd seen more than that, very close, in many Lines nearby—but she hadn't looked at all Lines. And then, charged full of adrenaline, driven by unthinking reflex, it had become impossible to marshal herself, to move between Lines and out of danger.

That was the opportunity Vask had created for her, maybe at the cost of his own life. She had time.

Time to rein in survival reaction, to pause for breath.

Time to recall what she had learned from Kastlin, experienced shifter of energies, a better master of his metabolism than she had been.

Time to tell her pounding heart that there *was* a way out of this, and she was about to find it. . . .

Yavobo made a flourish with his bloodied blade, a ritual motion followed by an inclination of his head. A nod to the sheep that deigned to be slaughtered.

He stepped forward.

Reva inhaled deeply, her chest rising with a great lungful of air. She put her head back, exhaling slowly, eyes closed for an essential moment, a segment of time where she was elsewhere, picturing herself gone. If he leapt at her now, she was done. If he walked, she had a chance. . . .

She drove consciousness of danger from her mind and sought that elusive place where one moment became many. She must reach that careful balance point, not actually moving across Lines, but poised upon the brink of doing so. It was enough to be simply out of phase with this material Now. If she could do even that much. It would be the hardest Lineshift she had ever done, but she had to try.

If she didn't, she was dead.

Yavobo raised his knife, savoring for a moment the choice of slashing the thin-skin's throat, so conveniently exposed, or sinking his blade into her gut, to tear the entrails forth as dishonorable foes deserved. Before he could decide she lowered her chin and looked square at him, her hazel eyes blazing with a look of—triumph?

His vision blurred, or unfocused, or his prey did, somehow. Reva's form shimmered and was gone, just as she had vanished from sight in the ocean.

"Soul-stealer!" the warrior hissed, dropping his knife like it had burned him, taking two hasty steps backward. The blade hung by its lanyard from his wrist, a smear of her blood wiping off on his thigh.

A token he would have taken a moment before as badge of victory he now rubbed off hastily with his palm. He had forgotten this, or hoped it not true, this thing about her nature he had observed before. Like the haunts of the lonely dunes under a midnight moon, she was more than human prey. She was a creature sent to test him, doubtless by ancestors offended by his actions, or curious about his abilities. . . .

Yet human or ghost, either could be killed, and he would not underestimate his quarry again. She was nearby, he was certain, for a soul-stealer never strayed far from its intended victim, not when final battle had been joined. He took the knife into his hand again, and began to search for Reva.

CXXXIX

A warning telltale on Adahn's desk console flashed persistently. He glanced that way quickly, unwilling to miss the drama unfolding in the antechamber. Then he recognized what the flashing light meant.

"Hey!" he blurted. "Who unsealed the doors?"

His tone demanded an answer, but his MazeRats had none for him. He rekeyed the lock sequences, sparing hasty glances toward the vid monitor. Hopefully Reva would not realize her way out was unbarred—no time right now to figure how that had happened, later he could wring the neck of the idiot who had defied his orders—

Security screens came back on. Then flicked off of their own accord. He heard the four-way locking bolts in his blast-safe door retract from the wall, saw the status trace that showed his office unsecured—

"What the fuck is going on here?" he shouted, an angry bellow to MazeRats who stirred in concern but couldn't help him. Harric himself controlled the master console, the position that ordered this level of physical security. And he wasn't even jacked in.

He remedied that in a moment, slotting into his desk. Instead of the orderly realm of his virtual command center, he found himself in a featureless cybervoid.

"Tsk, tsk, tsk." A slender figure with jagged lightning-shaped edges confronted him. Its nearly stick-figure proportions made the wagging spike of a finger look ridiculous.

"Who the fuck are you?" the crime boss demanded hotly.

"You're not welcome here," the intruder replied. "Back upstairs you go, now."

Where there had been void a steely-black wall flashed into existence between Harric and the netrunner. A round hatchway separated the two sims, sealed an instant later by the many-leaved plates of an iris valve, contracting shut.

Harric's netlink went dead, and he was back, stranded at his desk, a command console no longer his to order. Telltales revealed the extent of the intrusion: security screens had dropped, his blast door was open, even his personal force field at his desk had been disabled.

His complacency was shattered beyond repair. These were the things that kept him safe, kept him insulated from Reva, or Yavobo for that matter. He stood, moved by anger and worry, just as the bolt from the Sundragon punched through the wall and blazed through his office.

Two MazeRats fell, one holed, one losing an arm and part of his torso. The charge passed close enough to heat the air near Harric's face, and burned on nearly into Janus' office. It dissipated in a crackle of ionization around the half-vaporized hole.

There was an outcry of dismay and a whimper from the dying wounded; MazeRats in a neighboring room hammered at a door that had mysteriously locked itself against them. Harric looked up, panic threatening to grab hold of him. This was not leisurely command of a sterile killing from a safe vantage point. Somehow he was suddenly on the firing line, his systems preempted.

"Janus," he barked into the intercom, "get in here!"

The wall monitor was black, destroyed by the energy beam. Harric was blinded and ignorant. How to regain control of his systems? Was he in immediate danger, from the net intruder, from the assassin? Impossible to gauge.

"Lock that door manually!" he snapped to the three remaining MazeRats. He thumbed the intercom. "You reserves—go through the service hall, cut through Janus's office. Get in here quick."

He waited for his instructions to be carried out. And waited.

Janus didn't respond. The door wouldn't lock; every time a Rat secured the bolt, automatic systems released it. MazeRats weren't flooding into the room, no armed security was handy—

Then something slammed hard against his office door, thrusting it open against the Rat who was trying to lock it. A man's limp arm fell through the gap, to drop sprawled out on the floor. Startled, Adahn looked up, glimpsed Yavobo moving in the antechamber—then the skirling of a perimeter alarm tugged his eyes back to the estate map on his desk.

Harric hammered his fists helplessly on his desktop. Why hadn't the system cleansed itself of this invasion yet? Was the perimeter alert a false alarm triggered by the decker?

The blast door swung wide, shoved by the towering alien. Maze-Rats fell back before him, handling their guns uneasily, looking to Harric for guidance.

Yavobo stepped over the body blocking the doorway, met Adahn's wide eyes. "Something's terribly wrong," Harric told him in a rush. "We have an intruder in the house systems. We might be under attack."

The alien glanced around the office, at Sundragon damage and slain MazeRats, took in Harric's stance and smell of nervous fear. "I seek the woman," he said simply.

"The hell with her," the crime boss said angrily. "I need your help."

Cruel amusement lit the warrior's face as he threw Harric's own words back at him. "You are on your own," he said, then turned on his heel and left the office, striding through the blood-spattered antechamber.

Adahn had no time to curse or call him back, because internal alarms joined the perimeter alerts. Comlinks were dead, but that didn't matter anymore.

He could hear weapons fire in the halls.

CXL

First step in walking the Lines is to see them. Easy. You could do that in one place, a trick of vision, of altered perception.

The second step is to move across the Lines: to pick one Now to live in, to commit to one reality. To translate subjective consciousness, according to Vask's theory, into an alternate self in a parallel Timeline.

Somewhere between those steps was that balance point Reva thought of as standing between the Lines, perching on the razor-thin edge that separated various Nows, not committed to any of them.

Usually she traveled swiftly through that balance point. It was hard to maintain that state which Vask called phase-shifted. It was much easier to slip into one of the neighboring Realtimes instead. Walking the Lines.

Only here, all the Lines held Yavobo, and her death was very close.

So Reva clung to that balance, precariously at first, then with increasing confidence. This wasn't much different than walking surveillance, except that she wasn't going to step in and out of Realtime. She didn't dare. Yavobo was here in the antechamber; moments ahead, in various Nows, he left, then returned. In some he caught her—her fatal mistake, she'd come back to solid reality at the wrong time, or wrong place. In some Lines he looked around, hunting, not finding, and left the room again.

Mainline was like that and she breathed a little easier. She was on the right track.

When Yavobo marched past her phase-shifted self, he headed for the door she had entered by. That was when she realized the doors were no longer locked. With the alien down the hall, she picked another exit at random and moved toward it. Not the one where Vask lay unmoving: she hoped he wasn't dead, but she had to save herself first, if she wanted to help him later.

Beyond the Fixer she saw Adahn, gesturing to MazeRats—but the crime boss was no longer a priority, either. In this urgent moment her retreat was just that: retreat, while Yavobo's back was turned for brief moments.

She slipped out a side door while the warrior searched for her in the wrong direction.

Yavobo moved down the marbled entrance hall. Nothing.

Checked rooms whose doors had been thrown open. Nothing.

Observed the defunct service mecho, its torso sheared by blast-rifle fire.

He paused in his single-minded hunt and listened. The front of the great house was silent. He trod cautiously to the entrance, glanced outside. The woman's skimmer remained parked where she had arrived, and several others besides. Not skimmers: air cars, slewed in hastily abandoned positions. The warrior took in the scene, recalling Harric's words, and it all came clear to him.

Intruders. Reva had help, that was the only explanation for this. Of course she had not come alone. She had smelled a trap.

He turned and ran back up the grand hallway. Infiltrators would approach from more than one direction, that was a given. And the assassin would not let Adahn go so lightly, Yavobo was certain. Joined by reinforcements, she must be there, still, near Harric's offices.

He ran into the antechamber. The man he had thrown remained motionless on the floor, but Harric's office beyond was empty. A side door gaped that had been closed just minutes before. Had Reva come this way?

He went through, into a service corridor. He heard weapons fire from down the hall, and moved cautiously toward it.

CXLI

"Back me up, Flash!" Nomad yelled over his shoulder. "I'm running out of juice!"

A slick-faceted panther came too close to the lockout grid, and he loosed a blast at it. Then a decker in the form of a silver knight nailed him in the torso with an acid-orange beam, a disrupter program similar to his own weapon.

The energy hit him with a shattering electrical charge. His blue wire-frame chest bleached through green to washed-out yellow. Data blackouts began as he recoiled from the hit. Virtual reality melted away, leaving him in IntSec ops, jacked into his deck; then the ops center vanished as backup circuits struggled to hold him in the Net. The virtual grid flickered back into sight, its red bars sliding open one by one, freeing the tunnel mouth as enemy netrunners overcame the security lockout.

Nomad retreated to FlashMan's position.

"Couldn't hold 'em . . . ," he squeezed out.

"You alright?"

"No." Nomad staggered to his knees as the last of the lockout grid faded away. He saw a glass-black panther rush by to spring at Flash-Man. A second ICE construct slammed into Nomad's back and drove him to the ground on his face. He glimpsed Flash driven backward as well, data leads ripping from his head. Panther jaws closed upon the lightning-form's chest.

In the body, Nomad thumbed his emergency disconnect.

Nomad could hear before he could see again, though his language centers were scrambled and the sounds around him made no sense. Something pricked him in the neck; when objects swam into sight once more, an op center medtech was leaning over him with tabgun in hand. Nomad sprawled on the floor, shot full of brainstim, one smoking rigger lead dangling from his burned-out cyberdeck in the console nearby.

Commander Obray pushed through the crowd, squatted by his nearly fried decker. "What happened?" he asked sharply. Emergency aborts were rare.

Nomad mouthed words before they made their slurred way from his mouth. "Flash friends 'tacking Harric. You wan' cartel, move fast. Harric's running."

Obray looked to a lieutenant. "Scramble a raid party. Now."

CXLII

Karuu was numb. Events conspired to kill him and all he could think of was what he *couldn't* do. Couldn't hide, not inside Harric's estate. Couldn't risk getting shot, as long as Janus kept a gun on him. For once his inventiveness was failing him. At this rate it would amount to his death.

Could he run for it—? Shouts and gunshots in the hall cut that line of thinking short. He and Harric's lieutenant exchanged a startled look, then both came to their feet as MazeRats burst into the room from Adahn's office. Sparing no attention for the fugitive Dorleoni, they charged ahead, out the other door, into the hall, sheltering behind the door panel to fire upon intruders who were coming at a run.

Adahn came on their heels, mouth opened to order Janus. His mouth stayed open as he spotted Karuu.

"You!" he shouted at this convenient outlet for his rage and frustration. Karuu quailed, but the crime boss was upon him, the man's meaty hands clamped tight about his stubby neck. Harric spared a glance at the doorway where his MazeRats had not yet cleared the exit for him, then shoved Karuu back against the wall. He shook him like a scrap of cloth.

"All this shit started with you, you motherless turd!" Harric screamed red-faced. Before he could do more the door panel was blown down the hall and a concussion wave staggered everyone in the room. Lean, wiry commandos leapt over dead MazeRats in the doorway, and Harric whirled to face them, swinging Karuu about with him. The Holdout was swept through the air to dangle tiptoed before the crime boss, Harric's left arm about his neck. He struggled to pant for air.

Janus had dropped his gun and was ducking behind the desk as the last man stepped into the office. He was taller than his comrades, and clad in a spacer's gray coverall. He held only a needlegun, but his eyes widened as he recognized Harric from security pix. He brought his weapon to bear.

Before he could complete the motion Karuu saw Harric's right arm thrust forward with unnatural speed, palm out as if to halt the man.

"Don't move!" Adahn barked.

The intruders hesitated, for they saw the same thing Karuu did: the base of the man's palm swiveled downward, revealing the large-bore muzzle of a scatter cannon. The cyberweapon was installed in place of a forearm, housed in synthflesh that served Harric as an ordinary arm would. The bizarrely lethal device could blow away the cluster of commandos and the far wall in the wink of an eye.

"You're escorting me out of here, past your perimeter guard—"

With Karuu as a shield. To have his neck snapped as soon as he was no longer needed, of course.

The Holdout twisted his head toward his captor's beefy fist, close beside his jaw. Maybe this was a cyber-arm, too.

Maybe it wasn't.

The Dorleoni bared his tusks and struck. Ripping teeth sank into human flesh, and met in the middle of a very human hand, crunching finger bones that obstructed the way.

Harric let out a deafening scream and tried to yank his hand from Karuu's maw. Shiran Devin fired. Explosive-tipped needles ended Harric's outcry with abruptness and a spray of gore.

The falling body pulled Karuu to the floor with it. There he lay, jaws in a death-grip, face to face with a wide-eyed Janus, as renewed gunfire caused their attackers to draw back.

"Let's get out of here," said Adahn's former lieutenant.

Karuu couldn't have agreed more.

CXLIII

Reva walked softly down the corridor, resisting the urge to run as she watched for threats or danger. If she lost her concentration, she'd be back in Mainline or some nearby reality, maybe without the breathing space to shift away again. Her advance was cautious and slow, and she scanned the Lines ahead as best she could.

That's how she saw Devin.

The surprise of it threatened to drive her from that chancy balance point, plunge her unprepared into Realtime. She shut her eyes, held on to that center carefully. When she was secure again, she looked down the hallway once more.

At the end was an intersection, and across it ran the spacer. Several Devins, in several Realtimes: in Mainline he advanced behind Eklun and a handful of Skiffjammers, running down the hall, kicking in doorways and securing rooms as they came.

It was foolhardy and bold and incredible. She wanted to laugh with giddy relief. She had never needed or wanted help before, but it wasn't an offer she'd turn down right now.

The spacer and a handful of 'Jammers moved out of sight. She heard them shoot open the door to an office and flood within. Reva shifted down into Mainline, and hurried ahead to join them.

In the hall behind her Yavobo grinned fiercely and began to run. He moved in a sprint, abandoning stealth to close the distance between them.

The sudden rustle of motion behind her alerted Reva, and her heart leapt into her throat. She forced herself not to waste one precious second confirming what she already knew in her gut. Like a slow-motion runner in a nightmare, she tried to flee, willing muscles to accelerate, to carry her away from danger—

The hunter's dash that could bring a running keshun to ground caught Reva handily. She felt a weight drive into her from behind, something between a tackle and an overbearing rush. If she landed flat out, her enemy on her back, she would be at his mercy. She tried to angle her body even as he bore her to the ground, twisting so that she could bring her vibroblade into action.

The movement was futile. Yavobo's arm was around her waist and he slammed her down as she fell, left shoulder and head impacting the floor at the same time.

The world vanished in a flare of crimson pain. Vision receded for a moment, and Reva struggled to cling to consciousness. Yavobo flipped her over onto her back, sat atop her while she lay helpless, momentarily stunned.

He didn't even bother to pin her arms. Her left one was useless, waves of pain from the wounded shoulder a steady counterpoint to her racing pulse. Her vibroblade was clenched in her right hand, the straw clutched by a drowning woman. Yavobo seemed contemptuous of it. He held his own metal blade casually near her neck, within her line of sight.

Her breath came short and labored with the weight of the enemy upon her. Her nightmare confronted her, the relentless killer, the unstoppable machine. Like an echo of the person she had been, one who wouldn't quit until her target was dead.

She swallowed down nausea, and did the only thing left to her. She fought.

She drove toward his ribs with her blade that could slice plasteel without effort. He was ready for her, his arm twisting out of the way, hand striking down toward hers, long fingers wrapping around her fist and bringing it forward to squeeze, squeeze until she released the weapon. Small bones ground together in her hand and tortured pressure points shot fire up her arm. His iron grip compelled her to drop the weapon.

Unhanded, the monofilament wire went inert and tumbled to the floor beside her. Yavobo smiled and put his knife to her throat.

She faltered, the movement of his weapon a deadly fascination. Maybe it was just retribution. Revenge on her, as she had wanted on Lish's murderer. Or thought she wanted, for she was torn with the need to put the killing behind her. She used to believe she was only taking ghosts out of ghost Lines. She knew differently now.

Then she met the gaze of her stalker, and she realized the difference between them. The bloodlust in his eyes told the tale.

It was a look she had never worn. Never.

It wasn't moral superiority, really, but it was a difference. It made what was happening not so just after all. Something she could resist, still *wanted* to resist.

Yavobo gathered himself, the muscles in his neck and shoulder flexing. In a heartbeat he'd slice her throat and that would be the end of it. But it didn't take even that long to use a flechette caster.

He had kept her hand immobilized in his grasp. Her fingers were already straightened, from the harsh grip upon them. Reva hyperextended a muscle, and felt the flechette plate's three segments lock into one straight piece.

She flexed the trigger finger, once, twice, three times.

His eye was the most vulnerable part of his face, less than a handspan away from her weapon. At such close range the monomolecular edge on the flechettes speared through orb and skull and penetrated his brain. The minor charge they carried was more than sufficient to terminate his life.

Yavobo's eye dissolved into ruin. He wore surprise on his face as he fell to one side of her, dead. Like Lish.

It may have been self-defense, but it was hardly just another death. She rolled away from his body, nursing her wounded shoulder, and was sick beside the wall.

CXLIV

Devin followed Sergeant Eklun into the hallway, advancing under covering fire as 'Jammers tried to clear persistent MazeRats from their exit route. An exchange of fire scorched the air through a corridor intersection. For the moment, the advance of each group was blocked.

Reva pulled herself unsteadily to her feet. She took in the energy bolts stitching the air at the end of the hall, and turned to retrace her footsteps. There was no way to reach Devin through that killing fire.

She skirted the warrior who had nearly meant the end of her, staying in Mainline as she moved. She was too spent to walk the Lines, or even to look moments ahead through various Nows. She could only hope there was no greater danger than Yavobo ahead of her.

She found Vask stirring on the ground, and relief flooded through her. A scalp wound matted his hair with blood. He had a concussion, maybe worse, but he was alive. She helped him to his feet; they leaned on each other for support as she pointed the way out.

Adahn's office was empty, doors flung open on every side. Beyond one door was another office, and past that a hallway where Skiffjammers moved. Reva steered that way, and helping hands took them in. While Zay burrowed into an emergency medkit, the MazeRat fire from down the hall ceased. Shouts and running feet told the story confirmed moments later by a scout: the enemy was falling back. Someone else was on the scene, flanking the Rats, and soon to flank them.

Internal Security.

The time taken to regroup in the hallway was just long enough for Reva's fatigue to catch up with her. Her shoulder wound continued to bleed; pain from the traumatized injury was blurring her vision. She was growing weaker than she cared to admit. Devin helped her walk, sometimes run, as Eklun directed their retreat, using his comhelmet's HUD display to track their location on security maps and floor plans. He took them through a maze of service corridors and galleries to sheltered garden colonnades where their vehicles were parked in concealment.

Then they were piling into overloaded air cars, and lifting from the ground. Reva and her companions were sheltered from sight by the palatial bulk of the residence, not spotted by Bugs until they were aloft. Security, occupied with MazeRat resistance, spared desultory shots and a single pursuing vehicle for the fleeing 'Jammers.

By time they lost pursuit in city traffic, Reva had passed out against Devin's shoulder.

CXLU

The cleanup operation at Harric's occupied several days. Security agents confiscated mechos, arrested hired help, shut down the princeling's estate. The ripple effect was quickly felt throughout Bekavra. The remaining tribunes of the Red Hand cartel left the planet on urgent offworld business the first day of the Security action.

A few days later, thorough scanning revealed a network of secret tunnels deep beneath the residence. None showed up on security plans. It took the blush off the raid's success. By time the secret complex was secured, Janus, Karuu, and a number of MazeRats were long gone, along with some critical computer cores and data storage units.

Obray had to shrug and let it go. The remnants of Adahn's organization could do very little compared to the empire the crime boss had headed. An empire in ruins now, with strings of related arrests on this world and links to crooked operations on other planets. The grist would keep the justice mill grinding happily for weeks and months to come. It was a coup, by any standard, even with some rough spots along the way.

The first of those had come with Nomad getting blown out of the Net. At least FlashMan had come through the ICE attack unscathed; as he had once done when piloting the *Delos Varte*, he split himself into two sims, then bailed out of the attacked figure and moved to his second simulacrum elsewhere in the command Net. He'd kept estate defenses offline and enemy deckers occupied while Security wrapped up their raid on the place.

The independent was too good to waste in permanent lockup. Obray made him an offer he couldn't refuse. He dropped criminal charges and FlashMan agreed to work off punitive time in the ranks of IntSec's own netrunners. Not that he'd had much choice.

The worse confrontation had been the one with Vask two days after the Harric raid. There was a fine line between working undercover and actively helping the other side, and he'd pushed the limits on this one. Knew it, too, by his conduct, by his guilt-tinged debriefing. Kastlin's obsessive interest in the assassin seemed to be affecting his judgment. Obray had nearly taken him from this case. Nearly.

It was that threat, to pull Kastlin out of the field, that had led to a compromise. Vask told Obray why he was so interested in the assassin, why it was worth leaving her at large for now. When Obray pressed for more, the Mutate had claimed professional privilege, meaning his Academy oaths held precedence, that if he talked more he would violate some imperially chartered trust. . . . It was a balking point Obray had no way around. The claim of privilege rankled, but in view of the potential, here, he'd decided to go along with Kastlin's proposal. For now.

Things weren't all resolved, yet, in this matter. But Obray now understood that Reva moved through space differently than a Mutate normally did. Maybe Kastlin was right about the tactics to use with her, about the futility of trying to arrest the woman. After debriefing his field agent, the Commander had come to regard the assassin with the cautious respect one gives a boxed laircat. He'd seen Yavobo's body, and knew he'd rather have Reva on his team than with the opposition.

Maybe with time, Vask would succeed in wooing Reva to their side. He would live with their working arrangements for a while, and see where it all might lead.

☆   ☆   ☆

It's not a hard thing to do, Reva told herself. Come on. You've done this a hundred times.

She contemplated the boarding gate at Peshtano starport from her vantage between the Lines. The rampway led to a crowded spaceliner; once on board, she could blend in with other travelers to Qual.

For some reason she loitered, unable to join the throng of passengers. Yet where else was there to go? There was nothing for her on Bekavra. Devin talked of running freight, and Vask had disappeared as soon as he was out of the autodoc. She hadn't seen him for a day and a half, since her own resurrection and return to fitness.

She could stay between the Lines longer now, she noticed, as if riding that point of balance had become a better-honed reflex. But she couldn't spend all her time between the Nows, uncommitted to a Mainline, as much as she might like to.

There, her thoughts had strayed again. Not that she minded. It was easier than planning where to go. She had two refuges, her boltholes meant as emergency retreats. Now seemed the time to pay one a visit. One near, one far; both uninviting. Both places to be alone in.

She shifted her weight from foot to foot, edging slowly away from the gate. Since when do you mind being alone? she queried herself, and admitted reluctantly that she had grown accustomed to the closeness of humanity on board Devin's ship, people she'd known in the Lairdome and had grown to like.

Yeah, right. She halted that line of thought. They had only worked with her, for her skills, for what she could do.

She grimaced. What she could do was kill, but she wasn't so sure she had that in her anymore. Yes, if her life depended on it; she'd proved that at Harric's. But not like before. Coldly, routinely. As executions done for hire.

She felt a ghost-like pressure on her shoulder, then, an electrical tingle that made her jump. She whipped around, keeping herself between Lines with an effort, startled as she was.

It was Vask. She stood at the juncture of four or five Nows; four or five ghost-solid Fixers were overlaid in differing poses, all looking at her with a translucent, quizzical gaze. Rumpled brown hair, local high-button tunic. *Back to base,* he signaled her in waterspeak. Come back to Mainline, he meant.

She shook her head ruefully. He'd had the wit to find her, not only to reason where she would go, but to look for her in the one place that only Vask could spot her. She was surprised he even cared to do so.

She gave in to his persistence, and joined him in a private meeting alcove at one side of the terminal. Shifting into Mainline, as he'd asked.

"Don't do this, Reva," he said, as soon as they shared enough solid atmosphere to talk in.

She raised an eyebrow, a light brown one to complement her platinum blond hair, to go with the red slash-cut dress, the touristy traveling clothes that would let her mix into the starport crowd—

"You know what I mean." He frowned. "You don't need to run off like this. Fade away, like you were never here."

Anger surged through her, unexpected, violent. She felt herself flush. "You talk about running off? Where in the Deep did you go these last two days? I didn't hear any good-byes. I didn't think it was worth sticking around for any, either."

That last a barb, hoping to hit home. It did. Vask looked guilty. "I was taking care of something that wouldn't wait."

"Get back to it then," she snapped. "I won't keep you."

"And where do you think you're going?" he retorted, prodded by her anger.

"Wherever I damn well please. Away from here, for one thing. Too many Bugs around, now that Adahn's folded up. You'd be smart to leave, too."

Kastlin opened his mouth to respond, then closed it. He raised his hands in a calming gesture, or one of surrender. "We're getting off on the wrong foot here. Can we try again?"

She shrugged nonchalantly, leaned back in a casual pose. "Talk away."

"You know I've got connections."

"That's what being a Fixer's all about."

He pushed a finger across the sleek top of the pull-down table. "I've been making deals. You know about Devin's problem?"

She nodded. The Bugs, intent on securing the crime lord's estate, hadn't chased them very hard, but they'd left rented vehicles behind at Harric's estate, and those could be traced. Devin knew he must be a marked man already, that if he tried to lift from Bekavra, he'd be stopped or arrested.

"Well, no one's asking too closely about Devin anymore," Kastlin explained. "He can leave as anonymously as he came onworld. We can leave with him."

She took that in. "How'd you swing that?"

"I called in favors. A blind eye will be turned, if we're out of here soon."

"We?"

Vask shrugged. "I thought you'd like to come along." He looked at her with a challenge in his eyes. She was the first to look away.

"Come on, Fixer. You know better than that. . . ."

"Know what? That you're used to running away? That it's easier to duck out, or cross Lines, than to stay among friends?"

She glared at him. "I don't have any friends," she wanted to tell him—but couldn't. He was one of those friends she wasn't used to accounting for.

"Why are you so anxious to leave?" he continued. "You asked me not to leave you, when I wasn't so sure I should stick around. Now I'm asking you."

It was an unexpected appeal. He had hit her where she was vulnerable, and tears came to her eyes. "Dammit, Fixer," she breathed. "Don't do this to me."

He looked injured. "Do what?"

She closed her eyes. Don't let me think it matters, she answered in her head. Where I am, what I do . . .

It did matter, though. These people mattered, here, in Mainline. The consequences of their actions, of the choices they'd all made. The Line where she had wanted to stay, until Vask had disappeared and she'd felt abandoned.

It's time to quit running, she told herself. Put things in perspective, and stick Mainline out for a change. If you could face Yavobo, you can face this.

She opened her eyes again, blinked moisture away. "You make it tough to walk away, Vask. I'll come with you, for a time."

His face lit with a warm smile. "Good."

"Don't know for how long," she warned, "and I'm not making promises. You got that?"

"Yes."

"I can't work, and I . . ." Won't work. Couldn't, not that kind of work. "I need to get away."

"Understood."

"I need time, before I know . . . where to go from here, what to do. You can't push me on this."

"I won't. No one will."

She looked at him and believed he meant it. Tears threatened to come. This wasn't just a commitment to one Line, an agreement to travel with friends. This was the beginning of a search for herself. The doors that loomed open before her were frightening.

"I've never been . . . I don't know how . . . ," she faltered.

Vask reached out, touched her hand. "It's alright," he spoke quietly. "I understand."

She laced her fingers into his, a friendly anchor that kept her from toppling into an abyss of unknown territory. "If I'm not an assassin," she breathed, "what am I?"

He put his other hand on hers, but had no answer for her question. It was something she would have to discover for herself.

She returned his grasp, and held on.

Maybe it wouldn't be so hard to walk through those doors after all.

EPILOGUE

Reva left aboard the *Fortune,* with Devin and Vask and a crew of 'Jammers. She had a destination in mind. Not her personal bolt-holes, but an isolated place where they could relax and regroup, where there was leisure and amusement and the space to be alone and reflect.

Like captain and crew, she was unaware of the beacon transmitter concealed in an external sensor array. When they entered their destination system, the beacon fired a tachyon burst oriented away from ship's com systems. The intelligence satellite it found understood the signal readily, and passed automated word on to appropriate channels.

Commander Obray nodded when he got the update. It was good to keep a remote eye on the strayed sheep. Especially after reading the report from the genetic analysis they'd run on Reva's blood samples.

The woman had mutated DNA, and something nearly alien about her chromosome structure. It was quite a puzzler. The bloodstains where she had fought held a trove of genetic information, proof enough to give Kastlin's story weight. So Obray could live with their understanding for now.

Let Vask try to bring Reva around, get her to work for Security. If he failed—well, they would still be interested in the assassin, for different reasons. Maybe the Academy of Applied Psychonetics would share that interest as well. Maybe contract another Mutate or two in exchange for this wilder.

Of course, that was only a contingency plan. Obray would much rather have the woman on his team. It was nice to have special projects lined up on the side, though. Just in case you needed them.

He smiled to himself, and returned to the genelab report on his screen.